Dandelion on Fire
Sherry Torgent

BLUE INK
PRESS

For my mother

Chapter One

Hardy was socially awkward. Every day he sat behind Charity Hill in history class he was reminded of that glaring fact. He tried to talk to her—once—in second grade. He spent all week working up the nerve. He approached her on the playground and offered her a small bird's nest that he'd found after a storm. She laughed and skipped away, her blonde ponytail swinging. He supposed that's why they called them crushes. Because that's what ultimately happens to the poor sap who dares to long after a beautiful girl. She crushes him beneath her shoe like a bug and never looks back. The truth was, crushes didn't matter much anymore. A few more months and he would graduate from high school and start preparing to leave for college.

He straightened his black-rimmed glasses and rested his head in his hand while he doodled in the margins of his history book. Mrs. Reid's voice droned on in a maddening, flat tone that played at his ear like a buzzing mosquito. To make matters worse, she was going on and on about Greene Island and how their clean energy and responsible land management served as an example to the rest of the world. They should all be proud of the island's accomplishments. Hardy hated history. He hated the island.

"Hardy?" Mrs. Reid's voice pierced the room.

Hardy jerked to attention, knocking his history book to the floor with a loud thud. A ripple of laughter traveled through the classroom. He quickly picked up the disheveled textbook, his face burning. Mrs. Reid pretended not to notice his clumsiness and waited with rapt attention for his answer.

He cleared his throat into his fist. "Um…yep…don't know."

This was his standard answer when he had no idea what the teacher had just said. The odds favored a question. Hardy was a man of odds.

Mrs. Reid raised an eyebrow, frowned and called on her next victim.

Bullet dodged.

He glanced over at his best friend, sitting two rows over. Cricket flipped his sandy blond hair out of his eyes and mouthed *Brilliant*, grinning like an idiot.

Hardy sighed, slouched down in his seat, and stuck his pencil between his teeth. Boredom pressed against the back of his eyelids. He was sure that Mrs. Reid could have a second career lulling babies to sleep. Just as he felt himself falling into a nap, Charity turned in her seat and whispered "Hey."

He pushed himself back up in to his seat, clamping down on his pencil like a patient preparing to have his leg amputated. She stared at him with her blue, catlike eyes. He quietly regretted his decision to wear his T-shirt with the hole in the armpit, and crossed his arms in an attempt to hide the gaping hole.

"Would you mind massaging my shoulders for a quick second? I think I slept wrong or something," Charity said quietly, rolling one of her shoulders.

"Su…" He realized the pencil was still in his mouth and quickly removed it. "Sure. No problem." *Three words. Good.* He had managed three words to Charity without choking.

She smiled and turned back around.

Hardy looked up at Mrs. Reid and wondered if she would notice, but she was so absorbed in her dissertation that he doubted she would. He pushed his glasses up the bridge of his nose, and ran a hand through his mop of black hair. He stared at Charity's delicate shoulders feeling nervous, yet astounded at his good luck. He raised his hands, then lowered them. What if he did it wrong? He had never massaged anyone's shoulders. And this wasn't just anyone. It was Charity Hill, daughter of the Governor. His secret crush since grade school. In other words, untouchable. *Just do it, Hardy. How hard can it be?*

He reached up and placed his hands on Charity's shoulders and gently squeezed once or twice. *I'm actually doing this. I'm massaging Charity Hill's shoulders.* He increased the pressure. To his surprise, her shoulders began to relax beneath his fingers.

The sound of a single cricket echoed across the room. He recognized his friend's unusual talent—thus the nickname. Without breaking the rhythm of his gentle kneading, he cut

3

his eyes over to Cricket. The chirping stopped. Cricket shook his head back and forth and sliced his hand across his neck.

Hardy frowned at Cricket's attempt to ruin—

"Hardy Vance." Mrs. Reid's voice rang out.

Hardy's fingers froze. Cricket shrugged his shoulders, and gave him an *I told you so* look. Hardy turned his attention to Mrs. Reid who stood with crossed arms glaring at him. A quick look to his left and right revealed that he had awakened the class and sparked a curious interest.

"Is there a reason why your hands are on Miss Hill?"

He quickly removed his hands and placed them in his lap. "Um… She um…asked me to massage her…um…you know…shoulders." He didn't know how to explain the impossible. He bit his lip in an attempt to punish himself for sounding like an idiot.

Several people giggled. All girls by the sound of it.

"Charity, did you ask Hardy to massage your shoulders?"

"No, ma'am," she said, sounding distressed.

"That's what I thought," Mrs. Reid said with confidence.

Hardy shot up out of his seat as if by some involuntary reflex and pointed a finger at the back of Charity's head. "She's lying!"

The room exploded into stifled laughs.

"Hardy, you have earned yourself after-school community service for inappropriate physical contact."

"Mrs. Reid!" he protested. "I… She…I…" His stammering incited more snickering.

"Class, that will be enough," Mrs. Reid said, raising her voice.

He took a deep breath. Good. Now she would hear him out.

"Leave my class," Mrs. Reid said, sternly.

The realization of his predicament came to him like a giant punch to the gut. He looked around at the smug faces of the other students. *This isn't happening. There's been a mistake.*

"I'm talking to you, Hardy. Leave my class immediately and report to Administration."

His face flushed in anger and embarrassment. He bit the inside of his cheek, grabbed his backpack and history book, and headed toward the door like a dog with his tail between his legs.

"Okay, students. Now that that distraction is over, I'd like to offer a free lunch pass into the city for anyone who can find the cricket that seems to have made camp in our room all year."

The door slammed behind him.

Hardy made his way down the empty corridor, kicking lockers. His father was going to kill him. Tom had been very clear—mess up one more time, and there would be no leaving the island to go to college. Plus, he was supposed to take care of his grandfather after school. How was he going to do that if he had community service? It always felt like he was playing hide-and-seek with trouble. Trouble always found him.

Why had Charity lied? Why throw him under the bus? Who was he kidding—she didn't even know his name. Hardy took off his glasses and rubbed between his eyes, imagining how the conversation would go with his father.

You see it's like this, Tom. This girl was in serious pain, and being the kind, generous person I am…

She forced me to do it, I swear.

Mrs. Reid is a complete—.

None of his ideas were going to work with his father. Tom enforced a strict code of "no excuses" and was a stickler for the "three strikes rule." Hardy had already been in trouble at school twice this year—a fact Tom would no doubt remind him of before dropping the ax on his college plans. It hadn't even been *bad* trouble. The first time, he and Cricket had been innocently kicking around a paper ball before class when Hardy's shoe flew off and hit Ashley Hinton in the head. She cried, of course, so Hardy was immediately the bad guy. It wasn't like he *meant* to hit her, but that didn't matter to Mr. Bell. He got detention anyway. Then, there was the time in English when Josh Fountain took Hardy's pencils and threw them like darts into the ceiling tile. When Hardy stood on the desk to retrieve them, the desk buckled and collapsed to the floor. That landed him in after-school detention for destruction of school property.

No, there would be no talking his way out of this one. He would have to figure out something else—in other words, he'd have to lie. All he wanted to do was graduate and get off the island once and for all. He wasn't going to let some girl ruin that for him.

He opened the door to Administration and stepped inside. The glass walls and skylights filled the large room with natural light. The sweeping view of trees and rolling hills outside the back wall was a stark contrast to the industrial, white tables and chairs that dotted the room.

Hardy eyed the round reception desk at the center of the room. A line of students waited impatiently, shifting uncomfortably as they tried to balance books and backpacks. He decided to find an empty seat and just wait.

All the tables were occupied except for one at the back where a girl sat with her head buried in her arms. He wove through the other tables and quietly took a seat across from her. He stared outside at the new blooms of the apple trees that were lined up behind the school. His grandfather Olen always said there was wisdom in trees. Well, Hardy needed a big dose of wisdom right now, and no stupid tree was going to help him with that.

He had zoned into a non-blinking stare when the girl across from him bolted straight up. She didn't say a word, she just glared at him in silence. Her eyes were shocking. One blue. One brown. He didn't know which one to look at. Her white-blonde hair hung below her shoulders in a great flowing mass of loose waves. Her coloring was pale. Her lips the color of raspberries. Feeling awkward, Hardy crossed his arms.

"Hardy Vance," she said methodically.

He squeezed his eyebrows together. "Sorry, do we know each other?"

"You don't know me," she said.

He uncrossed his arms and scooted his chair closer to the table. "And how is it that you know me, exactly?" *Nobody else does.*

The strange conversation was cut short by the appearance of the Principal, Mr. Bell. He motioned with his fingers.

"You two, come with me."

They both stood simultaneously, each a little surprised that the other had been included in Mr. Bell's instruction. Hardy eyed the girl's long, black floral skirt and baggy tee. He was fairly certain she was barefooted. Who was this girl?

They followed Mr. Bell through one of the glass doors on the other side of the room into an office that held nothing but a large, oval table surrounded by plastic chairs.

"Have a seat," Mr. Bell said, settling his large frame into a chair. Hardy and the girl both dropped into seats across the table from him.

Mr. Bell had a bushy mustache that kindly hid his lack of an upper lip. His tousled salt-and-pepper hair indicated that he had likely been under some stress recently. He plopped a laptop on the table, opened it up, and started typing.

"Hardy Vance, meet Darcy Page, your new best friend," Mr. Bell said without looking up.

"I think there's been a mistake," Hardy said.

Mr. Bell stopped typing and leaned back in his chair. "Mrs. Reid said you would say that. Genius, that woman," he said, pondering the thought. He shot forward again and continued typing into his laptop. "You two will be assigned to Hill Home for the elderly for the next two weeks. Assignment begins Monday at four o'clock sharp. Hill Home of Dunby. Don't be late."

Hardy couldn't believe this was happening. Charity was the one that had gotten him into this, now he was going to be volunteering at one of her family's elder care facilities. He looked at the door, hoping somehow Charity would find the decency to show up and save him.

"As for today, you will both go to the town hall in Grey-stone to volunteer. Final bell will be ringing any minute. Any questions?" he said, looking up.

Hardy was about to open his mouth, but something about Mr. Bell's small, dark eyes prevented him from speaking. He decided he would be better off trying to find Charity and getting her to clear things up.

"Fine then," Mr. Bell said, satisfied. "Hardy, since you're a senior and Darcy a freshman, I will hold you responsible for making sure she does her service. She's been known to…how shall we say it?…skip out on occasion."

Hardy almost blurted out *"That's not fair."* But Mr. Bell was known for his witty answer to that remark: "Of course life isn't fair. That's what makes life fair for everyone."

"Make haste." And with that, Mr. Bell closed his laptop and left.

Hardy turned to the girl. "Darcy, is it? Look, I need to find somebody before we go."

"Okay," she said robotically.

There was no way he was going to take care of old people for two whole weeks. He was going to find Charity and make her fix this.

As soon as they stepped out into the hall, the bell rang, signaling the end of school. Hardy made out for Mrs. Reid's classroom, dodging the oncoming flood of students headed in the opposite direction. He was frantic to get there before Charity had a chance to leave. He bumped into more than one person. "Jerk," one of them called after him. He got to the room just as Charity was leaving with two of her friends. By this time, he had already broken out into a nervous sweat

9

and was breathing heavily through his mouth.

"Charity," he said, stopping in front of her. "I need you to come to Administration and tell them what really happened."

Both of Charity's friends smiled.

Charity feigned confusion. "I'm sorry, do we know each other?"

"You're kidding, right? Tell me you're kidding." Hardy said, agitated.

"Come on, girls." With that knife to the heart, she skirted around Hardy, and her lackeys followed close behind.

Unable to process what had just happened, Hardy leaned against the wall and put his hands on his head.

"You're upset," Darcy announced.

He had forgotten about Darcy. She was standing off to the side glaring at him with her weird eyes. He wondered why she thought that stating the obvious was somehow helpful.

"Of course, I'm upset," he snapped.

"We should go," Darcy said.

Charity had made a fool out of him, and there was nothing he could do about it. This was happening whether he wanted it to or not. "Fine," he said, peeling himself off the wall.

They made their way in silence out of the building to the bike racks. Darcy grabbed her bike and followed Hardy to retrieve his.

"Listen, I've got something I have to do," Hardy said.

"Okay." Darcy started to turn her bike around.

"Wait. Where are you going?"

"Home."

Hardy sighed. "You can't go home. We've got to report to the town hall."

"You said you had something to do."

"I do, but…" Hardy was stuck. He was supposed to go check on his grandfather Olen, but he also couldn't let Darcy leave. Mr. Bell said he was responsible for her.

"Will you go with me to do my errand?" he asked.

He heard Tom's voice echo in his head as soon as the words were out of his mouth. *Never tell anyone about Olen.*

Darcy stared at him with an unmoving, blank face. Hardy's eyes shifted back and forth between her blue and her brown eye. He decided the brown eye was less intimidating to look at and focused on that one.

"There's just one small thing," he said.

Darcy's face remained emotionless.

"You can't tell anybody about where we're going."

"Why?"

Hardy tugged at his right ear. He would have to be careful with his explanation. If Darcy thought that Olen was some big secret, she was more likely to blab. He decided on an alternate truth.

"If my parents find out that I got in trouble at school again, I won't be able to leave the island for college. The less people who know what we're doing, the better."

Darcy raised and dropped her hands. "Okay."

Relieved, Hardy smiled. Darcy would tag along on days when he had to check on Olen. His new excuse for being home late would be study group. Problem solved. He might just get away with this without Tom knowing.

Hardy rubbed his hands together. "All right. Let's go then. Hopefully you can keep up." He detected a slight movement in Darcy's face, something like a smirk, but it was hard to tell by her flat expression.

They walked their bikes through the meadow of solar panels that sat behind the school. A handful of sheep grazed among the rows—Nature's lawnmowers. Greene Island was a beautiful place, no doubt. The crystal-blue seas surrounded green hills and fertile farmlands. It was as if a beautiful piece of the mainland had broken off and floated out to sea. One could easily forget that they were on an island when they were inland walking in the woods, away from the rocky shores that held back the vast ocean.

But, despite its beauty, the island had one lingering problem. Its undying reputation for being cursed. The instrument of that curse was an angry princess named Viola who had lived on the island nearly three hundred years ago. The idea that she had cursed the island had become so ingrained in their society that it now became a convenient excuse for whenever anything bad happened. If a farmer lost one of his prized animals under any kind of superstitious circumstances, it was always blamed on *The Curse of Viola.* The same with anybody who died too young—it was Viola herself wielding the sickle of death. Some islanders went further still and fed the belief that Viola continued to roam the island, shifting to a new body as she pleased.

Hardy didn't buy into any of it. There was only one unexplained phenomenon that Hardy couldn't ignore—

Cricket. The thing that he could do was beyond explanation, and it wasn't making cricket noises. It was a secret that nobody knew about except for Cricket and Hardy. That's the way they meant to keep it. Hardy never believed Cricket's strange ability had anything to do with Viola's curse. Still… He wondered sometimes.

At the far edge of the meadow, Darcy followed him up a short footpath through some trees that led to a bicycle path. The trail was the former home of an old railroad that used to run from the north island to the south. Now the tracks were gone, and in its place was a dirt path edged on both sides by a waist-high thicket of freshly sprung weeds.

Hardy mounted his bike. He waited and watched Darcy, wondering how she was going to ride a bike in a long skirt. Without missing a beat, she dragged the back of the dress up through her legs and tied it in a knot near her waist. Sandals had miraculously appeared on her feet.

Not so big on looks. Ditto on modesty.

Darcy had no problem keeping up. In fact, at times she rode far ahead of him. That explained the smirk earlier when he offered to slow down his pace.

He just hoped she would keep her mouth shut about Olen. He pushed away his doubts in bringing her along by reminding himself that it was a necessary risk. He had several balls in the air right now, and he couldn't allow any of them to drop.

The tall grasses soon gave way to towering trees, encasing them in a kind of protective wall of nature. It was beautiful riding underneath the open sky between the regiment of trees. He thought perhaps he would miss this, anyway. It occurred to him that someone else would have to check on Olen after he left for college. He supposed his older brother Tate would pick it up again. It certainly wasn't going to be Tom.

After a long ride, they stopped and pushed their bikes into the woods. Hardy propped their bikes against a tree, and they continued without speaking down a steep bank that led to a small river. Even though the silence between them was awkward, Hardy was grateful for it. He hated small talk.

He sidestepped down to the river bank and lifted several piles of dead brush, tossing them aside. The old, weathered canoe had stayed well hidden. He lifted its bow up onto the bank.

Darcy studied the canoe. "We're going downriver?"

This is it. She's going to get scared, panic, and then bail.

Hardy put his hands on his hips. "Yes," he said. "That's where my grandfather lives."

To his surprise, she seemed pleased. And by 'pleased' he meant there was no sign of displeasure. She skirted around him and stepped into the canoe, seating herself at the front. He wondered how someone could have the face of an angel and the demeanor of an ax murderer. He thought maybe he should be scared of her. He could be playing right into her hands. She'd get him alone and then slit his throat, with the knife she kept hidden underneath her long skirt. No one would know. That was one possible scenario, anyway.

He realized he was staring at her and quickly untied the canoe's rope from a large root and threw it into the boat. He dropped his backpack in, scrambled to the center seat, and pushed offshore with the oar that was lying in the hull.

Chapter Two

Darcy was pleasantly surprised that Hardy's errand turned out to involve a trip downriver. It was a little curious that his grandfather appeared to be a kept secret, but then she knew about secrets. She had been living with hers now for the past five years. She only wished the eye wasn't blue. It was too different from her real brown one. People tended to stare at such strange things as a girl with different colored eyes. But she had learned to live with the stares and the secret.

She focused her blue eye on the passing trees.

Quercus robur. Oak.

Pinus radiata. Pine.

"You don't talk much, do you?" Hardy asked after several long minutes of rowing in silence.

Darcy ignored him and continued to stare at the parade of trees that marched along the banks of the narrow river. Virtual images flashed in front of her until a tree hit a match. *Corylus avellana*. Hazel.

There was no room for conversation when her eye was engaged. No one could understand her mind, and she didn't expect that Hardy would be any different. She had given up trying to make friends a long time ago. It was just easier—keeping to herself. Besides, she knew Hardy had just become her glorified babysitter. There was no need to try to be friends. She held her face up to the cool breeze and continued to identify the trees.

***

Hardy wondered what Darcy was thinking as she stared out into the trees. As soon as she had entered the boat, she had become completely entranced by the river. It was as if it was her first time in a canoe. Maybe he could—teach her a few things. Big brother and all that. If nothing else, he could score some Brownie points with Mr. Bell by keeping her in line.

Like a small child, Darcy leaned over the side, checking out each small fork in the river as they passed it. It was a virtual maze of water back in these woods. That was probably why his grandfather had stayed so well hidden all these years.

Getting close, Hardy steered the canoe toward a dense thicket on the river's edge. He stuck the paddle's blade behind him and dragged it forward to slow the canoe. "You'll have to duck to get past the Snake," he said.

Darcy looked tentatively behind her. "Snake?"

"You'll see," he said, smiling.

Hardy guided the canoe right into the bank of shrubs.

"Duck down," he instructed.

Darcy bent over and the canopy of green brush grazed across her back. They melted into the thick foliage and glided under the gnarled, twisted trunk of a large oak that bowed over the water like a giant sea serpent.

"That's the Snake," Hardy said as they cleared the tree.

"It must be two hundred years old," Darcy said, studying the twisted trunk.

Hardy raised an eyebrow and cleared his throat. "Uh, yeah. Something like that."

A few feet past the ancient tree, Hardy drew the canoe up next to a sandy bank, put on his backpack, and made the jump to dry land. He grabbed the stern and pulled it onto the shore of sand and small rock.

He held his hand out to Darcy. "Okay. Come on."

Darcy stared at his hand like the concept of helping someone out of a boat was foreign to her. She finally took it and stepped out onto the soft bank.

Hardy pointed to a narrow footpath that led up a steep slope that was covered in pitch pines and hickory trees. "This is it."

"Your grandfather lives here?" Darcy asked, looking around.

"You promised to keep this under wraps," Hardy reminded her.

"I said I would." Darcy untied her skirt and let it fall back over her legs.

Hardy took a deep breath and released it. "Good."

He led her through the trees up the rutted pathway until they reached a clearing of tall, thick weeds. A roof and a small columned porch appeared above the overgrown thicket. He put his arm out to stop Darcy.

"What's wrong?" Darcy whispered.

"Just wait."

Hardy cupped his hands together against his mouth and mimicked the sound of a mourning dove: "Coo-oo, ooo ooo ooo." This was the signal to his grandfather that Hardy was there. You didn't want to take him by surprise. Olen had a shotgun.

All was quiet in the woods. There was no movement from the small rustic cabin.

Hardy cooed once more. He had never had to do it more than once. He started to worry that something was wrong. Finally, the door opened and Olen's hunched frame, crowned by his shoots of white hair, stepped out onto the porch. Despite the warm afternoon, he wore a gray, button-up sweater and burgundy bow tie.

"Come on," Hardy said, relieved at the sight of Olen. They walked through the weeds into the mostly dirt front yard and climbed the three steps to the weathered porch. Olen was squinting intently at Darcy. Darcy seemed equally enamored with Olen. Hardy felt like the uncomfortable third wheel.

"Darcy, Olen. Olen, Darcy," Hardy said.

Olen peered at Darcy over his thin glasses. "Well, boy, I didn't think you had it in you."

Hardy blushed. "What? No, Olen, that's not—"

"She's a bit of a sprite, mind you, but the petite ones are often little firecrackers inside." Olen smiled with his yellowed, stained teeth and winked at Hardy.

Hardy wanted to find a rock and crawl under it. Darcy's expression seemed little affected by Olen's remark.

"It's not like that," Hardy tried to explain.

"Eh?" Olen said, peeling his eyes off Darcy and looking at Hardy.

"I'm kind of… watching her."

"Whatever you say, boy." Olen grinned.

"You're dead," Darcy said abruptly, focusing on Olen.

Hardy's stomach lurched into his throat. Either she knew Olen's secret, or she was the psychopathic killer Hardy had imagined her to be.

Olen stopped smiling and narrowed his eyes. He took a step toward Darcy, studying her face. "Well I'll be," he said, looking surprised. "I thought you had Heterochromia, but you don't, do you?"

Darcy didn't reply.

"Wait. Hetero—whatever that is you said. What's that?" Hardy hoped it wasn't contagious.

"Heterochromia of the eye. The irises are two different colors. Surely you've noticed, boy."

"Oh, that. Yeah, of course I noticed," Hardy said, feeling inadequate. "So what?"

Olen took Darcy gently by the shoulders and looked into her eyes.

"By George, you're an Illuminator, aren't you?"

Darcy nodded like she knew what Olen was talking about. Hardy was still trying to wrap his head around what was happening.

"You better come inside," Olen said, turning and opening the screen door.

"Wait! What?" Hardy asked.

Darcy and Olen ignored Hardy and went inside.

Hardy wondered if bringing Darcy along had been one huge mistake. Did she know about Olen? That he had died in a drowning accident thirty-two years ago? Now she knew the secret—Olen wasn't dead. But how? Hardy had never met her before today. Then again, she *had* known his name. He spun around in a frantic circle. Taking a deep breath, he pulled the screen door open and stepped inside.

The cabin was just as it was the last time Hardy had been there. The back wall held built-in bookcases full of dust-covered books. The ladder in front of the bookcases led up to an unused loft. Hardy tried to imagine his father as a child climbing the ladder to go to bed, but his mind was never able to picture it. Maybe because Tom never talked about his childhood.

An unmade single bed sat underneath the window on the right wall. Olen hurried to straighten it, tossing the covers back in place. On the left side of the room was a cast-iron stove and a small room, basically the size of a closet, which served as a kitchen. The only other furniture was an old burgundy lounger that sat next to the kitchen door, and a small table with two wooden chairs pushed up against the wall between the two front windows.

Olen apologized as he scurried about the room picking up clothes. "Sorry about the mess. I'm not used to having company."

Hardy took his backpack to the kitchen and quickly un-loaded the sugar, flour, and strawberries Olen had asked for. He needed to get Darcy out of there—stat. If Tom knew that

Hardy had exposed Olen by bringing Darcy…Well, he didn't want to think about it.

"Did you bring the strawberries?" Olen called out.

"Yes. We can't stay, Olen. We have to be somewhere. Listen, I forgot your newspaper, I'll remember next time."

When Hardy reappeared, Darcy was sitting in a chair by the table, facing into the room. Olen was pulling up a chair in front of her.

"Do you mind if I examine you?" Olen asked Darcy.

Hardy dropped his backpack on the floor and rushed forward, grabbing Olen by the arm. He lowered his voice to a whisper so Darcy couldn't hear. "What are you doing? Darcy doesn't need a doctor. Whatever it is you think she has—"

"It's fine, Hardy. I want him to," Darcy said.

Hardy dropped his hand from Olen and looked at Darcy.

"Please," Darcy said.

Hardy held up his hands and stepped aside. "Fine. Whatever."

Olen shuffled to the back wall and pulled an old, black doctor's bag off a lower shelf.

Hardy locked his hands on top of his head in disbelief. He had lost complete control of the situation, and he didn't even know what the situation was.

Olen planted himself in front of Darcy. He pulled out a stethoscope that looked prehistoric and stuck it in his ears. When he slid the scope up Darcy's shirt, Hardy turned away and started pacing. All was quiet except for the flapping of Hardy's tennis shoes against the rough, planked floors.

Olen stopped and turned to Hardy. "I need quiet, Hardy."

Hardy stopped and stood, staring at the bookcases, his jaw tensing with impatience. After what seemed like several minutes, but which in fact had only been a matter of seconds, Olen cleared his throat.

"Your heart rate is strong. Fascinating. May I look at the eye?"

Hardy turned around and watched Olen grab Darcy's face and peer into her blue eye.

"How long have you had it?" Olen asked.

"Since I was ten."

"How is it powered?"

"Mostly solar. But there is an auxiliary hook-up if I need an emergency charge."

Hardy started biting his nails. Power? Solar? He had no idea what they were talking about. Olen pulled down hard on Darcy's lower lid.

"I see the auxiliary hook-up," Olen said. "Come see, boy."

Hardy wasn't sure he wanted to see anything, but he was too curious not to look.

"Look left, Darcy," Olen instructed.

Hardy peered over Olen's shoulder and then jumped back. "What the—what's that?"

"An auxiliary hook-up. A tiny hole similar to the ones on cellphones."

Olen released Darcy's eye and placed his hand on her cheek. "You've been given a great gift. Make sure you use it wisely."

Darcy placed her hand on top of Olen's and smiled.

Hardy was surprised to see she had teeth and that her smile made her look… pleasant.

"Would *someone* please explain to me what is going on?" Hardy asked impatiently.

Olen stood and returned his stethoscope to his bag. "Darcy here is what you call an Illuminator."

"You said that already. What does that mean?" Hardy asked, watching Olen return his bag to its shelf.

Olen turned back to Hardy. "It means her eye is, for lack of a better term, a computer."

Hardy glanced at Darcy. She sat quietly and appeared to be scanning the books on the back wall.

"She's connected at all times to the island's network," Olen continued. "She can access virtually anything they've given her access to. You could say her reality was augmented."

Hardy laughed. "That's ridiculous. How would you know this, anyway? You've lived in the woods like…forever."

"The research started back when I was practicing medicine. I was privy to certain projects. I just never thought I'd live to see the day that it would actually come to fruition."

"Is he right?" Hardy asked Darcy.

"Yes." Darcy stood and walked past Hardy to the back bookcase. He stared after her in disbelief. "What about what you said about Olen? You said he was dead. What does that mean?" Hardy knew what it meant but he wanted to know if she did—if she was actually this Illuminator thing.

Darcy pulled a book from the shelf and rubbed the front cover with her hand. Olen dropped himself into the old lounger and pulled the lever to recline like he was settling in to watch a movie.

"As soon as you told me his first name, my search engine automatically pulled up the article about his drowning thirty-two years ago. Plus, I have facial recognition even if there's been age progression."

Hardy felt like an idiot. Here he thought he had something to offer this girl, teach her something even. This was the second time today a girl had made a fool out of him. Fool me once, shame on me. Fool me twice—

Hardy was furious. "You didn't think your illumi thingy was important to tell me about?"

"Illuminator," Olen corrected.

Hardy gave Olen a chastising look.

Olen pushed the lever down on the side of his chair. "I'll get us some tea," he said. He shuffled toward the kitchen.

"We're not staying," Hardy barked.

Darcy flipped through the book she was holding. She seemed to be ignoring Hardy.

"Well?" Hardy pushed.

Darcy looked up from the book in her hands. "No, I didn't think it was important."

"Well, it is!"

"Why?" Darcy asked innocently, closing the book.

"Why?" Hardy repeated, struggling to find the words. *Because now you know Olen's not dead, and I feel like a fool.* "I don't know, it just is."

"Will you treat me differently now that you know?"

Hardy felt like she was doing something weird with her blue eye, like scanning his face to see if he would be truthful.

He wondered if she could read minds.

"No." He lied. "I mean, you can't like, read my mind or anything, can you?" Hardy bit hard into his index fingernail.

"No. Don't be ridiculous," Darcy said, narrowing her eyes.

"X-ray vision?" Hardy said, casually crossing his arms across his chest.

"No," Darcy said loudly. "It's not a super power."

"It is to me," Hardy said fiercely.

Darcy sighed, and dropped the book to her side. "Well, it's normal to me. It's not a big deal."

"Yeah, but now you know Olen's not dead," Hardy whispered harshly.

"And now you know I'm an Illuminator."

Hardy relaxed a little. "People don't know?"

"No."

Olen returned balancing a bowl of strawberries and three Ball Mason jars of brown liquid on a piece of scrap wood. "Here we go. Sorry it's not much," Olen said, setting the makeshift tray on the small, wooden table.

Darcy approached the table and set the book down. "Thank you." She took one of the jars and drank the full contents.

Hardy's mouth fell open. He knew what Olen's supposed "tea" tasted like—dirt. Darcy set the empty jar down and shoved the tip of a large strawberry into her mouth.

"I'm curious as to how you two came to know each other," Olen said.

Hardy shook his head at Darcy, indicating his desire for her not to say anything.

She paused only long enough to swallow. "Hardy got after-school community service for inappropriate touching. I got it for sleeping in class. We stopped here first." She bit into the rest of her strawberry.

Olen peered at Hardy over the top of his glasses.

Hardy sighed. "It's not what you think."

"How many times is this now?" Olen asked.

"It wasn't my fault. This girl—"

Olen held up a hand. "No need to explain."

"Tom can't find out. He said if I got in trouble again, I wouldn't be able to leave the island for college."

Olen smiled. "There's little chance of it coming from me. So, who was the unfortunate girl?"

Hardy snatched his backpack off the floor. "No one."

"Charity Hill," Darcy blurted out.

The smile disappeared from Olen's face. "Is that right, boy? Was it Charity Hill?"

Hardy's lips tightened with agitation. He gawked at Darcy and her big mouth. She held his gaze and shrugged.

"Hardy," Olen said.

Hardy squeezed his eyes shut and took a deep breath. "Yeah…but I told you, it's not what you think."

Olen stuck his finger in Hardy's face. "Stay away from that girl. Do you hear me?"

Hardy turned his head away from Olen's annoying finger. "It's not a big deal. It was just a misunderstanding."

Olen dropped his finger. "I have no doubt it was." He went back to the table and picked up a jar. "Promise me you'll stay away from her."

"Why? How could you possibly even know who she is?"

Hardy asked, perplexed and annoyed by Olen's concern.

Olen took a sip of his tea and smacked his lips together. "I don't have to know her. I know the Hill family." He set the jar back on the table. "And I know what I'm talking about."

Hardy wanted to be done with this conversation, and this visit. "Time to leave."

Olen picked up a strawberry. "I want to show Darcy something before you go." He walked to the screen door and blew a short burst of whistles.

Hardy flung his empty book bag across one shoulder. "Were leaving now, Olen," he said sharply.

Olen held up a hand. "Be patient, boy."

The sound of little clawed feet hitting the steps was followed by the appearance of a whipping, rust-colored tail, until finally the tiny face of a red squirrel peered up and over the last step. It stood on its hind legs and sniffed the air.

As Hardy stared at the little rodent, a weird sensation came over him. A rush of pins and needles ran through his scalp. A slight dizziness settled into his vision. He took a step back. The stress of the day was apparently getting to him.

"There you are, Angus. Come for your treat, have ye?" Olen motioned for Darcy to come over to the screen door. He handed her the strawberry. "Here. Give it a try. He'll take it right from your hand."

A blurry white light started pulsing around the squirrel's head. Hardy seemed to be the only one noticing it. He watched the whole exchange in a kind of tunnel vision.

Darcy slowly opened the screen door. Angus turned and

darted down a step. Darcy looked back at Olen who urged her forward with his hands. She took two steps forward and kneeled down, holding the strawberry out on the palm of her hand. Angus jumped back up onto the porch and crept cautiously toward her. He quickly nabbed the berry with his tiny paws and sat on his hind legs. He turned his prize until the stem was down and sank his small, white teeth into its soft flesh.

Darcy twisted around and grinned at Olen.

Hardy was unable to tear his eyes from the flickering, white fire that surrounded Angus. This weird vision thing had happened once before, about six months ago when Cricket's dog got hit by a car. The eye doctor had said it was migraine aura. A rare but real sign that a migraine was approaching.

Olen must've noticed the strange look on Hardy's face. "You okay?"

"Um… Do you… See that?" Hardy asked.

Olen looked back out the screen door. "See what, exactly?"

Hardy wasn't sure how to describe it. "Um…Flickering light."

"Around Angus?"

Hardy nodded.

"I suspect you've been told it's migraine aura," Olen said. "Have you had it before?"

"Once." Hardy tore his gaze from the squirrel and looked at Olen. Without saying anything, Olen returned to the table and scribbled something on a pad of paper. He ambled back to the bookcases and rummaged through a wooden box until

28

an envelope appeared in his hand. He shoved the note into it and licked the tip of the flap.

Hardy had no idea what Olen was doing. Surely he wasn't trying to write him a prescription for migraine medication? Maybe Olen was getting senile.

Olen returned to the table and picked up the book Darcy had chosen from his bookcase.

Angus finished the last of the berry and dropped the stem on the porch. He hopped up to Darcy and stood on his hind legs, looking to see if more treats were available. She held out her empty hand which he quickly sniffed. Then, with a quick snap of his tail, he bounded down the steps and out into the woods. The blurry light seemed to follow and disappear with the squirrel. Hardy's vision returned to normal.

Darcy stood and wiped her hand on her long skirt. She was still smiling. Hardy pushed open the screen door, and Olen followed him out onto the porch.

"Come on. We've got to get back to town," Hardy said to Darcy.

Olen held out the black book to Darcy. "I want you to have the book."

Darcy stared at it like she wasn't sure what the proper thing to do would be. She shook her head.

Olen gently took Darcy's hand and laid the book on her open palm. "I insist."

Darcy smiled and wrapped her fingers around the book. "Thank you."

She quickly embraced Olen who froze in place, surprised at the sudden affection. Hesitantly, he patted her on the back.

Without another word, Darcy turned, ran down the steps, and headed toward the river.

Hardy placed a hand on Olen's shoulder. "I'll see you Monday, okay?"

"Sure. See you Monday." Olen was staring into the woods after Darcy.

Hardy sensed a certain sadness in Olen's voice. Maybe it wasn't always easy living alone. He promised himself that next time he would stay longer.

He raced down the steps and was almost out of sight when Olen called to him.

"Hardy!"

Hardy spun around. "Yeah?"

"Wait." Olen rubbed his hand across his mouth and stared down at the envelope he was still holding.

Hardy stood impatiently, shifting his feet from side to side. He didn't want Darcy disappearing on him.

"Give this to your father," Olen said, holding out the envelope.

"Okay," Hardy said, making his way back to the cabin and up the steps. Olen had *never* sent a message to his father. *Ever.* Hardy didn't even know the last time they had seen each other. He was pretty sure it was when his father had run away from the tiny cabin at age fourteen and told everyone that Olen had drowned.

Hardy took the envelope from Olen's frail hand. He couldn't help but wonder how the day could get any weirder.

Chapter Three

Olen watched Hardy disappear into the woods. The Program would come for him now. The girl had seen him—identified him. He had awakened with the great hope of the morning, and now his day would end with the great dread of death. He was surprised it hadn't come earlier. When his son had walked out of the woods years ago, Olen had thought that he would be found out then. But Tom had been clever. They had believed his story. Tom had explained how he had lived in the woods with his father for fourteen years. Olen had drowned, and Tom had no choice but to come out of the woods. Tom was a bright kid. He had planted a shoe downstream and a shirt caught up in the brambles. There was an old hunting shack near the supposed drowning. No doubt Tom had shown it to the officers as the place where they had lived. Tom had at least tried to keep Olen from being found out. That's how the papers had explained it, anyway.

They had been happy, just the two of them, for a long time. But children grow up, start asking questions. In the end, Tom had just wanted the truth. *Why did they have to live in the woods?* But the truth was dangerous, and Olen never wanted him to have to carry the burden of that truth. He had tried to explain to him that they had to live in the woods because there were people out there that wanted to harm them. That wasn't enough for Tom. There was no stopping the boy after that. Olen figured Tom spent a good two months planning the day he would leave.

He walked down the steps of the cabin and looked at the innocent beauty that surrounded him. The strong oak and the spring pine. He never got tired of it, and he would miss it. He stuck his hands in his pockets and held his face to the remaining rays of sunlight that broke through the treetops. He never regretted his decision to come to the woods and bring his son. They had been safe there. But he did have one lingering regret. He had never told Tom that he loved him. Yes, he had cared for him, supplied his basic needs, but he had withheld the one thing that Tom needed the most. If he had only said those three little words, trusted him with the truth, maybe Tom would have never left. And just now, when he had called to Hardy, he wanted to send Tom a different message than the one he handed to Hardy. He wanted his only son to know that he loved him. Pride could be an evil thing in a man. And even now, on the eve of his death, he couldn't push past its great wall. He supposed it was the idea that it was too late to fix the past. He feared the words would ring hollow, and Tom would hate him for saying it now instead of years ago when he should have.

Olen walked into the woods. At least he had gotten to know his grandsons. First, Tate, who was married now. Then Hardy, who took over checking on him. He was surprised the first time Tate had shown up. Surprised not only that he did have a grandson, but also that Tom had felt some sense of obligation to the crazy old man who lived in the woods. It was probably more than Olen deserved.

Ah, there it was. The great oak tree with its rotted-out hole. The perfect hiding place and home for his beloved squirrel, Angus. They were hidden here—the papers. He felt comfortable with the fact that at least The Program wouldn't find them. There was a small hope in the back of his mind that perhaps Hardy would find the papers. The boy was a bit of a scatterbrain, but Olen was hoping his mischievous nature would be enough to lead him to the tree. Hardy had a knack for trouble, after all. And this was trouble. Big trouble.

Olen rubbed the rough bark of the tree with his hand then stuck it blindly into the black hole. Woven sticks jutted out at odd angles. Angus had built himself quite a fortress. Olen moved around it, his fingers finding nuts, something slightly wet. He dug past the refuge and scraped below the pile of treasures until his fingers found the smooth texture of plastic. He felt the sharp edges, the seal seemed to be intact. Good. Angus hadn't destroyed it. He pulled his hand out and brushed it off on his pants. He looked around, taking it all in one last time and headed back to the cabin. The idea was crazy. After all, he was leaving it up to a kid to do what he should have done a long time ago. And even if Hardy was able to reveal the truth, would anyone believe it? It was a long shot, no doubt. But even long shots won races sooner or later.

Olen dragged his tired feet through the dried leaves of last fall. New green life was peeking through the dead of winter and renewing the forest once more. When the cabin came into view, he stopped and stared at it like a stranger. His bones ached. He was tired. The truth was, he was getting too old to survive in the woods. He could barely make it down to the river to bathe anymore. Some days his hip hurt so badly all he could do was lie in bed all day. A new home without this body began sounding more like a relief. Besides, it was time to be reunited with the love of his life. His wife, Sarah. The Program had killed her. Now, they would come for him—at last.

***

Hardy strained to pull the oar against the gentle current. Between Darcy pronouncing Olen dead, the discovery that Darcy was some kind of virtual genius, the strange letter to Tom that was currently burning a hole in his pocket, and the throbbing in his left temple, he was feeling a bit worn-down and irritable. He cast a bitter stare at Darcy, focusing on her sparkling blue eye.

"Please stop staring at me," Darcy said.

"I'm sorry. I'm just a little freaked out about the whole eye thing. Who else knows?"

"My family."

"That's it?"

"Yes."

"Why is it such a big secret?"

"I don't know. I'm supposed to be some kind of secret prototype. It would be easier if you would just treat me like you didn't know."

"Yeah, it would. But it's too late for that."

Silence settled between them. Hardy's oar parting the water and birds whistling their songs across the water were the only sounds.

"So...in class...you basically know everything already?" Hardy asked.

"Yes."

Hardy whistled. "Lucky."

"Boring."

Hardy took a break and let the oar rest in his lap. "Why do you have to go to school then?"

"I don't know."

"Well I would certainly ask if I was you."

Darcy stared down at the book she held in her lap without responding.

Hardy sensed that he had hurt her somehow. "Darcy, I—"

"I did ask questions at first. But there were no answers given, so I stopped asking," Darcy said quickly.

Hardy dug the oar back into the water. "Sorry," he said.

"For what?"

"I don't know. Having to go to school when you don't need to, I guess."

Darcy stared out into the passing trees.

"So...back there...how did you know Olen was a doctor?" Hardy asked.

Darcy tapped a finger next to her blue eye without looking at him.

"Right—access."

After that, Hardy left her in peace. The conversation had deepened the lines on her forehead, and he felt bad for pushing for information.

Darcy held on tightly to her book and scanned the trees that lined the river. Her blue eye darted back and forth. They didn't speak again until they arrived in Greystone.

***

"That was fun," Darcy announced, looking refreshed and exuberant after their long bike ride.

Hot and irritable, Hardy wiped his forehead on his sleeve. If only he had a car. But Tom had insisted that there was nowhere Hardy needed to be that wasn't within a thirty minute bike ride. Well, Tom was wrong. *Whatever.* No car— Just something else to hate about his life.

They dismounted at the traffic circle in front of Greystone Town Square and pushed their bikes into the bricked open-air market. The statue of the veiled lady stood before them— the legendary Princess Viola who had supposedly cursed Greene Island almost three hundred years ago. A few people stood staring at her—tourists. Locals never lingered near the statue, much less looked at her. They were too superstitious.

A ladder leaned against her side. Apparently, she was due for some maintenance. Hardy felt for the poor chum who got that chore. Superstitious or not, the statue was eerie with its ghostly face that peered at you from behind its veil of stone.

The square itself was flanked by three-story buildings washed in pale pinks and yellows, capped off with clayed tiled roofs. Second- and third-story window balconies held boxes full of spring flowers. Sidewalk cafés bustled with people enjoying afternoon tea at the end of a cool spring day. Waiters laid new white tablecloths as the tables emptied.

The town hall sat at the back of the square—a Gothic marvel of brick arches that supported a second-story, white-columned balcony. A clock tower stood at the hall's right corner. Climbing the steep steps to the top of the tower was popular with school kids and tourists. The reward for the climb was a close-up look at the antique clock's metal workings, and a picture-perfect view of downtown Greystone and its harbor.

To Hardy, it was all old and boring. He just wanted to get this over with so he could go home. They slid their bikes into a rack and passed through the center arch of the town hall.

They both stood in the cavernous lobby unsure of where to go. Now that he was there, Hardy found himself fuming again over the injustice of what Charity had done to him. Not to mention he was now stuck with this Darcy girl who was not only weird, but also smart. He almost laughed out loud about how he had thought he might teach her something.

A short, elderly, bald man with round glasses came barreling around the corner wearing a scholarly navy blazer, khakis, and a worn pair of brown Oxfords. A stack of glossy pamphlets were clutched in his right hand. He approached the unmanned reception desk and deposited the pamphlets in a plastic holder. "The bell tower is closed for the day. Come back tomorrow at ten o'clock."

Hardy cleared his throat. "We were sent by Mr. Bell at Southeast High."

The man pulled up the sleeve of his jacket and glanced at his thin, Swiss watch. "You're late."

"Sorry. He didn't give us an exact time," Hardy explained.

The man touched the rims of his glasses and settled them higher on his nose. "Generally, after-school service means *after* school."

Hardy decided ignorance was his best defense and said nothing. Darcy's head was tilted to the ceiling like she was a safety inspector. When neither Hardy nor Darcy responded, the man turned and headed back toward the hallway he had appeared from.

"Follow me."

Hardy and Darcy followed him down a long hall of office doors with frosted glass windows.

"I'm Dr. Finch, the curator of all things related to our historical town square."

Hardy felt a yawn coming on. He hoped there wasn't going to be a history lesson. All this had been very exciting at five when he had first climbed the bell tower. Now it was nothing but snooze-worthy.

Finch opened the door with a brass plaque nailed below its window that said 'Dr. Cain Finch'. He marched straight to his desk and shifted through one of the stacks of paper he had on his otherwise immaculate desk. Darcy drifted to the towering wall of old books that lined the left wall, and began scanning the shelves. *Here we go again*, Hardy thought. A long, wood table sat at the back of the room in front of two tall windows that looked out through the hall's brick arches to the small shops across from it.

Finch seemed pleased by Darcy's interest in his book collection. He came back around to the front of his desk. "Most of those books are hundreds of years old."

"Actually, only a few dozen are," Darcy responded.

Hardy choked back a laugh that came out as a cough.

Finch's face went white. "How could you…?"

Darcy was oblivious to Finch's embarrassment at being called out on his embellishment of his book collection.

"Yes, well…back to business." Finch handed them each a sheet. "Fill this out and sign it." He handed them another sheet. "Read this carefully. There will be a test." He gave them both pencils and left the room.

A test? When Hardy heard those words he groaned. He took a seat at the table facing the windows. Darcy sat directly across from him.

The first page looked like a legal paper of some kind. Probably used to keep you from suing them in case of injury. Hardy filled it out and signed it without reading it. The second page had "The Legend of the Veiled Lady" written across the top. So, they had to read about Viola and her curse. *Great.*

He glanced up at Darcy. She was staring right at him. He adjusted his glasses which were still slippery with sweat after the long bike ride. "You're supposed to be reading," he reminded her.

"I am. This is quite fascinating."

"But you're not even looking at the page."

"I prefer the digital copy. I'm connected to the hall's server."

Hardy sighed, realizing she was reading it from her virtual eye. Still, the staring straight ahead was disturbing.

"Would you mind…reading in another direction?"

Darcy turned her chair sideways and stared at the right wall. Hardy lowered his head into his hand and began reading.

Legend of the Veiled Lady

Back when there were kingdoms and uncharted lands, the King sent his youngest son Philip, who was lazy and spoiled, to a wild and untamed island. There he was to make his mark and prove to his father that he was worthy of more. The King's elder son, Felix, rejoiced in the King's decision because, even though he was heir to the throne, he knew his father favored his irresponsible younger brother, and he saw his brother's banishment as a victory.

Philip, feeling angry and dejected, sailed to the island with a fleet of ships and a large contingent of colonists. They found the land to be fertile but difficult, for no one had ever populated the land and cultivated it.

After a year of back-breaking work and failed crops, Philip stood on the beach and cursed the day he was born. He had failed, and now he must return to his father and beg to be taken back, for his spirit had been broken. He now saw the error of his ways.

It was then that she appeared. At first Philip thought he was seeing things, for there were no boats anywhere on the horizon. She walked naked out of the sea, her wet hair hanging down her back. She shivered, and Philip covered her with his cloak. Water dripped from her long, red lashes as he looked into her emerald-green eyes. He saw something there that he didn't understand, but right then, he knew that he loved her. "Who are you?" he asked. "Viola," she whispered.

Philip and Viola were married that day, and new hope came to the island. Together they devoted themselves to the land, and the island prospered. The people of the island felt that Viola had brought good fortune with her, and therefore all the people loved her. Her children were revered and counted as blessed. The island became a prosperous port and a shining beacon in the King's kingdom. The King was a happy man, for Philip had proved himself as a worthy son.

All was well until the King died. Felix became King, but jealousy of his brother still burned in his heart. Felix sailed to the island, killed his brother, and took Viola as his wife. On their wedding day, as they stood in a meadow, Felix handed Viola a dandelion and told her to make a wish, for he would give her anything her heart desired. She took the dandelion in her hand and blew, and the white seeds spread into the air and hung there as if suspended in time. Suddenly, the floating seeds lifted into the air like a veil from her face and disappeared into the sky. Felix felt something cold move through him. Something that felt like fear. As Felix looked into Viola's darkened eyes, he dared not ask her what she wished for. Felix took Viola from the island, leaving her children behind as orphans, ensuring they would never be able to take the throne.

The people mourned the loss of their Prince Philip and Princess Viola, for they had dearly loved them. After that day, it is said a dark cloud came over the island, and a curse came upon the land. For crops and animals died of disease, and the island no longer prospered.

The legend is that Viola's descendants still roam the island, carrying with them traits of an extraordinary nature. But what those traits are and whether or not the island was ever cursed, no one can say.

Viola's statue stands today in Greystone Town Square.

Hardy finished reading and looked up. Darcy was roaming around the room, and had stopped to look at a collection of historical pictures that hung behind Finch's desk. He stared back down at the paper. The old legend was hogwash, of course. But that one sentence—*Viola's descendants still roam the island, carrying with them traits of an extraordinary nature.* He couldn't help thinking about Cricket's strange ability. He reminded himself he didn't believe any of it and pushed the ridiculous idea out of his head.

He stuck his hand inside his pocket and felt the stiff edges of the folded envelope—Olen's mysterious letter to Tom. He slid it out of his pocket and unfolded it. It was probably just some advice about Hardy's weird migraine symptoms. He turned it over and noticed that the seal hadn't stuck. The flap was loose. He toyed with its edges. It would be so easy just to slip out the note and see what it said. Olen hadn't wanted him to read it. Hardy remembered him licking the envelope. What if Olen had decided to say something about Charity? He seemed pretty adamant about Hardy staying away from her.

Hardy lifted the flap and pulled out the small slip of paper. He opened it slowly. There were only eight words written on it.

It's time to tell Hardy the truth
Olen

The truth? About what? Annoyed by the cryptic message, Hardy shoved the note back in the envelope and licked the flap. He placed it on the table and rubbed it shut and stuck it back in his pocket. Tom would never know that Hardy had read it. He rested his elbows on the table and massaged the light drumbeat that was pounding in his temples. Hardy and Tom never had real conversations, so he didn't expect Tom would even discuss the note. It was better just to pretend it never existed. Tom never talked about his time in the woods with Olen. So, if there was any truth to be told, Hardy was sure he would never hear it.

Hardy was about to speak to Darcy when he caught a glimpse through the window of short, blonde hair that looked an awful lot like Charity's. He jumped up out of his chair and ran to the window. There were two dark-haired women holding boutique bags, chatting outside a small shop. He looked left and right, but there was no sign of a blonde. He could have sworn he'd seen Charity. Maybe it had just been wishful thinking.

Dr. Finch entered the room, interrupting Hardy from his frantic search and Darcy's self-guided tour of the office. Hardy turned around and put his hands in his pockets. The scowl on Finch's face indicated he wasn't too pleased to find Darcy perusing his things. He came to his desk and glared at Darcy over the top of his glasses.

"Darcy Page, I'm going to assume you are prepared for the test since you found it convenient to snoop."

43

Hardy felt a slight pang of sympathy for her. Darcy, however, didn't miss a beat. She stood facing Finch, unfazed by his prickly demeanor.

"More than prepared. I'd be glad to recite the legend to you in full, if necessary," Darcy said.

Hardy suppressed a smile by biting his lip. Maybe she wasn't so bad.

Finch stared at her with a look of shocked disdain. He opened his mouth to speak but Darcy continued.

"If that is insufficient, I can also discuss the sculptor, how long it took to sculpt it, when it was put in Town Square, and how the statue never deteriorates." Darcy paused and added, "Which has yet to be explained."

Finch blinked several times and turned red. He looked as if he might be choking.

"Follow me," Finch croaked.

Sweet. No test. Hardy was starting to think that his day was finally looking up. Strangely enough, it was due to Darcy.

It was obvious by the supplies Finch was collecting out of a utility closet that they were to do some kind of cleaning. He just hoped it wasn't toilets. Finch filled a bucket with a container marked 'Distilled Water' and set it in the hall. He took down a yellow, two-gallon container and handed it Hardy. He gave Darcy gloves and a clear bag of white, fluffy material that looked like cotton.

"You two will be cleaning Viola."

Oh no. Not that. He had had plenty of weird for one day. "Are there any other options?" Hardy asked. He glanced at Darcy who rolled both of her eyes. Hardy was mesmerized.

How did she do that? No one would ever know that her blue eye wasn't real. Hardy was still staring at Darcy when Finch clapped his hands together.

"Pay attention, this is important." Finch mimicked long, gentle strokes in the air with his hand. "Wipe the statue, not rub, with a piece of cotton wool barely moistened with the cleaning mixture in the yellow container. After you clean a small section, rinse it with another piece of cotton dampened with the water in the bucket."

Hardy started biting his nails—the one nasty habit that he couldn't seem to kick—often used when bored, nervous, or stressed. Currently, he was all three—trifecta.

"Is that clear, Hardy Vance?" Finch asked.

"Got it."

Finch frowned, obviously concerned as to whether Hardy had actually *gotten it*.

"Tourists tend to ask questions, I hope you will revert to the story you just read in order to answer them," Finch said. He looked at his watch. "You have one hour."

Hardy gnawed on the cuticle of his pinky finger, but paused to ask a single question. "That whole curse thing is all just a fairy tale, right?"

Looking put out, or perhaps annoyed, Finch walked down the hall to his office and shut the door.

Hardy bent over to pick up the bucket of water. "Okay, then. Onward to clean the creepy statue."

"She's not creepy," Darcy said. "Her name is Viola."

"Whatever you say. I'm sticking with creepy."

Darcy sighed and headed toward the main entrance.

The end of the workday had ushered in the young professionals who were now filling the sidewalk cafés for their afternoon teas or cappuccinos. Wrought-iron benches held the loners who preferred reading and eating their takeout out of white paper bags. Traffic circling in front of the square sounded off with grinding engines and honking horns.

Hardy walked around to the front of the white, weathered statue and set his load down. This was the first time he had looked at the statue of Viola—really looked at her. The statue stood in the middle of a slightly elevated circle of grass that was contained by a low brick wall. Linked black chains held by short stakes surrounded her in a protective circle. The only way to get close to her was to climb a small section of steps in front of her and stand next to the chains that kept her just out of arm's reach.

It was the way she looked that made Hardy feel like he was standing on a grave. The artist had created an illusion of a thin, fabric veil that hung delicately over her face. Through the veil you could see the imprint of a crown of flowers around her head, a pair of hollow eyes, and a long, delicate nose. Her crossed hands rested on her long, flowing gown. Her left hand held a seed-head of a dandelion—the instrument of her curse. She was a translucent masterpiece, a shadow of a living soul.

A shudder ran through Hardy's body. Her shaded eyes looked down on him as if she was watching him. He reminded himself that he didn't believe in curses. Still, rereading the story of the legend had resurrected the idea in his mind, and he wasn't relishing getting anywhere near Viola, legend or not.

Darcy started putting on plastic gloves. Hardy took the

46

containers up the steps and climbed over the chain link.

"I guess I'm going up the ladder," Hardy said.

"If you don't mind. My eye and heights don't get along so well."

Hardy put on his gloves and tore off a piece of cotton from inside the bag. He moistened it with the cleaning mixture and stared up at Viola from the base of the ladder. No matter where he stood, it seemed like Viola was staring at him. His day already felt cursed. How much worse could it get?

He climbed the ladder until he reached her veiled head. He gingerly reached out and dabbed her forehead, pushing the cotton between the crevices of the stone flowers braided beneath the stone veil.

"So, Viola. I could really use a little of your good luck side."

"What?!" Darcy yelled up.

Hardy jumped at Darcy's sudden outburst. The ladder swayed lightly beneath his feet.

"Nothing!" Hardy yelled back, frowning.

Darcy shrugged and bent down to work on Viola's sandaled feet.

Hardy readjusted himself and wiped Viola's lifeless eyes. He lowered his voice to a whisper and continued to talk to the statue.

"There's this girl named Charity. Like the most gorgeous girl on the island—but she humiliated me, and I ended up the one in trouble." Hardy continued wiping down her veiled nose.

"So, if there's any way you can help me out—" He didn't

get to complete the thought when he heard a small voice in his head say, *Charity is going to be hit by a bus*. Hardy smiled. "Well, I think that's a little drastic. Maybe just...a flesh wound."

This time the voice was louder. "Charity is going to be hit by a bus!"

Hardy realized that it was Darcy yelling and not his imagination making up a voice for Viola. Darcy was staring at the traffic circle in front of them. Charity was headed straight for it. Sure enough, a bus was just making its way up the hill, headed for the roundabout. Hardy's heart began to race. "She'll hear it."

"No, she won't. She's got in headphones."

Hardy glanced at Viola. Surely this had nothing to do with what he had just said...to the statue.

"Twenty-five seconds!"

Hardy realized he had a decision to make. Risk embarrassing himself and try to save Charity, or watch her get hit by a bus. He quickly climbed down the ladder. "Are you sure?" Hardy said frantically, bouncing on his heels.

Darcy's blue eye was darting back and forth between the bus and Charity. "The driver doesn't see her. He's talking to the passenger sitting behind him. Charity's looking down at her phone."

Charity walked into the street and stopped, her fingers moving across her phone. The bus was coming up fast—the driver wasn't slowing down. It was now or never.

Hardy took off running. The bus turned into the roundabout. He was afraid he wasn't going to make it. He pushed himself harder. All he could hear was the sound of his lungs fighting for air and the pounding of his heart in his temples. He screamed Charity's name over and over again. The muscles in his legs stung with pain. He could smell the rotten fumes of the bus's exhaust, hear the shift of the engine as it bore down on her in that last horrible moment. He slammed into Charity at a full run and felt the wind of the bus brush past as they hit the ground.

Chapter Four

Light seeped through Hardy's eyelids. He must have slept hard because he didn't even remember going to bed. In fact, he suddenly realized he could barely remember anything. He rummaged around his brain. After-school community service, weird girl named Darcy, checked on Olen... Oh, the bus. Charity. A sharp pain shot through his head. He cringed. When he tried to lift his head and realized it was as heavy as a bowling ball, he pried his eyes open to a small slit. He wasn't at home. Fluorescent lights glared above him. A needle-like pain pinched the crook of his right arm. The smell of disinfectant and clean sheets pulled him into reality. He was in a hospital room.

Hardy's half-opened eyes moved slowly back and forth. Cricket and Darcy were sitting on opposite sides of his bed staring intently at each other. They were so focused on each other they didn't notice that he had opened his eyes. The sound of a cricket chirping was the only sound in the room.

"I know it's you," Darcy said to Cricket.

The cricket noise stopped.

"I don't know what you're talking about," Cricket said innocently.

The cricket noise started again.

"Your lips may not be moving, but I can detect a slight movement in your jaw where you're pushing the air through," Darcy said.

The cricket noise stopped again.

Cricket leaned back in his chair and folded his arms without breaking eye contact with Darcy.

"Hey," Hardy managed to say.

Cricket jumped up out of his chair and leaned over Hardy, smiling. "Hey, buddy. How are you feeling?"

"Crappy."

"Yeah, I bet you do. You hit your head pretty hard. Busted it right open. They said there was blood everywhere. Gusher proportions."

Hardy held up a hand. "Okay, okay. I don't need the graphic details."

"You're a real hero, chum. Can I have your autograph?" Cricket patted his shirt and shorts pockets looking for a pen.

"Ha, ha. Very funny." Hardy winced as another sharp pain shot through the back of his head.

"Hey, you okay? You want me to get the doctor?" Cricket said, looking concerned.

Hardy shifted in the bed. "I'm fine."

Darcy coughed into her hand.

"Is Charity okay, Darcy?" Hardy asked.

"Yeah, speaking of Darcy. Who is she, and why is she

51

here?" Cricket asked, sounding annoyed.

"We have after-school community service together," Hardy explained.

Cricket shrugged. "And...why is she *here*?"

Darcy stood. "I'll go."

"Darcy..." Hardy didn't know what to say. He did find it kind of strange that she had waited at his bedside.

"It's fine. I just wanted to make sure you were okay." Darcy moved around the bed and headed for the door.

"Darcy." Hardy said.

She stopped and turned around.

"Um...thanks," Hardy said, not knowing what else to say.

She nodded and left. For some reason Hardy felt bad about her leaving.

"Thank goodness she's gone. I tried everything to get rid of her. That's one weird girl. I mean what's up with the creepy eyes. One blue and one brown? It's like she can look through you, or something."

"Don't be such a jerk."

"Dude, she just met you today and she's hanging out at your bedside? Can you say—stalker?"

"It's not like that. We went through a lot together." *You're dead. Darcy is an Illuminator.*

Cricket held up his hands in surrender. "Okay, whatever you say."

Dread set in as Hardy realized his parents would probably know everything by now. Tom would know about the after-school community service. Any chances of getting off the island just went to zero.

"Are my parents here?" Hardy asked.

Cricket motioned over his shoulder with his thumb. "Yeah. Outside talking to the doctor."

Hardy looked around Cricket and through the partially open blinds could just make them out talking to a man in a white coat.

"How much do they know?" Hardy wanted to be prepared.

"About the accident?"

"No, you idiot. Do they know why I was in Greystone?" *Because if they know that, then they know everything.*

"I don't think anything. They got a call from the hospital and came straight here. I think all they know is that you saved Charity's life."

"What about Darcy? Did she tell them anything?" Hardy fought the urge to start biting his nails.

"She told them you two were hanging out by the statue when the whole thing went down."

"Did they ask her what we were doing there?"

"What's with the twenty questions?"

"You know why. My whole future hangs in the balance. Now answer the question."

"No. I think they were too worried to care about why you were there."

Hardy took a deep breath. He could still get away with them not knowing about the trouble at school. He was beginning to feel quite differently about Darcy. She had not only saved Charity's life, she had saved his.

The door opened, and Hardy's parents followed the doctor in. His mother looked relieved to see Hardy awake and rushed to his side. Her eyes looked tired, her black hair hurriedly pulled back into a ponytail.

She took his hand. "Hey, honey. How are you feeling?"

"Fine. Can we go home?" He wasn't exactly fine, but he definitely didn't want to be stuck in a hospital room surrounded by strange people.

Hardy looked around his mother at his father. Tom stood by the door with his hands in his pockets looking uncomfortable and edgy. His generous stature didn't match his quiet demeanor. He had a presence that made people stand up and notice. It wasn't often that one would see an older man with a barrel chest and arms like a wrestler. His looks demanded attention wherever he went, but his body language suggested he was more comfortable in the shadows. It appeared that Tom planned to stay by the door.

A young, clean-cut doctor stepped up to Hardy's bedside and stared down at him. "I'm Dr. Anderson. Do you remember what happened?"

Hardy glanced at his mother who was calm, relaxed, and smiling. But then, this was her element—her place of work. Tom shifted nervously in the background.

"Not really. At least nothing after grabbing Charity."

"Well I'm not surprised. You have a mild concussion and a pretty bad gash on the back of your head that required several stitches. You lost a lot of blood which is not uncommon with a head wound."

"Can I go home?" Hardy asked.

"We'd like to keep you overnight for observation. Just to make sure nothing develops."

Hardy looked at his mother. "Mom, please," he pleaded.

His mother turned toward the doctor. "Dr. Anderson. I can keep a check on things. Do you think you can let us take him home?"

The doctor flipped through Hardy's chart. "Hardy, you're lucky your mother is a nurse. I'll go sign your release papers. You're going to need to take it easy for the next few days. Listen to your mother."

"Thank you," Hardy said, with a half-sigh.

He winked at Hardy and headed for the door.

"Mr. Vance, if you'll come with me, we'll get the appropriate paperwork taken care of and see if we can get you folks out of here."

Tom opened the door and left with the doctor. It appeared that he was just as anxious to get out of there as Hardy was. At least they had that in common.

His mother held up a tote bag she had been holding. "I brought you a change of clothes. Do you want some help getting dressed?"

Cricket snickered. Hardy flashed him a look.

"No, Mom, I can manage just fine."

Hardy pulled the covers off and dumped his legs over the side of the bed. His head felt like it was in a vice. A wave of nausea hit him, and he fought the urge to throw up.

"Okay. I'll be just outside if you need me," she said.

As soon as his bare feet hit the cold floor, Hardy started second-guessing the need for help. The room tipped ever so slightly. He reached back and placed a hand on the bed to steady himself.

"Are you sure you don't want Mommy to help you?" Cricket teased.

"Shut up and hand me my pants."

Hardy managed, but just barely, to put a shirt over his head and slide into a pair of jeans.

Just as he zipped up, someone knocked and came into the room with his mother. For a minute, he thought he might be hallucinating again. It was Governor Marcus Hill, Charity's father. Hardy recognized the dark, chiseled features from TV. The Governor was much taller in person, and his manicured good looks were very intimidating.

"Hardy, the Governor would like to speak with you if you're up to it," his mother said, like it was something she said every day.

Governor Hill approached Hardy and held out his hand. His shake was strong and confident, just like a leader's should be. He took Cricket's hand and gave it an equally strong pump.

"I'd like to thank you for saving my daughter's life, Hardy."

"Anyone would have done the same thing. Sir."

The Governor smiled with his perfect teeth. "On the contrary young man, it takes a lot of courage to throw yourself in front of a bus."

"Is Charity okay?" Hardy asked.

"She has a broken left arm, but she'll be fine."

"Oh...um...I'm sorry."

The Governor put a hand on Hardy's shoulder and squeezed. "Are you good at keeping secrets, Hardy?"

What? Had Charity told him about what had happened at school? Hardy felt like the beans were about to be spilled.

"I suppose," he murmured.

"If I was a betting man, I'd say you probably are."

The Governor's grip on Hardy's shoulder tightened to where it was uncomfortable. If he was trying to send Hardy some kind of message about keeping his hands off his daughter, Hardy was receiving it loud and clear. He started feeling dizzy again.

"Don't look so worried, Hardy. I was only going to say that just between you and me, Charity can be a little unfocused at times."

Relieved, Hardy tried to smile. But he really only wanted the Governor to leave before he threw up on his expensive, Italian leather shoes.

"Well, I've got to get back to the business of our people." The Governor turned to Hardy's mother. "Mrs. Vance, it was nice to meet you. You must be very proud of your son."

"Yes, Governor, I am. Thank you for coming by."

"It was my pleasure." The Governor pointed at Hardy. "Hardy, take care of that head, and stay out of trouble."

Hardy nodded. "Yes, sir. Governor, sir."

And with that, the Governor was out the door.

Hardy's mother was smiling like she had just won the lottery. "Wasn't that nice of the Governor to come by?"

There was something Hardy didn't like about the Governor that he couldn't quite put his finger on. It was the way he had said *secret*, as if he knew Hardy was hiding something and wanted him to know it. Charity had probably told him about the incident at school, painting Hardy as the bad guy. The Governor's words of thanks were probably nothing more than obligation. A publicity stunt.

"Yeah, nice," Hardy responded.

A nurse came in with a wheelchair. Hardy was never so glad to see a pair of wheels. He shuffled across the floor and fell into the chair.

Chapter Five

Marcus dropped his keys onto a tray in the foyer. He picked up a stack of mail and absently glanced through it. Nothing but bills. The smell of roasted chicken drifted down the hall. It had been a long day. All he wanted to do was to get out of his suit and tie and check on his daughter.

"Marcus, is that you?" His wife called from the kitchen.

"Yes, Lizzy."

He and Elizabeth had been high school sweethearts. He still remembered the first time he'd caught her eye. It was the last basketball game of his freshman year. With only two seconds left in the game, he made the winning shot from mid-court. The cheerleaders ran onto the court and the crowd followed. The petite cheerleader with the blonde ponytail that was crushed against him was Lizzy. The rest was history. Now, she was his first lady, working to raise awareness about domestic violence. Despite the dignified woman she had become over the course of their twenty-five year marriage, she would always be his Lizzy.

She came down the hall rubbing her hands on a white, linen dish towel. Marcus pulled her into his arms and embraced her. "Mm…Am I glad to see you."

"Rough day?" Elizabeth asked.

Marcus released her and smiled wearily. "You could say that. How's Charity?"

"She's in her room resting. I think she's upset because she's going to miss the rest of volleyball season."

"I'll go up and talk to her."

Elizabeth reached out and stopped him. "Someone is here to see you."

Marcus frowned. "Who?"

"Mr. *Smith*."

Marcus sighed and rubbed his forehead. "Where?"

"Your study. Should I keep dinner warm?"

"No. This won't take long."

Elizabeth gave him a reassuring smile and returned to the kitchen.

Marcus walked quickly through the grand living room to his study at the back of the house. When he opened the door, *Smith* was standing by the wall of glass that overlooked the backyard.

"What are you doing here?" Marcus asked.

"You have a beautiful backyard. The pool is spectacular."

Marcus walked over to his desk and awakened his computer. The screen came to life. He quickly scanned his inbox. "I don't want you coming to my home."

"The Program sent me."

"My father is dead and, last time I checked, I was Governor. The Program doesn't concern me."

"You're Governor thanks to your father and his legacy. He started The Program."

"You've made your point. What's so urgent that couldn't wait until tomorrow?"

"Olen Vance has been found."

"I know." Marcus unbuttoned his pinstriped jacket and sat down. "I don't know why you're so worried. He's been quiet for over forty years."

"You should never make the mistake of underestimating Olen Vance. It's only because of the girl that we know about him. The Program thought he was dead."

"If he was going to expose the research, don't you think he would've done it by now?" Marcus asked.

"As long as he's still alive, he's a threat. He'll have to be taken care of."

"Fine. Anything else? My wife has a dinner prepared."

"We need the place searched."

"For..."

"Papers."

"If you're worried about incriminating evidence, why not just burn the place down?" Marcus asked.

"These are research papers. We need them if we're ever going to perfect the DIE research. No one has been able to reproduce Olen's work."

Marcus leaned back in his chair and placed his fingertips together. "Very well. Let me know when...it's done. I'll send someone out to search the place."

The unwelcomed visitor nodded and headed toward the door.

"What about Hardy?" Marcus asked, feeling a painful twinge of guilt for the boy who had just saved his daughter's life.

"Don't worry about Hardy. The Program will be keeping an eye on him."

Chapter Six

Hardy slept through Saturday. Now Sunday was upon him. He toyed with the idea of getting out of bed. His mother had checked on him constantly, plying him with liquids and food between sleeping spells. There still hadn't been any real discussion about the accident or why Hardy was in Grey-stone. He hoped maybe they would simply be glad he was all right and not ask a lot of questions. Or he could always fake amnesia. Didn't people often forget things after a knock on the head?

He stared at the white, tent-shaped ceiling of his small loft, debating whether he should brave his parents and climb down the ladder to the living room. He absently grabbed his glasses off his side table and put them on his face. He rolled to his side and pulled back the curtain of the small window that looked out across the back of his house. He squinted at the sudden burst of sunlight and quickly let the curtain fall back into place. There was no more putting off the inevitable. He rolled out of bed, dug Olen's mysterious note out of Friday's jeans, and climbed down the ladder.

The door to the bathroom was open. Tom was on his knees over the tub. Pieces of plumbing lay in disarray on the floor. Tom spoke without turning around. "You can use the toilet, but you'll have to use the outdoor shower if you want to wash up." Tom stood and left the bathroom.

Well, some things never change, Hardy thought. He couldn't help but wonder if he had somehow, once again, disappointed his father by getting a concussion. They were like oil and vinegar, he and Tom. Tom was muscular and strong with big hands and a head of reddish-brown hair. Hardy was tall and skinny with a mop of black hair and glasses. Sometimes he played with the idea that he was adopted, but then he would look at his mother's petite frame and thick, black hair and dismiss the idea.

Hardy stepped up to the mirror and tried to look at the stitches in the back of his head, but all he could really manage to do was feel their rough edges. He splashed cold water on his face and wandered into the kitchen.

His mother was standing over a pan of bubbling eggs. His father was seated at the small square table peering through his reading glasses at what looked like a fix-it manual.

Anna smiled when she noticed Hardy. "Hey, there, sleepyhead. How are you feeling?"

Hardy looked at his father. Tom glanced at him over the top of his reading glasses and then buried his face back into the thin paperback.

Hardy rubbed a hand through his unwashed hair. "Hungry."

"Good. Sit down. These are almost ready."

Hardy planted himself across from Tom, hiding the envelope in the seat under his leg.

Milk and fresh strawberries had already been placed on the table.

"Tom, can you get us some plates?"

Tom rose obediently and grabbed three plates off the open shelf beside the sink. His mother fumbled in a drawer for some utensils and handed them to Tom, who returned to the table, set the stack down, and returned to his book.

Anna brought the hot pan of eggs to the table and set them down on a hot pad. She began to examine Hardy's stitches on the back of his head.

"He's fine, Anna. No need to baby him," Tom said, taking off his reading glasses.

"I'm just checking for signs of infection."

Hardy brushed her hand away. "I'm fine, Mom."

"Okay. Okay."

They ate in silence. Hardy's mother kept staring at Tom like she was waiting for him to say something. Finally his father spoke. "Do I need to ask if you did what you were supposed to do on Friday?"

So there it was. Tom assumed that, since Hardy was in Greystone on Friday, he had likely skipped out on Olen.

Anna glanced nervously at Hardy and put a fork full of eggs into her mouth.

"I did. He's fine," Hardy said, gritting his teeth.

Tom put his last bite of egg into his mouth and drained his milk. That's when Hardy tossed the envelope across to him. Tom stared at its blank surface. "What's this?" Tom asked, without touching it.

"Olen wanted me to give it to you," Hardy said with smug satisfaction. He knew it would make Tom angry. Olen's name was never to be spoken in the house. It felt good to break the golden rule.

Tom's face turned bright pink. He grabbed the envelope, picked up his book and glasses, and left the table. Hardy was pretty sure he would never hear another word about the note.

Anna forced a smile. "Don't mind him. He's stressed over the leak in the shower. You know he thinks he has to fix everything."

She always made excuses for him. Whatever. Hardy didn't care about the stupid note. Four more months, and he was out of there. He just needed to get through the community service without Tom finding out.

Hardy stood up and took his plate and glass to the sink. "I'm going to shower outside. Oh, and...um, I'm going to join a study group for history, so...I'll be home late for the next few weeks."

"Okay, honey," she said, smiling at him. "I'm really glad to see you taking more of an interest in school."

That was easy. Excuse for being home late—done.

Hardy grabbed a towel from the bathroom and slipped out back through the kitchen door. Despite the bright sun, the morning was still cool. He hoped there was hot water. He laid his glasses down on the patio table and entered the four-walled stall.

He undressed and threw his boxers, tee, and towel over

the top of the door. He turned the water on and stood back, waiting for it to get hot.

His head felt much lighter now, and the warm water soothed his stiff muscles. While soaping up, he noticed quite a few bruises that had turned dark purple. He still couldn't believe he had saved Charity's life. Like she would care. She would probably blame him for the broken arm. He wondered if there was a category at school for inappropriate arm breaking.

He had just rubbed soap all over his face when he heard a voice that sounded like it was coming from within the shower stall.

"Hey, Hardy."

"What the—?" Startled and blinded by soap, Hardy fell against the shower door and covered his privates with one of his hands. He tried to open his eyes, but the soap immediately seeped in and began stinging. He quickly leaned into the water and rinsed his face with his free hand. When he looked up, a blurred Darcy was peering over the shower stall.

"Darcy? You scared the crap out of me. Do you mind?!"

"Don't worry. It's nothing I haven't seen before. I have two brothers."

Hardy wanted to scream. He was horrified. "It's hardly the same...never mind."

He did a quick rinse and cut the water off. He jerked the towel down from the door and wrapped it around his waist and opened the stall door. Darcy was standing there barefoot in a long, flowery dress, daisies woven through her long, wavy, blonde hair.

"Isn't it a beautiful day?" Darcy asked.

Hardy wiped a hand over his face. "What is so important that it couldn't wait until I was out of the shower?" he asked, tightening the towel around his waist.

"I want to go see Olen."

"It's Sunday."

"I know, but I want to go today. I need to ask something about the book he gave me."

"Darcy, I'm recovering from a concussion. I'm not going to go trekking out into the woods just so you can talk to Olen about some book."

And as if Hardy wasn't already traumatized by Darcy's sudden appearance over the shower stall, she stepped up, grabbed his face, and pulled it down to her so that they were eye level. She stared into his eyes, her blue eye twitching back and forth. He was torn between ripping her hands off his face and maintaining the towel around his waist. She jerked his head down further and looked at the back of his head. She was surprisingly strong.

"You're fine," Darcy said, releasing his head.

Hardy's face flushed and his jaw tensed. He picked up his glasses off the patio table and pushed them onto his face. "I'm sorry. I don't think I made myself clear—I'M NOT TAKING YOU TO SEE OLEN!" Hardy was genuinely flustered now. He was outside, half-naked, arguing with a girl he just met two days ago.

Darcy just stared at him. "Okay." She turned and walked toward the green pasture that ran across the back of their house.

Hardy felt a sudden surge of satisfaction, having put her

in her place; then it was replaced by unexplained panic. Darcy had given up way too easily. Hardy ran after her, finding it awkward to move quickly in a towel. His bare feet, tender after being in shoes all winter, rose and fell to the ground like he was walking across hot coals. He finally caught up to her and reached out a hand to stop her.

"What do you mean, okay?" Hardy said, narrowing his eyes.

"I mean, okay. I'll go by myself." Darcy turned to leave.

"What?! No! You will not go by yourself," he said, trying to keep his towel intact.

"So you'll come?" Darcy asked.

Hardy bit his lower lip.

Darcy smirked and looked around Hardy. "I think your dad is looking for you."

Hardy glanced back. Tom was standing on the patio with his arms crossed.

"Wait for me by the boat," he said quickly. He couldn't risk her going out to Olen's on her own. What if someone saw her, or Olen shot her?

Darcy smiled, and his anger melted away. There was something about her smile that transformed her entire face from weird girl to just...girl.

Hardy crunched his toes in the grass all the way back to the house. Tom did not look happy.

"Do we need to have *the talk*?" Tom said, eyeing Darcy.

"No..."

"Isn't that the girl from the hospital?"

"Yes, sir, but she's just..." Hardy didn't know what to call her. "A friend."

"What village does she live in?"

"I don't know."

"You're friends, but you don't know what village she lives in?"

Hardy really wasn't up for one of Tom's interrogations.

"We just meet at school. We're in that just getting to know each other stage."

"Your mother is going to church, and I'm going to pick up some parts I need for the shower. She wants you to stay at home and rest."

"Okay."

Tom left and went back inside.

This Darcy girl was going to be a thorn in Hardy's side.

***

Hardy walked down the steep slope to the river. Someone had pulled the canoe out of the thicket and it floated lazily several feet off the bank, still attached to its rope. There was no sign of Darcy. It figured. He had come all the way out there for nothing. Darcy was probably off chasing butterflies. He knelt down and took hold of the rope, slowly pulling the canoe back to the bank. Just as he reached his arm out to grab the edge, Darcy sat straight up from inside the canoe like a dead corpse rising from a casket. He dropped the rope and fell backwards.

"Darcy!" Hardy yelled, his heart racing.

This was the second time today she had scared the crap out of him.

"Sorry. I was just staring up at the sky while I waited. I

think I dozed off."

Hardy stood up and brushed his shorts off, pushing down his anger. He jerked the canoe back to shore, forcing Darcy to grab onto the side of the boat to keep from falling.

"Move to your seat," Hardy said gruffly. A small throb began beating at his temples.

It was a beautiful spring day, and glimpses of blue sky and sunlight poured through the overhanging trees. If only Hardy could enjoy it. He couldn't help but stare at Darcy. Her face was raised to the sky, her eyes closed. The daisies tied in her hair with ribbon were starting to wilt. She was definitely a free spirit. Something he knew nothing about.

When they arrived at Olen's, they hiked up the wooded hill and stood behind a band of tall weeds just within sight of the cabin. The cabin was closed up tight. Hardy had never been there before on a Sunday, and he hoped they wouldn't scare Olen by showing up unannounced. Hardy gave the required *Coo-oo, coo...coo...coo*, and waited. Nothing happened. Darcy made a move to head toward the cabin. He held her back with his arm.

"Not yet. He could be sleeping."

"*Coo-oo, coo...coo...coo,*" Hardy blew through his cupped hands. He could feel Darcy fidgeting next to him.

The cabin door remained closed.

Darcy pushed Hardy's arm out of the way and ran up the hill.

"Darcy, wait!" he called out.

Hardy noticed that, even though she was barefoot, she

ran across the rough ground like she had shoes on. He took off after her. His head was pounding now. Every step was like a jackhammer straight to his head. He watched Darcy run up the steps through a haze of small stars that were forming in the back of his eyes. He wondered if he would pass out. Something was wrong, he could feel it. Maybe it was the concussion, but something in him felt weird. He was spiraling into something. A sense? A feeling?

By the time Hardy caught up with Darcy, she had flung open the screen door, taken one step inside, and frozen. Hardy stepped around her. They both stared at the vacant eyes that looked at them from the lazy chair. Darcy rushed to Olen's side. Hardy didn't move. Olen's face was still and pale, his skin sinking into his frail cheeks. Darcy grabbed Olen's face with her hands and searched his eyes. Small stars danced and multiplied like a virus in Hardy's eyes. He backed up and held onto the door jamb to steady himself. He strained to take air into his lungs as if there was no oxygen in the room. Darcy's fingers fell slowly from Olen's face. She laid a hand over his eyes. Now he looked like he was sleeping.

"He's dead," Darcy said, turning to Hardy.

The stars evaporated, and a tight knot in the center of Hardy's chest took their place. "What?" Hardy said, wondering if he had misunderstood her.

"I said, he's dead," Darcy snapped.

Hardy put his hands on top of his head and stared at Olen in disbelief. "No. We were just here Friday. Everything was fine. He's probably just…"

But even as he tried to wish it away, he knew she was

72

right.

Darcy shook her head, her face red with grief. She brushed past Hardy and ran out of the house. The screen door slammed behind her.

Hardy looked around the cabin in disbelief. The bed was made, clothes put away. No dirty dishes were lying about. Olen's glasses lay neatly folded on the little table by the window. His cabin was never this clean. It was as if he knew he was going to—Hardy didn't finish the thought.

The knot in Hardy's chest was growing tighter, like a twisting towel. His breaths were coming in short bursts. He was well on his way to hyperventilating. At least he wasn't seeing stars anymore. He walked slowly over to Olen. Olen's skin was colorless, opaque.

"Olen, I'm sorry." He looked down and noticed that Olen's right hand was clenched into a fist like he was holding onto something. Hardy swallowed—hard. He knelt down and turned Olen's fist over and pulled the fingers back one by one, as if peeling an orange. By the time he got to the pinky, he began to think he had been mistaken. There was nothing there. A small breeze blew through the screen door, causing the slightest movement in the palm of Olen's hand. There was something there—a tiny white feather.

Chapter Seven

Hardy, Tom, and his brother Tate stood over Olen's body. It was strange—all three of them there at the same time. Tate had stopped coming several years ago when he had married Vivia and moved out of the house. Hardy knew that Tom hadn't been there since he had run away all those years ago. He watched Tom's face, wondering if he would finally open up about Olen and they would get a glimpse into their father's past. But Tom stood stiffly, with no emotion. Hardy should have expected that. That was Tom's way. Closed off. Inaccessible. Even unto death.

"Hardy, go out back and see if you can find a shovel," Tom said.

Hardy trudged around the back of the cabin and found a large, rusty shovel leaning against the cabin. He couldn't help feel like Tom would somehow find a way to make this Hardy's fault. After all, he was the last one to see Olen alive. And what was he doing out there on a Sunday when he was supposed to be home resting?

As he came around the front, Tom and Tate were bringing Olen down the front steps. The sun disappeared behind the clouds.

"Let's take him down by the river where the soil will be softer," Tom said to Tate, leading him toward the dirt path.

"No!" Hardy yelled, jogging up to Tom.

Tom paused, shifting the weight of Olen in his arms.

"He has a favorite tree," Hardy said.

"Son, it doesn't much matter where he goes now, does it?" Tom said, his face red with the strain of Olen's weight.

"It does. It matters." Hardy had never really stood up to his father before. His adrenaline surged with fear and anger. Hardy had treated Olen as a chore. He wanted to at least do this for him. Put him where he would want to be.

"It will be harder to dig—"

"I'll dig it," Hardy interrupted.

Tom looked at Tate who was silent on the matter and only shifted his feet.

"Fine. Where is it?" Tom asked.

To be truthful, Hardy wasn't sure exactly where it was. Olen had only shown it to him a handful of times. The tree was where Olen always shared his favorite saying with Hardy. *There's wisdom in trees.* It wasn't far. He knew that much. He would just have to wing it—act like he knew where he was going.

"This way," Hardy motioned with his thumb over his shoulder.

They headed into the woods just to the right of the cabin. The further they walked, the more worried Hardy became.

75

The trees were growing thicker, and one tree looked like the other. He could hear Tom and Tate's labored breathing behind him. Hardy started biting the nail of his left index finger. *Come on, come on.* He knew it was close. Finally, he spotted the large oak. Its rotted-out hole was like a black bull's-eye against the gray trunk. He ran up to the tree and placed a hand on it. "This is it."

Tom and Tate laid Olen's body down on top of green grass sprouting from the forest floor. "Start digging," Tom said to Hardy.

Hardy was surprised to find that he was angry, and he had no idea why. He stuck the shovel into the ground several feet away from the tree and rammed his foot down hard onto its blade. His head protested with each push and pull of dirt. He ignored the pain and worked furiously on the hole, putting all his pent-up anger into the dirt.

A strong wind began blowing through the tops of the trees, the branches cracking in protest. Dark clouds moved in overhead. Hardy dug deeper, and the sky grew darker. A low rumble vibrated in the distance. Weather often turned quickly on the island. Storms blowing in from the ocean could change sunny skies to dark clouds within minutes.

"There's a storm coming. Tate, relieve Hardy or we'll be here all night," Tom said.

Hardy sat down, leaned against the oak tree, and wiped the sweat from his pounding head. He watched Tate dig, his biceps bulging under the strain. Tate was muscular, just like Tom. The two of them even looked alike—freckled, light-skinned, reddish-brown hair. The only real difference was Tate's full beard and mustache. They were physically everything he wasn't.

He stared through the treetops at the ominous, fast-moving clouds. Those were the kind of clouds he felt like he was living under.

Hardy glanced over at Olen. One of Olen's eyes was partially open. He crept over and knelt down next to him and shut it closed with his finger. That's when he saw the lighter lying on the ground near Olen's pocket. He picked it up and looked at it. It was an old flip-top, gold lighter—plain, except for an inscription on the back. *Alea Iacta Est.* He had no idea what it meant, but it felt like maybe Olen was somehow giving it to him, so he stuck it in his pocket.

He studied Olen's face. He had never seen a dead body. He decided it wasn't scary but peaceful. He wondered what it meant that Darcy seemed to be more upset by Olen's passing than any of his own family members. She had pulled the flowers out of her hair and hidden her face in her knees the whole way back down the river. When they came close to the river bank, she stepped out of the boat into the water and took off up the hill without another word. He didn't understand why she was so upset over someone she had just met. Darcy continued to surprise him.

"The grave is ready," Tate said, leaning over the handle of the shovel.

It started raining.

***

Darcy ran to her front door and leaned against the wall of its recessed entrance. Her breath came in short, powerful

77

bursts. The rain was coming down in sheets, and she was drenched through. She had spent the last few hours wandering, looking for anything that would distract her mind. Only under the threat of rain did she force herself to return home. She stared at the doorknob, willing herself to open it. This was her home. Their tenement—a four-room hole in a long cobblestone building. It was a lonely house with nothing holding it together but cracking mortar and worn wood beams. Her heart ached for the thing it was missing—her father.

Darcy had made a connection with Olen. She felt like her father would've been like him had he lived. Water ran down her face. She wasn't sure if she was crying. It was hard to tell with only one normal eye. The rain—the beautiful rain. Today it only brought her sorrow.

The door jerked open, startling her.

"What are you doing out here? You're soaked. Get inside."

Darcy's mother—Eva. A woman broken by loss. Eva lived her days in a haze of bad memories. It didn't matter that it had been five years. Eva would live every day as a reminder to Darcy that it was Darcy's fault that her father had died. Today would be no different.

Darcy stood just inside the door dripping water onto the floor.

"Where have you been?" Eva snapped.

"Out," Darcy said, wiping a hand down her wet face.

"Don't smart mouth me, young lady. I work two jobs to keep this roof over our heads. Don't you forget it."

How could I when you remind me every day?

"Get back there and do your brothers' laundry. Unlike you, they have jobs. The least you could do is help out."

Eva left Darcy standing in the small living room. The lonely, white-plastered walls offered no comfort. The small fireplace was lifeless. A thick layer of ash lay under its grate like the charred embers of her life. The old, brown tweed sofa on the opposite wall: empty. And there was *his* chair— her father's. An old recliner rocker—rusty orange, outdated, patched with duct tape. A place where he had held her, tick-led her, and let her comb his hair. She sank down into it, closed her eyes, and rocked.

***

"Where have you been? I've been worried sick," Anna said. "Wait right there. Let me get some towels."

Hardy and Tom stood like wet sponges just inside the door. Hardy was numb. The pounding in his head had stopped. Now it just felt swollen, heavy.

Anna handed Tom a towel and wrapped one around Hardy. She frowned as she examined and rubbed Hardy's face.

"Tom Franklin Vance. The last thing Hardy needed was for you to drag him out into the woods to bury your father. Look at him."

Tom rubbed the towel back and forth through his bristly hair. "I would agree with you, except that Hardy didn't see much issue with it when he went traipsing out there in the first place."

Anna crossed her arms. "Hardy, go get a hot shower. It's

fixed now."

Hardy knew this was his mother's way of dismissing him so she could say what she really wanted to say to Tom. Hardy headed straight back through the living room to the bathroom.

"He just came home from the hospital and—" Anna's voice was cut off as soon as Hardy shut the door. He sat down on the toilet seat and buried his head into his hands.

"You have to stop babying him." Tom's voice came muffled through the door.

Hardy reached over and turned the water on in the shower. They would argue now. His mother would defend Hardy. His father would tell her she was wrong.

Right now, he didn't really care. He reached into his pocket and pulled out Olen's lighter. He had never seen Olen smoke. He opened the lid and struck the grooved wheel with this thumb. To his surprise, it threw up a flame. He flipped the lid shut and set it on the sink. *Alea Iacta Est*. He made a mental note to look up the strange words.

When Hardy emerged from a hot shower and a change of clothes, the house was quiet. Whatever had been spoken between his parents was done. He found his mother in the kitchen, busy putting the last touches to dinner. Tom sat in his chair next to the wall reading something, sticking to his usual practice just before a meal.

"Are you hungry, dear?" Anna asked Hardy.

"Not really."

"Eat, anyway. You need to stay nourished."

Hardy sat across from Tom. His mother set down a big platter full of spaghetti and meatballs in the center of the table and plopped down between Hardy and Tom.

His mother served, piling more on Hardy's plate than was humanly possible to eat. Tom took large bites while Hardy pushed the meatballs around on his plate.

"Are you okay, honey? I know it must've been difficult for you finding your grandfather like you did," Anna said.

"He's fine," Tom said, followed by shoveling a forkful of pasta into his mouth.

"If you don't mind, I'd like to hear it from him," Anna responded curtly.

They both looked at Hardy.

"I'm fine, Mom. I'm just tired. Digging the grave wore me out." Hardy knew that last bit would throw his mother into a tailspin.

Anna's faced turned bright red, and she started choking on the bite she was in the process of swallowing. Tom cut his eyes at Hardy and jabbed his fork into his food. Anna didn't say anything then, but Hardy knew Tom would hear about it later. *How could he let a boy with a concussion dig a grave? What was he thinking?* Hardy had said it on purpose. Anger tore through his veins, and he began to wonder if he hated his own father.

"Tom, there's something you should know—about Olen," Hardy announced.

Tom stopped with his food halfway to his mouth and set his fork down. Olen's name was not to be spoken in the house, and Hardy had just broken the golden rule—again. His mother closed her eyes. Tom stared at Hardy waiting for him to speak—daring him to.

"I read the note." Hardy coughed into his hand. "I mean… Friday, when Olen asked me to give you the note. I read it."

Tom's face flared with the red of restraint. Anger. Hardy felt himself crumbling under his father's stern expression. The pressure of tears built behind his eyes. He would not cry. He would not.

Anna placed a hand on Hardy's arm.

Hardy swallowed the lump that had risen in his throat.

Tom's eyes blazed with fury now. He immediately rose from the table, grabbed his plate that was still half-full, and dropped it into the sink. The sound of crashing dishes echoed across the small kitchen. He charged outside through kitchen's back door.

Hardy looked at his mother. Bitter tears seeped into his eyelids.

"It's okay. Don't worry about it. I'll talk to him," she said, reassuringly.

Yeah. You'll talk to him and, as usual, nothing will change. He won't talk to me about the note. He won't talk to me about anything.

Anna followed Tom out the door, but the door stayed ajar. Hardy could still make out their low murmurs from the patio.

"Was that really necessary?" Anna asked. "You should talk to him about the note."

"That's never going to happen," Tom said angrily. "Olen had a lot of nerve sending me a message like that with my boy."

"Well, he obviously thought Hardy should know."

Tom laughed. "I don't really care what he thought. He was wrong."

"Was he?" Anna asked.

"I don't expect you to understand," Tom mumbled.

"We get it, you know," Anna said, losing patience. "You had a crappy childhood. Your father kept you hidden in the woods for fourteen years. That can't always be your excuse. Not anymore. Hardy needs a father."

"Tate turned out just fine," Tom retorted.

"You're right, he did. But you two have more in common. He wrestled, like you. And now you both work for the island's power company. Hardy is not Tate. What do you give to Hardy?"

"He's got a roof over his head, food on the table. I haven't denied him anything," Tom said fiercely.

"You've denied him the most important part—you!"

Tom sighed. "There's nothing in me that Hardy needs."

"You're wrong, you know. Every boy needs a father. You of all people should know that."

"I don't know how to be a father. Not like you want me to be."

Hardy couldn't take it anymore. He couldn't listen to the hushed voices any longer. Tom was right about one thing. There was nothing Hardy needed from him. Not anymore. He thought he did. He was wrong. He threw his chair back and went to his loft.

"Maybe it's time you started trying—" Anna's voice faded.

Chapter Eight

Monday came too quickly. Hardy thought that stitches, plus concussion, plus a death in the family would've at least been good for a few days off, but with Tom, days off meant you had to be unconscious or incoherent. Since Hardy knew his first and last name, he was sent to school.

He couldn't stop thinking about Olen. Even though they were never close, he realized that he had never really tried to know Olen like a grandson should. Now he was carrying Olen's lighter in his pocket and he didn't understand why he felt the need to. Maybe it was regret he was carrying in his pocket.

When he pulled up to the school, Hardy was surprised to see several TV vans with big saucer satellites parked in front. Men and women with headsets were talking into cameras and looking back at the school.

He coasted to the first bike rack with an empty spot and jumped off his bike. Immediately, he sensed that the other students by the racks were staring at him and whispering. He rubbed the rough spot on the back of his head where his stitches were. After he secured his bike, he pulled a ball cap out of his backpack and put it on.

He lowered his head, slumped his shoulders forward to balance his backpack, and headed for the entrance. He didn't want any reporters stopping him to ask him random questions that he would have no clue how to answer. That was a social nightmare that could only end in stuttering and a new viral video.

He began crossing the courtyard at the front of the school when someone yelled out, "There he is!" The mass of reporters and cameras started moving in his direction. He looked behind him to see if he had missed the person of interest.

"Hardy!" The reporters all yelled in unison. They ran toward him. He froze and looked around him, still unsure if they were calling his name or someone else's. Before he knew it, he was surrounded, and nameless faces were shouting at him.

"What made you run in front of that bus to save Charity Hill?"

"Have you talked to Charity since the accident?"

"Did you suffer any injuries?"

For a minute, Hardy was so overwhelmed he couldn't speak. The shouting stopped and was replaced with an awkward silence. Microphones were now hanging over his head like swarming flies. Curious students pressed in.

"I...um...I did what anyone would do." Hardy repeated what he had heard someone say on the news after being asked why they helped pull someone from a house fire.

A woman with bright red lips forced her way forward. "Is it true that the Governor visited you in the hospital?"

"Um…" *Hardy, are you good at keeping secrets?*

A cold sweat broke out on Hardy's forehead. "Um…Yes." He reached behind his head and made sure his ball cap was covering his stitches.

"What did he say to you?" The red-lipped lady asked.

"He, um…just said…" Hardy stuck his hands in his pockets. "Thank you."

There were several chuckles in the growing crowd. The people standing in the back started looking behind them. The reporters shifted to make room for someone who was coming through. Charity stepped out of the melee and stood beside Hardy. Her left, lower arm was covered in a navy cast.

"Charity!" The reporters all yelled at her, trying to garner her attention.

The sound of camera clicks moved in a circle around them. The stitches on the back of Hardy's head began throbbing. Sweat dripped down his back.

"Charity! What do you have to say to your hero?" A man with a WGRA-TV hat yelled over the top of the other reporters' heads.

This ought to be good, Hardy thought. Maybe she would tell them that she thought the tackle had been inappropriate touching. He lifted his cap and wiped the sweat from his forehand with the back of his hand. He pulled his cap down lower over his eyes and stuck his hands back in his pockets. He could smell Charity's hair. It smelled like flowers.

"I only have one thing to say to him," Charity said. The

crowd grew silent waiting to hear her declaration.

Here it comes. Hardy's public humiliation. He dropped his chin to his chest and stared at his tennis shoes. Every muscle in his body tightened with anticipation. Then he felt the sleeve of his T-shirt being tugged and Charity's soft lips landing on his cheek, resting there. The smell of perfume and sweet fruity lip gloss crashed into him. He forgot who he was, where he was, and the fact that dozens of people were watching. He was completely lost in some kind of weird abyss that he couldn't pull himself out of. Light and sound disappeared like he was swimming underwater. Charity pulled away. Hardy's senses crashed to the surface. Everything seemed suddenly loud.

The reporters and students broke out into loud cheers. Hardy stood with his mouth agape. Charity smiled and pushed her way back through the crowd. The whole mass of people chased after her, leaving Hardy in shock and uncertain of whether he had just blacked out. He straightened his glasses which now sat crooked on his nose. He could smell the remnants of her cherry lip gloss on his cheek. *Charity Hill just kissed me.* He grinned, looking around, but there was no one there to share his triumph. He glided through the front doors of the school, whistling, as if the ground beneath him was air.

***

Hardy remembered very little between the opening bell and sitting down outside for lunch. It was like he was in some kind of trance. Charity sat down the grassy hill from him with her volleyball friends. He stared over his food at her until Darcy dropped her tray on the table across from him, snapping him back to reality. He blinked and realized that Darcy was now blocking his view.

"I need to talk to you about Olen," Darcy said.

She plopped the black book Olen had given her down on the table and stared at him.

"Not now," Hardy said, scooting over to try and get a better view of Charity.

Cricket slammed down his tray next to Darcy, once again blocking Hardy's view. Cricket grinned from ear to ear and Hardy returned it. Hardy had crossed the great divide, and they both knew it.

"I'm completely speechless. Our nerd quotient just dropped from like a nine to a three," Cricket said.

Darcy rolled her eyes.

The whole nerd quotient thing was true, at least for Hardy, anyway. Cricket was nowhere near Hardy's low rung of the ladder but, by default, Cricket's friendship with Hardy often put him there. Hardy didn't know many people who would make that kind of sacrifice for a friend.

"Speaking of nerds, why is *she* here?" Cricket asked, motioning with his head.

Darcy pushed her shoulders back and sat up straight. "I have just as much right to sit here as you do."

Cricket ignored her. "Seriously, Hardy. This is not going to help your new image. She's a freshman and…well…weird."

"Don't worry about it. She's harmless," Hardy said.

Darcy gave Cricket a smug smile. He responded by forcing her tray out of his so-called space.

She frowned and shoved her tray back into place. Her blue eye twitched furiously. This was not good. She was up to something.

Darcy leaned close to Cricket's ear. "I doubt anything is going to improve your nerd quotient with a name like yours."

Cricket gritted his teeth. "What did you say?"

Darcy crossed her arms.

Oh, no. Hardy had sworn never to reveal Cricket's true name to anyone. When they were kids, they had cut themselves with Cricket's pocket knife as a blood oath. But with Darcy's abilities—*she would know his real name.* Cricket would assume Hardy had told her.

Hardy held up his hands. "Cricket...I didn't tell her." He looked at Darcy, pleading with his eyes. "Darcy don't."

Darcy placed both hands flat on the table and pressed her face close to Cricket's. "LINUS."

Cricket's face flushed red. His chest heaved with hot, angry breaths.

"PORCIOUS."

Cricket's eyes cut into Hardy, accusing him.

Hardy shook his head. "I swear. I didn't."

"WRIGHT."

Cricket grabbed his tray and headed straight for the nearest trash receptacle. Hardy chased after him.

"Cricket!"

Cricket dumped the entire tray into the trash and turned to face Hardy. "You swore you would never tell another living soul."

"I didn't," Hardy insisted.

Cricket laughed. "And you have the nerve to lie to my face?" He held up the palm of his hand. "Did you forget this?" The scar of their pact was slashed across the palm of Cricket's hand. "We made a blood oath."

Hardy sighed. "We were like eight, Cricket."

"Blood oaths are for life," Cricket spat. "Go on, go back to your little weird-eyed girlfriend. I'm sure you'll be very happy together. You probably had a jolly good laugh about it when you told her my real name."

"Are you done?" Hardy asked.

Cricket shrugged.

"Darcy is not... normal," Hardy said.

Cricket clapped his hands together and smiled. "Well at least you're truthful about that."

"No...What I mean is...You need to ask her about how she knows your real name."

"I know how. You told her."

Hardy held up his scarred palm. "I swear to you, I didn't tell her."

Cricket cocked his head and considered Hardy's plea of innocence. "Why can't you just explain it to me?"

Hardy glanced back at Darcy who was busy eating her sandwich as if she hadn't a care in the world.

"I promised her I wouldn't," Hardy said.

Cricket shook his hair to the right to get it out of his eyes. "Oh, this is rich. Now you are sharing secrets?"

"It's not like that."

Cricket raised an eyebrow.

"She knows about Olen," Hardy said.

"What? Are you insane or just stupid?"

"I know, I know. I didn't have a choice. I had to take her with me to see him on Friday. She was going to leave and go home. Mr. Bell said I was responsible for her. I didn't have a choice."

"Oh, you had a choice all right. You just made the wrong one."

"It seemed right at the time. There's something else you should know."

"What else?"

"Olen is dead." The words felt wrong coming out of Hardy's mouth. Like it wasn't the truth, except it was.

"What? When?"

"We found him yesterday."

"We, as in you and Darcy? Never mind. Hardy, I'm sorry. Why didn't you say anything?" Cricket laid a hand on Hardy's shoulder. "Are you okay?"

"Yeah. I guess. Look, can you come back to the table so we can clear up this name thing?"

Cricket nodded, and they returned to the table. This time they both sat down across the table from Darcy.

"Will you please tell Cricket how you know his real name?" Hardy asked Darcy.

Darcy set her sandwich down and looked at Cricket. "No."

"Do it for me then," Hardy said.

Darcy locked eyes with Hardy. He thought he saw her weakening, but it was hard to read her icy stare.

"Look, I trust him. Can't that be enough? He won't tell anyone," Hardy pleaded.

"Tell anyone what?" Cricket asked.

"Fine." Darcy cleared her throat and folded her hands in front of her. "I'm an Illuminator."

"Wow. Really? Why didn't you say so?" Cricket said sarcastically. "What does that even mean?"

"Her blue eye isn't a real eye. It's a computer. She can access all kinds of…stuff."

Cricket's eyes narrowed. He plopped his elbows on the table and leaned toward her. "You really had me going there. What do you think I am, an idiot?!"

Darcy stood, leaned across the table, and grabbed Cricket's face between her hands. He tried to pull away from her, but her grip was like a vice. Her blue eye twitched back and forth across Cricket's now red face.

"What, is she—?" he tried to say with fish lips.

"Don't talk," Darcy snapped.

Cricket froze under her hands. After thirty seconds, she released him and sat back down.

Cricket rubbed a hand down his chest. The white imprints of Darcy's fingers lingered on his face.

Darcy began her monotone analysis, focusing her eyes on Cricket. "Your heart rate is sixty-five. Blood pressure 120/70. You have a slight heart murmur which is not a big deal. Your vision is 20/30 in your left eye, but your right eye is dominant so there is no significant loss of vision." She sat back and took a big bite of her sandwich.

Cricket didn't say a word. He just sat there, like someone had frozen him in the battle room of *Ender's Game*. Hardy couldn't help but smile a little. Watching Darcy in action was… entertaining.

"Can you read my mind?" Cricket asked quietly.

"No," Darcy said between chews.

"Good." Cricket relaxed a little. "X-ray vision?"

Darcy sighed and set her sandwich down. "No."

"Sorry. Just wondering what the boundaries are," Cricket said. "So, you have access to my school records?"

"Maybe."

"Can you change my grades? Like make F's into A's?" Cricket asked. "Wait. You'd better make it B's. A's would be too obvious."

"No." Darcy picked up her tray. "I have to go."

She disappeared down the hill.

"Was it something I said?" Cricket asked.

"Probably. I don't think she likes talking about her... eye."

"Dude, that's crazy awesome. We could like get her to do our homework and stuff," Cricket said, elbowing Hardy in the ribs.

"Leave her alone," Hardy said.

Hardy noticed that Darcy had left the book Olen had given her on the table. He grabbed it and shoved it into his backpack.

"Sorry I doubted you. I really am sorry about your grandfather," Cricket said.

"Thanks."

"At least you don't have to go hiking out into the woods all the time now. I know how much you hated it."

"Yeah." Hardy had thought he had hated it, but now he wasn't so sure.

"Hey, see those two girls sitting across from Charity?"

93

Hardy looked down the hill at Charity's table. Two girls, a blonde, and a brunette sat with their backs to Cricket and Hardy.

"Yeah." Hardy's eyes rested back on Charity. His stomach did a quick flip as he remembered her thank you kiss.

"I will be taking one of them to prom," Cricket said.

"Psst. Right."

"No. I'm serious. I...um, overheard them in the locker room talking about me. They think I'm cute."

"You went into the girls' locker room?" Hardy asked.

"No. Not went, went. Ya know, incognito."

This was it. The thing. The thing that always whispered into Hardy's ear—*strange things happen on Greene Island.* Cricket's "incognito" was outside the realm of what one would consider normal. Way outside. Cricket could leave his body. Float through walls. Go anywhere.

"Cricket, that's just sick."

"I averted my eyes. I swear. I'm not a pervert."

"Uh-huh."

"I'm going to go down there and see what they're saying."

"Not now, the bell's about to ring." Now was not the time for Cricket to play ghost.

"Relax, it will only take a minute. Make sure nobody touches me."

Cricket put his head down on the table, and his body went limp. Cricket had left his body. Right now he was drifting through the air down the hill ready to eavesdrop at Charity's table, undetected. Hardy never got used to it. It freaked him out. He always worried something would happen and Cricket wouldn't make it back and then he would be—dead. When Cricket was gone from his body, he didn't breathe. The few times Hardy felt like Cricket had been gone too long and had shaken him, Cricket was furious. Touching him, forcing his spirit back into his body, was akin to a body slam.

Hardy was staring down the hill at Charity's table when he realized Darcy had come back. She stood at the edge of the table looking at Cricket's lifeless body.

"Darcy. Hey. You forgot your book." Hardy unzipped his backpack and held the book out to her.

"I know," Darcy said without removing her eyes from Cricket.

"He's um…napping," Hardy said.

Darcy's eyes turned large and scared. She reached out to Cricket. Hardy grabbed her arm.

"He's fine," Hardy said.

"He's not breathing, Hardy." Darcy tried to pull her arm from Hardy's grip. Seeing that Hardy showed no concern, Darcy examined Cricket more closely. Her eyes drifted up above Cricket's head and followed an invisible something down the hill to the table where Charity and her friends were sitting. Hardy didn't know what to do. It was obvious that Darcy was figuring out what Cricket was doing. He let go of her arm. Her eyes returned to Hardy.

"Darcy, there's something you should know." He lowered his voice, even though there was no one nearby. "Cricket can leave his body. You know…like a spirit."

Darcy's eyes widened. "He's a Sleeper," she whispered.

The bell rang.

Chapter Nine

After school, Hardy and Darcy rode their bikes twenty minutes north to Hill Home just outside the village of Dunby. Today they began their two-week stint of community service, and Hardy was not looking forward to it. At least he wouldn't have to worry about checking on Olen anymore. A surge of guilt twisted through his gut, thinking of Olen's clenched fist and empty eyes. And then there was the curious tiny feather. He had taken the feather, put it in a plastic baggie, and stuck it in the drawer beside his bed. The gold lighter in his pocket pressed against his leg with each push of the pedal. These two things were all he had left of Olen.

The white-columned house stood grandly at the top of a hill. It was surrounded by manicured green lawns and hardwood forests. They passed a large, white sign hanging from chains welcoming them to Hill Home of Dunby.

They took a brick path that led to the back of the estate and put their bikes in a long, black rack, and followed the sidewalk that led up to a windowed door marked with a plaque that said "Employee Entrance."

Hardy had no idea what to expect. He knew virtually nothing about the numerous Hill Homes for the elderly that were scattered across the island. All he knew was that they were founded by Governor Hill's father, were supported by the island's government, and old people came there when they were near their end. That was the extent of his knowledge. He was certain that Darcy had probably read every available article, accessing all of it inside her head.

He pulled the door open and they were immediately hit with the smell of brown gravy and peas. The kitchen was just inside on the right. Its double swinging doors were propped open. Ribbons of steam rose from huge, silver pots. A man in a tall, white hat poked and prodded the contents with a long spoon. The chef looked up and saw Hardy and Darcy. He pointed with his spoon. "Down the hall, take a right."

The hall was carpeted in a rich emerald color, and the walls were covered in a beige wallpaper that alternated between floral stripes and a scene of two women churning butter under a tree. Small crystal chandeliers hung from the ceiling. The place had a musty smell that reminded Hardy of old furniture and library books.

Just around the corner, a round-cheeked black lady stood by an open door, dressed in pink scrubs. She frowned when she saw them coming.

"Come on, you two, we're about to start." She disappeared into the room. Hardy and Darcy hurried inside.

The room offered several rows of chairs facing a wooden

podium. They were given a handout and told to take a seat. There were at least six others—a mix of younger and older adults. Hardy and Darcy were the only teens.

Hardy sat down in the back row, and Darcy sat beside him. The lady in pink swished to the podium at the front of the room. Even though she was on the plumper side, her arms looked like sledgehammers. He imagined her pulling him into a headlock just to set him straight.

"I'm Nurse Troxler. My friends call me Mama. Let me make it clear. You are not my friends, and I'm not your mama. You will call me Nurse Troxler."

Hardy noticed a few people sink down into their chairs.

"You are here because you screwed up. You will do what you're told, when you're told. No questions asked. Any questions?"

Hardy wondered if anyone would be dumb enough to actually ask a question. Darcy started to raise her hand. Horrified, he quickly pushed her hand back down to her lap and shook his head.

"Good," Nurse Troxler said. "You were each given a handout. I expect you to take it home and read it."

Hardy whispered out of the side of his mouth to Darcy. "Do you have this...upstairs?"

"Yes."

Hardy folded the handout and stuck it under his leg. He would accidentally forget it on his way out.

"While you are here, you will assist our staff in the care of our patients. They deserve to be treated with the dignity that their many years have earned them."

Hardy leaned over to Darcy. "So, what's this stuff about

Cricket being a Sleeper?"

"He could be a part of Viola's legacy," Darcy said quietly.

"I seriously doubt it."

Nurse Troxler's voice droned on. "However, don't be fooled by their humbled position. Some will try to convince you that they are being held against their will while others will swear to you there's been a mistake, pleading for you to call their son or daughter. Some will try to give you things. DO NOT TAKE ANYTHING FROM A PATIENT. You will be kind. You will do your assigned task. That's it."

Darcy leaned toward Hardy. "Viola supposedly passed down some unique traits to her children."

"Examples of what you might be asked to do: light cleaning, making beds, putting away laundry, assisting patients from their bed to a chair…"

"Nobody believes that stuff," Hardy whispered back.

"…help with daily walks, soaking dentures, brushing hair…"

"Some believe it," Darcy said.

"…helping men shave, refilling water…"

"Are you saying that Cricket is somehow related to Viola? That's insane."

Darcy looked right at Hardy this time. "Yes, that's what I'm saying."

"…delivering books and food trays."

"But he's nobody, much less royalty," Hardy said.

"His last name, Wright, is in the royal family tree."

Hardy was stunned. Could it be true? Could Cricket really be a descendant of Viola? It certainly would explain a lot. Why he was able to do what he did. But then, that would mean all those supposed tales and legends about Viola were true.

"Any questions?" Nurse Troxler finally asked.

Yeah, Hardy thought. I have a lot of questions, but not about this stuff. Only, his questions were going to have to wait. Darcy started to raise her hand again. He shoved it, more forcefully this time, back into her lap. The stitches on the back of his head began to ache.

"Good. You all will now take a drug test and be fitted with standard blue scrubs that you will wear whenever you are on duty. You'll find a bathroom at the end of the hall. Pee in a cup, write your name on it, and bring it back to me. When you're done, I have a box of uniforms by the door to hand out."

This was beginning to feel a lot like prison.

After the humiliation of peeing into a cup and carrying it down the hall, Hardy and Darcy changed into their cotton scrubs in the designated locker rooms and reported to the front desk for their work assignments. The front desk was on the ground-floor lobby just inside the grand double doors of the main entrance. Two, large, white-paned windows afforded a view of the home's large, columned front porch which was lined with white rocking chairs and hanging ferns. The lobby was empty except for a small elderly lady with a sweater around her shoulders sitting in a wicker chair by one of the windows. Her chin had dropped to her chest, and her eyes were closed.

A twenty-something man stood behind the desk shuffling papers. His name tag said "Trevor." He was broad-shouldered and short-necked, with arms that stretched the limit of his scrub's sleeves. A partial tattoo that appeared to be the tail of a red and green serpent showed below his right sleeve. Something about him looked familiar, but all Hardy could conjure was Friday night wrestle mania on TV. Darcy was staring—no, more like glaring—at Trevor's face. Hardy wondered what popped up in that eye of hers for Trevor.

Trevor asked their names, wrote something down on a clipboard, and handed them both a slip of paper. "If you have any questions, don't hesitate to ask," Trevor said, sounding bored. He looked around them for the next person in line. Hardy and Darcy started to move away from the desk when Trevor called after them. "Oh, and keep the cover over the bird. He never shuts up."

Hardy looked down at his slip of paper. Sure enough, number one—clean out birdcage by front window (supplies in storage closet 12b). He sighed and looked toward the entrance. A sheet was draped over a large A-frame structure hanging from a metal base. He guess it could've been worse: they could've been asked to clean toilets.

Darcy headed toward the cage.

"I'll get the stuff, don't worry about it," Hardy called out to Darcy.

Hardy found 12b down the hall and gathered newspaper, trash bags, plastic gloves, and a yellow container labeled "parrot food." When he came around the corner, Darcy had the gray and white parrot out of the cage and propped on the back of her right hand. The bird was whistling and bobbing its head. *Good grief.* He glanced at the desk. Luckily, the muscled nurse was gone.

He rushed over to Darcy. "What are you doing? Put that thing back."

"His name is Petey."

"Name is Petey!" the bird squawked.

Hardy anxiously scanned the lobby. "Do you want to get us thrown out on our first day? Now put him up."

"He likes me." Darcy put her face close to the bird.

"OUCH—EYE!" The bird gently kissed the cheek next to Darcy's blue eye.

Darcy held the bird out close to Hardy's face. Petey stuck out its head and pecked on the left lens of Hardy's glasses. "FOUR EYES!"

Darcy let out a stifled laugh.

Hardy frowned. "Very funny." He grabbed Petey and shoved him back into the cage. The bird flapped its wings wildly and landed on the wooden post in the middle of the cage, clenching and unclenching its thick claws.

He turned to Darcy. "I suppose you think that's funny?"

Darcy smiled. "Kind of."

"Let's just stick to cleaning the cage." Hardy handed her a garbage bag. "Here."

"He's cute, huh?"

"THE DIE HAS BEEN CAST!" Petey shrieked.

"Yeah. Adorable," Hardy said.

The bird watched Hardy closely as he took the paper from the bottom of the cage and dumped it into the trash bag Darcy was holding.

"I need to talk to you about, Olen," Darcy said.

"OLEN!" Petey cried.

Hardy looked around the lobby, worried about the bird's outburst, but only a few visitors were passing through. "Would you be careful what you say?"

"Sorry. I didn't know it would repeat everything I said."

"What is it that's so important?" Hardy shoved new paper into the bottom of the cage. When Darcy didn't say anything, he stopped and turned to her. "Well?"

"I can't be sure, of course."

"Sure about what?"

Darcy looked down and fidgeted with her hands. "There were signs."

Hardy was growing impatient. "Signs? Could you be a little more specific?"

Darcy peered up at Hardy. She looked scared. "When we found...Ol...him. There were footprints outside."

"Yeah, so."

"Footprints of someone else."

"Who else, Darcy? No one knows about that place but my family."

"Someone...had been there before us," Darcy said nervously.

Hardy rubbed the back of his head grazing the rough stitches. "How could you possibly know something like that?"

Darcy stared at Hardy and raised an eyebrow.

"Right—you compared the footprints to ours..." Hardy said.

Darcy nodded.

Hardy glanced at the bird. It was sitting completely still, head cocked to the side, as if listening.

"My gosh. What does this mean? What are you saying?" Hardy asked.

"I think your grandfather was murdered."

Petey jumped onto the side of the cage and bobbed its head from side to side. "MURDER! THE DIE HAS BEEN CAST!"

Chapter Ten

Hardy couldn't sleep that night. He lay in his bed staring at the ceiling of glow-in-the-dark stars that he had stuck there when he was ten. *Murder*. He couldn't get the word out of his head. Why would anyone want to kill Olen? Who even knew Olen existed, besides his family and Cricket? It didn't make any sense. Darcy said she saw footprints that didn't belong to either one of them or Olen. Maybe she was wrong. After all, there was no sign of foul play at the cabin. Nothing was out of place. *Exactly*—nothing was out of place. Everything was clean, as if Olen knew he was going to...die. Still, outside of that, nothing about Olen suggested murder. The body had no wounds, no injuries. The only strange thing had been the tiny feather closed inside Olen's fist.

Hardy rolled over and opened the drawer of his bedside table. He removed the plastic baggie with the feather in it and grabbed Olen's lighter from his side table. He flipped open the lid and scraped his thumb over the coarse wheel. A small yellow flame jumped to life. He held the baggie up to the light and stared at the strange feather. It was shaped like a tiny propeller—white-feathered top, brown stem. He had no idea what kind of feather it was, or if it even mattered.

Tom had been angry about the note Olen had sent through Hardy. *It's time to tell Hardy the truth.* Could Tom have been angry enough to make sure Hardy never learned what the *truth* was? Was he capable of murder?

He flipped the lid of the lighter shut, leaving him in the dark again. He wanted to call Darcy and tell her about the feather. The note. He didn't think she had a phone. He had never seen her with one. He rolled back over, turned on his light, and grabbed his laptop. Propping up against his backboard, he unfolded his screen and pressed the power key. She was a virtual computer: it shouldn't be too hard to contact her.

Hardy logged onto the school website and pulled up the student directory to find Darcy's e-mail. He scrolled down through the P's until he found "Page." Darcy Page. Hardy pumped out a quick note—*Call me. Hardy*. Send.

He stared at the screen. If Darcy was everything she appeared to be, it wouldn't take long. And he was right. Within seconds, his computer came to life, and Darcy was staring at him through his screen. He could barely see her. She was like a gray shadow except for the eerie glow of her blue eye.

"You woke me up. What time is it?" Darcy asked, rubbing her brown eye.

"Late."

Darcy's hair hung in a mess around her shoulders. The scene in front of him went from her ghostly white face to her hands grabbing a sweatshirt off a chair, to the screen going temporarily black, back to her face reappearing on his screen.

"Are you on a laptop?" Hardy asked.

"No. You know I don't need that. I'm looking at you in a mirror so you can see me. Otherwise, you'll just see what I'm seeing."

"Okay—that is really cool."

Darcy sat down in front of what appeared to be an old antique dresser mirror.

"Can you turn a light on or something, I can barely see you?"

"No. What's going on?"

"I can't stop thinking about what you said about Olen. You know…about him being murdered."

"Can we talk about this tomorrow?" Darcy asked quietly. She glanced behind her into the darkness.

"Olen gave me a note to give to Tom the day we were there."

"Do you know what it said?" Darcy whispered, sounding more interested.

"I wasn't supposed to read it, but yeah—it said, *It's time to tell Hardy the truth.*"

"What did your father say about the note?"

"Nothing. He was angry, though. Then a few hours later we find Olen dead."

"You think he had something to do with it?"

"I don't know. I want to show you something." Hardy held the plastic bag in front of the screen.

"An achene from a Taraxacum. A weed."

"A ache—what? From a Tara—what?"

"A seed from a dandelion." Darcy glanced nervously behind her. "I need to go."

"I found it at the cabin," Hardy said, setting the bag down.

Darcy stood up and got closer to the mirror. Her white, distorted face filled Hardy's screen, her blue eye flashing as she blinked. "Where?"

"In Olen's hand."

Darcy sat back down into her chair. "Oh no."

"What? What is it?"

"There aren't any dandelions on Greene Island."

"I thought you said it was a weed."

"It is, but not on Greene Island. Not anymore. What does Viola's statue hold in her hand?"

"Viola? Oh yeah—oh—a dandelion."

"She put a curse on the island with it, remember?"

"Not that again. That's just—crap."

Darcy crossed her arms. "Some people don't think so."

"DARCY!" A rough male voice called out in the dark behind her.

She stood up again and came close to the mirror. "I have to go. I'm sorry."

Hardy's screen went black.

"Darcy! Darcy!" he yelled at the screen.

Great. Now he was even more confused. No dandelions on Greene Island? Then how does the seed of one end up in Olen's cabin?

Hardy typed dandelion into his search engine. He clicked on the first result. He scanned the page looking for—he didn't know what he was looking for. All he found was weed, worldwide, edible in their entirety. Beneficial, nuisance. He skimmed through a bunch of other facts, but nothing that would indicate anything bad outside a mild allergic reaction.

He sighed and shut his laptop. Nothing was going to be resolved tonight. He shoved his laptop onto his side table along with the lighter and the seed. He switched his light off and pulled the covers over his shoulders. Tomorrow. Tomorrow he would find out what else Darcy knew. He drifted off to sleep wondering if his father was a murderer and what dandelions had to do with it. He imagined the police taking his father away in handcuffs and the whispers of islanders saying: *It was Viola's curse that drove him to it.*

***

"Who are you looking for?" Cricket asked, tearing open a salt packet and sprinkling it on his fries.

"Darcy," Hardy said, searching the faces of students coming outside to eat at the picnic tables.

"Ugh. Why?" Cricket said, removing the top bun of his burger.

"I need to talk to her. Have you seen her today?" Hardy asked, frowning.

Cricket tore open a ketchup packet with his teeth and squeezed it onto his hamburger. "Uh, no. She's a freshman. Why would I see her? For that matter, why would you want to see her?"

Hardy pushed his tray of food to the side. He had lost his

appetite.

"Look, you're not going to ruin my chances of taking Megan to the prom by associating with Darcy," Cricket said, pointing the empty ketchup packet at him.

"So, you decided on Megan, huh? Well, this is a little more important than your prom date," Hardy snapped.

"Please enlighten me then," Cricket said sarcastically, shoving the burger into his mouth.

Hardy leaned forward. "Darcy thinks Olen was murdered."

"Mm huh," Cricket mumbled through his full mouth.

"Uh-huh? That's all you have to say? I just told you Olen may have been murdered."

Cricket swallowed and dropped his burger onto his tray. "Come on, Hardy. Darcy is running circles around you. Why would anyone kill Olen? He's lived in the woods for years. Nobody knew he was there. And he was…old."

"She saw footprints that weren't ours or Olen's."

"What else?" Cricket asked, running his tongue over his back teeth.

Hardy didn't want to mention the note or the dandelion seed. Cricket would only laugh. Probably. "Isn't that enough?"

"Frankly, no. Was Olen injured? Was anything missing?"

"Well, no. But the place was spotless which was completely out of character for Olen."

"Big deal. So he decided to clean up for once in his life."

"Could you at least try to take this seriously?" Hardy asked.

Cricket chugged half of his canned Cola and let out a

long burp. "I'm sorry. Darcy is weird. I don't trust her."

"Whatever." Hardy stood up and grabbed his tray.

"Where are you going?" Cricket asked.

"To look for Darcy."

Cricket lifted his hands in resignation and let them fall hard on the table.

"What do you want, Mr. Vance?" Mrs. Wiggins asked, dropping a stack of papers down in front of her. The phone rang. "Administration," she answered pleasantly. "One minute please." She pressed three buttons and turned her sour face back to Hardy.

"I need to know if Darcy Page is at school today." Hardy said, leaning over the reception desk.

"You know we don't give out private information on a student."

"I just want to know if she's here. That's all. I'm not interested in her social security number."

"Sorry. Can't help you," Mrs. Wiggins said. She dropped into her chair, licked her index finger, and started shuffling through her stack.

He took a deep breath and smiled. "You know, Mrs. Wiggins, you're looking quite lovely today."

She laughed, frowned, and flipped to another page with her wet finger.

Hardy turned around and rubbed a hand through his hair in frustration. That's when he noticed Mr. Bell quickly passing between work tables, headed for the exit to the hallway. He ran after him. "Mr. Bell!"

Mr. Bell continued toward the door. Hardy made a mad dash and planted himself in front of Mr. Bell just as he was reaching out a hand to push open the door.

"Mr. Vance. I'm in a bit of a rush, so if you don't mind —" Mr. Bell said.

"You said I was responsible for Darcy, remember? We have community service today, and I haven't seen her."

Mr. Bell stared at Hardy over the top of his glasses. "Very well." He turned and headed straight for the receptionist's desk. Mrs. Wiggins was still licking her finger and flipping through her papers. "Helen, is Darcy Page here today?" Mr. Bell asked.

Mrs. Wiggins gave Hardy a reproachful look. Hardy suppressed the desire to smile.

"No. She called in sick," she said, sounding annoyed.

Sick? She seemed fine last night.

Mr. Bell straightened and turned to Hardy. "Satisfied?"

"Uh…yeah. I should go check on her, though," Hardy said, frowning and feigning concern. "Like you said, I'm responsible for her."

"Very well. Helen, please give Hardy Darcy's address," Mr. Bell replied. He quickly headed for the exit. The bell rang.

Hardy dragged himself to class and spent the rest of the day biting off whatever remained of his already massacred fingernails. Nasty habit, he knew, but excellent stress reliever.

***

After school, Hardy stood next to his bike and unfolded the piece of paper with Darcy's address. His stomach dropped. The address was for Rhode Village, often referred to as "Road Kill Village", due to the distasteful joke that its occupants ate the said nickname for dinner. In other words, the village was poor. It was once a popular place to live, nestled between birch woods and rolling green hills. Then the windmills came. The lush hills became mounds of dirt plugged with the giant spinning blades of progress. The residents complained of the constant whoomp, whoomp sound that traveled through the village at night into people's dreams. Anyone with the means left, abandoning their homes, taking their businesses with them. The poor moved in.

Hardy had paid little attention to the vulgar jokes. He never had the need to venture into Rhode Village until now. He shoved the paper into his pocket and took off on his bike.

He barely had time to get to Darcy's and then make it to Hill Home on time. He pedaled as fast as he could, the back of his calves burning. The closer he got, the more he questioned whether going to see her was such a good idea. She had left him hanging last night. Cutting him off before she explained more about the dandelion seed. He needed to know what she knew.

He eventually came to the wide hillside of the tall spinning turbines. Nothing green existed between the simple wired fence and the brown hills that held the white monsters except for unfriendly patches of grass. It looked like a desert, a no man's land, where life had been scared away by the hum and buzz of the mechanical rotating arms.

Hardy turned off the small, two-lane paved road into a one-lane dirt road that was scarcely wider than a path. Just below him lay a long strand of honey-colored stone cottages with gray, wood-shingled roofs. Darcy lived in one of these. Like condos, they were connected, each sharing walls with their neighbors. Across from the cottages, a small stream gurgled and wound its way through the small village.

Past the steep-pitched roofs of the cottages, stood the remains of a village where people once came to buy homemade scones and wildflowers. Faded shop signs hung like memorials from chains above boarded-up doors.

The saddest sight was a small church surrounded by weeds. The steeple that once held a cross was gone, as if a wrecking ball had knocked it free. Like the other shops, the windows and doors were boarded up with plywood. The rest of Rhode Village was a hillside sprinkled with shacks people called home.

Hardy coasted slowly by the cottage doors, trying to remember the number on the piece of paper. He passed a man hanging in the shadows of his recessed door, his presence only detectable by the red ashes glowing at the end of his cigarette. Hardy hunched down over his handlebars, trying to make himself smaller, less exposed.

He slowed down and pulled out the paper. Sixteen was the cottage number. He quickly realized that none of the doors had numbers on them. He was running out of time. If he didn't find it soon, he was going to be late to Hill Home.

He passed a woman of considerable size sitting on a stool that had disappeared underneath her generous lap. She sat outside her door peeling potatoes, letting the peels fall to the ground and tossing the naked spuds into a pot of water that sat next her. Hardy hesitated, but necessity won over fear. He turned around and pedaled back, stopping in front of her.

"Excuse me, can you tell me where sixteen is?"

When she looked up, he noticed her mouth sunk in over her gums. No teeth. She smacked her lips together a few times. "Why that be two door that a ways."

"Okay. Thanks," Hardy said.

Her cheeks sank into a scowl. "I hopes you ain't a messin' with that Nash boy. He trouble."

Hardy slowly pulled away, wondering who Nash was. He coasted forward two doors. The door was purple. Its peeling paint revealed a faded red beneath. He leaned his bike up against the window box of the small window beside the door and walked into the small recess. He knocked twice and waited. He looked behind him, feeling somewhat trapped in the darkened doorway. He heard a metallic click, and the door opened a crack. Darcy's brown eye peered out at him.

"What are you doing here?" Darcy asked. She didn't seem happy to see him.

He shoved his hands into his pockets, feeling awkward. It wasn't like they were close friends or anything. "I came to check on you."

"I'm fine, just a bit under the weather. Goodbye." Darcy started to shut the door.

Hardy stuck his shoe in the closing door, and pushed it open with his hand. He stepped inside. The ceiling was low with large brown beams running across it. The small square room consisted of an old, beat-up recliner doctored with duct tape and a brown sofa pushed against the wall. The dark fireplace just inside to the left held a mountain of winter's ash. The place smelled of burnt wood and strong drink.

Darcy closed the door, walked past Hardy, and turned around. She tightened the tie of the white robe she was wearing, and crossed her arms in front of her. "I said I was fine. You can go now."

He studied her face. Something was off. She was too anxious to get rid of him. Plus, she didn't look sick, she looked—sad. "Is anyone else here?" he asked, looking past her.

"No."

"What happened last night? Why did you cut me off so quickly?" he asked.

"You know what, I'm actually starting to feel a little better. If you'll wait for me to change, I'll go to Hill Home with you." She turned to leave the room.

Hardy knew a dodge when he saw one. He reached out and grabbed her by the arm. Darcy cried out in pain. He quickly released her and held up his hand. He had barely touched her. She kept her back to him, holding her left arm. Without thinking, he slowly turned her around and slid her robe off her left shoulder. She moved her hand. There were dark, oval-shaped marks on her arm. Bruises. Large fingerprints. A man's, by the size of them.

"Darcy," he whispered.

She pulled her robe back up over her shoulder. "I fell last night, stumbled in the dark."

"Darcy, who did this to you?" he asked, concerned.

"I told you, I fell."

"No, you didn't."

Darcy averted her eyes and shifted her feet.

"Did your father do this?" Hardy pushed.

"No!" Darcy yelled. Anger and pain flashed in her eyes. "He's dead!"

He held up his hands. "Okay. Okay." Pushing her to talk wasn't getting him anywhere. He took in the meager furnishings again. "We could call someone. Get you out of here."

Darcy sighed and folded her arms. "Take a look around, Hardy. I'm not going anywhere."

"Where's your mother?"

"Work," she said, staring at the floor.

"We could call her."

"Where do you live, Hardy?" Darcy asked, staring him straight in the eyes.

"What? What has that got to do with—?"

"What village?" she snapped.

"Hampton," he said quietly.

"Village of the pod dwellings. Decent folk. Respectable, even. Where do I live, Hardy?"

He looked around at the poor furnishings, starting to feel like a fool.

"That's right. We po folk, Hardy. We got what we got," Darcy said in an accent not unlike the lady without the teeth.

Hardy wiped a hand across his mouth. "I'm sorry...Darcy." He realized she wasn't wrong.

"Wait here. I'll get dressed."

Hardy collapsed into the duct taped lounge chair. There

was a picture sitting on the table next to it. He picked up the photo and stared at the faces. There were three of them lined up like toy soldiers on the beach. Tallest to shortest. Two brothers and Darcy squinting against the sun. Darcy and the brother standing next to her were smiling. The oldest brother stared hard at the camera like he was angry. Hardy opened the back of the frame. Three names were written on the back of the old picture. Nash. Danny. Darcy. There was no doubt in Hardy's mind—Nash was the one who had done this to Darcy.

***

Darcy unrobed and stared in the dresser mirror at the matching set of dark bruises on her upper arms. Nash's fingerprints.

He had come home late, argued with their mother about his drinking, and then collapsed onto his bottom bunk and began his chainsaw snoring. Danny, oblivious, slept heavily in the single bed across from them. Not even the drone of the giant windmill blades could drown out Nash's snoring. Darcy had just shoved a pillow over her head when the e-mail alert came in. Her school account. Boring. But then she realized what time it was. Too late for school e-mail. She opened the e-mail in her head. *Call me. Hardy.*

She had carefully climbed down the bunk ladder. She knew how Nash was when he drank. Unpredictable, mean. But, he was laid flat out on the bunk below her, still in his clothes, mouth open. She didn't think anything would wake him. She had been wrong. He heard her talking to Hardy. It woke him up. Did she have any idea how important his sleep was? Could she comprehend how important his lousy job was in keeping the family afloat? It was bad enough that he had to deal with their nagging mother: he didn't need a crazy sister who talked to herself in the mirror.

With each admonishment, his fingers had dug deeper into her flesh. Danny had roused from his sleep and made a feeble attempt at helping, but Nash told him to shut up, and, as always, he caved and rolled over.

Darcy didn't cry, didn't yell. She took it. She took it because in her mind she deserved it. After all, it had been her fault—her father dying. She had been the reason they all lost the only good thing any of them had ever had. The life they once shared—gone forever. There was no getting over that.

Chapter Eleven

Hardy's questions about Olen's death would have to wait. After what he had just seen on Darcy's arms…It just wasn't the right time to bring it up. He had wanted to help her, but she had shut him down at every attempt. He had no idea what to do. At least Hardy's father had never hurt him — physically. They rode to Hill Home in silence, changed into their scrubs, and lined up at the lobby front desk.

Trevor yawned as he handed out the assignments. When Hardy's turn came, Trevor handed him a card and smiled. *Assist Nurse Troxler with second-floor patients.* Crap. The one who gave them the 'do what you're told' speech and had arms that could break Hardy in half. He looked at Trevor, hoping he had read it wrong.

"Good luck," Trevor said smugly.

Hardy headed for Darcy who was already over at the birdcage poking her face into its wire bars. The bird was tenderly kissing her cheek.

"Ouch!" Petey cried.

"What's your assignment?" Hardy asked.

"Four eyes!"

Darcy smiled.

"I really hate that bird," Hardy said.

"I get to take care of Petey and help Trevor with patients."

"I don't know which is worse. I'm stuck with Nurse Troxler."

Darcy poked her fingers into the cage and Petey gently played with them. "Mama?"

"What?" Hardy asked.

"Nurse Troxler. Her friends call her Mama."

"Well, like she said, we're not her friends and we won't be calling her Mama. I'll meet you out back at six o'clock?"

"Sure."

"You okay?"

Darcy stuck her fingers inside the cage. "I'm fine. Right, Petey?"

"THE DIE HAS BEEN CAST!" Petey screeched.

At least Hardy didn't have to listen to that irritating parrot. He took the winding staircase up to the second level.

At the top of the second floor was a smaller nurses' station with an adjacent elevator. Nurse Troxler was talking to the station nurse. Hardy waited by the stairs, not wanting to interrupt. The station nurse noticed him and stopped talking. Nurse Troxler turned around. "Well, what are you waiting for? Come on. We've got patients that need tending to."

Hardy covered the distance between them and held out his hand. "Nurse Troxler, a pleasure. Hardy Vance."

She ignored his hand. "Take that cart of books and newspapers over there by the elevator and go room-to-room to see if anyone's interested in reading material."

Hardy dropped his hand awkwardly to his side. He felt her large brown eyes on him as he went to the cart. She was not one to be messed with. He would have to be careful not to get on her bad side.

He pushed the cart a few feet past the elevator and turned, stopping dead in his tracks. Trevor was in the hallway with Charity. *What was she doing here? And with him?*

Trevor's neck flared bright red as he spat angry words at her. Charity pleaded helplessly with her hands. Hardy didn't think after that. He abandoned the cart and made a beeline down the hall. "Hey!" Hardy yelled out, quickly covering the last few feet between them.

Charity turned toward Hardy: tears were streaming down her face.

"Get out of here, Vance. Can't you see we're having a private conversation," Trevor said sharply.

Charity stared at her feet and rubbed at her tears with her fingers.

"Are you okay, Charity?" Hardy asked, ignoring Trevor.

Trevor bumped Hardy with his large chest. "Are you deaf, Vance? I said beat it."

Hardy didn't know what to do. It wasn't like he owed Charity anything, especially after she had stuck him with community service. Plus, he really didn't want to cause any trouble on his second day. But then again, he wasn't known for making good decisions.

"I'll leave if Charity tells me to," Hardy said.

"You're dumber than you look then." Trevor grabbed a handful of Hardy's shirt and shoved him hard against the wall.

A dull pain shot through Hardy's head, his vision blurred.

"Stop!" Charity yelled. "Let him go now or we're done!"

Trevor loosened his grip but continue to hold Hardy against the wall. "You don't mean that," Trevor said, sounding hurt.

"I do, Trevor. I mean it."

Trevor seemed to melt under her words. He released Hardy and pushed him one last time into the wall.

"I'm leaving now, with Hardy. When you grow up, you can call me."

Charity, suddenly confident and in charge, linked her arm with Hardy's and led him down the hall. Hardy was still waiting for his head to clear.

"What just happened?" he asked, rubbing the back of his head.

"It's nothing. He's just being a jealous jerk."

"Jealous? Of what?"

"You."

"Me?"

"Trevor's my boyfriend." Charity released her hand from under Hardy's arm.

When they came around the corner, Hardy was relieved to see that Nurse Troxler was no longer by the desk. Charity walked over to the railing that overlooked the lobby below and leaned back against it.

"Trevor? That guy is your boyfriend?" Hardy asked. *He's*

a jerk.

"Yes. Trevor Irene? He used to go to Southeast High?" Charity said, trying to jog Hardy's memory. "He was a senior when we were freshmen."

"Wow," Hardy said, stunned.

"You should stay away from him," Charity said.

"Why? What did I do?"

"I kissed you on local TV in front of everybody. Remember?"

Yeah, he remembered all right. Best day of his life.

"Plus, I told him it was your idea, you know, for publicity," Charity said.

"What? Why would you do that?" Hardy said exasperated. He leaned forward and rested his hands on the railing. *Unbelievable.* No doubt Trevor would now make Hardy's life miserable.

"He gets angry," Charity said.

"Yeah, I noticed." Hardy said. He slammed his hands on the railing. "Listen, Charity. I'm here because of you. And now your jealous, testosterone-charged boyfriend hates me."

Hardy was not going to let her off the hook so easy this time. She stepped close to Hardy and placed a hand on his chest. No doubt she could feel his heart racing. She embraced him, wrapping her arms around him and laid her head against his chest.

"You saved my life, and I only wanted to thank you. But Trevor is such a jealous jerk," she murmured against his chest.

Her tears soaked through his shirt. The sweet smell of her hair drifted upward. He could feel himself weakening under her embrace.

"Hardy. I'm so sorry," she sniffed. "I always end up making a mess of things. I'm sorry you're doing community service because of me. I should have told the teacher the truth about what happened in class. I hope you'll forgive me."

She held Hardy tighter and shook with small sobs. Feeling her warm, delicate body next to him, his anger fled. He put his arms around her and buried his face into her hair. He knew she wouldn't clearing his name with Principal Bell—she had taken it too far to go back now. Still, he would forgive her. He held her for a long, glorious moment before she released him and wiped her tears.

"Thank you for understanding, Hardy." She looked up at him with her watery, blue eyes and kissed him lightly on the lips. She disappeared down the stairs, leaving him in a stupor. He followed her with his eyes as she crossed the lobby and went out the front door. That's when he noticed Darcy staring up at him from beside the birdcage.

"Mr. Vance!"

Hardy spun around. It was Nurse Troxler. She came directly to the railing and peered over. The only one in the lobby was Darcy, who smiled and waved. Nurse Troxler took a step back from the railing. "It appears you'd rather flirt with your little girlfriend than do any actual work."

He held up a hand. "This is not what it looks like."

She folded her arms across her large chest. "You young people think you're so smart—you don't know anything."

"I can explain, really," he pleaded.

"Follow me."

Hardy gritted his teeth and stared at the front door. Char-

125

ity always managed to leave him with the consequences of her actions. What was wrong with him? When he was around her he was just—stupid.

He rushed after Nurse Troxler, who was very quick on her feet for someone so short and stocky. A tower of food trays stood by the elevator doors. He caught the scent of beef and tomato sauce seeping from the covered plates.

"Grab the cart and follow me."

Hardy pushed the tray tower behind Nurse Troxler. When they turned left down the hall, he was relieved to see that Trevor was no longer there. Nurse Troxler stopped at the first room.

"Well—grab a tray. Don't just stand there."

Hardy slipped a tray out of its slot and followed her into the darkened room. She made directly for the blinds and lifted them with a single pull. Light came flooding into the room.

The crumpled, frail body lying in the raised bed opened her eyes and blinked several times.

"You need to keep the blinds open, Mrs. Gobble. The sunlight is good for you."

The white-haired lady pulled herself up slightly in the bed and glared at Hardy. "It's about time you brought me something to eat. They're starving me around here," she said.

Hardy looked at Nurse Troxler who ignored the comment and rolled the old woman's bed tray up to her bed. "Nobody's starving you, Mrs. Gobble. You've had breakfast and lunch today."

Hardy slid the tray of food on the tray table and lifted the cover. Mrs. Gobble glared at him with her worn, watery eyes. She reached out a gnarled hand and placed it on his arm.

"Can you take me home now, son?"

Hardy froze. He thought of Olen. Alone. Cold in the ground.

Nurse Troxler took the water pitcher and headed to the bathroom. "This is Hardy, Mrs. Gobble, not your son."

When Hardy heard the water turn on in the bathroom, he took Mrs. Gobble's hand into his and squeezed it gently. "Soon, Mom. Soon, we'll go home."

Mrs. Gobble smiled at him, and he handed her a fork.

"It won't do you any good getting too close," Nurse Troxler said as soon as they were back in the hallway.

"I'm sorry, she seemed like she—"

"Come on, next tray."

Nurse Troxler barreled into the next room. Unlike Mrs. Gobble's room, it was brightly lit with the late-afternoon sun. She immediately grabbed the bed tray and rolled it front of the elderly gentleman who appeared to be sleeping. His thinning, salt-colored hair barely covered his head. A soft rattle came from his throat.

"I know you're not sleeping, Mr. Stanford. You never sleep with your glasses on," Nurse Troxler said.

The man opened one eye. "It was worth a try, don't you think?"

"Are you going to eat for me today?" she asked.

The man ignored her and peered at Hardy from under

his white bushy brows. "Who's this? The undertaker? Come to size me up for a box, boy?"

"No, sir." Hardy set the tray down.

"Hmph!" the man grunted.

Nurse Troxler took the cover off the plate and dug a fork into the meat loaf. "Now don't give me any problems, George. Open wide."

George ignored her and stared at Hardy. Hardy shifted his feet and crossed his arms.

"I can feed myself. I'm not an invalid," George protested.

She set the fork down. "Is that why I keep finding your food in the trash or in Mrs. Gobble's room? You're scaring her, you know. She thinks you're trying to steal from her."

"Hmph!" George raised a finger and pointed at Hardy. "I want the boy to feed me."

Nurse Troxler looked back at Hardy. "You want Hardy to feed you?"

"That's what I said. You can leave," George said.

Hardy shook his head. He definitely did not want to feed some crotchety old man and wipe the drool from his mouth.

"Well then, George, if that's going to make you happy and you'll eat, then Hardy it is."

"Nurse Troxler, I don't—"

"I'll be back around after I deliver the rest of the trays," Nurse Troxler said, heading toward the door. "You behave yourself, George."

Hardy stood staring down at George. George stared at his food.

"God broke the mold when he made that woman. One of a kind, that one. Mean as a snake on the outside, but the kindest heart you'll ever find," George said.

Hardy's diagnosis: senile *and* crazy. Hardy lifted the fork of meat loaf to George's thin, blue lips.

"You first," George said.

"Me first, what?"

"Take a bite."

Hardy looked at the brown rough meat hanging off the end of the fork.

"They kill people in this place, boy. Don't you know anything? Might be in the food. Who knows?" George said.

"I really doubt they're putting anything in the—"

George snatched the fork from Hardy's hand and held it out toward Hardy.

"Fine." Hardy took the meat loaf off the fork with his fingers and popped it into his mouth.

George waited until Hardy swallowed. "How do you feel?"

Hardy grabbed at his throat and held his breath until his face turned red. George's eyes grew wide. Hardy released the air from his lungs. "Whoops. False alarm." Hardy smiled.

"I suppose you think that's funny," George said stoically.

"It kinda was."

"Not bad, kid. Not bad."

Hardy reached for the fork, George jerked it away. "I can feed myself." George pushed his fork into the potatoes. "What's your name, boy?"

"Uh…Hardy."

"I know that, you dimwit. What's your full name?"

"Hardy Vance."

George stopped with the fork halfway to his mouth. "Any relation to the Olen Vance that kept his son in the woods for fourteen years?"

Hardy was surprised to hear someone, anyone, mention the story. He supposed it was in all the papers at some point, but he had never met anyone who actually remembered it.

"He was my grandfather."

George worked his gums back and forth. Hardy thought he saw some kind of recognition in his pale blue eyes.

"Did you know him? Olen Vance?"

George shoved the potatoes into his mouth without answering.

Hardy stuck his hand in the pocket of his scrubs and felt the cool metal of Olen's lighter. He drifted over to the window and stared down at the bricked courtyard below. Red Japanese maples grew in large pots next to a three-tiered fountain complete with circling goldfish in the large base. Benches sat on either side. It was very peaceful-looking, but peace was far from Hardy's mind. He needed to talk to Darcy. The idea that Olen could have been murdered was gnawing away at him. Tom said he was going to the store to get parts. He had plenty of time to go out into the woods, argue with Olen. Hardy imagined Tom holding a pillow over Olen's face. That would explain no signs of injury. Maybe the white dandelion seed in Olen's hand wasn't a seed at all. Maybe it was a feather from a pillow. Darcy could have been wrong. But then again, Olen was old. Natural causes. It happened all the time.

"I want to know how my bird is," George said with a full mouth.

"Excuse me?" Hardy said, turning around.

"Petey, my bird. Get your head out of the clouds," George said, spitting potatoes.

Well that explains a lot. A crazy old man—a crazy old bird. "He's annoying, that's how he is." Hardy snapped. He was getting tired of this old guy's attitude.

George chuckled. "So, he's doing just fine then. That one will live well beyond me, mark my words."

Hardy started feeling guilty for raising his voice. "I'm sorry. He called me four eyes, and he continually squawks about dice."

George pushed the tray away and wiped a napkin across his mouth. His eyes narrowed behind his glasses. "Is that right?"

"He's fine. Really." Hardy reached for the tray.

George grabbed his wrist. "You be careful, boy. Things go on here—bad things."

Hardy stared into George's pink-rimmed eyes. "Don't worry, George. Everything is going to be just fine." A shooting pain ran through the back of his head. Would this day ever be over?

Chapter Twelve

The next day, Hardy debated whether he should bring up Olen. Darcy seemed a little withdrawn still, and he didn't want to seem indelicate to her situation at home. Maybe this was a sign for him to drop the whole murder thing. It was possible that Darcy was wrong about the footprints. And even if Tom was somehow responsible for Olen's death... Well, it wasn't like Hardy was going to turn in his own father. Maybe it was just time to move on.

Beginning to feel a sense of closure, he whistled as he walked down the hall. He was on his way to read the newspaper to Mr. Glenn in room 210 when he spotted Trevor leaning up against the wall practically spitting into his phone. His fingers gripped the phone so tightly, Hardy half-expected to see it explode into tiny pieces in his giant hand. Hardy moved quickly past him, avoiding eye contact.

"Hardy!" Trevor called after him.

Hardy stopped reluctantly and turned around. Trevor

held his phone against his chest. "Get over here."

He took a deep breath and cautiously approached Trevor. He didn't want to get slammed against the wall again.

Trevor held out a small, rectangular, black box. "Take this to Mrs. Gobble's room."

Hardy held out his hand. "And do what with it?"

Trevor carefully placed the box in Hardy's hand. "Just do it. Got it?"

"Yeah." Hardy gave him a fake smile, then turned and rolled his eyes. He walked down the hall to Mrs. Gobble's room. Right before he stepped into the room he heard Trevor say, "Charity, I said I was sorry. What else do you want me to do?" *Figures, it would be Charity.*

"Hello, Mrs. Gobble," Hardy said, approaching her bedside.

She looked up at him and reached out a cold hand. "Are my hydrangeas blooming yet? Did you check for me?"

He sat the box down on her bed tray and took her delicate hand between both of his. "Yes, and they are as beautiful as you are."

She smiled sweetly. There was a weak joy in her eyes.

"How about I come back later and take you out onto the porch to see them?" he asked.

"That would be lovely, dear."

"I've brought something for you." Hardy took her hand from his and placed it on the box.

"Oh, a gift."

"I'll be back later."

"Okay, dear."

When Hardy reached the door, he looked back. She was

struggling to open the box. "Here, let me help you," he said, returning to her bedside.

"Oh, thank you, dear," Mrs. Gobble said, releasing the box.

Hardy lifted the lid and that's when it happened. The explosion of white. Snow. Except snow didn't suspend and hang in the air, did it? Time faded away. Sound ceased to exist. The heaviness of his body melted away. He was caught in a dissolving cloud with Mrs. Gobble that fell like soft snow upon their faces. Surely he was dreaming. Mrs. Gobble was smiling and holding her hands in the air, happy. She reached out to the sea of white like a child reaching for bubbles. Hardy's skin began burning like a thousand bee stings. His clothes felt like they were on fire, searing his skin like hot coals. He wanted to tear at them, rip them off, but he couldn't move.

The room began spinning. He was sure the floor was opening up, or the wall was caving in. The whole room was being pulled into something, like water circling down a drain. Faster it spun until the walls disappeared and the room was filled with bright light. Everything else in the room disappeared except for the light. The light separated like a piece of paper being ripped in two, revealing a narrow, suspended bridge that shot out into the sky. Clouds tumbled and churned at the end of the bridge as if time sped forward. Mrs. Gobble's smile faded, and her eyes rolled into the back of her head. Suddenly, she was sitting up, alive and vibrant. She floated from her bed and moved toward the bridge. Hardy didn't understand how she was able to move without walking. What was happening? He was dreaming.

He had to be. He closed his eyes as the last of his body was pulled into darkness and then oblivion.

***

"Hardy, wake up."

He heard the voice like it was someone calling him from a distance. He sped toward the voice until his eyes opened. A blurry Nurse Troxler, along with Darcy, and another young, female nurse, leaned over him.

"Can you sit up?" Nurse Troxler asked.

Confused, Hardy pushed himself up. He was on a gurney. "What happened?" he asked, trying to get his bearings.

"You passed out," Nurse Troxler said. "Sarah, get him some water."

"What?" Hardy asked.

Nurse Troxler frowned, but her eyes were sympathetic. "We found you in Mrs. Gobble's room, out cold."

"I don't understand? Why would I pass out?" Hardy looked at Darcy. She avoided eye contact.

"Mrs. Gobble has passed away," Nurse Troxler said. "We think you may have witnessed it."

"Can I have my glasses please?"

Darcy stepped forward and gave Hardy his glasses. He unfolded them and put them on. "You mean she's dead?"

"It appears to have been a massive heart attack. She had a heart condition," Nurse Troxler said.

Sarah returned with the water and handed it to Hardy. He emptied the contents in three swallows.

"Would you like us to call your parents?"

"No!" Hardy and Darcy said at the same time.

"I'm fine. Really," Hardy said. But was he fine? Something happened in that room. The problem was he could barely remember any of it. Snow. Light. That did sound a lot like passing out. But it felt like there was more to it. Why had he been in Mrs. Gobble's room? Wasn't he going to read the paper to Mr. Glenn? Hardy realized Darcy was holding his left hand. Probably taking his pulse. All three women were staring at him.

He pulled his hand out of Darcy's. "Trevor had something to do with this," he blurted out without knowing why.

Nurse Troxler frowned. "Why would you say something like that? Sarah found you."

He rubbed his forehead. "I don't know. I saw him in the hall—before. I think." But it was all so fuzzy. Something was gnawing away at the back of his mind—Trevor was somehow involved. Hardy just couldn't remember how.

"Now if you're going to start talking crazy, I'm going to have to send you home."

"I'm fine," Hardy said quickly.

"Okay, if you say so. For whatever reason, which I cannot begin to fathom, the patients think the world of you, Hardy. Pull yourself together and then get back to work."

"Will you at least ask Trevor about it?" Hardy pushed. He wasn't even making sense to himself.

Nurse Troxler looked at Sarah.

Sarah shrugged. "I did see Trevor in the hall looking a little anxious right before I went in Mrs. Gobble's room to give her medication."

"Very well. If it will get you back to work, I will talk to

Trevor."

Nurse Troxler and Sarah left, leaving him alone with Darcy. He dropped his feet to the floor and stood up. His head felt like a grenade had gone off between his eyes. Darcy immediately wrapped her arms around him.

"I'm glad you're okay," Darcy said into his shirt.

The gesture caught Hardy off guard, but he found himself holding her back, surprised that he *needed* to hold her. Cling to something real — safe.

Darcy released him and stepped back. "What happened?"

He tried to remember. The pounding in his head made it hard to concentrate. He had been in Mrs. Gobble's room. Hydrangeas — wait, no. Snow? Trevor?

"I don't know. I'm sure it has something to do with Trevor, though," he said.

"You should stay away from him," Darcy warned.

"Why?"

"He has several felonies and a misdemeanor."

"What? That's impossible. They would never let him work here."

"They would if his record had been expunged."

"Expunged?"

Darcy sighed. "Erased."

"How is that possible?"

"Who knows? Why don't you ask Charity? Governor Marcus is the one who cleared Trevor's record."

***

"Hardy, you're going to be late for school!" His mother's voice boomed from below.

It took Hardy a minute to realize he was in his bed—fully clothed. He must have fallen asleep doing homework. He opened his eyes and was greeted with a blurry ceiling. He blindly reached a hand over to his side table and searched for his glasses. His hand fell on a laptop, half-eaten bagel, balled-up paper. No glasses. That's when he realized he was still wearing them. He sat straight up and took off his glasses. They must've been smudged somehow. He cleaned them on his T-shirt and plopped them back on his face. He stared at the dresser straight ahead—blurry. He took the glasses off and looked at them. Had he got his glasses mixed up with someone else's? He looked around the room. The chair in the corner covered with dirty clothes—clear as a bell. The picture of him holding a swim team trophy—clear. He leaned over to the small window next to his bed and pulled back the curtain. He could see everything—perfectly. He could see without his glasses. He pressed his eyes shut and rubbed them with his fingers. When he opened his eyes everything was still in focus. It was a miracle. Except something in Hardy told him otherwise. It didn't take him long to realize that something didn't just happen to Mrs. Gobble, *something had happened to him*. Hadn't he felt weird ever since? *I once was blind but now I see?* Trevor. Trevor had sent him into Mrs. Gobble's room. Hardy held the palms of his hands to his eyes. The box. He remembered a black box. He pushed to remember what was in it. The only thing he could come up with was snow. Impossible.

"Hardy! Get down here now!"

Hardy hastily threw on a clean T-shirt, climbed down the loft, and hurried to the kitchen.

"Here's some toast—" His mother stopped speaking mid-sentence when she caught sight of him. Her hand flew to her mouth. "Sweetie. I believe you need to shave. And, where are your glasses?"

"What?" Hardy touched his face. It was furry. He had never had anything more than peach fuzz. He ran to the bathroom and looked into the mirror. He couldn't believe it. He didn't just have a five o'clock shadow, he had like a ten o'clock shadow. He had started growing a beard—overnight.

His mom smiled at him from the doorway. "You can use one of your father's razors." She pointed at the vanity. "Bottom drawer."

Hardy rubbed a hand across his new look. "I think I'll keep it." He had a few questions for Trevor, and he wanted to make sure he didn't destroy the facial evidence. He remembered what George had said the first day he had helped him with his food. *You be careful, kid. Things go on here... Bad things.* Suddenly, the old man didn't seem so crazy. Now he just needed to explain to his mother why he wasn't wearing his glasses.

"Mom, remember those contacts you got me last summer? I'm wearing them now."

***

Evidently, Hardy looked quite different with no glasses and rugged facial hair. He had garnered more attention in one day than he had in his entire four years at Southeast High. That is, if you could call long stares and whispering attention. He was almost positive that Charity had made eye contact with him in the hall on the way to second period. If only he cared. He was preoccupied with trying to remember what had happened in Mrs. Gobble's room yesterday. He bit his nails through two periods, and headed outside to meet Cricket and Darcy for lunch.

Hardy sat with his head in his hands until Cricket plopped down a tray of pizza and fries across from him.

"Well, I heard the rumor. I just didn't believe it," Cricket said.

Hardy rubbed his face in his hands and squinted at Cricket.

"What happened to you? Yesterday you were Clark Kent, today you're Superman."

"Very funny."

Cricket shoved the end of the pizza slice into his mouth and continued to chew and talk at the same time. "Dude…this is going to do wonders for your rep."

Hardy scratched the new growth on his face. *Who cares? Mrs. Gobble is dead.* Hardy had a sinking feeling that something was wrong about the whole thing. Something was very wrong.

"Hey, maybe I can get you a prom date with Megan's friend, Zoe."

"Not interested." *Where was Darcy?* He searched the hill, waiting for Darcy's long, wavy hair to appear over the crest.

"Why not?" Cricket said, shoving a fistful of fries into his mouth. "She's cute. We can double date."

"Like I said, not interested." The last thing Hardy wanted to do was to go to some stupid dance. He spotted Darcy's blonde hair and felt himself relax. She would know what to do.

"Give me one good reason? This is our senior year and —"

"Because I already have a date! Okay?!" Hardy didn't have a date, but he was hoping it would put Cricket off.

Cricket swallowed, almost choking. "Who?"

Darcy was almost to the table.

"Never mind. Just drop it."

Cricket dug at the food stuck in the back of his teeth with his tongue. "No. I'm curious now. Who is it?" Cricket folded his arms across his chest.

"Darcy." Hardy blurted out the only girl he could think of who would actually agree to such a thing.

Cricket laughed. "Is that right?"

Darcy put her tray on the table and sat down. "What happened to you?" Darcy asked upon seeing Hardy's face.

"I don't know," Hardy said. *But I sure hope you do.*

Cricket held up a hand. "Hold it right there. I want to hear it from Darcy."

"Hear what?" Darcy said, confused.

Hardy started biting his nails, or rather, the nubs that were left of his fingernails.

Cricket leaned his elbows on the table and folded his hands together. "Hardy here says he's taking you to the prom."

Hardy gave Darcy a subtle pleading look that he hoped would translate into *please*.

"Well?" Cricket said, obviously believing he had caught Hardy in a lie.

Darcy began mixing her salad together. "Yes. He's taking me to the prom."

Without moving an inch, Cricket glared at Hardy. "Are you insane?!" Cricket asked. "No offense, Darcy."

"None taken." Darcy calmly began eating her salad.

Hardy had no idea how he was going to get out of this one. As usual, he had dug himself into a corner. He would straighten all this out later with Darcy.

"What's the big deal?" Hardy asked.

"What's the big deal? She's a freshman—and, well—look at her. She looks like she stepped out of the 60s." Cricket argued. "Sorry, Darcy. Still on for helping me with calculus tonight?"

"Yes," Darcy said.

Hardy glazed over the whole 'helping with calculus' thing. He was much too concerned that Darcy seemed unfazed by the barrage of insults. Why was she taking this from Cricket? After what Hardy had seen at Darcy's house, he had developed a strong desire to protect her that he couldn't explain. A surge of angry adrenaline propelled him across the table. Before he even realized what he was doing, his hand grabbed a fist of Cricket's shirt, lifting Cricket from his seat.

"Don't you ever talk about Darcy like that again!"

Darcy touched Hardy's arm. "Hardy, it's okay."

Hardy turned his angry face toward Darcy. She looked frightened. "No it's not, Darcy. It's not okay." He pushed Cricket back into his seat, grabbed his things, and left.

"Geez, what was that all about?" Cricket asked.

"I don't know." But Darcy did know. She rubbed her arms, the bruises safely hidden underneath her long-sleeved shirt.

***

Hardy was bent over, unlocking his bike when two pink-toenailed, sandaled feet appeared in his line of vision. He'd know those feet anywhere.

"Hi, Hardy," Charity said.

Hardy unzipped his backpack and deposited his bike lock. "What do you want, Charity?" Even Charity Hill wouldn't be able to cast her usual spell over him today.

"Why so glum, Hardy, really? I only wanted to invite you to join the prom committee."

He smiled and zipped up his backpack. "No thanks."

"We need more guys—you know—to make sure it's not too girly."

He pushed his arms through the straps of his backpack. "I'm not going to the prom, Charity. I'm sure you'll find someone else." He stood on one pedal, threw his leg over the seat, and rode off to meet up with Darcy.

As soon as he was clear from the school, Hardy realized what he had just done. He had left Charity Hill, the girl of his dreams, his forever crush—in the dust. Now he knew for sure something was wrong with him. Just last week, he would've jumped at the chance to be on any committee that would bring him closer to her.

He stood up on the pedals and pumped harder, cresting

the hill overlooking the campus. Darcy was sitting in the grass picking daisies. When she saw him, she stood up and brushed off her long, floral skirt. He pulled into the grass and stopped.

"Look, about lunch… and the whole prom thing," Hardy started to explain.

"Forget it. I understand. You needed a cover."

That was the thing Hardy liked about Darcy. She understood him. Not many people did. That was why he so desperately needed to talk to her.

"I think something happened to me yesterday in Mrs. Gobble's room," he said.

"Like what?"

Hardy laid his bike down the grass. "I don't know. Look at me!"

"You got contacts and grew a beard."

He threw his hands up. "No, Darcy, I don't have contacts in. And this beard? It grew overnight."

"You don't have in contacts? How can you see?"

"Exactly! I can see. I can see everything with 20/20 vision."

She reached out and took Hardy's face into her hands. Hardy let her look into his eyes. He covered her hands with his. "Help me, Darcy. I'm scared."

"Okay, Hardy," she said gently. "I'll try."

***

Darcy peered into Hardy's eyes. It was true. His vision was 20/20, if not slightly better. She studied the cornea, the back of the eye. She could feel his warm breath on her face. She checked everything she possibly could. Heart rate, blood pressure, body temperature. She held on a moment longer, looking at him this time. She hadn't realized what long eyelashes he had. How beautiful and rich his dark eyes were. He looked into her eyes, not realizing she had already stopped analyzing his vitals. He needed her. She could see that much. Her heart began racing. She quickly released her hands from his face, stepping back as if she had touched a hot stove.

"Everything is elevated. Heart rate, blood pressure."

He stood staring at her. He was handsome. She wondered why she was just noticing this now. Her face flushed. "You're perfect...I mean your vision is perfect," she stammered.

"Okay, then. What does it mean?"

"I'm not sure. But you're right. Something did happen to you."

Hardy started pacing through the grass, rubbing his hands through his thick, black hair. Darcy put out a hand to stop him. "We'll figure it out together, okay?"

He grabbed her and held her tightly in his arms, burying his scruffy face into her neck. "Thank you, Darcy."

She closed her eyes. She couldn't remember the last time anyone had held her. She hoped he couldn't feel her pounding heart—feel the desperation for affection in the fingers she dug into his back.

Chapter Thirteen

Hardy had no idea how he was going to figure out what Trevor was up to. Shoot, he didn't even know why he thought Trevor had anything to do with Mrs. Gobble's death and Hardy's sudden transformation. If only he could remember…

It was doubtful he was going to find out anything today. Darcy was helping Nurse Troxler give female patients' sponge baths, and Hardy was stuck babysitting George again.

"Where were you yesterday? I near about starved," George said.

Hardy had already sampled George's food, and George was eating like a rabid animal. He sat and watched the old man's jaw work into a frenzy.

"No one is trying to poison you, George. You should just eat your food."

"Don't worry. I don't plan to be here much longer."

"You're getting released?"

George peered at Hardy over the top of his glasses. "Something like that." George scraped the rest of the mashed potatoes off the plate and shoved them into his mouth. "Interesting look you're sporting there."

Hardy rubbed a hand across his black cheek. "Yeah."

"So, I heard Mrs. Gobble kicked the bucket."

"Uh-huh."

"Heard you were there when it happened." George picked up his napkin and wiped his mouth.

Hardy was hoping this was just George being curious and he would soon drop it.

"Heard they found you out cold."

Hardy sighed. "Is there a point to this?"

"What do you remember?"

"Not much." Hardy stood up and reached for George's tray. "You done here?"

"Any detail could be important. Think."

"She had a heart attack, I panicked. The rest is history. End of story."

George's face grew cold and hard. "Listen to me, boy. We both know that's not what happened."

Hardy's palms begin to sweat. "I don't know what you mean."

"Mrs. Gobble didn't have a heart attack, and you didn't pass out."

Hardy took the tray and headed for the door. He wasn't up for George's paranoid babble.

"She was murdered," George said to Hardy's back.

Hardy stopped. He considered turning around, spilling

147

everything that had happened to him in the past week. But wasn't George just a crazy old man? What could he possibly know about anything? He was a typical paranoid islander.

Hardy kept going. His head was spinning. He was desperate to get out of the room. The walls were closing in on him.

"Watch yourself, boy!" George yelled after him.

As soon as Hardy made it out the door, he leaned against the wall in the hallway. His heart was racing. What if it was true? *Murder.* First Olen, now Mrs. Gobble. It didn't make any sense. None of it did. He closed his eyes and waited for his heart to slow. He needed to find Darcy. There was no moving on now. Something was going on, and he and Darcy needed to figure out what it was.

Hardy made his way downstairs. Nurse Troxler and Trevor were standing by the entrance in what looked like a heated discussion. There was no sign of Darcy.

"I'm sorry to interrupt, but have you seen Darcy?" Hardy asked.

Nurse Troxler's face momentarily registered shock. "What happened to you?" she asked.

Hardy had no doubt she was referring to his unshaven face and lack of glasses.

He nodded toward Trevor. "Why don't you ask him?" he said bitterly.

Trevor glared at Hardy as if daring him to say more.

Nurse Troxler ignored Hardy's comment. "Hardy, there's been an incident."

"An incident?" Hardy asked.

"Yeah, your little girlfriend has run off," Trevor said smugly.

"What?" Hardy asked.

Trevor smiled.

Hardy erupted and lurched for Trevor. "What did you do to her?!"

Nurse Troxler pushed Hardy back. "Calm down."

Trevor smirked. Hardy's hands balled into fists.

"Trevor. Wait in my office. We have some things we need to discuss," Nurse Troxler said calmly.

Trevor's smirk turned to a frown. He left—reluctantly.

Hardy was feeling the growing frustration of not being able to remember what happened in Mrs. Gobble's room. "Nurse Troxler, I'm telling you Trevor had something to do with Mrs. Gobble's death."

"That's interesting, since you were the one found in her room on the floor. Besides, I told you I was going to look into it, and I am. But for right now, I need to address the situation with Darcy."

"What happened? Is she okay?"

"While she was assisting me with Mrs. Wilson's sponge bath, Darcy told the patient she had skin cancer. The patient naturally became upset, and said some unkind things to Darcy."

Hardy headed for the door. "Hardy, wait!" she yelled after him, but he was already down the front steps.

Hardy found Darcy behind the home in the large, grassy

lawn that overlooked a field of wildflowers. She sat with her arms around her knees absently twirling a wild daisy between her fingers. He sat down beside her.

"Hey," Hardy said.

"Hey."

"I heard about what happened. Do you want to talk about it?" he asked.

"Not really."

"It's okay, you know. It's not the end of the world."

Darcy looked at him. "If only that was true. I can't even look at a person and see them in the normal way. I just blurted out that she had skin cancer. I couldn't help it. I saw the spot, and my eye just took over."

"Darcy—"

"I'm poison, Hardy."

"No, you're not. I think you're—amazing." It surprised Hardy to hear himself say it.

"You don't really know me, Hardy. You don't know what I've done in my past."

As much as he wanted to help her, he was not equipped to handle confessions, or any serious conversation for that matter. He patted her awkwardly on the back. "Come on now, how bad can it be?"

Darcy picked the petals off the daisy, one by one and threw them into the grass. "I killed my father. The only person who ever cared about me."

Okay, so that did seem pretty bad. Hardy stuck his chin into his hand and stroked the edges of his beard. "You mean, like in the library with a candlestick type of thing?" He knew that was the wrong thing to say, but Darcy seemed unaffected by his social ineptness and continued to talk about her father while she stared out into the untamed meadow below.

"He was a pilot—single-engine plane. Took tourists on sightseeing tours over the island. He loved it—flying." Darcy smiled and closed her eyes as if savoring the memory. "Sometimes he would take me up. He'd say from up here, the whole world is yours. He said I could be anything I wanted to be. I believed him."

"You can be anything you want to, Darcy."

She threw the empty stem and opened her eyes. "No I can't, Hardy. Look at me. I'm an artificial monster. I don't know how to be a human being."

"That's not true."

Tears released from her brown eye, transforming into gray spots as they hit her blue scrubs.

"Do you want to tell me what happened… to your father?" he asked gently.

Darcy hesitated. Her grief-stricken eyes looked into Hardy's. He nodded slowly, wanting her to know that she could trust him. She swallowed hard and continued to stare out into the distance.

"He'd been gone for a week. He had been at some convention on the mainland for independent pilots with small businesses. We rode to the small airport in Freeport to welcome him home—my mother and two brothers. When we went out to the tarmac, he was already there. He was on the other side of his plane looking underneath it. I was so excited to see him, I let go of my mother's hand and took off toward him. My mother called after me, but I kept running.

When I got to the plane, my father saw me, but he didn't look happy to see me. I saw fear in his eyes and I didn't understand. He lunged for me, and we both fell to the ground." Darcy wiped at the tears that continued to flow down her face. "The plane was still running. The propeller—I didn't see it, Hardy. We were both on the ground. The right side of my face was burning in pain. I could still see him out of my one eye, crying for his arm that wasn't there anymore. Still, he kept yelling that it was going to be okay."

Darcy stood, but struggled to keep her balance, as if she could feel the earth spinning. Her real eye was swollen with grief and leaked a steady stream of tears. Hardy jumped to his feet and reached out to her, but she shook her head and backed away. "He...he...died," Darcy stammered. "He lost his arm...he got...he got...an infection. I killed him! I killed him, Hardy!" Darcy turned as if frightened by her confession and started running away. Hardy ran after her and quickly locked his arms around her. She struggled to free herself from this grasp, but sorrow emptied her body of any fight she had left, and she sank to her knees, bringing Hardy with her. He turned her to him, and they sat in the meadow, him holding her tightly against his chest. Her body shook in silent sobs. All he wanted to do was make Darcy's pain go away. She was a sheep amongst the wolves, and Hardy just wanted to protect her. How had he ever thought his life was so terrible?

He held her until her body stopped shaking and his shirt was soaked with tears. He stroked her hair with his hand. "Darcy, it was an accident," he said into the top of her head.

She shook her head against his chest. He gently pulled

her away and looked into her eyes, holding her wet face in his hands. "It was. It was a horrible accident."

She struggled to shake her head within his hands.

"Yes, it was. It was, Darcy. You were just a child. Your father wouldn't want you to blame yourself."

"Why not? My mother does."

New tears came from her eyes and fell across his hand. "Why would you say that?" Hardy asked.

"I can see it in her eyes every time she looks at me."

He could see that Darcy was telling the truth and anger swelled inside him. How could a mother blame her child for a terrible accident? How could a mother allow her daughter's arms to carry bruises?

"She's wrong. Say she's wrong," he said roughly.

Darcy shook her head once again.

He gripped her face tighter in his hands. "You can. Say it."

"I can't, Hardy. I can't. Please."

"SAY IT!"

"She's...wrong," Darcy stammered.

Hardy released Darcy's face and wiped her tears with his fingers. "It's time to put this behind you. Your father would want you to be happy."

"I don't know how," she said, sniffing.

He smoothed her hair back from her forehead and smiled. "We'll figure it out."

Darcy collapsed into the grass and stared up at the sky. Hardy lay next to her.

"Thank you, Hardy."

"For what?"

"Nobody ever said the things to me that you did."

He rolled to his side and rested on an elbow. He took her hand and she turned her head toward him. "They should have," he said.

She gave him a weak smile and tenderly touched his face. Without thinking, he slowly lowered his lips toward hers.

Her warm breath melted into his face. "Are you going to kiss me, Hardy Vance?"

"I was thinking about it," he said softly.

She smiled at him.

That's when he saw it. Inches from her head. A perfect, white, feathery ball, delicately balanced on its brown stem. He froze.

"What's wrong?" Darcy whispered, seeing the fear in his face.

There it was, in all its glory. A dandelion—Viola's curse. The memories came flooding back. The snow in Mrs. Gobble's room hadn't been snow at all. It was a dandelion. Hardy remembered. He remembered it all. Trevor had given him a black box to give to Mrs. Gobble. He had helped her open it, and the seeds exploded into the room.

"What is it, Hardy?" Darcy said, sounding worried.

"A dandelion."

Darcy twisted her neck trying to look around her. "What? Where?"

"Don't move," he said slowly.

Hardy reached into his pocket and pulled out Olen's gold lighter. He flipped the lid and struck the wheel. The flame leapt to life. He leaned over Darcy and held the flame out to the whisper of white. It drew the flame and erupted into fire.

Hardy scrambled to his feet and pulled Darcy up with him. He stared at the empty stem, his heart racing.

"Where did you get that lighter?" Darcy asked.

"What?" Hardy held out his hand with the lighter in it. "It was Olen's."

"Alea Iacta Est," Darcy said.

"Yeah, I know what it says." Hardy shoved the lighter back into his pocket. He took her gently by the arms. "Listen, I remembered what happened in Mrs. Gobble's room."

"Do you know what it means? The words on the lighter?" Darcy asked.

He dropped his hands from her arms. "Darcy, now is really not the time for a Latin lesson."

"The die has been cast," she said louder.

Darcy had obviously not heard what he had said, so Hardy repeated it slowly. "Please listen to what I am saying. I remembered what happened in Mrs. Gobble's room."

"You're not listening, Hardy. Alea Iacta Est, means the die has been cast. The bird in the lobby has been saying it over and over."

"George," Hardy said.

Chapter Fourteen

When they returned to the home, Darcy went to find Nurse Troxler to try and patch things up. Hardy knew he should be confronting Trevor, but instead he headed straight for George's room. It was no coincidence that George's bird was repeating the same saying that was on Olen's lighter. The old coot had even asked if he was related to the Olen Vance that had kept his son in the woods. George definitely knew something, and Hardy was going to find out what it was. Trevor would have to wait.

When Hardy reached George's room, he found him gathering clothes and books and shoving them into a large tote bag. It looked like he was packing up to leave.

"Hardy, back so soon?" George asked, shoving a pair of brown slippers into the bag.

"We need to talk."

George smiled. "I'd love to, but right now I'm going outside to enjoy some rocking chair time on the porch."

Hardy followed him onto the porch, wondering why George had felt the need to bring half of his room with him.

George planted himself in one of the white rockers and pulled a book out of his bag. Hardy stood over him.

"You still here, kid?" George stared up at him.

"I told you we need to talk." Hardy reached in his pocket and pulled out Olen's lighter. He opened his palm so George could see the inscription.

"No thanks. I gave up smoking years ago. Now if you don't mind, I have some reading to do." He opened the book in his hand and began scanning the page.

Hardy stuck the lighter back in his pocket and snatched the book out of George's hands.

"Hey! Give me that back," George snapped, reaching for the book.

"Would love to, after we talk."

George crossed his arms. Nurse Sarah came out the front door pushing Mrs. Jacobs in her wheelchair.

Hardy knelt down next to George and lowered his voice. "Why don't you tell me about your bird?"

"Petey? What about him? He's lost his marbles. You've seen him," George said, practically yelling.

"You know what I'm talking about, George," Hardy said incredulously.

George removed his glasses and rubbed the bridge of his nose. "I want to see Petey."

"You will, after we talk." Hardy was beginning to lose his patience.

"Nope, I want to see him now, or no talking." George put his glasses back on his face.

Hardy sighed and lightly pounded his fist on the armrest of the rocker. "So, if I bring you the bird, you'll talk?"

George nodded.

What could it hurt? The bird's wings had been clipped. If humoring the old man got Hardy some answers, then one ornery bird coming up.

Petey did everything he could to avoid Hardy's grasp. The bird made quite a scene jumping from one side of the cage to the other while screeching "ouch" over and over again.

"Come on, you stupid bird or I'll show you what ouch really is."

Hardy finally managed to wrangle him out of the cage. The bird dug its sharp claws into his arm as if frightened.

When Petey saw George, he fluttered to him and sat on George's extended arm.

"There's my Petey. Good boy." Petey settled in on George's arm and began grooming himself.

"Okay, you got your bird. Now start talking," Hardy said.

"You best leave well enough alone."

Hardy squatted back down to George. "Are you kidding me? Look at me," he said bitterly. "Something happened to me in Mrs. Gobble's room, and I think you know what. And you know what else? I think you know all about my grand-father, too."

George remained silent and stared out at the lush, mani-cured lawns.

Hardy was about to take George's precious Petey away from him when Nurse Sarah called out to him.

"Hardy, can you come watch Mrs. Jacobs while I go get Mr. Glenn?"

"Don't move. We're not done here," Hardy said quietly to George.

Hardy threw on a fake smile and relieved Sarah. "Thanks, Hardy. Sometimes she tries to get up. I don't want her to fall."

Hardy kept a close eye on George. The old man wasn't as crazy as he wanted everybody to believe. Hardy bit his nails as he watched the bird kiss George on the lips.

"I love Jesus," Mrs. Jacobs said.

Hardy patted her on the shoulder. "I know you do, Mrs. Jacobs. That's awesome."

George looked at his watch, stood up, grabbed his bag, and walked toward the steps that led down to the circular driveway.

"Where are you going, George?" Hardy asked.

"Calm your shorts. I'm just going down to see the tulips."

"Don't go far," Hardy warned.

He watched him take the steps one at a time, the bird perched on his shoulder. George headed straight for the tulips that lined the drive and walked next to them, feigning interest.

"I love Jesus."

"Yes, Mrs. Jacobs. Me, too."

A black car pulled into the long drive at the top of the hill that led down to the home. George was getting further and further away from the porch. Hardy leaned over the railing and called out to him. "George, you're going too far."

"I need my sweater," Mrs. Jacobs said.

"Okay, Mrs. Jacobs. Just a minute."

George kept walking.

"George!" Hardy called out.

"I'll just go get my sweater."

Hardy turned and held up a hand. "Stay right there, Mrs. Jacobs."

Hardy called out to George again. George was almost on the other side of the circular drive where it joined the road that led out of the home. The black car entered the circle. "George!"

When Hardy glanced around to check on Mrs. Jacobs, she was up and shuffling toward the door. He rushed to her side. "No, Mrs. Jacobs. Come sit back down. I'll get your sweater." He glanced over his shoulder. The black car had passed the front porch and was stopped beside George. Hardy gently took Mrs. Jacobs by the shoulders and steered her back to her wheelchair. George was opening the door of the car. Hardy's heart raced. What was going on? Was George trying to make some kind of getaway?

"Come on, Mrs. Jacobs. Almost there."

Panic coursed through Hardy's veins. George was getting into the car. Hardy gently, but quickly, lowered Mrs. Jacobs into her wheelchair and held up a hand. "Stay right there, I'm going to get your sweater." Mrs. Jacobs nodded.

Hardy skipped the steps and leapt over the railing to the ground. He sprinted down the driveway toward the car. "George, stop!"

George disappeared into the front seat. Hardy caught the passenger side door just before it shut. He flung the door open and grabbed George's arm. "OUCH!" Petey cried out.

"Where do you think you're going?!" Hardy yelled.

"Let me go, kid."

"No! There's no way I'm letting you leave." Hardy glanced over at the driver who was hiding behind a hat, beard, and dark sunglasses. George struggled to pull himself out of Hardy's grip while the bird continued to hysterically flap its wings.

"Let go, Hardy," the driver said.

The driver knows my name? Hardy stopped pulling on George but didn't release his grip.

"Let go, fall backwards, and chase after the car."

"What? Who are you? What is this?" Hardy said frantically.

"It's me, Hardy."

"Do I know you?"

The man lowered his mirrored sunglasses.

"Tate? What the—?" What was his brother doing here and why was he taking George? And where did he get a black Cadillac?

"Do what I say," Tate said firmly.

"But I can't just let you take—"

"DO IT! I'll explain later," his brother shouted.

Hardy let go of George. The door shut so fast that Hardy stumbled backwards and fell—no faking required. The car screeched away. Hardy scrambled to his feet and ran after the car. "Stop!" The car sped down the long driveway. He only ran about ten feet before he stopped and looked back at the porch. Nurse Sarah stood at the top of the steps with her mouth open.

***

It was nine o'clock before Hardy got home. He wondered how he was going to explain his lateness to his mother. Tom never asked, but his mother on the other hand…

Tom was sitting on the couch, reading glasses resting on his nose, book in hand. He seemed to be alternating between reading and staring at the TV over his glasses. He barely looked up as Hardy closed the door.

"Where's Mom?" Hardy asked.

Tom shifted his eyes from the TV to Hardy. "Working a night shift at the hospital."

Hardy couldn't believe his luck. The last thing he needed was an interrogation. The police had done quite enough of that already. He didn't know how much more lying he could do. It was beginning to weigh heavily on his conscience.

Tom picked up the remote and upped the volume on the TV. "Have you seen this?"

A woman's voice blared from the TV. "Just over three hours ago, a patient at this Hill Home facility was taken while walking on the grounds."

A woman reporter with shoulder-length, brown hair and a blue suit stood in front of Hill Home holding a piece of white paper and a microphone.

Hardy's stomach dropped. He shifted uncomfortably on his feet.

"It was around 5:30 p.m. when a patient whose name has yet to be released was walking in these grounds just behind me." The reporter looked over her shoulder and back down at her white paper. "Witnesses reported seeing a black sedan

162

come around the circle driveway where the patient then entered the car."

Hardy moved toward his loft. Tom held up a hand. "Just a minute."

"A worker at the facility tried to stop the car, but was unsuccessful. It is unknown at this time whether the patient left willingly or was forced into the car."

Tom turned off the TV. "What's the world coming to when they start kidnapping old people?"

What about killing old people? "Yeah. Awful. Well, goodnight."

Hardy had one hand on the ladder to his loft when his father spoke the words that every teenager dreads to hear. "Come sit down, Hardy. Let's talk."

Tom removed his glasses and closed his book.

Hardy shrugged off his backpack and fell into the couch. He tried to remember the last time Tom had wanted to talk. He was pretty sure it was the last time he had gotten into trouble at school. He could tell his father was uncomfortable because he was massaging the back of his neck. There was no doubt in Hardy's mind—Tom knew about Hill Home.

"There comes a time in a boy's life when things start to happen."

Hardy was confused. This was not what he was expecting. "Things?" Hardy asked.

"Yes. Changes in one's...body."

Hardy moved forward to the edge of the couch. "Whoa. Wait. Are you trying to give me the talk about the birds and the bees?"

"Your mother thought I—"

Hardy stood up. "I'm seventeen!" Hardy's fight or flight response kicked in and he definitely wanted to flee.

"It's just that you're obviously going through some more changes with the beard and your new friend."

"Tom. I'm fine, really."

"We just wanted to be sure that you understood how important it is to focus on school and remind you that—"

"Tom, please stop. I know. You don't have to worry."

Tom stood and stuffed his hands into his pockets. "Well, okay. If you're sure."

"I'm positive."

Hardy hurried up the ladder to his loft. He pushed the palms of his hands into his eyes and looked at himself in the mirror above his dresser. He definitely had a beard now. It looked more like it needed a mowing now instead of a shave. He was relieved that Tom didn't know anything about the antics at Hill Home. Another bullet dodged.

He paced his room wondering what he should do next. The only thing he knew at this point was that Trevor had done something to him and Mrs. Gobble, George—and apparently Tate—knew something about it, and Tom was hiding something that Olen thought Hardy should know. This had gotten personal. He *needed* to know what was going on.

He wanted to call Tate, but he had lost that privilege three cellphones ago. The first phone had gotten washed in the back pocket of his jeans, the second he dropped in the hall at school only to have someone step on it, and the third was stolen. With Tom, it was a three strikes policy. No more cellphones for Hardy.

He sat on his bed and put his head in his hands. There

was no way he was going to be able to sleep until he talked to Tate. He would wait until Tom went to bed and do the only thing he could do. Sneak out.

Chapter Fifteen

Tom stayed up until midnight reading. Hardy waited another thirty minutes for good measure then threw on a hoodie, grabbed a flashlight and headed out on his bike. It was close to 1:30 in the morning when he arrived at Tate and Vivia's cottage.

They lived in one of the quaint villages that tourists loved to visit. Most of the homes were stone cottages with flower boxes and wood-shingled roofs. Nothing like the modular homes in the village where he and his parents lived.

Hardy opened the gate of the white picket fence, and followed the stone path that ran through Vivia's small vegetable garden. He stood at the door of the dark cottage. He hadn't been to his brother's house in…Well, he couldn't remember. The nine-year age difference had always been a barrier between them. Plus, Vivia had a way of doting over Hardy that drove him a little crazy. He knew it was because Vivia couldn't have children of her own. Fussing over Hardy had been a poor substitute, but he endured it for her sake.

He pounded loudly on the small red door and waited. Almost immediately, a dim light seeped through a window. Tate answered the door in a T-shirt and boxers and stared sleepily at Hardy. Hardy pushed his way past Tate and looked around the dark living room. He half-expected George to be camped out on their sofa, but it was empty.

"By all means, please come in," Tate said.

"Where is he?" Hardy snapped.

"Where is who?"

Hardy walked straight to the kitchen at the back of the room and turned on the light.

"Do you know what time it is?" Tate asked.

Hardy spun around. "Did you really think I would just let this go? You must think I'm a real idiot!"

Tate held up his hands. "Calm down. You're going to wake up Vivia."

Hardy laughed. "Oh, I'm sorry. Have I come at a bad time? I don't care about Vivia!"

"Hardy?" Vivia appeared at the edge of the kitchen squinting at Hardy through her emerald-green eyes. Her long brown hair was piled on top of her head in a messy bun. She wrapped her pink robe around her and tied it shut. Tate seemed grateful for the interruption and padded to the sink to get a glass of water.

"Is everything okay? Has something happened to Tom or Anna?" Vivia asked.

"No, they're fine," Hardy said curtly.

Vivia immediately approached Hardy and went into her concerned mother routine. "Wow, your beard is almost as thick as Tate's." She rubbed the hair back from his forehead. "Where are your glasses? You feel warm. Are you sick?" she said, resting her hand on his forehead.

Hardy grabbed her wrist gently. "Vivia, please don't."

"Okay, sweetie. I'm just concerned about you. It's not like you to show up here in the middle of the night."

Tate leaned against the sink, crossed his muscular legs, and casually sipped his water.

"Why don't you ask Tate? He knows why I'm here."

Vivia looked to Tate for an explanation.

Tate set down his glass of water. "Vivia, can you give us a minute?"

Vivia kissed Hardy on the cheek and left. Hardy waited until he heard the bedroom door shut. "Where's George?"

"Right here." George said, appearing from the second bedroom off of the living room.

Hardy raised his hands and let them drop. "Great. Do you have any idea what I just had to go through because of your little stunt?"

"Sorry, kid." George shuffled over to the small kitchen table and sat down. He was still wearing the same clothes he had left Hill Home in.

"Sorry! Is that all you have to say? The police are looking for you."

"What can I say, kid? I needed a change in scenery."

Hardy rubbed a hand across his mouth and looked at Tate. "This guy is hilarious, huh? A real comedian."

"I think we should all sit down," Tate said, heading for the table.

George was as cool as a cucumber and it made Hardy's

blood boil. Hardy crossed his arms. "I'll stand, thanks."

"Suit yourself, kid. This could take a while," George said.

"Don't call me kid. The name's Hardy."

George shrugged.

"Come on. Sit down," Tate said, pointing to an empty chair.

Hardy sighed. "Fine."

Hardy reached into his pocket, pulled out Olen's lighter, and slapped it down on the table. He sat down between George and Tate. "Where's your dumb bird?"

"In the guest bathroom. Thanks for your concern."

"You want to explain to me why your bird repeats the words on my grandfather's lighter?"

George picked up the lighter. His white eyebrows raised. "Nice piece. Circa 1960s."

Hardy slammed his hand down hard on the table, making George jump. "Stop the crap! I want some answers!"

Tate placed a hand on Hardy's shoulder. "Take it easy. This isn't helping."

Hardy held up his hands in surrender. "You're right. I'm sorry. Could someone just tell me what's going on? Perhaps Petey would like to join us."

"No. Sleeping. Doesn't like to be disturbed," George said.

Hardy gritted his teeth.

"I think it would be best if you explained, George," Tate said.

"Yes, George. Please do," Hardy said sarcastically.

"Your grandfather and I grew up together. Actually graduated from med school together."

"So, you lied to me. You asked me if I was related and

never said a word about knowing him."

"You never asked."

"I'm sure in your mind that made it okay."

"I tried to warn you it was dangerous at the home. I didn't want you dragged into it."

"Dragged into what?" Hardy asked.

"I have suspected things have been going on at the home. I wanted to check it out for myself."

"Does this have anything to do with the fact that I now have perfect vision and have grown a full beard in two days?"

"Probably. You've been exposed," George said.

"Exposed to what?!"

"A deadly dandelion in Mrs. Gobble's room."

"But…she's dead, and I'm alive."

"The healthy sometimes survive, get stronger. That was always the mystery of the thing. Most subjects pass away quickly, others survive and get stronger. As long as you're not exposed again, you should be fine," George explained.

"How do you know all this?" Hardy asked.

"The mysterious toxic dandelion was one of many secret research projects that fell under the umbrella of what was called The Program. Olen and I were part of the dandelion team. The plan was to try to modify the dandelion to harness only its ability to strengthen and not to kill. Unfortunately, that proved to be too difficult. The Program changed our work to focus on the dandelion's ability to kill. Olen, along with a few more, protested, but we were overruled. Olen ultimately destroyed years of work and disappeared. When I suspected The Program research had been resurrected and was being used in Hill Homes, I decided to check it out for myself."

Hardy couldn't believe that Olen had been involved in something so—big. He wondered if Tom knew. Was that the truth that Olen wanted Tom to tell Hardy?

"Did you know Olen was alive?" Hardy asked George.

"No. Tate told me. Nobody knew where he was until his son turned up several years later and said he had drowned. I thought he was dead like everyone else. Tate said he died recently. I'm sorry."

"I'm so confused," Hardy said, putting his elbows on the table and pulling at this hair.

"I think I should tell you the story that started all this," George said.

"No more lies, George. If that's even your name. How did you get into Hill Home, anyway?" Hardy asked.

"I may know a few people on the police force. One of them may have needed to check their poor old father into Hill Home. I'm sure it'll all be straightened away," George said, dismissing it with a hand. "It's still George, though. But the last name is Bolt."

Hardy took a deep breath trying to tame his irritation.

Tate finally spoke. "I know it's a lot to take in. I didn't know either," he said, trying to reassure Hardy.

They were all quiet for a moment while George collected his thoughts.

George cleared his throat and began his story.

"We were inseparable, Olen and I. Olen's daddy was a cattle rancher and mine was his right-hand man. But something happened one day that changed everything for the both of us. This is how Olen told it to me."

Olen ran as fast as his ten-year-old legs would take him. His father's tent was just down the way, but it felt like miles through the grassy meadow. Olen had awakened early with excitement. Today they would bring the cattle into Greystone Town Square for auction. All six hundred head. They had spent several days herding the cattle down from the northern island. Today, they would make the last part of the trek. Except there would be no trek, no auction.

The cook called after him from his food cart. "Slow down there, Red. Don't need you turning an ankle."

Olen ignored the unwanted nickname referring to his head of red hair, and barreled through the flaps of his father's tent. He bumped clumsily into the small wood table his father's coffee rested on. The upturned coffee spilled across the table onto his father's now vacated chair.

"Olen! What have I told you about—?"

"Dad...you have...to come," Olen said, breathing heavily.

"Go out of here, and come back in like a proper gentleman."

"But Dad..."

His father pointed at the tent flaps as he tried to clean up the mess with a hand towel. "Go!"

Olen reluctantly left the tent. Boone Vance was not a man you argued with. Olen exited the tent just as two of the cowhands rode up on their horses. His father came out of the tent. A pink sun was just breaking the horizon. The men's concerned faces were hidden in the dim light. But Hardy knew why they were there.

"What's going on, boys?"

"You better come with us, Boone."

"Someone hurt?"

172

The men shifted in their saddles and looked at each other.

"It's serious then?"

They nodded.

"Bring me my horse." Boone disappeared back into the tent and returned with his boots on and his hat in hand. He grabbed the reins of his horse, mounted, and pulled Olen up behind him.

Olen held tightly to his father's waist. He was afraid. He knew what his father was about to face. He closed his eyes tight. He felt the rhythm of the horse's hooves beating the ground, the sound pounding itself into his memory like a hammer. He would never forget that fateful ride. How could he?

Olen knew when they had broken the cusp of the hill. Every muscle of his father's body tightened. Boone's strong arms pulled the reins to a stop. Not a sound broke the eerie silence as his father took in the horrid scene. Even the horses stood quietly as if they understood the destruction. Olen opened his eyes when he felt his father's body slide off the horse. Boone removed his hat and stood gazing upon the horror of it. His life, his livelihood — gone.

The field was littered with the dead bodies of his herd. Only a few dozen remained huddled together away from the carnage, almost as if they were afraid. Boone didn't speak, but Olen could see the heartbreak in his eyes. Boone knelt and dropped his head into his hand. Olen wanted to go to him. To put a hand on his back, tell him it would be okay. But that would be a lie.

"How?" Boone said it so softly that only Olen was close enough to hear. "How?!" Boone yelled out, his face red with anger, frustration.

"We're not sure, boss," the foreman said.

"Then give me your best guess."

"The field was covered with weeds. It could've been anything.

Poisonous probably."

Boone stood and faced the foreman. "What weed do you think it was?"

The foreman and his second stood shifting uncomfortably with their hats in hand. "We think it was the...the um...the dandelion."

Boone nodded, his jaw moving with tension. "The curse of Viola," he said, looking across the field.

The foreman stared at his feet. "It's the only thing that makes sense."

Boone spat and put his hat back on. "I'll tell you what makes sense. The herd got a hold of a poisonous weed, not a harmless dandelion. I don't ever want to hear that story come out of your mouth again. Ya hear?"

"What do you want us to do? With the dead cattle?" the foreman asked.

Boone rubbed his eyes between his forefinger and thumb. "Burn 'em. Burn the whole field."

"Okay, boss."

Boone mounted his horse. "So, we won't be going to Greystone?" Olen asked.

"No, son. No, we won't."

When they returned to the camp, Olen ran back to the tent he was sharing with Cook, and sat on his cot. He knew there would never be another trip to Greystone. This would ruin his father. Yet, Olen was angry that this would be his first and last cattle drive. He felt ashamed that all he could think about was himself. Whether his father wanted to admit it or not, this was the curse of Viola. The others knew it—so did Olen. But superstitions were not something his father believed in, so Olen knew it would never be spoken of again. Not to his mother, not to anyone.

Olen reached for his pack and lifted the flap. He dug through the boxes that held all his dead specimens: flying insects, ground insects, plant life. At the bottom was his glass jar. He lifted it out and held it to the light that seeped through the tent flaps. There were ten perfect dandelion seed balls preserved in his jar. He had collected them last night from the field. Now they would become something more than just fun for a boy's playful curiosity. He promised himself that one day he would figure it out. He would stop the curse—the thing that had broken his father.

A sudden burst of light entered the tent. Olen quickly shoved the jar back into his pack.

"Come on, Red. Help me pack. We're going home," Cook said.

They all sat in silence as Hardy tried to absorb everything. Again, he was hit with the guilt that he had never taken the time to get to know his own grandfather and had only looked at him as a chore, a duty. Then he remembered the seed. The dandelion seed buried in Olen's clenched fist.

"I still don't understand what any of this means." Hardy said.

"Your grandfather was involved in some very serious research," George said. "He wanted something good to come out of the tragedy that ruined his family's livelihood. You see, the cattle that survived grew stronger, healthier. Olen thought there was something to it, so once he became a doctor, his research focused on something that would help people, sick people. But our government changed our mission to the properties that expedite death. That's when Olen stopped it all. He burned all the research, the specimens, and disappeared."

"Olen had a dandelion seed in his hand when I found him," Hardy said quickly.

George nodded. "So it's true then," George said solemnly, picking up the gold lighter.

"What's true?" Hardy asked.

"Alea Iacta Est. The DIE has been cast."

"What does it mean?"

"Direct Instant Extermination. They've restarted the DIE Program, and they're using it to eliminate the weakest members on the island."

Chapter Sixteen

It was Saturday. Darcy rode her bike to the Vance house and knocked on the door. She became worried when Hardy didn't show up for school on Friday. He said he remembered what happened in Mrs. Gobble's room. Then the patient with the bird that repeated the words on Olen's lighter had disappeared. She hadn't spoken to Hardy since.

A petite woman with shoulder–length, black hair and olive skin answered the door. Darcy immediately saw the resemblance to Hardy in her lightly creased, dark eyes.

"Can I help you?" Anna asked.

"I'm Darcy."

A look of recognition crossed Anna's face. "Oh, yes. From the hospital. Come in, come in," she said, stepping aside.

"I came to see Hardy."

"That was kind of you to check in on him," Anna said, closing the door. "Hardy, you have a visitor!" she yelled.

There was no response.

"Why don't you go on up?" Anna said, pointing to the ladder at the end of the living room.

Darcy climbed the ladder to the loft and was immediately hit by the smell of body odor. Dirty clothes were piled up high on a chair in the corner. A few pieces were strewn across the floor where Hardy had discarded them.

Darcy's eyes rested on a brown, plaid lump that protruded from the bed. She pulled back the cover to reveal what looked like a small, furry animal.

"Mmm," Hardy groaned, covering his head with his arms.

Darcy poked at the lifeless blob. It rolled over and opened its eyes.

Hardy squinted at her through a hairy, black face.

"You're gross," Darcy said.

"Thanks. Nice to see you, too." Hardy tried to roll back over.

Darcy stopped him with her hand. "You need to get up, shower, and shave."

"No thanks. You know the way out. Besides, I'm sick."

She sat on the bed and grabbed Hardy's face between her hands. He closed his eyes and grabbed her wrists.

"Stop. I don't need your diagnosis, Dr. Page," Hardy groaned.

Darcy tore her arms out of his grip and laid across his chest, pinning his arms beneath her. His breath smelled like a garbage can. She pried one of his eyes open with her fingers. He continued to try and free his hands. She peered into his moving, bloodshot eye and scanned his vitals. Satisfied, she released him and sat up.

"You're fine," Darcy announced.

"I don't feel fine," Hardy snapped.

"The patients have been asking about you."

Hardy sighed and scratched the thick beard on his face.

"Those patients need you. Besides, we both know there's something going on there." When Hardy didn't respond, Darcy continued. "Mrs. Gobble is dead. George disappeared from the home. There's some kind of connection to Olen. What about the lighter?"

Hardy rolled onto his side, his back to her. "There's stuff you don't know, Darcy. This is bigger than a couple of teenagers."

"We have to do something."

"I can't," Hardy moaned into his pillow. "I'm no hero. I'm nobody."

"I believe in you."

He turned back to her and stared wearily into her eyes. She recognized the look of hopelessness.

She pushed her hand into his. "We could figure it out together—for Olen."

As she held his gaze and squeezed his hand, she felt his resistance fade. She smiled at him. "Now, please shower. You smell worse than both of my brothers put together."

"Will you wait?" Hardy asked.

Darcy nodded.

Darcy flipped through a woman's magazine while she waited in the Vance's small living room. It was awkward to be in a place so modern and clean. This must be what a real home felt like. Someplace clean where people took care of you when you were sick.

Darcy glanced up to find Anna staring at her from the kitchen doorway drying the inside of a glass with a dish towel.

"Sorry. Didn't mean to interrupt," Anna said.

Darcy closed the magazine and laid it down on the coffee table.

"So, you and Hardy go to the same high school?" Anna asked.

"Yes, ma'am."

"Please, call me Anna."

"Okay."

"Are you graduating this year?"

"No. I'm a freshman."

Anna raised her eyebrows in surprise. "I see. Do you have classes together?"

Darcy shifted nervously in her seat, worried about where this was headed. "No."

Anna flipped the dish towel over her shoulder. "How did you two meet?"

Darcy swallowed hard. Just as she opened her mouth to speak, Hardy bounded down the ladder to his loft and dropped to the floor. Anna's eyes widened, and her hands flew to her mouth.

Darcy jumped up. "I don't think so," she said, eyeing his overgrown, hairy face. What had been a scruffy beard had morphed into a bushy mess.

Hardy pushed his hands into the pockets of his shorts.

"What? Too much?"

"The Abe Lincoln look is a little outdated," Darcy said.

Hardy stroked his hairy chin. "No?"

"Definitely, no." Darcy said, crossing the room. She grabbed his arm. "Where's the bathroom?"

"To your left," Anna said.

Darcy dragged him into the small bathroom off the living room and pushed him in front of the mirror.

"I don't want to shave it off," Hardy said into the mirror.

"I know, but you can't wear it like that. I can trim it for you."

Hardy raised an eyebrow in surprise, but Darcy ignored it and started rummaging in the drawers and beneath the sink for an electric razor and some scissors. She thought she saw him staring at her out of the corner of his eye. It felt different—the way he looked at her when he didn't think she was looking. Darcy buried the thought.

"Here we go," she said, finding the necessary tools. She pulled a small towel from a recessed shelf beside the sink and wrapped it under Hardy's chin.

"Are you sure you know what you're doing?" Hardy asked.

Darcy raised an eyebrow.

Hardy tapped a finger under his eye. "Right. Access."

Darcy stood on her tiptoes and started snipping slowly and meticulously. "I actually used to do this for my father. He let me practice playing beauty shop. When I was done, I would hand him a mirror and he would tell me how marvelous it looked, even though it was pretty much a massacre."

"Is that supposed to make me feel better?"

"Don't worry. I became a lot better at it," Darcy said, hair falling on the towel.

They smiled at each other's reflections in the mirror until the connection felt awkward. She completed the trim in silence, avoiding Hardy's gaze.

"There," she said, turning off the electric razor. She carefully removed the towel and shook the clipped hair into the toilet.

Hardy held his face up to the mirror and rubbed his cheeks with his hand. "Wow. You weren't kidding. I almost look handsome."

He was handsome. Darcy suddenly became overwhelmingly aware of how small the space was between them. She headed toward the door just as Hardy turned around, and they bumped into each other. Hardy instinctively reached out and held her arms. Darcy held her breath.

"Thanks," Hardy said.

She tried to swallow. "You're...welcome," she croaked, the words catching in her throat. She broke his grasp and skirted past him, anxious to get out of the tight quarters.

When they got into the living room, Hardy yelled out to his mother. "Mom, I'm going out!"

Anna's face promptly appeared in the kitchen doorway. "Oh, much better. Thank you, Darcy."

Darcy nodded, embarrassed somehow at being able to trim a beard.

"Where are you off to?" Anna asked.

The truth ran through Darcy's mind—*we're going to try to figure out why Olen was murdered and old people are turning up dead at Hill Home.*

"The beach, probably," Hardy said.

"Be careful, then. Take sunscreen."

"We'll be fine."

Anna glanced at Darcy's fair skin and blonde hair.

"Okay, I'll just grab that real quick." Hardy ran back to the bathroom.

"It was good to see you again, Darcy. Please come again."

Darcy smiled shyly.

Hardy reappeared with a blue tube in his hand. "Got it. Let's go," he said, grabbing Darcy by the arm and dragging her through the front door.

"Sorry about my mom," Hardy said, once they were clear from the parent zone.

"I like her. She's nice."

"Yeah, I guess she's pretty cool."

Darcy wondered if Hardy had any idea how lucky he was.

***

It was just pure coincidence that Darcy had never met George. If she had, perhaps she would have identified him as George Bolt, and Hardy would have made the connection to Olen. Maybe even prevented what happened to Mrs. Gobble—to himself. But Tate had been clear the other night—Hardy was to steer clear of anything and anyone who might be connected to The Program. In Tate's mind it was over. This was something from Olen's past, and it had nothing to do with them. But could Hardy really stand by and do nothing? Olen and Mrs. Gobble were dead. He had spent a day and a half in bed wishing he didn't know what he knew. Now, Darcy had pulled him out of the fog, held his hand, made him believe he could still do right by Olen and all the other patients at Hill Home.

He filled Darcy in on everything—Trevor and the black box, the dandelion exploding in Mrs. Gobble's room, George's story, The Program. She listened quietly, intently. A few times her blue eye seemed to be searching the net. Maybe looking for more information. After Hardy was done, Darcy said they had no choice but to try to find out the truth and expose it. He knew they should stop now. What difference could a couple of teenage kids make? But Darcy believed in him. That was enough to make him want to try. They decided to go back to Olen's and look for anything that might shed some light on The Program. Darcy couldn't find anything in her vast access to information about The Program or who was involved in it. It was as if it didn't exist.

As usual, Darcy kept well ahead of Hardy on her bike. After two days of lying in bed, Hardy found himself struggling to keep up. The sun was beating down on his back, and a blast of hot air hit him every time a car passed. He reached back to wipe the sweat from his neck when a loud horn blast forced him into the rough shoulder of the road. He struggled to steady the front wheel of his bike and keep himself upright. He squeezed his handbrake and came to a rough stop as a beat-up, gray Ford truck pulled up next to him. The passenger window rolled down.

"Whoa, Vance. A-bro-ham Lincoln called and wants his beard back."

It was Luis Romero. The slightly annoying, stocky jock friend of Cricket's who often became their third wheel. He reminded Hardy of a Samoan wrestler, except on a much smaller scale. Hardy tolerated him well enough, but it was his constant use of the word "Bro" in all its creative forms that really irritated him.

"Luis," Hardy said.

Hardy peered around Luis to Cricket, who was in the driver's seat.

"What's up?" Cricket asked. "I came by your house Friday night. Your mom said you were sick."

"Yeah. I'm fine now."

"Good. Throw your bike in the back and get in."

Hardy looked ahead to Darcy who had just noticed Hardy had stopped. She straddled her bike, staring toward them, hand shading her eyes from the sun.

Both Cricket and Luis followed Hardy's gaze.

"Ohhh," Luis drew out. "Who's the unlucky lady?"

"No one," Cricket and Hardy said at the same time.

"Well, *no one* seems to know you."

"Shut up, Luis," Hardy said.

"Did you forget today's the senior picnic at Dunwoody beach?" Cricket asked.

"Yeah, bro. We do it early before all the tourists take over our beaches," Luis added.

"Oh," Hardy said.

"Come on. You're not going to miss this," Cricket said.

Hardy started biting his nails. "What about...her?"

Cricket sighed. "Tell her you forgot. She'll understand."

"Yeah, I guess. Okay."

Hardy rode toward Darcy. Why did he feel so bad? They were supposed to be solving the crime of the century and he was going to go indulge in senior mania. The two weren't even remotely comparable, but Cricket wouldn't understand. He would never forgive Hardy if he chose Darcy over him.

Hardy stopped next to Darcy, wondering what he should say.

"You're going to your senior picnic," Darcy said.

"How did you—?"

"I can see stuff from far away."

"Another detail you failed to mention."

Darcy shrugged. The truck pulled up beside them.

"Hey, Cricket," Darcy said into the open window.

Luis squinted at her with his dark eyes and thick eyebrows. "And you are?" Luis asked.

"Darcy Page. Freshman. You're Luis Gomez. Senior. Excellent wrestler, but lousy in math."

Hardy smiled and looked at the ground. If Luis was surprised at Darcy's revelations, he didn't show it. He stared at her with a look of curious amusement.

"Come on, let's go," Cricket urged, sounding annoyed.

Hardy pulled open the tailgate of the truck, lifted the bike into the bed, and slammed the long door shut.

Luis was still staring at Darcy as Hardy opened the passenger side door.

"Move over," Hardy said.

Luis hauled his thick body out of the truck and waved a hand for Hardy to get in. "Bros first."

Hardy rolled his eyes and climbed into the middle seat.

Luis surprised them all by taking Darcy's delicate hand into his thick fingers. "Nice to meet you. I hope I'll see you again real soon." Luis kissed the top of her hand.

Darcy's mouth fell slightly open.

Luis smiled at her, climbed into the truck, and slammed the door.

Cricket and Hardy stared at him in disbelief.

"What? Come on. Let's roll," Luis said, biting his lip and pounding the dashboard twice with his hand.

Hardy watched Darcy become smaller in the side view mirror until she disappeared. What kind of guy dumped a girl on the side of the road? Evidently, he did. He knew Darcy deserved better. But this was his senior year. It was time to celebrate. That's what Cricket would say, anyway. Then why didn't he feel like celebrating? He settled into a sullen mood that was something like dread mixed with relief.

Luis rattled on about some action movie. Good, Hardy wouldn't have to talk. He let Luis's voice carry him all the way to Dunwoody beach.

Chapter Seventeen

Dunwoody beach wasn't just a beach. During the summer months, it was a public haven for the hordes of tourists that visited Greene Island. On the grassy slopes that overlooked the beach were several covered pavilions filled with picnic tables and grills. A sand-filled volleyball court, tetherball, and a playground for kids completed the recreation area.

Part of the large, adjoining parking lot was currently taken up by covered tents from Southeast High, offering games of chance, rewarded with the usual cheap prizes that most people didn't want, like miniature footballs and squirt water bottles. Hardy expected half of it would end up on the beach under a layer of sand. Later on, some tourist's kid would dig the prize up with a shovel and think they hit the jackpot. A large banner declared that all proceeds went to Hill Homes.

Cricket and Luis headed straight for the rail tie steps that led down to the beach. A good portion of the island's beaches were born from rocky cliffs. Dunwoody was no exception.

A small workout was needed to get down to the beach.

Hardy paused at the top of the steps. Cricket and Luis jogged down the long, steep steps like anxious children. Paper-thin clouds stretched across the blue sky like watered-down paint. The ocean waves curled and crashed, spilling their white foam onto the beach. A steady wind blew from the south.

The beach was covered with a maze of multicolored towels filled with Southeast High students laid out like white corpses. He expected half of them would show up to school on Monday bright red. At least he didn't have to worry about getting burned. Luckily, he had inherited his mother's dark-toned skin and not Tate or Tom's freckled, pale skin.

Hardy soaked it all in, taking his time navigating the steps. The twenty-minute ride had done nothing to improve his mood. The last thing he wanted to do was socialize, but he told himself he could do anything for a couple of hours. The anxiety of interacting with actual people was always overcome by the hope of leaving soon.

Like the morons they were, as soon as Cricket and Luis hit the sand, they pulled their T-shirts over their heads and sprinted for the ocean, screaming and pounding their chests like primitive animals. They sent up a spray of sand, leaving a wake of girls screaming and cowering on their towels. Hardy stood at the base of the steps and watched the melee. Cricket and Luis dove into the surf and reappeared several yards out. Cricket turned and motioned for Hardy to come out. Hardy waved him off. Cricket dived into an oncoming wave.

He was pondering what to do with himself when Charity

caught his eye. She was playing beach blanket volleyball. In this version of the game, a team used blankets to catch and send the ball over the net. No hands were allowed to touch the ball. Her cast arm didn't seem to be an issue. She was wearing a white tank over her pink halter swim top, and a pair of hot pink gym shorts. Her short hair was pulled back from her face with a white headband.

Her team flipped the ball up and over the net. The other team caught it in their blanket, but the ball had momentum and ended up rolling off and falling to the ground. Charity's team dropped their blankets and started high-fiving each other. Apparently, they had won.

Charity turned and looked right at Hardy. The only thing worse than staring was getting caught staring. His face burned like a hot hand slap. She spoke to two of her friends and then, to his surprise, headed in his direction.

Her friends spread out, trying to recruit more players to replace the losers, who apparently weren't interested in a rematch. Charity jogged over to Hardy. Her face was beaded with sweat. She was beautiful even when she was breathless and sweaty. He stuck his hands underneath his armpits, trying to resist the urge to start biting his nails.

"Hey, Hardy," Charity said, sounding winded.

"Sup?" Hardy said, with a quick flick of his chin. *Sup? Who says that anymore?* The social ineptness was beginning. He bit his lower lip.

"Where have you been? I didn't see you at school Friday."

Hardy squinted against the bright sun. *Must keep words to a minimum.* "Sick."

"Well, you're obviously better. You want to play volley-ball? We need more people."

More losers, you mean. Hardy released one of his arms from its incarceration and scratched the back of his neck. "Not really my thing." *Good, Hardy. Four words is a good rule to stick with.*

Charity tugged on his arm. "Oh, come on. It's easy." She held up her cast for him to see. "Even I can play."

She's touching my arm. Red alert. Code red. He was going to say something dumb.

"Okay." *Wait. What? No.* He meant NO! *Mental note— apparently the four-word rule does not prevent stupidity.*

Charity smiled. "Come on." She ran ahead of him. "I love the beard, by the way," she said, turning and running backwards.

When it came to Charity, Hardy turned into a five-year-old. He rubbed his face and blinked his eyes. He could do this. A ball and a blanket. How hard could it be?

Charity's friends had managed to recruit a fresh group of players. Charity captained a team. The football team's kicker, Josh Fountain, headed up the other. He and Hardy were the only two boys.

Josh flipped a coin to see who would pick first. Hardy expected he would be picked last, but Charity won the toss and called out his name. He stood motionless for a minute thinking maybe this was one of his fantasies playing out in his head. Charity's ponytail-clad friend, Megan, gave Hardy a nudge and he went and stood by Charity. He just hoped that he wouldn't embarrass Charity with his not so stellar athletic skills. Swimming was the only thing his tall, lanky body lent itself well to.

The groups were picked. Eight per team. Two blankets per side. Hardy and Charity held onto the back corners of one of the blankets. Josh's group of four served the ball out of the blanket from the backcourt. Hardy's group managed to catch it and flip it back over. He glanced over at Charity and she smiled at him. Oh, yeah. This was worth the risk of humiliation.

After several minutes of back and forth balls, sweat pooled and dripped down Hardy's back. That's when he realized that having a beard in the summer—not so great.

Josh was looking annoyed that his team wasn't crushing what he probably considered a "no contest" team that consisted of Hardy and a bunch of girls. Hardy's team prepared to serve. Josh clapped his hands together, trying to rouse his team. The score was tied. This was match point.

The ball was low and looked like it might not make it over the net. The group at the front of the opposing team scrambled forward, but the ball fell like a cannon ball just on the other side of the net. Charity's team had won.

Josh, being the sore loser that he was, snatched up the ball and spiked it over the net. The ball hit Charity smack-dab in the side of her face. She immediately bent over and held her face in her hands.

"You jerk! Look what you did!" Megan yelled at Josh.

Someone called Josh's name from the beach, and he took off.

Hardy put a hand on Charity's back. "Are you okay?" The rest of the girls gathered around her.

"I'll go get some ice," Megan said, and took off running

for the first aid tent.

Hardy felt useless. Should he rub her back? No, probably not. Sing to her? Stupid—she's not a child. Before he knew what he was doing, he was lifting Charity up into his arms. Surprisingly, she didn't protest. She buried her face into his chest, and he carried her over to the shade beneath the cliffs.

Megan ran over with a blanket and an ice pack. She spread the blanket, and Hardy carefully placed Charity on it. Charity sat with her knees pulled up to her chest. Megan handed her the ice pack and Charity held it to the bright red mark on her cheek. "Thanks, guys."

"Josh is such a jerk. He didn't even apologize," Megan said. "I'm going to go give him a piece of my mind."

"Megan, forget it," Charity called after a running Megan.

Hardy sat down next to Charity and pulled gently at the hand that held the ice pack. "Here, let me take a look." There was a quarter-sized red mark on her cheekbone. "Looks like it hit you squarely on the cheekbone, so it's not too bad."

Charity pressed the ice pack back to her cheek. "Are you sure?"

"Yeah. Bonus—you won't have to use any blush for a while."

Charity laughed. "Oh. Ouch. It hurts to smile."

Hardy was alone with Charity on the beach, and so far he wasn't blowing it. He decided he operated better in a crisis situation.

"Hey...um...Thanks," Charity said.

"For what?"

"For rescuing me—again."

A surge of heat rushed to Hardy's face. He hoped his

beard hid most of it. "Well, you know. I turn into Superman when I think no one's looking. This nerdy persona is just a cover."

She was smiling and staring at him now. "Except…you're not so nerdy anymore."

Now that the crisis was over, Hardy felt himself sinking back down into his pit of awkwardness. Any minute now he would say the wrong thing and ruin everything. He clammed up and stared at his feet.

"Listen, I was wondering if you would do me a favor," Charity said.

"You need some more ice?" Hardy started to get up.

She reached out and grabbed his arm. "No. Not that."

Hardy sat back down.

"I was wondering if you would be my date for the prom."

Hardy froze. He could not move one bone in his body. He wasn't sure he was even breathing. He was likely hallucinating. He must've gotten overheated. Maybe his breakfast hadn't sat well. He was sick. Fever probably. He needed water. He started looking around to see where he could get some water.

"Hardy? Did you hear me?"

Hardy chewed the inside of his cheek. "Um…yeah…um. Could you repeat that again? The sun is getting to me." He fluttered his hand near his ear. "My hearing is a little off."

"The prom. Will you be my date?"

Yep. That time he heard her loud and clear. His throat developed a large lump that he couldn't swallow. It was gross. Maybe one of his tonsils had separated from the side of his throat.

"Oh. Do you already have a date?" Charity asked.

"No" came out like a croak. Hardy cleared his throat. "I mean…No. I don't. What about Trevor?" *Your psychotic boyfriend.*

She put the ice pack down and stared out at the surf. "He forgot to ask off for that night and now it's too late."

"No offense, but the last thing I need is Trevor beating me up, so no thanks." Hardy started biting his nails.

"I told him I was going to ask someone. I'm not going to my senior prom alone."

"Still," Hardy said, already imagining Trevor's left hook to his face.

She turned to him and held onto his arm with both hands. "Please, Hardy. We'll go as friends. I promise Trevor won't touch you."

Hardy stared into her perfect, almond-shaped eyes. Did that color blue even exist anywhere else? *Say no*, the voice inside his head said. *She's going to crush you like a bug.*

"Okay," Hardy heard himself say.

Charity smiled. "Thank you, Hardy. It will be fun. There's going to be a party at my house afterward." She stood up. "I'm going to go find Megan. I'll see you later, okay?"

Hardy stood up. "Yeah, sure. Okay. Later."

She walked out of the shade into the kaleidoscope of towels.

Hardy looked around him. This was big. No, this was huge. No—monumental. He shoved his hands into his hair. He wanted to scream from the cliffs for everyone to hear that he, Hardy Vance, was taking Charity Hill to the senior prom. He turned in circles looking for someone to tell. Everyone was oblivious and absorbed in their own little social worlds. He jogged back down the beach to find Cricket. Then he remembered. He had told Cricket he was taking Darcy to the prom. His stomach plunged like an elevator that was about to hit bottom. He'd figure it out. It wasn't a big deal. Nothing was going to ruin this moment for him.

***

Darcy was almost glad Hardy had gone to the senior class picnic. It postponed the inevitable, and gave her longer to consider how she was going to break the news that she was the reason Olen had been murdered.

She stared at Olen's now abandoned cabin from the edge of the woods. There was no sign of life. She slowly made her way through the weeds. Reaching the steps, she smiled, remembering the red squirrel—Angus. Everything looked the same, as if she would find Olen right inside the door. She climbed the steps, opened the screen door and turned the doorknob. It was dark inside, but she could see right away that the place had been ransacked. The curtains were drawn. She pushed them open with her hands to let light into the small space. Dust danced in the broken rays of light. All of Olen's books had been torn off the shelves, opened, and discarded on the floor. The mattress on the bed had been upturned and slashed. White stuffing littered the floor around it. Olen's Burgundy chair had been overturned and pulled apart.

She picked up an open book from the pile on the floor and closed it. "I'm sorry, Olen." She brushed the dust from its hard, blue cover. "I'm sorry I killed you."

A shadow suddenly blocked the light coming through the door. Startled, Darcy turned and dropped the book.

"I think you have some explaining to do," he said.

A man with ginger-colored hair and a beard stood in the doorway. A series of faces flashed in front of Darcy and stopped on a match. Tate. Tate Vance. She couldn't help but notice how Hardy looked nothing like his brother. Tate was muscular in a mountain man kind of way, while Hardy was tall and lean.

Tate picked up a bat by the side of the door and scanned the room for other intruders.

"No one else is here," Darcy said nervously.

Tate relaxed his grip on the bat but continued to hold on-to it. "Now would be a good time to start talking. Who are you, what are you doing here?"

Darcy kept her eyes on the bat. She wasn't exactly afraid, but she was unsure if Tate could be like her brother Nash when he got angry.

"I'm Darcy Page. I'm a friend of Hardy's," she said, her voice unsteady.

"I'm not going to hurt you."

Darcy stared warily at the bat.

Tate leaned it back up against the wall and held up his hands. "What are you doing here?"

"I came here once—actually twice, with Hardy."

Tate pinched the bridge of his nose. "I guess you had nothing to do with—this then?"

"That's not entirely true," Darcy confessed.

Tate's eyes narrowed. "Care to explain?"

"It's kind of a long story."

Tate gestured toward the wooden table between the front windows. "I've got all day."

They both sat down. Tate crossed his arms and settled in. Darcy explained about her eye and the first day she had come there with Hardy.

Tate sat in stunned silence, rubbing his beard. "So, Olen examined you?"

"Yes."

Tate lifted his eyebrows. "I'm sorry, I just find it hard to believe you're a… Whatever the name you used."

"Illuminator."

"Yeah—that."

"I knew your name. I have face recognition," Darcy offered as evidence.

"Hardy could've told you my name. Showed you a picture."

"What would convince you?"

"I don't know. Nothing, probably."

"Well, let me see what I can find out about you." Darcy began a full scan on Tate Vance on all available servers. She scanned with her blue eye, but she could see Tate out of her normal eye shifting nervously in his seat. It wasn't long before she found exactly what she was looking for.

"Interesting. Oh, that's funny," she said.

"What?"

She stopped the scan and stared into Tate's skeptical, yet concerned eyes. She couldn't help but smile. She knew she had him. Tate put a fist up to his mouth and cleared his throat. Perhaps he sensed it in her face.

"You hold the Southeast High wrestling record with 119 wins. Your best season was your senior year with a 30-2 record. But you blew your knee out at the regionals which kept you from possibly winning your second straight silver medal."

Tate tapped his fingers on the table. "All of that is public record."

Darcy sighed. "That I would take the time to memorize? No offense, but your stats are ancient. I was, like, eight when you graduated from high school."

Tate shrugged. "Maybe you're a wrestling fan."

Darcy rolled her eyes. "Okay. I didn't want to do this but you leave me no choice. You got into a little trouble once."

Tate's face was stoic. "Hah. You're wrong."

"I see. So you weren't caught trespassing on the McKinney farm on the North Island dressed like a girl?"

Tate's face turned red. "How did you—? Hardy doesn't know..." His voice trailed off.

Darcy stared at his gaping mouth and crossed her arms, feeling satisfied that she had not only convinced him, but also wiped the smug look from his face.

Tate stood up and paced the room for a few minutes, stopping a few times to glance at her, as if he might say something.

She examined her nails as if she cared about her cuticles.

He finally stopped and rested his strong hands on the table and spoke in a low, terse voice. "That was an initiation stunt. It was supposed to be wiped off my record."

"It is. I have quite an extensive access to information."

Tate bit his lip and pointed a finger at her. "Not a word about this to Hardy or anyone else."

"Of course not."

He began pacing again. "Why did you say you killed Olen?"

"Well, not directly. It took me a little while to make the connection."

"What connection?"

"My eye...it records everything."

"And?"

"I think someone found Olen through me. My eye identified him as Olen Vance. A man who was supposed to be dead. It must have triggered some kind of red flag."

"What do you mean, *red flag*?"

"The day we found Olen—"

"You were here that day?" Tate sighed. "Never mind. Continue."

"Anyway, I had noticed extra footprints around the cabin that day. I was worried that something had happened to Olen and I ran to the cabin. That's when I found him—we found him—dead. Later, when I went back to review the video from that day, it was gone. Someone had erased the file."

Tate stopped pacing and stared at Darcy in horror. "Good grief. What are you saying?"

"I'm sorry, I think Olen was murdered because of me." Tears flowed down her cheek.

Tate ran a hand across his mouth. "Darcy...it's not your fault. Look at this place. Olen was involved with something

200

none of us knew anything about until a few days ago."

Darcy stood. "I should go. I shouldn't have come here."

He reached out a hand to stop her. "Wait. I told Hardy and I'm going to tell you—I don't want either of you getting involved in whatever—" he paused, looking around the ransacked room. "This whole thing is. It's too dangerous."

Darcy nodded. The tears kept coming, though she willed them to stop.

"Look, about Hardy. He'll feel the same as me. He won't blame you," Tate said reassuringly.

Darcy suddenly felt hopeful. "You think so?" She rubbed her fingers across her wet cheek.

Tate nodded. "Yeah. I do." He looked around the room again and scratched the back of his neck. "Do you want to help me clean up this mess?"

Darcy nodded. They both moved toward the pile of books at the back of the room.

"Listen, I hate to ask this, but are you recording...this...us?" Tate asked.

"No. I figured out a way to disable the function."

Tate picked up a handful of books. "Okay. Good," he said, sounding relieved.

Darcy smiled. "Your secret is safe with me, you know."

"I guess your eye is supposed to be a secret, too?"

"Yes."

"We're even then. Shake?" Tate shifted the books to one hand and extended his other. Darcy slid her fingers into his firm grip.

Darcy bent and gathered some books into her arms. Tate pushed his load into the bookcase. "You can't like...read my mind or anything, can you?" Tate asked, casually.

Here we go again, Darcy thought. "No."

"X-ray vision?"

"No."

"Too bad. That would have been cool."

Yep. Tate was definitely Hardy's brother.

Chapter Eighteen

Darcy pushed her bike down the small dirt and gravel lane that led to her apartment. She enjoyed the sound of the brook's water that ran along the side of the road. The gurgling rush of water over stone resurrected the memory of walking in it barefoot with her father in the stifling heat of summer. Her father would tease her by kicking up the cold water onto her bare arms. Her skin would rise with goose bumps and she would try to splash him back. Happy memories, with no new ones to replace those that she had lost. She played the ones with her father over and over in her head like a favorite song.

Meeting Hardy's brother had been a surprise. She only hoped Hardy would be as understanding about her part in Olen's death as Tate was. She had seen nothing at the cabin about The Program or why they might want Olen dead. But it was obvious that someone had ransacked the place looking for something. She hoped Hardy wouldn't be discouraged. Despite Tate's warning, Darcy wasn't ready to give up just yet.

"Darcy!"

Darcy looked over to see Mrs. Twiss occupying a low stool just outside the recess of her apartment doorway.

"Hello, Mrs. Twiss." Darcy pushed her bike across the dirt lane to join her.

She squinted at Darcy with one eye open and the other closed. She laid the paperback book she had been reading into her lap.

"How is Mr. Twiss? Is his back better?" Darcy asked.

Mrs. Twiss pushed her tongue between her lips a few times, finally letting her mouth relax over her toothless gums. "Well, he still ain't worth a lick, but I reckon I keep him, anyways."

"I hope he feels better soon. Is there anything I can do?"

"No, but you best take care. That brother of yours on a drunk. Come a swayin' down the road like a tree in a storm."

Darcy's stomach dropped. If Nash was drunk, there was no telling what was waiting for her at home. Her grip tightened on the handlebars. "Thank you—for the warning." Darcy walked her bike the last few feet to her apartment.

"A good switch would have done that one some good," Mrs. Twiss called after her.

Darcy leaned her bike against the empty flower box outside their one front window. They were going to plant flowers in it—she and her father. Now it sat empty with a crust of hard dirt that not even weeds could poke through.

She put her hand on the doorknob and took a deep

breath. As soon as she stepped into the room, the odor of strong whiskey engulfed her. She could almost taste its bitter, oaky flavor on her tongue. Nash was lying out on the couch, with one hand behind his neck, TV blaring, a glass dangling from his other hand.

"Where you been?" Nash barked.

"Out. Where's Mom?"

Nash sat up and dropped his worn boots to the floor. His eyes were glazed over. "I asked you a question."

Darcy passed through the small living room into the kitchen, searching for her mother. She was the only one who could deal with Nash when he was like this. The kitchen was empty, but her mother's purse was on the kitchen table. She hurried to her mother's room and knocked on the door. There was no answer. She cracked the door opened and looked inside. The bed was made, the room empty.

"Hey!" Nash yelled from the living room. "I'm talking to you. Don't walk away from me!"

She heard Nash's boots dragging across the wood floor. She ran into their shared bedroom and locked the door. Danny wasn't there. Nor was her mother. She was alone—with Nash.

She stood with her back to the locked door, waiting, hoping Nash was too drunk to make the effort to come after her. The apartment grew silent until a sudden pounding on the door vibrated through her back. She closed her eyes.

"I know you're in there. Open up!" Nash said, slurring his words.

She heard an empty bottle fall to the floor. A soft belch.

"I will break this door down if you don't open it up,

now." His voice was tight and angry.

Darcy knew he would do it. She turned around and put her hand on the knob, flipped the lock to the left, and slowly opened the door. Nash had one hand leaning on the door jamb. He stared at her from under droopy eyelids.

"In case you forgot, I'm the man around the house now — your daddy ain't here no more."

"He was your father, too."

"Psst." Nash pushed past her, dropped to his bottom bunk, and started pulling his dust-covered cowboy boots off. "No." He pointed at her, dropping the first boot to the floor. "You was his one and only. We was just another man's leftovers."

"That's not true. He loved you and Danny like his own."

Nash laughed and grabbed his other boot. "I'm sure that's what you keep telling yourself. Except it isn't true." The other boot fell to the floor. He stood up and peeled off his armpit-stained T-shirt. "You was his favorite—true blood. But now he's gone and you got nothing."

Darcy's blood pounded in her temples. Nash was a liar. Her father had loved the boys. He accepted them as his own when he married their mother. That didn't change when Darcy was born. He treated them all the same. She hated Nash for dishonoring her father's name.

"He was ten times the man you'll ever be!" Darcy knew she shouldn't have said it as soon as it came out of her mouth. It was dangerous challenging Nash when he was drunk.

Nash wiped his face with his dirty T-shirt and dropped it on the floor. "If he was so wonderful, why did he marry a woman who didn't even love him? Huh? Tell me that."

"Shut up, Nash." She was sick of his drunken lies.

Nash smiled. "Oh, I see. You had no idea."

Darcy felt like she couldn't breathe.

"Let me paint you a little picture," Nash said. "Widowed mother with two young boys meets handsome pilot while waiting on him at his favorite diner. They get chummy. She's still quite a looker, so it doesn't take long before he's on one knee asking for her hand in marriage. She's got no money and no prospects, so she says yes."

"You're a drunken liar!"

Nash undid his belt. "You're right. I am drunk, but I'm no liar. Your daddy knew shortly after they were married that there was no love on her side, so she gave him you, so you could give him what she couldn't. The love of his life."

Darcy stifled a sob by covering her mouth.

Nash bent over and stepped out of his jeans and fell into his bunk with his socks still on. "Take care of those dirty clothes. I need them cleaned for work tomorrow." He closed his eyes.

Darcy didn't think she was capable of hate, but her pounding heart felt as if it would explode and turn the room into a million pieces.

"Nash, you shouldn't tell your sister such tales."

Darcy turned to find her mother standing in the doorway with a cigarette between her fingers. Her brown eyes were stamped with the hard life she had led.

"Mom, it's not true, is it?" Darcy asked.

Her mother folded her arms and drew on her cigarette, blowing the smoke slowly out of the side of her mouth. They both looked at Nash, but he had already passed out and was snoring.

"Of course not. Now take care of that laundry." She pointed at it with her cigarette and left Darcy standing there staring at an empty doorway.

She saw it in her mother's face the minute she asked. The brief squeeze of her eyes—undetectable by anyone else—except Darcy. It was true. She knew now what she'd always somehow felt but had never been able to identify. Her mother had never loved her father and, in turn, had never loved Darcy.

Chapter Nineteen

Hardy dug through the piles of old notebooks inside his locker looking for his calculus book. Monday had arrived too soon. The weekend had been one of the best of his life. He was not only taking Charity to the prom, everyone *knew* he was taking her to the prom.

At church on Sunday, he had never received so many slaps on the back and fist bumps. Maybe Charity would finally see what a jerk Trevor was and then...well...anything was possible. Hardy smiled. Not even getting his stitches removed from the back of his head this morning could dampen his mood.

"Bromancer."

Hardy pulled his calculus book from underneath the rubble and slammed his locker shut. Luis's big brown face was grinning at him.

"Hilarious, Luis." Hardy turned and started down the hall. Luis took up alongside him.

"Hey. You know Darcy's schedule?"

Hardy frowned and glanced at Luis. "No. Why?"

Luis stuck his hands in his pockets. "I don't know. She's kinda cute."

Hardy stopped in the middle of the hall and turned to Luis, causing several minor shoulder bumps from passing students. "She's a freshman."

Luis shrugged his shoulders. "I know. Cricket told me."

Hardy was speechless. "Luis, I really don't think Darcy is a good idea."

"Why not? She's...different. You know, not all obsessed with her looks. Kind of fairy-like with that hair. I'm a big *Lord of the Rings* fan."

Hardy started biting his nails.

Luis held up a hand. "Whoa, wait. If you have a thing for Darcy—"

"What? No!"

"Okay then, help a brother out."

Hardy hesitated. Something about this bothered him that he couldn't quite put his finger on. "She has third period lunch. That's all I know."

Luis adjusted his backpack. "Crap. I have second. But not to worry. I have my methods for getting out of class. Later, bro."

Luis disappeared into the crowd of students all moving in a kind of chaotic autopilot down the narrow hall.

For some reason Luis's interest in Darcy annoyed him. He didn't want to have to worry about Darcy, or anything else for that matter. He wanted to enjoy his senior year, take Charity to the prom, and get off Greene Island.

He had decided he was going to tell Darcy that he didn't want to pursue finding out what was going on at Hill Home or why Olen may have been murdered. They were just a couple of teenagers. Why did they think they could do anything about it? Besides, Tate had told him to drop it. Hardy had one more week at Hill Home. Why risk everything now? Tate was right. He and Darcy shouldn't get involved.

But Hardy's plan to talk to Darcy at lunch didn't happen. She never showed. He waited for her at the bike racks after school, but there was no sign of her. He felt a small pang of worry and wondered if he should ride to her house and check on her. No. He was moving on. He made the short bike ride to Hill Home alone.

When he reported to the front reception desk for his assignment, Darcy was there with a few others waiting for Trevor. Hardy touched her arm, and she turned around.

"Where were you today?"

"I had a headache."

Hardy focused on her brown eye, trying to see if she was being truthful. "Are you sure that's all it was?" he said, recalling the bruises on her arms.

"Yeah. That's all it was," she said flatly.

He wasn't sure he believed her, but decided not to push. He released her arm. "Okay."

Trevor came strutting up to the desk with a clipboard in hand. "Listen up, chumps. Mama is out, so it's going to be me and you for the rest of your miserable day."

A small lump lodged in Hardy's throat. What did Trevor mean, Mama is "out"? Hardy started biting his thumbnail. She said she was going to talk to Trevor and now she was out. He dismissed his paranoid thoughts. It was probably nothing. People miss work all the time. Besides, he had already decided to let things lie.

"No slackers, and no drama," Trevor said, looking straight at Darcy. "Your assignments are on the clipboard. Get busy." He dropped it on the desk and left.

The group huddled around the clipboard looking for their names. Hardy looked over a few shoulders. His assignment was sweeping the front porch, picking up trash on the front lawn, and circulating books to patients. He looked for Darcy's name. She had the same assignments.

He backed up and waited for Darcy. Without speaking, they gathered brooms and trash bags from the supply closet and headed out to the front porch. They swept on opposite ends. All the rocking chairs were currently unoccupied.

Darcy was definitely not herself and Hardy had no clue how to handle it, nor did he want to. He told himself it was none of his business. Her life was hers, and his was his.

They finished the porch and took trash bags out onto the lawn. They hadn't been at it long when Darcy stopped and stared out toward the surrounding woods.

"What? What's wrong?" Hardy asked.

"Trevor."

Hardy followed her gaze. Trevor had crossed the side lawn and was heading into the woods.

"We should follow him," Darcy said.

"Why?" Hardy asked.

"He's up to something. He's being careful—looking around making sure no one is following him."

"I don't think that's a good idea."

Darcy frowned. "What do you mean? This is our chance to see what he's up to. Find out something—for Olen."

"Yeah. The thing is…" Hardy said, searching for the right words.

Darcy sighed, dropped her trash bag, and headed in the direction of the woods.

"Darcy, wait!"

She ignored him and kept walking. He gritted his teeth and chased after her.

"I really think we should drop this," he said, coming up beside her.

Darcy stopped. Trevor disappeared into the woods. Darcy studied Hardy's face. He started getting that feeling that she was looking through him. He crossed his arms and stuck his hands under his armpits. "What?" Hardy asked.

"I'm doing this with or without you." Darcy turned and continued walking toward the woods.

Hardy scrambled after her. "We need to drop this. It's too dangerous."

"I'm not scared," Darcy said, moving quickly.

"Why do you even care about this? Olen is not even related to you."

Darcy stopped suddenly, causing Hardy to trip over his own feet and fall to the ground. He slapped the ground with his hands in frustration. Darcy stared down at him.

"You want to know why I care? Because…Olen dying…It was my fault."

Hardy stayed on the ground and rested his arms on his knees. "What do you mean it was your fault? No it wasn't."

"It was. My eye…it records. I mean it doesn't now, but it

did."

Hardy pushed himself up off the ground. "What does that mean?"

Darcy's face flushed, her hands clenching into fists. "It means, Hardy Vance, that everything at the cabin the first day you took me there was recorded."

Hardy stared at Darcy, still unable to connect the dots. Her face was blaring with frustration.

"They found him because of me! Get it!"

Then he understood, and the pit of his stomach twisted like a knife. "Are you sure?"

"Yes, Hardy. I'm sure," Darcy said quietly.

"Wait. Were you recording when you spied on me in the shower?" Hardy asked, mortified at the thought.

"I wasn't spying on you," Darcy said, exasperated.

Hardy turned around in circles, torn between anger and regret, wanting his life back to normal.

"Well? Don't just stand there. Say something," Darcy said loudly.

"Give me a minute, okay?" Hardy said, digging a shoe into the ground. Did this really change anything? He *wanted* to move on, leave this Olen mess behind. He squinted toward the woods and heard Olen's voice. *There's wisdom in trees.* He would be risking everything if he followed Darcy into those woods. All the plans he had made to get away from his life, the island, would be in jeopardy if this thing went south. But, if he could bring justice to Olen, didn't he owe it to him to try? Tom certainly wouldn't want him pursuing Olen's killer. But then, he still wasn't sure that Tom wasn't somehow involved in it.

Darcy appeared to be scanning the perimeter of the woods. He knew that part of this for her was penance for what had happened to her father. For the first time in his life, he cared more about her feelings than his own.

"Okay. Let's do this," he said.

"What about what I just said? About it being my fault that Olen is dead."

"None of this has anything to do with you. It's not your fault."

"That's what Tate said you would say."

"Wait. Tate?"

"I'll explain later. Come on." Darcy grabbed Hardy's hand and they ran toward the woods. There was no turning back now.

Darcy plowed through the woods like a dog on the trail of a scent. There were no paths of any kind that Hardy could see. It appeared to him like they were just wandering aimlessly.

"How do you know he went this way?" he finally asked.

"I can see signs."

Hardy couldn't see anything but tree trunk after tree trunk. He was beginning to get that sinking feeling that they were lost.

"Maybe we should turn around," he said, slapping a low-slung branch out of his way.

"Hush. We're getting closer."

How could she possibly know *that*? From what he could tell, there was nothing out there. Trevor was probably already back at the home. This was starting to feel like a wild-goose chase—one where they got lost. Hardy fought the urge to start biting his nails.

"Darcy, I really think we should turn around."

Darcy stopped suddenly, grabbed Hardy by the sleeve, and pulled him down behind some large, blooming rhododendrons. "Shh."

"What? Do you see him?" Hardy asked.

"Look." Darcy quietly parted an armful of the red blossoms. In front of them was a large clearing with no trees. Trevor was walking across it.

"What in the world is he doing out here?" Hardy whispered.

Darcy put her finger to her lips. Trevor stopped briefly, looking around as if he had heard something. Hardy froze and held his breath while Trevor's eyes searched the surrounding woods. Satisfied no one was there, Trevor headed out of the clearing into the trees across from them. Suddenly, there was a flash of light in front of Trevor, and he disappeared.

Hardy stood straight up. "Did you see that?! He just disappeared into thin air!"

"Not thin air," Darcy said, standing up. "Something else."

"What something else?" Hardy asked.

"Come on," she said, moving toward the clearing.

Hardy grabbed her arm. "Wait. Where you going? We don't know what's over there. What if we disappear?"

Darcy jerked her arm away. "Stop being a baby. It's an illusion, you idiot."

She stepped out into the clearing and headed for the line

of trees that Trevor had disappeared into.

"I'm sorry, did you just call me an idiot?" Hardy said, feeling a bit of an ego bruise.

Darcy ignored him. "I've never seen anything like it."

"Anything like what? Trees and more trees?" Hardy said sarcastically.

"You're not looking close enough. They're not trees. It's a reflection of trees that you're seeing."

"You mean, like a mirror?" Hardy asked, studying the spot Trevor disappeared into.

"I mean exactly a mirror. The whole thing is a mirror."

"What...*thing*?"

"Come on. Let's check it out."

As they got closer, Hardy finally began to understand. Their reflections began showing up across from them as if their doubles were walking toward them.

"Holy cow. What is this?" he asked.

"It's a building made from mirrors. You wouldn't even know it was here."

"Okay, this is just weird."

As they got closer and closer, the edges became more defined, the shape becoming more rectangular. A mirrored box with no doors.

"What if Trevor sees us?" Hardy asked.

"He can't see out."

"And how do you know that, exactly?" Hardy was feeling frustrated by Darcy's abilities. Especially when he had none.

"I just know, okay? Quit asking questions."

"What now, genius?"

Darcy put her hands on the mirrored walls—walking slowly—sliding her hands across their smooth surface. "There has to be a hidden door."

"Kudos, Sherlock. I think you've cracked the case."

Darcy continue to ignore him, which just irritated Hardy even more.

"It has to be here somewhere," Darcy said, continuing to move and feel her way along the wall.

Finally, she stopped. "Here. It's right here."

"I don't see anything."

"It's a palm scanner. I can see his palm print."

Hardy bit his lip and looked to the top of the trees. *Great.* She also has thermo scan capability. He didn't think it was possible to feel even more useless than he already did. But there was no time for pride. "What do you think is in there?" he asked.

"If I had to guess—I would say dandelions."

Hardy ran a hand through his hair. "My gosh—we have to get in there. Can you do some computer voodoo and get us in?"

"I've already done a search. This place doesn't exist anywhere I have access to. There's no way for us to get in."

A light bulb went off, and Hardy felt like he was about to redeem himself. "That's where you're wrong. I know one person who can get in."

"Who?" Darcy asked, surprised.

"Cricket."

Chapter Twenty

It was Tuesday evening when Hardy and Darcy visited Cricket at his home.

"You both have gone off the deep end. Count me out." Cricket was sprawled out on his brown leather sofa eating chips out of a big bag.

"Haven't you heard one thing I've said? They're killing old people—at least, we think they are," Hardy said.

Cricket showed no interest in hiking out into the woods to investigate the mysterious mirrored building. He seemed even less convinced that it was full of killer dandelions or that there was anything called The Program.

Cricket held up a greasy hand and swallowed. "Oh no, I heard you. I just think it's all a bunch of horse manure."

Hardy looked at Darcy for help. She frowned and crossed her arms.

"I found a dandelion seed in Olen's hand. I watched a pa-tient open a box with a dandelion in it before she died,"

Hardy spat.

Cricket wiped his hands on his shorts and chuckled. "Uh, more like some old lady died, and you passed out in her room. I hardly call that murder."

"What about the story from when Olen was a boy? Huh?"

Hardy watched in frustration as Cricket held the bag of chips up to his mouth and tapped in the remaining contents. Cricket threw the empty bag on the coffee table. He took his time chewing and swallowing.

"All you know is that some cattle died like a million years ago and that some old dude named George and your grandfather studied a weed. How do you jump from that to they're using toxic dandelions to kill people?" Cricket asked.

Hardy should have expected this. Cricket had a way of twisting the facts to get himself out of doing something he didn't want to do.

"What about Olen's cabin?" Darcy said. "Someone tore the place apart."

"I don't know—squatters?" Cricket suggested.

Hardy wanted to pull his hair out. "Who slashed the mattress and chair?!"

Cricket shrugged.

"Why are you being like this?" Hardy asked.

"You mean, sensible?"

"No, stupid," Hardy snapped.

"Oh, I see. I don't do what you want, so now I'm stupid?"

"Look, the truth is, we need your help. I know you don't believe any of this, but can you do this as a favor to me?"

Cricket cleaned the chip residue from his teeth with his tongue. He looked past Hardy to Darcy. "What about her?"

Hardy turned to glance at Darcy. She was leaning against the wall glaring at Cricket.

"What about her?" Hardy asked.

"Olen's not her grandfather. What has she got to do with any of this?"

Why was Darcy such an issue for Cricket? Hardy raised and dropped his hands. "I need her."

Cricket laughed, rubbed his hands down his shorts, and stood up. He walked up to Hardy and put a finger on his chest. "What you need is to stop all this foolishness and focus on enjoying your senior year. Prom is in less than two weeks, and you're taking the most popular girl in school. Instead of focusing on that, you're out in the woods chasing her boyfriend."

"You're a jerk!" Darcy blurted out.

Cricket narrowed his eyes and pushed Hardy to the side with his hand. "Excuse me?"

Hardy was stunned. Darcy looked like a bull preparing to break out of its pen.

"You heard me, Linus Porcious Wright."

Oh no. Not the blood-sworn, never to be mentioned name.

Cricket turned bright red, his jaw tensing with anger. Darcy moved right up to his face. She was a good foot shorter, but she suddenly seemed huge.

"Do you really think we would be coming to you with some imagined story, if there wasn't something to it?" Darcy blasted into Cricket's face.

Cricket stiffened and locked eyes with Darcy. He

221

breathed heavily through his nose, fighting to restrain himself.

"How old is your grandfather, Wright?" Darcy asked.

Cricket just glared at her as if he wanted to rip her head off. His red face looked painful, as if sunburned.

"HOW OLD?!" Darcy shouted.

"Seventy-nine," Cricket said through gritted teeth.

"Mrs. Gobble was seventy-five. She died because they killed her, just like they killed Olen. Your grandfather has a bad heart valve. How long before he ends up at Hill Home?"

Hardy watched the color fade from Cricket's face like a deflating balloon.

"I don't know how my grandfather has—"

"He has everything to do with it. He could be next. Then what will you tell yourself? At least I got to enjoy my senior year?" Darcy pushed past Cricket and stormed out the door, slamming it behind her.

Hardy stuck his hands into his pockets and held his breath, waiting for Cricket to explode. Instead, Cricket stared at his feet and shook his head.

"She's some piece of work, that one," Cricket said.

"Yeah, she is that."

To Hardy's surprise, Cricket laughed.

"What's so funny?" Hardy asked, feeling relieved.

"I don't know. She's so…so…"

"Darcy," Hardy finished.

"That, and annoying beyond words," Cricket said. "Listen, I'm sorry. I should have been more…"

"Look, it's okay. I know it all sounds a little crazy."

"Yeah, but you're my best friend, and best friends stick

together." Cricket held up his scarred palm. "Blood brothers, remember?"

"Blood brothers." Hardy raised his own scarred hand and clasped Cricket's. "So you'll help us."

Cricket sighed. "Yeah."

Hardy grinned. "She got to you, huh?"

Cricket pointed a finger at Hardy. "Don't push it."

Hardy held up his hands in surrender. "Okay."

"What now?" Cricket asked.

"We make a plan."

***

Wednesday at lunch, they solidified their plans for that night. They would go out to the mirrored building in the cover of night and Cricket would "sleep" and find out what was inside. It seemed simple enough.

"Okay, so you'll meet us at the edge of the woods at nine o'clock tonight?" Hardy asked.

Cricket was sitting across from Hardy, thumb-typing into his phone. "Yeah. As soon as I get off work."

"You have the coordinates?" Darcy asked.

Cricket continued to type into his phone without answering.

Hardy reached across the table and pushed Cricket's phone down. Cricket rolled his eyes. "Yes, yes. Aye, aye, captain," Cricket said, saluting Darcy.

"Why are we going at night, anyway?" Cricket asked.

"So no one sees us," Hardy said.

Out of the blue, Luis plopped down a tray next to Cricket. Hardy jumped.

"Gee, bro. What's got you on edge?" Luis said. "Hey, Darcy."

"Hi, Luis," Darcy said.

Luis rubbed his hands together as he surveyed his lunch tray. He chose a roll and bit it in half. "So, what are you talking about?" he said with a full mouth.

Hardy inwardly sighed. Luis had found a way to change his lunch. The last thing they needed right now was for him to poke his nose into where it didn't belong.

"Nothing," Hardy said tersely.

Luis pointed the remaining roll at Hardy and Darcy, and swallowed. "It ain't nothing. I've seen you guys whispering over here like you've got something to hide."

No one said anything. Luis opened his milk carton and chugged it down in two gulps. He burped and squeezed the carton with his big, brown hand and let it drop on the table. "So, I'm right then?"

"Actually, Luis, we were talking about video games," Darcy said.

"We were?" Cricket asked.

Hardy kicked him under the table.

Luis kept his critical gaze on Hardy and Darcy.

"Right. Video games," Cricket said.

"Which one?" Luis asked, sticking a whole chicken finger into his mouth.

"I was telling them about a game I play online, but they laughed at me," Darcy said.

Luis eyed Darcy's unopened milk carton. She picked it up and placed it in front of him.

"What game?" Luis asked, opening the milk.

"You've probably never heard of it. Mostly kids play it," Darcy said.

"Try me," Luis said, tossing back the milk.

"Magic Mirror."

Luis choked and pounded his chest with his fist.

"You heard of it?" Darcy asked, poking a fork around her salad.

"Maybe," Luis croaked.

"You play?"

"What's your in-game?" Luis asked suspiciously, milk lingering on his chin.

Hardy had to hand it to Darcy. She knew how to create a distraction.

"Valdus RedBlood," Darcy responded.

Luis slapped his hand on the table making all the trays jump. "You're Valdus RedBlood? No way. Uh-uh. Valdus RedBlood is a bro."

"Nope. Me."

"I don't believe you. He's legendary. A PvP master."

Darcy held out her hand to Cricket. "Can I borrow your phone?"

Cricket stared at Darcy's outstretched hand as if she had asked him to donate a kidney.

"Please," Darcy said.

Cricket reluctantly slapped the phone down in her hand. Darcy bent over the phone for a few minutes and then held it out to Luis. Luis reached across the table to take it.

Cricket grabbed Luis's arm. "Not until you clean those greasy hands."

Luis rubbed his hands on his shorts and held them up for Cricket to see. Cricket relented. Luis took the phone and glared at the screen. A look of complete shock spread across his face. "I don't believe it. You're him. He's you. You're my idol."

"Thanks, Luis," Darcy said, smiling.

Hardy rolled his eyes.

"Luis, do you really play that dumb game?" Cricket asked. "It's for ten-year-olds."

Luis handed the phone back to Cricket. "You wouldn't understand. Some things are just hard to let go of, no matter what your age. So, watch your mouth or I'll toss you to the ground right now."

Cricket chuckled. "Whatever, dude."

"Listen, Darcy. Do you think you could help...I don't know...give me some tips on how to improve my rank?"

The bell rang. They all started gathering their book bags and trays. Luis quickly shoved the rest of his chicken tenders into his mouth.

"Can I walk you to class?" Luis mumbled to Darcy through his half-eaten chicken.

"Sure," Darcy said.

Hardy and Cricket watched Luis and Darcy head down the hill together. Cricket laughed and slapped Hardy on the back. "They're perfect for each other," he said.

But those were not the words that came to Hardy's mind. In fact it was just the opposite. "Yeah...perfect," he said absently.

Chapter Twenty-one

It was funny how plans made in the light of day suddenly seemed like a bad idea in the cover of night.

Hardy and Darcy lay on their stomachs in a ditch across from the mirrored building. They were both dressed in black for the covert activity. Darcy's long hair was pulled back into a ponytail. The woods were pitch-black except for the glow of Hardy's flashlight which only offered a pinprick of light at best.

It wasn't that Hardy was afraid exactly—it was that he felt vulnerable without light. The sound of flapping wings and low squeaks coming from the treetops above him didn't help. He started imagining multiple, disastrous scenarios, one which involved him pulling a vampire bat's teeth from his neck and contracting rabies.

"Where is he?" Darcy asked.

"He'll be here," Hardy said wearily.

They had waited for Cricket at the edge of the woods for

twenty minutes. When he didn't show, Hardy thought maybe he got confused and thought they were supposed to meet *in* the woods.

"It's almost nine-thirty."

"So, it's one minute later since the last time you mentioned it," Hardy whispered harshly.

"You don't have to be so touchy."

"Stop bringing it up. He'll be—"

"Shh, I thought I heard something," Darcy whispered.

"Me, too." Hardy turned off his flashlight. "Can you see anything?" he asked quietly.

"Yes, someone is coming. I can see their thermal images."

"*Their?* What?" Hardy said, nervously.

"There's two people coming through the woods," Darcy said.

Two people? Something was wrong. Hardy's worst-case scenario shifted from rabies to double homicide. "Is it Trevor?"

"I don't know. I can't recognize faces in the dark at this distance. Maybe."

Hardy rolled over onto his back, Darcy followed suit. Hardy grabbed Darcy's hand. "Be still." Hardy's heart was pounding so hard it hurt. What if they got caught? What if Cricket had already been caught?

The sound of twigs breaking beneath heavy steps grew closer. Flashlights swept over the space above their heads. Hardy held his breath. Darcy was squeezing his hand so tight he wanted to cry out. If they had to, they'd make a run for it. "Prepare to run," he whispered.

Then the lights went out. Nothing happened. Nothing

moved. The only sound was the crickets and cicadas battling between scratching legs and high-pitched buzzing. The two strangers had vanished. Hardy thought perhaps they had gone inside the mirrored building. He and Darcy waited, not daring to move.

Like a lightning bolt striking the ground, two bodies fell down into the ditch one on each side of Hardy and Darcy. Distorted faces illuminated by flashlights screamed at them through the darkness like attacking ninjas. "Ahhhhhhhh!"

Darcy matched the screams with her own piercing scream that had the intensity of a horror movie actress. Hardy scrambled to his feet and fumbled to turn on his flashlight. Shaking, he shined the light on the dark shadows. Laughter filled the air.

"Cricket? What the—?" Hardy stammered.

"Hey, bro," another voice said.

Hardy swung the flashlight over to the other body. "Luis?" Hardy took a deep breath and bent over his knees, trying to pull his stomach out of his throat. Cricket and Luis continued to laugh.

"I wish you could have seen your face," Luis said, cracking up.

"You guys scared the crap out of us." Hardy pointed his flashlight at Darcy. Her face was eerily white and her eyes wide with terror. "Are you okay?" he asked.

Without saying a word, Darcy ran into the woods. "Darcy, wait!" Hardy called after her. "You idiots. Look what you've done now."

"I better go after her," Luis said, and took off.

Hardy stood up and shined his flashlight directly into

229

Cricket's face. Cricket held up a hand to block the light from his eyes. "Chill, dude. We were just messing around."

"Why is Luis here? I don't recall asking him to come," Hardy said between gritted teeth.

"I needed a bodyguard."

"FOR WHAT?!"

"I wasn't going to come out to these creepy woods by myself."

"Oh, so Mr. Tough Guy is not so tough when it comes to the dark."

Cricket pointed at Hardy. "Hey. There's nothing wrong with a nightlight."

Hardy clasped his hands behind his neck and started turning around in circles. "I can't believe this. I can't believe you brought Luis. Did you tell him everything?!"

"No. I didn't tell him anything."

Hardy got right in Cricket's face and shined the flashlight underneath their chins. "And what does he think he's here for?" he said, slowly and sharply.

"Dude, you need to get out of my face."

Hardy poked Cricket in the chest with his free hand.

"Really? This is how you want to play this?" Cricket asked.

"Yeah. This is how I want to play this." Hardy stabbed him in the chest again with his fingers.

Cricket held up his hands. "I'm warning you. Stop now, before it's too late."

"Maybe I don't care." Hardy reached out to make another stab, except this time Cricket grabbed his arm. Before Hardy knew it, they were on the ground wrestling like they were eight years old again. Within seconds, Cricket was on top of Hardy's back, the side of Hardy's face smashed into the ground, and his arm was pinned behind his back.

"Are you done being an infant?" Cricket asked, pushing on Hardy's face.

"Yes," Hardy snapped. "Now let me up."

Cricket released his hold on Hardy. Hardy scrambled to his feet and brushed the forest floor from his face and spat into the ground.

"What is wrong with you?" Cricket asked.

"I'm sorry. It's just...you brought Luis...and then Darcy..."

Cricket laughed. "What? She can't take a joke?"

"You scared her, man," Hardy said, rubbing the dirt out of his hair.

"And? We're teenagers. We scare each other."

"Her life is not like ours." Hardy said, recalling Darcy's bruises.

"I know. She's an Illuminator. She's weird," Cricket said wiggling his fingers in the air.

"That's not—" Hardy took a deep breath. "You know what? Never mind. You wouldn't understand."

"Look, I'm sorry," Cricket said, taking a step toward Hardy.

Hardy nodded and stared at his shoes. "Let's just forget about it."

"Deal," Cricket said, clasping Hardy's shoulder.

"Come on, the building's over here."

Cricket followed Hardy across the clearing. "Whoa. This is freaky," Cricket said, seeing their flashlights reflect off the building. Cricket reached out a hand and touched its smooth surface. He drew up close and stared into the mirrored wall, lighting up his face with his flashlight. "I AM YOUR FA-THER," he said in his best Darth Vader voice.

"Stop fooling around, Cricket."

"Okay, Colonel." Cricket dropped down on the ground and leaned back against the building.

"Wait a minute. Does Luis know you're a Sleeper?" Hardy asked.

"Uh, no. Just you and weird Darcy." Cricket grinned sheepishly.

"Please, stop. Her name is Darcy."

"What about WD for short? Weapon of MASS distraction." Cricket held up a hand like he was waiting for a high-five.

"Yeah, hilarious," Hardy said, ignoring the hand. "How did you expect to go inside and check it out without Luis seeing you passed out?"

"Well, he's not here now. Problem solved."

Hardy sighed. "Whatever. Let's just get this done before they come back."

"Fine by me. What exactly am I looking for?"

"I don't know."

"Well, that makes a lot of sense."

"Just look around and see what's in there. This is where we saw Trevor go in."

Cricket propped his head up against the wall. "Don't let any bugs crawl into my ears. See you on the other side. Oh, and don't touch me." Cricket grinned and then he was gone.

Cricket melted through the mirrored wall into a white, sterile chamber. Silver suits hung like discarded snake skins from hooks on the wall. Bulky, protective headgear sat on benches underneath. This was not what he was expecting. A hatch with a center wheel and a small, round window was the only other door in the small space.

He hung in the air like vapor, watching a dark red glow coming through window. It was obvious you were supposed to suit up before you went on the other side of that door. What if he got in there and then burned up or vaporized? There was no time for doubt. When he was away from his body, he wasn't breathing. It was now or never. He flew through the small window and froze, waiting to see if he suffered any ill effects. He didn't self-combust. That was a good sign. So far, so good.

He found himself in a giant room filled with row upon row of dandelions in various states of growth. They grew under red lighting. Red, glowing, creepy lighting. Hardy wasn't lying about what was in there, but deadly dandelions? Cricket felt the pull of his body—the desire to breathe calling him back—the sting of no oxygen. He needed to hurry. Not much time left.

He flew slowly over the section where the dandelions had gone to seed. The white balls sat delicately on their stems like golf balls on tees. A strange sensation vibrated through Cricket as he glided above them. He got the distinct feeling that the plants were *watching* him. They responded to him as he moved. It was subtle, but they definitely moved,

233

reached, as he passed by. It was as if they sensed his presence. He stopped. The dandelions on each side of him leaned toward him all at once. The soft, white seeds quivered as if wanting to release, as if they didn't need someone to blow them free. Cricket froze. He didn't dare move, but quickly realized he couldn't move. He was paralyzed, with no way to return to his body. The need to breathe created unimaginable pain—like someone's hands were on his throat, choking him.

***

Hardy bit his nails as he stared at Cricket's lifeless body. This night was turning into a nightmare. He should have known Cricket wouldn't play this straight. Now Luis was running around the woods with his schoolboy crush, looking for Darcy. And Darcy's face. He didn't just see fear in her eyes. It was terror. Cricket was such an idiot. Hardy hoped all this was worth it.

What was taking him so long? Hardy paced in front of Cricket's body. How long could Cricket go without oxygen? Two, three minutes? Cricket didn't like it when you brought him back. The re-entry was more violent when someone touched him. *Never touch me,* he always said. Forget it, Hardy wouldn't be responsible for another death. He reached out a hand and touched Cricket. Cricket's body heaved violently. He fell to his side, gasping for air, coughing uncontrollably.

Hardy squatted next to him and put a hand on his shoulder.

Cricket held up a finger. "Just give me a minute," he said hoarsely. After another coughing fit, he sat up and leaned back against the building. "You were right. The place was full of dandelions."

"I knew it! We have to get some kind of evidence. Did you see anything else?" Hardy asked.

Cricket shook his head and pressed the palms of his hands to his eyes.

"Maybe you could try again. See if there's an office or something you missed."

Cricket grabbed Hardy by the shirt collar and pulled him close to his face. "I will *never* go back in there. Do you hear me?"

"What are you doing?" Hardy said, grabbing Cricket's wrists.

"I need to know you hear me," Cricket said fiercely.

"I hear you, I hear you."

Cricket's grip loosened, and Hardy sat down on the ground next to him. "What happened in there?" Hardy asked.

"I'll tell you what happened in there—I almost died."

"What? How?"

"I don't know. I was moving above the white dandelions and...it was weird. It was like they were watching me, so I stopped and hovered."

"And?"

"They all leaned toward me at once, and I couldn't move. I couldn't come back to my body. And then...I don't know. I felt myself dying."

Hardy locked his hands on top of his head. "What if I

hadn't touched you? This was all a really bad idea."

"Forget it. I made it out in time."

A light flashed into the clearing from the trees.

Luis and Darcy burst out of the woods at a full run. Something was wrong. Darcy kept looking over her shoulder. "Run! Now!" Luis yelled, barreling toward them.

A loud shout erupted from the woods. Someone was coming. Hardy didn't hesitate. He grabbed Cricket by the back of his shirt and lifted him up off the ground. Cricket could barely stand, much less run. Luis sensed something was wrong and stopped to hold up Cricket with his broad shoulders. They stumbled off in one direction while Hardy and Darcy ran in the opposite direction. Better to divide and conquer. A large figure came out of the woods, a man, screaming for them to stop.

Hardy and Darcy sprinted through the clearing toward the safety of the trees. Darcy was plunging through the darkness like she was running in an open field in broad daylight. Hardy immediately fell behind, struggling to see by the light of a flashlight in a full run through a maze of trees. The thing about the dark was that there was no way to tell how close someone was to you. Hardy could hear the labored breathing, the pounding of feet, but he didn't know if it was his, or the stranger that was pursuing them. He tried to focus on Darcy's blonde ponytail as a kind of carrot on a string. Just when he thought he was getting the hang of it, he slammed into a tree, rolled off its surface, and stumbled back into the dark. He was immediately tackled to the ground from behind. His flashlight fell from his hand and rolled out of reach. He struggled to get to his feet, grasping at the ground with his fingers. He clawed his way out of the man's grasp and was almost free when a hand caught his ankle. Hardy flipped over and tried to kick his leg free. The pursuer shined a flashlight directly into his face. With one last kick that came with a distinctive crunch, Hardy freed himself from his attacker. He scrambled to his feet, and Darcy grabbed his hand. They ran into the woods together, letting it drape them in the safety of darkness. Except they weren't safe. The man had seen Hardy's face.

Chapter Twenty-two

Hardy and Darcy ran until they burst out into the fields next to Hill Home. There was no sign of the man from the woods. They had lost him, thanks to Darcy. It had been so completely dark that, without her navigating, they would've been lost or, worse, caught.

Hardy bent over and put his hands on his knees, trying to catch his breath. Darcy held a hand to her stomach. They were silent except for the huffing sounds coming from their stinging lungs.

The moon was full. And now, no longer hidden by the trees, it lit the meadow in a warm light. Hardy straightened and realized that Darcy had wandered several feet away.

"Are you okay?" he said, approaching her.

Darcy was holding herself, staring up at the sky. Her hair had come unbound and was draped over her shoulders like a white blanket. She turned and grabbed Hardy, wrapping her arms around his neck. He was startled, but feeling her cool fingers on his neck and the warmth of her hair, he slowly wrapped his arms around her waist and held her tiny, delicate body. His hands resting on the small of her back.

"It's okay, Darcy," he said, putting his hands into her soft, wavy hair. She breathed into his neck. He held her tighter. He wanted to hold her. He buried his face into her hair, smelling earth and flowers. But then, as if waking from a dream where he was falling, Hardy quickly pulled back and held Darcy stiffly at arm's length. They stared at each other in the dim light. He froze. *What just happened?* Nothing happened. Nothing *would* happen. He quickly dropped his arms from Darcy. She stared at the ground.

"I'm…um…sorry about all that back there. Cricket scaring you and stuff."

Darcy looked up and nodded, her white eyelashes fluttering like moths in the moonlight. Hardy wanted to reach out to her, but something was stopping him. He didn't want her to get the wrong idea.

"I should get home," Darcy said.

"Yeah, of course."

They started walking through the field along the edge of the woods to the place where they had hidden their bikes.

"You were right—about the dandelions," Hardy said.

Darcy stopped and stared at him.

"Cricket said the place was full of them," Hardy said, avoiding eye contact. For some reason he was having a hard time looking at her.

"We have to do something," Darcy said.

"I know."

Darcy turned and started walking again. Hardy watched

her for a minute, thinking he might catch up to her and pull her into his arms one more time. Wanting to—hold her. Wanting to… He brushed the feelings off. There was absolutely no way he was feeling anything for Darcy. Not now. Not when he was so close to getting everything he ever wanted with Charity.

***

It was eleven o'clock p.m. when Hardy heard a knock on the door. Unable to sleep after the adrenaline-filled chase through the woods, he had spent the last hour staring at the ceiling. His stomach sank when his father opened the door and flashing blue lights bounced off the living room wall and up to his ceiling. He was worried this might happen. He knew the man in the woods had seen his face. He hadn't told Darcy. He figured if it came to this, he would take the fall on his own.

He listened to the hushed voices and waited.

"Hardy. Can you come down here please?" Tom called up.

Thank goodness his mother had the night shift at the hospital. Her disappointment was more than he could deal with tonight. He was used to disappointing Tom.

Hardy slowly descended the ladder from his loft. They say people can be eerily calm right before the ax drops.

Two police officers stood in their small living room. A deep V formed between Tom's eyes at the sight of Hardy. "This is Officer Bryan and Officer Pierce. These gentlemen say that some kids were trespassing on Hill Home property tonight. Would you know anything about that?" Tom's face reddened as if he had already determined Hardy's guilt.

Hardy crossed his arms and shook his head.

The heat of Tom's anger was now spreading to his ears. "You were identified as one of the kids by an employee. Are you denying you were there?"

Hardy assumed that by *employee* they meant Trevor. He should have known. "Yes. I deny I was there." He knew he should fess up, but he also knew the stakes of confessing. Somehow, knowing that it was Trevor who ID'd him made it easier to lie.

"Where were you earlier then? You weren't here," Tom pressed.

Hardy could see the disgust in his father's face, and for some reason it made him angry.

"Mr. Vance, I'm afraid we're going to have to take the boy downtown for questioning," Officer Bryan said.

"Dad!" Hardy reached out to Tom waiting for him to do something—say something to help him.

"Son, you'll have to answer for your actions."

Hardy's heart sank. His dad didn't believe him. One of the officers removed a pair of handcuffs. Hardy's stomach twisted into a knot.

"That won't be necessary, gentlemen," a voice said from the doorway.

It was George. His gray hair uncombed, his clothes baggy and wrinkled, like he had just rolled out of bed.

"Who are you?" Tom asked.

George approached Tom and held out a hand. "George Bolt."

241

Tom reluctantly shook George's outstretched hand.

George turned to the officers. "This boy was with me until ten. I can vouch for his whereabouts. He would've been home sooner but I made him stay and have a late supper."

Tom looked utterly shocked. Hardy tried to hide his disbelief. He didn't know how George knew, or why he was there, but a tidal wave of relief washed over Hardy.

Tom turned to Hardy. "Is that right, Hardy? Were you with this man?"

Hardy quickly stuck his hands under his armpits to hide his nervousness. "Yep."

Tom squinted at George. "And what business do you have with my son?"

"Oh well, I know your boy Tate. I asked him if he knew anyone who would help me with my yard, seeing as I can't manage it as well anymore with the bad back." George was leaning sideways into his hip, really playing it up.

Tom's expression was mostly suspicious. "And you just happened to be driving by and thought Hardy might need an alibi tonight?"

Hardy shifted nervously from foot to foot, wondering how George was going to skirt out of that one.

George laughed and slapped his leg. "Good grief, no. I got me a police scanner." George scratched his head. "It's a little hobby of mine. An old man gets lonely. The voices keep me company late at night when I can't sleep. Fascinating stuff. Anyway, I heard the address for a possible trespassing suspect, and I recognized it as Hardy's address." George moved next to Hardy and put his arm around him. "After what this young man has done for an old man like me, I knew I had to get over here right quick."

Tom frowned. Hardy smiled and put his arm around George.

Officer Bryan sighed. "The problem is, George, the boy has been identified by an employee as one of the kids."

George walked closer to the officer and adjusted his glasses. "And where did this employee *see* Hardy, exactly?"

Officer Bryan coughed into his fist. "In the woods."

George put his index finger to his lips and contemplated. "The woods?"

"Yes," Officer Bryan responded.

"The dark woods? And who was the employee?"

The officers looked at each other.

"Dan Bryan, your mother would not like to hear you disrespecting an old man. I've known you since you were a boy playing naked in mud puddles, and you know me well enough."

Officer Bryan's face flushed red. "Trevor Irene."

George held up a finger. "Ah ha! Now here's where it gets interesting." George turned to Hardy. The courtroom atmosphere grew as George worked the room. "Who are you taking to the prom, Hardy?"

"You're going to the prom?" Tom asked, looking incredulous.

"Please hold your questions until the defendant has answered," George said.

"George, this isn't a courtroom," Officer Bryan said. Officer Pierce suppressed a smile.

George held up a hand. "Indulge an old man. Hardy?"

"Charity Hill."

"Charity Hill?" Tom said, unable to hide his shock.

"And is Charity your girlfriend?" George asked Hardy.

Hardy stuck his hands in his pockets. He was beginning to realize where George was going with this. *Genius.* "No. We're going as friends."

"And why is that?" George paced.

"Her boyfriend had to work."

"I see. And who is her boyfriend?"

Hardy could feel his heart leaping from his chest with excitement. "Trevor Irene."

The revelation stunned the officers. They looked at each other and shifted uncomfortably on their feet.

George turned to the officers. "The same employee who turned in Hardy. Officers, I think what we're seeing here is a jealous young man who saw an opportunity to incriminate my client."

"For Pete's sake, George. He's not your client," Officer Bryan said.

George raised a finger high into the air. "Nevertheless, I have made my case. The boy was with me: the so-called accuser has a personal vendetta. Case solved."

Hardy imagined that if a gavel had been present, no doubt George would have banged it. Officer Pierce smirked, apparently finding George's tirade amusing.

Officer Bryan stared at George, contemplating. He tilted his head and pressed the radio device at his shoulder. "Negative on the trespassing call. The kid was with a Mr. Bolt. He has an alibi."

A voice blared back over the radio. "Roger that. Hey, is that old George Bolt? Tell him I'll see him in the morning at our Romeo Club."

Officer Bryan sighed. "10-4."

Everyone looked at George. He shrugged. "What?"

No one would say it, but everyone was wondering what the Romeo Club was. George held up both hands. "It's not what you think, boys. It stands for 'Retired Old Men Eating Out'."

Officer Pierce chuckled. Officer Brian looked done.

"Mr. Vance, sorry to have disturbed you. You folks have a good evening," Officer Bryan said. He nodded, and they let themselves out.

"Well, I reckon this old man needs to get back home, too."

"Mr. Bolt. Thank you." Tom extended his hand.

George grasped Tom's hand and pumped it twice. "No thanks needed. That's a good boy you got there." George gave Hardy a two-finger salute and left.

Hardy and Tom were left standing alone. The tension in the air was thick. Tom stared at the floor, rubbing the back of his neck. Hardy waited for an apology that didn't come. It didn't matter that Hardy had lied. The fact was that Tom hadn't stood up for him.

"Well, I guess I'll go back to bed," Hardy said.

"Okay. Goodnight," Tom said, avoiding eye contact.

Hardy wanted to say more. Wanted Tom to explain himself. Why did he always think the worst of Hardy? Why couldn't he just—love him? Instead, Hardy turned, climbed the ladder, and fell back into bed. Within a few minutes, he could hear the news playing on the TV like nothing had happened.

Chapter Twenty-three

Hardy absent-mindedly secured his bike to the school bike rack. He had barely slept, his mind racing after discovering what was in the mirrored building. They had no proof, nothing to expose the horror of what was happening at Hill Home. And to think there were nine more homes just like it on the island. What now?

He rubbed the palms of his hands into his eyes. Someone tapped him on the shoulder. He jumped, ramming a knee into his bike pedal. It was Charity.

"Wow. A little jumpy this morning, aren't we?" Charity asked.

Hardy rubbed his knee. "Uh…hey…"

Charity handed him a square of silky material covered in a floral pattern. "I just wanted to give you a sample of my dress so you can match your tux to it."

Hardy had no idea what she was talking about, but he

took the material from her.

"Okay, thanks. Yeah, I was planning to go tomorrow to rent the tux."

Charity smiled. *Man, was she beautiful*. He rubbed the material in his hand then stuck it in his pocket.

"Great. It will be fun. Don't forget about the party at my house afterwards."

A cold sweat broke out on the back of Hardy's neck. "Yeah…about that. What about Trevor?" *He knows I was in the woods last night.*

"We broke up."

Hardy's inhale got stuck in his throat like he was choking on a piece of food. "What?" he said, coughing into his fist. *He's going to kill me. I'm dead.*

"He's too possessive. I'm tired of it." Charity reached out and put a hand on Hardy's wrist. He watched her hand travel up his arm. Hardy was either holding his breath or hyperventilating. He wasn't sure which one. "Besides," she continued, "maybe I want to see—"

"Bromeo!" Someone yelled out. Hardy didn't need to look to know who it was. Charity withdrew her hand and looked toward Luis who coasted to a stop right next to them.

"Well hello, Miss Hill. You're looking lovely as usual," Luis said.

Charity smiled. "Hey, Luis."

Brilliant. She knew Luis's name but barely knew who Hardy was until a few weeks ago.

She rested a hand on Luis handlebars. "Hey, listen, I wanted to invite you and your prom date to the after-party at my house. Can you make it?"

"Yeah. Sounds great."

"Good. Well, I have to get the class. I'll see you guys later." Charity gave a little wave of her hand and she was off.

Hardy wanted to punch Luis in the face. Not only did he ruin the moment, he got a party invite. Hardy followed Luis's eyes which were following Charity as she made her way inside. He punched Luis in the arm. "Hey."

Luis grabbed his arm and looked at Hardy. "What?"

Hardy rolled his eyes. "Never mind."

"That is one good-looking girl," Luis said, shaking his head.

"Shut up, Luis."

"Sorry. She is. And now I'm going to her party." Luis held up a hand, waiting for Hardy to give him a high-five.

Hardy just stared at it.

"Don't leave a bro hangin'."

"I didn't realize you knew Charity," Hardy said, annoyed.

Luis dropped his hand and flexed his biceps. "I'm a wrestler. Everyone knows these guns. They don't call me the Terminator for nothing."

"Whatever. I need to get to class." Hardy stuck his thumbs into his backpack straps.

"Hey. I wanted to let you know I'm going to ask Darcy to the prom."

"Absolutely not," Hardy and someone else said at the same time. Cricket stepped up next to Hardy.

Luis frowned. "What's your guys' problem?" Luis's frown faded. "Oh, I get it. You two don't think I'm good enough for her."

Cricket laughed.

"No, that's not it," Hardy said.

"Then what is it?" Luis asked.

Yeah. What is it? Hardy had no clue. He knew what Cricket's reasons were—she's a freshman—she's weird, Darcy. But what were Hardy's?

He pointed a finger at Luis. "Don't you dare do anything to hurt her. You get me?"

Luis held up both hands. "Whoa, bro. What's the big deal? I thought you weren't interested in her."

"I'm not *interested*. But I swear, if you do anything, and I mean hurt one hair on her head, I will beat you to a pulp."

Luis and Cricket chuckled. "As if you could," Luis said.

Hardy poked a finger into Luis's chest. "I'm stronger than I used to be." And he was. He had gotten away from Trevor in the woods last night.

"Okay, okay. Chill, why don't you?" Luis said, holding up his hands.

Hardy backed away.

"You know, for someone who claims to not be interested in Darcy, you really seem to go out of your way to protect her." Luis frowned and pushed his bike past Hardy to another rack.

Hardy breathed heavily through his nose and rubbed his eyebrow. A small throb pulsed at his right temple. A headache was coming on.

Cricket raised and dropped his arms. "Terrific. Now, Darcy is going to be hanging with us at the prom."

Hardy glared after Luis as he headed toward the school. "She hasn't said yes, yet."

Cricket laughed. "She will."

"How do you know?" Hardy asked, wondering if Cricket knew something he didn't.

"This may be her only chance—like ever. I doubt she'll turn it down."

"Could you just give it a rest?" Hardy snapped.

Cricket frowned. "What crawled up your—"

"The police came to my house last night. Okay? The guy in the woods was Trevor. He saw my face," Hardy said sharply. *And Charity just broke up with him.*

Cricket's face went white. "Whoa. The police came to your house?"

A couple holding hands passed right in front of them. Hardy waited until they were clear and lowered his voice. "Yeah. So don't ask me what crawled—"

"And?" Cricket said interrupting.

Hardy rubbed his pounding forehead. "Someone showed up and gave me an alibi."

"What? Who?" Cricket asked, surprised.

"George Bolt," Hardy said, shifting his backpack.

Cricket's mouth was practically hanging open. "The old dude from the home you told me about?"

Hardy nodded. "Yeah. That would be the one."

"But you said you didn't like the old crony."

"I know, but you should have seen him. He had the officers eating out of his hand," Hardy said.

"Wait. How did he know you are in trouble?" Cricket said skeptically.

"He said he heard it on his police scanner." Hardy pinched the bridge of his nose. Talking about it was making his headache worse. Or maybe it was imagining what Trevor was going to do to him.

"Do you believe him?" Cricket asked.

"I don't know. I guess. But he knew other stuff, too."

"Like what?"

"About my prom date, Trevor and Charity," Hardy said, gesturing wildly.

"Dude, that's kinda weird," Cricket said, staring into space. "You're one lucky son of a gun."

"I know," Hardy said. Right now he just wanted to change the subject and put it behind him. "Hey, look. I'm sorry about last night. If something would've happened to you in that dandelion building…"

"Well, it didn't. So don't worry about it."

"I am worried. This stuff is turning out to be dangerous. I can't let my friends get hurt in the process."

Cricket clasped Hardy's shoulder. "Listen, we're best friends. I'm not going to leave you hanging, okay? If you need me, I'm there. Just no more weird buildings in the woods."

"Deal." Hardy pulled the square of material Charity had given him out of his pocket. "Hey, I need to go rent a tux. Charity gave me this. I don't even know what to do with it."

Cricket laughed. "I tell you what, let's go Saturday night after I get off work. I need to rent one, too. Meet me at seven?"

The bell rang.

***

Hardy and Darcy stood at the front of the reception desk at Hill Home and waited for their assignments. Today was their last day. Trevor was nowhere to be seen. Hardy dreaded the minute Trevor laid eyes on him. It didn't matter that the police had let Hardy off the hook. Trevor knew he had been in the woods—he had seen Hardy. At least Darcy was safe. That was all that mattered. At least, that's how he tried to console himself before the inevitable face smashing he would get from Trevor.

There had been no opportunity at school to discuss what happened last night. Charity had climbed the hill and sat with Hardy at lunch. Darcy, Luis, and Cricket sat across from them. Darcy maintained her usual calm composure, Luis grunted and belched over his food, and Cricket kept a cocky grin on his face. Hardy had to fight the urge to get up and run away from the social nightmare. Instead, his right leg bounced uncontrollably for twenty minutes under the table. Charity had rambled about the prom theme—Paris lights, and the after-party which she described as epic. Hardy stared at Darcy most of the time, looking for some kind of reaction. After all, he had faked asking her to the prom. But there was nothing but polite interest on her face. He was pretty sure the only thing he ate for lunch was his nails.

Now standing there with Darcy, he got the distinct feeling that something was wrong between them. He had no idea why he felt that way. On the surface, everything seemed fine. In reality, it just didn't matter right now. It was up to him to do something about what they had discovered last night, and Darcy was the only one whom he could truly depend on to help.

The group of workers were becoming restless, some threatening to leave. Right on cue, Trevor came barreling around the corner. He didn't look happy. Not only did he have a white bandage across his nose, he also had matching purple bruises under his eyes. Everyone took a small step back, mumbling to each other, wondering what happened to Trevor's face. Hardy knew exactly what had happened to it—his foot.

"Okay, losers," Trevor said, walking behind the desk. "Mama is permanently out. You're stuck with me until a replacement can be found. Do your job, don't complain, and we'll get along fine." Trevor slammed the clipboard down on the counter with his hand and stared straight at Hardy as if sending him a message. *You will pay.* Hardy swallowed the sick feeling rising in his throat. The group slowly drifted away from Hardy like he was contagious. Trevor left, and the group stood in a stunned silence.

Dread hit Hardy like a kickball to the stomach. This wasn't over, and he knew it. Trevor would wait and make Hardy sweat before he ripped him apart. And now Nurse Troxler was gone. Had she confronted Trevor about Mrs. Gobble's death? Panic set in. What if something had happened to Nurse Troxler? Maybe Hardy should leave now, confess all to his father, take his punishment, stay on the island, ruin his life… No, he couldn't. He wouldn't. It wasn't just for Olen now, it was for every elderly person in Hill Homes all over the island.

Everyone crammed together around the clipboard, careful to keep their distance from Hardy. Everyone except Darcy, who took his hand and pulled him forward. She had put her hair into a single braid with a pale blue ribbon wrapped around the end. He could smell a hint of vanilla in her hair as he looked over her shoulder. She had a way of calming him that he couldn't explain.

His assignment was written in big capital letters. CLEAN TOILETS IN ALL ROOMS ON HALL B. A few people evidently noticed and were smiling as they skirted around him. Hardy's face flushed and grew hot at Trevor's attempt to embarrass him. He didn't think it was possible to hate anyone so much, and the fire of it burned in his gut. Darcy pulled her hand from his vice grip and asked him if he was okay.

"I'm fine," he said, pulling Darcy out of the range of listening ears. He tried to put his anger aside. "Listen, I'm worried about Mama—Nurse Troxler. I insisted she talk to Trevor about Mrs. Gobble's death, and now she's gone?"

"It does seem strange. I'll see what I can find out." Darcy turned to leave.

"Darcy."

She turned back to Hardy.

"Be careful," he said. *I'll never forgive myself if anything happens to you.*

Darcy nodded and left Hardy standing there feeling lost the moment she walked away.

Hardy hauled around a bucket with a brush, toilet cleaner, and rags, all afternoon. After fifteen rooms, and two toilets containing unspeakable things, he had had enough. He was coming out of his last room when Darcy caught him by surprise. Her eyes were darting up and down the hall. She looked nervous.

"What's wrong?" Hardy asked.

"It's Nurse Troxler," Darcy said, pulling her braid through her hands, over and over.

"What about her?"

"She's here."

"She's back at work?" Hardy asked, confused.

"No. She's a patient."

"What? Where?"

"Hardy, you don't think they're going to…?"

He set his bucket down and gripped Darcy by the arms. "Over my dead body. Do you know where she is?"

Darcy shook her head. "But I overheard Trevor talking to someone on the phone. He said, *she wouldn't be a problem anymore after today. Tell the Governor not to worry*."

Hardy stuck his hands in his hair and gritted his teeth. "The Governor?" He didn't want to believe it, but it made sense. Marcus Hill was the one who cleared Trevor's record. The Hill Homes were started by his family. Of course, Marcus Hill would know what was going on.

"Do you know who Trevor was talking to?" Hardy asked.

"No," Darcy said softly.

This was Hardy's fault. He had insisted Nurse Troxler talk to Trevor about Mrs. Gobble.

"Okay. I'm going to find Trevor," Hardy said.

"I'll go with you."

"No!" Hardy snapped. He briefly shut his eyes, trying to regain his composure. "No, Darcy. I don't want you to get hurt. I'll find you. Stay somewhere safe, with other people."

Darcy nodded. Hardy left the bucket in the hall and took off.

Chapter Twenty-four

Hardy checked every patient room on the top and bottom floors. There was no sign of Trevor or Mama. Maybe Darcy had misunderstood what Trevor had said. He just couldn't shake the feeling that something was wrong. Why hadn't Trevor sought him out—confronted him over the woods, over Charity? Unless there was something more important, more urgent. *Like getting rid of Mama.*

Desperate and winded, he decided to try the hall with the employee lockers. As soon as he turned the corner, he caught a glimpse of Trevor's snake tattoo turning left toward the kitchen. Hardy jogged down the hall and stopped at the corner. He placed his back against the wall and peeked around the corner. Trevor had stopped in front of a door across from the kitchen and was looking around to make sure no one was watching. Hardy jerked his head back against the wall, hoping Trevor hadn't seen him. When he peered back around, Trevor was inserting a skeleton key into the door's old lock. There was a black box in his hand.

This had to be it—where Trevor was keeping Mama. Hardy's heart pounded. He shoved his head back into the wall and closed his eyes. He heard the door close. A knot lodged in his throat. *Stop, Hardy. Stop. Do something. Do anything.* He was a coward. What could he do? How could he stop Trevor? There was no time to think. He heard the door open and forced himself to look. Trevor turned the key inside the lock and headed in Hardy's direction.

Hardy ran to the men's locker room on the other side of the hall and slipped inside. He cracked the door and waited for Trevor to pass by. Once Trevor made it down the hall and turned the corner, Hardy sprinted to the door, hoping by some miracle it wasn't locked.

His hands gripped the cold, hard knob. It wouldn't turn. He beat on the door with his fist. "Nurse Troxler! Open the door!" Desperate, he backed up two steps. The door was old. Maybe he could break it down. He rammed his right shoulder into the door. A bolt of electric pain shot down his arm. He was about to pound on the door again when a red fire extinguisher came down on top of the doorknob, and the knob fell to the floor. The door cracked open. Darcy stood with a fire extinguisher in hand.

"You stay here, understand?" Hardy cautioned.

Darcy nodded.

Hardy stared at the small hint of light that seeped through the cracked door. A light burned from somewhere inside. He stuck out his right arm and pushed the door open with his fingers. He could see the end of the bed sticking out, the rest hidden by the bathroom wall. He moved slowly into the room. It was quiet except for the rustle of bed sheets. He stepped past the bathroom.

"Nurse Troxler?" he said softly.

Hardy barely recognized her. She wore no make-up, and her short hair was pinned back away from her face. Her eyes were wide with fear. She was holding a rolled-up magazine. The black box was ominously sitting on her bed tray.

"Come any closer and I'll beat you to death."

Hardy held up his hands and inched closer. "It's me, Nurse Troxler. Hardy Vance."

"Hardy Vance? The little troublemaker from Southeast High?"

He grimaced at the word 'troublemaker'. "Yeah, that would be me." He took another step forward.

"Stop right there, or I'll scream."

Hardy froze and backed up a step, still holding his hands up. "Okay. Don't scream. I'm here to help you."

"You can't help with my clogged arteries. But I'm getting my surgery tomorrow. Going to be good as new."

He bit his lip and stared at the black box. He could make a mad dash for it. She might get in a few swipes, but nothing that would stop him from getting that box. She studied his eyes and glanced at the box. She put her hand on it and drew it closer to her.

"You're here to steal from me, you little—"

"Mama, no." Hardy reached out a hand toward her.

She picked the box up. "This is a gift from my sister in Seattle. No way are you getting your grubby little hands on it. Now get out of here."

Hardy shook his head and inched forward. "It's not a gift

from your sister. Trevor is trying to hurt you."

Mama's eyes grew even larger, and she pointed toward the door. "Get out!"

It was now or never. Hardy couldn't let her open that box or she was as good as dead. He charged her bed, reaching for the box. She screamed and held the box high in her hand. His fingers were inches from it when she whacked him across the face with the tightly rolled magazine. It knocked him sideways, and his fingers collided with hers. The box slowly tumbled out of her hands. "No!" Hardy yelled, watching it fall. He dived across her toward the other side of the bed. She furiously pelted his back with the magazine. The box grazed his fingertips and fell to the floor. The lid slid off and, in a blink of an eye, a white haze exploded into the air. Hardy's hand swam in the middle of the delicate white seeds. Mama's screams filled the room and everything changed.

He pulled himself up off the bed and stumbled backwards. Everything happened in slow motion now. Mama was no longer angry. She was smiling, holding her hands out to the floating seeds. *No, no, no.* This wasn't happening. His body felt like lead. He couldn't lift his feet. A light wind spilled into the room. Did someone open a window? The air was cold and warm at the same time. Like springtime, when the air is cold and the sun is warm. A small pinprick of light appeared on the far wall. He watched it spin, fold, and enlarge. Faster the light spun, the wind growing stronger. He strained against the powerful gust, though nothing in the room was moving. The blinds were quiet, the sheets calm. How was this possible? The swirling vortex of light swallowed the entire back wall and exploded, flooding the room with bright, pure light, the likes of which Hardy had never seen. He held up an arm to shield his eyes. And, like magic, the wall disappeared and he was staring at a bridge of wood planks suspended in mid-air, with nothing holding them from above or below. Water flowed underneath the planks. White and black clouds churned together in the sky. He looked at Mama. She was getting out of bed.

"Mama, no!" he yelled above the roaring wind.

She hesitated. "Should I go, Hardy?"

There were two of her now. One was lying in the bed, asleep, the other standing, staring at him.

"No, Mama. Stay right there," he yelled, holding up a hand.

That's when he heard a voice. *Noli Timere. Don't be afraid.* He understood Latin? *I understand Latin.* He looked back to the bridge. There was a man standing on it now. He had brown, wavy hair and a beard. The rest of him was hidden in a light fog that floated over the bridge. Hardy's heart almost stopped. He knew this man. He had never seen him before, but he knew him. A pulsing orb of light surrounded Hardy. He couldn't breathe, but he could feel. He felt love. Pure, clean, perfect love. He fell to his knees. Tears came down his face as he stared into the man's eyes. He was ruined.

"Hardy, should I go?" Mama asked.

He looked at Mama through his veil of tears. Her eyes were frozen in confusion. He nodded. "Yes, Mama. Yes. Go."

He watched her float toward the bridge as if she had no

legs. When she reached the bridge, her legs suddenly reappeared, and she walked toward the man who was now holding out his hand to her. Hardy rose up on one knee, trying to stand, but the wind kept him from rising. He wanted to go, too. *Don't leave me. Let me come.* The voice spoke again in his head. *Noli Timere. Don't be afraid.* He fell to the floor, and the room went dark.

Hardy. Hardy. A voice called his name from somewhere very far away. He felt like he was underwater and a voice from above was trying to reach him. He didn't remember getting in the water. He blinked. Her face, beautiful—glowing like an angel. The image was—ethereal.

"Am I dead?"

The angel tugged on his arm, trying to pull him out of the water. "Come on. We have to get out of here."

***

Darcy ran into the room and dropped down to the floor next to Hardy. "Hardy!" He was on his stomach. His eyes closed. She rolled him onto his back and put her ear close to his mouth. Thank goodness—he was breathing. She rushed to Mama's bedside. Her eyes were wide open, frozen, staring into nothingness. She lifted Mama's wrist and felt for a pulse. Nothing. Mama was gone.

She fell back on her knees next to Hardy and patted his whiskered cheeks. "Hardy. Hardy. Wake up."

He muttered and turned his head, but didn't open his eyes. She grabbed him by the shoulders and gently shook him. "We have to get out of here."

His eyelids fluttered. She took his face in her hands and squeezed. "Open your eyes, Hardy."

He blinked several times. "Am I dead?" He muttered.

Darcy pulled on his arm. "Sit up. Come on."

Hardy sat up, his body limp. He opened his eyes halfway and smiled. "Hey, Darcy."

"Come on, we have to get you out of here," she said, pulling, encouraging him to sit up.

Hardy resisted. "Whoa. Whoa. Wait," he said, pulling his arm out of her grip. "You look really good in that blue dress," he said, slurring his words.

Darcy sighed. "I'm not wearing a dress." She grabbed his arm again. "Please get up."

"Okay, fine." He let her help him to his feet. He stumbled and grabbed onto her. "Whoa." Hardy stared into her eyes. "You're really pretty, you know that."

"Let's get out of here before Trevor comes back."

"Trevor. I really hate that guy."

"I know." Darcy pushed her shoulder under Hardy's armpit, and they managed to make it out into the hall.

Something was wrong with Hardy. She messaged Cricket with her eye and prayed he would get there in time—before Trevor found them. She dragged Hardy down the hall, his body leaning on her. She could barely support the dead weight. He was soaked in sweat.

"Did you know I can see dead people?" Hardy mumbled.

"That's great. Just keep moving, okay?"

What if Hardy died? He was in the room when the dandelion exploded. She didn't want to lose the only friend she had.

After starting and stopping several times, Darcy managed to get him down one hall and left into the hall that led to the entrance. She could see the door, but it felt like it was a mile away. There was still no sign of Trevor. One final push, and hopefully Cricket would be outside, waiting.

Hardy's knees buckled, and his dead weight fell to the floor where he sat with his head hanging to his chest. "I'm tired, Darcy. I just need to lie down." He started to stretch out on the emerald green carpet.

Darcy grabbed him under the arms from behind and lifted. "Soon, Hardy. Soon. Cricket is picking us up. Just a little bit further."

"Cricket's coming?" Hardy pushed up with his feet.

"He's right outside the door." Darcy hoped he was right outside the door.

"Okay." Hardy put his arm around Darcy and stumbled forward.

They had only taken a few steps when Hardy tripped. They fell sideways into the wall. Darcy was pinned beneath Hardy.

"Is this place spinning? Because I'm really dizzy," Hardy said.

Darcy tried to push him off of her when she spotted Trevor coming toward them. Oh no. If he saw Hardy like this, it was over. She lifted Hardy's head from her shoulder. "Hardy, look at me."

His half-closed lids looked at her, but didn't appear to be focusing.

"I'm going to kiss you, and I want you to kiss me back." Darcy glanced toward Trevor who had spotted them and was now scowling.

Hardy chuckled. "I knew you'd only be able to resist me for so long."

It was now or never. "Shut up and kiss me."

She pulled Hardy's lips to hers. His lips were soft and hot. His facial hair enveloped her lips like a warm cocoon. She felt his limp body suddenly begin to gain control, his legs planting into the ground. Then he kissed her, really kissed her. Held her face. Breathed into her. Her mind left her, her hands traveled up Hardy's arms. She forgot about Trevor, she didn't care. She'd never felt so... Maybe the room was spinning.

A voice broke through the haze. "You two! Get back to work. Now!"

Darcy pushed Hardy away and turned her head. Trevor had walked by them and was turning the corner. She sighed with relief. She looked back at Hardy who seemed slightly more aware but still groggy.

"I think we should do that again," Hardy said, slurring every word. He moved closer to her, pursing his lips.

She placed a hand firmly on his chest. "No, Hardy. We have to go. Remember? Cricket's waiting."

"Cricket's waiting?" he muttered.

"Yes. Come on."

Darcy's heart was pumping blood so fast that the sight in her blue eye flashed in and out with white static. She grabbed Hardy around the waist, and they struggled down the hall together. Her depth perception was coming and going. She tried blinking, focusing, but her vision continued flickering. Just a few more feet to the front door. Thank goodness, not many people were hanging out in the lobby. Only a few patients sat in their wheelchairs staring at them with a vague interest.

Darcy fumbled with the knob to the door and managed to get it open by balancing Hardy on her hip.

Relief flooded over her when she saw Cricket's pickup truck parked at the bottom of the steps. He was leaning against the passenger door with his legs crossed. When he saw Darcy struggling to support Hardy, he ran up the steps and shoved a shoulder under Hardy's arm.

"Thank goodness you're here," Darcy said, allowing the bulk of Hardy's weight to shift to Cricket. The flashing in her eye began to stabilize.

"What happened?" Cricket asked.

"Cricket? Hey, bro," Hardy said, grinning like an idiot.

"Yeah...let's get you to the truck."

"Is she coming?" Hardy uttered.

"Who? Darcy?" Cricket asked.

"That's a pretty name...Darcy," Hardy said, lobbing his head toward her.

"Okay...this is getting weird. Come on." Cricket navigated Hardy down the steps with Darcy's help.

Cricket grabbed the handle to the passenger side door. "Has he been drinking?"

"No."

"Okay, buddy. Into the truck." Cricket shoved Hardy inside.

Hardy immediately fell over and stretched out over the whole bench seat.

"Good grief," Cricket said.

Darcy pushed Hardy's feet off the seat and slid in. Cricket ran around to the driver's side, pushed Hardy up off the seat, and squeezed in. Hardy's head fell backwards against the back window.

Cricket started the truck and glared across Hardy at Darcy. "Do you mind telling me what is going on?"

"Just go. I'll explain later," Darcy said, nervously staring at the door of the home.

Cricket sighed and shifted the truck into drive. Hardy's head lurched forward, and he opened his eyes.

"Cricket, when did you get here?" Hardy asked.

"We're going to take you home," Cricket said.

"No!" Hardy yelled out, grabbing two fistfuls of Cricket's shirt.

Cricket struggled to maintain his grip on the steering wheel. "A little help, please," he snapped.

Darcy laid a reassuring hand on Hardy's shoulder. "It's okay, we're not taking you home."

Hardy released Cricket, and collapsed into the back window again.

"What now, genius?" Cricket asked.

"I don't know. Give me a minute. He needs medical attention." Darcy felt Hardy's forehead. He was burning up.

"Did you drug him or something?" Cricket asked.

"No, don't be ridiculous."

"I'll tell you what's ridiculous. This—you—all of it."

Darcy's stomach rolled into knots. Wasn't it true? She *was* the reason Hardy was in all this mess. She felt the pressure build behind her brown eye. *Don't cry. Not now.*

"Hey!" Hardy said, coming to. He shoved a finger into

Cricket's face. "Don't you talk to Darcy like that."

Cricket pushed Hardy's finger aside. "Don't worry about it, Hardy. Just sit back and relax."

Hardy leaned over and put his arm around Darcy. "This one has been taking care of me, haven't you, honey."

"Honey?" Cricket repeated.

Darcy wanted to cry—scream—run.

"Yeah. This girl is a great kisser, too." Hardy started stroking Darcy's hair.

"What?" Cricket asked, glancing over at Darcy.

"He's delirious, can't you see that?" Darcy spat.

"I'll say! What are we supposed to do now!?" Cricket shouted.

"Stop yelling at me. I can't think," Darcy said loudly.

"No, you can't. I have to agree with that one."

"He needs a doctor," Darcy said.

"George is a doctor," Hardy said. He fell over into Darcy's lap and held her legs like a pillow.

"Do you know where the old dude lives?" Cricket asked Darcy.

Darcy put her hand into Hardy's damp hair and pulled it through her fingers. She initiated a search for George's address. Hardy looked like a little boy—innocent—sweet. *He kissed me. He won't remember.*

"Darcy!" Cricket yelled impatiently.

"1215 Kismet. Hurry."

Hardy murmured something into Darcy's thigh. She lowered her ear to his lips. "What, Hardy?"

"*Noli Timere,*" Hardy whispered.

"What did he say?" Cricket asked.

"Noli Timere," Darcy said quietly.

"What does that mean?" Cricket asked.

A tear fell from Darcy's eye and landed on Hardy's face. "Don't be afraid," she said.

Chapter Twenty-five

George lived out in the middle of nowhere down a long dirt road. At the end of the road stood an old, stone cottage with a roof taken over by green moss. Wildflowers enveloped the cottage in tall clusters of purple and yellow. A gray, weathered table sat out front, weeds grasping at the legs of its matching chairs. Darcy just hoped George was home.

"Are you sure this is it?" Cricket said, cutting the engine.

"Just go see if he's home," Darcy said.

Cricket looked down at Hardy's pale face and frowned. "Is he...?"

"He's still breathing, if that's what you mean. He's hot, though. He has a fever."

Cricket was only a few feet away from the truck when George stepped out of the front door and aimed a shotgun right at him.

"I'd stay right there if I were you," George threatened.

Cricket raised his hands. Darcy squirmed nervously in

her seat. They had nowhere else to go.

"Turn yourself right back around, get in your truck, and drive."

"We need help," Cricket said, looking back at the truck.

"Well, you're not going to get it here. This is your final warning. Get gone," George barked.

Cricket gave Darcy a "what do I do now?" look. Darcy pushed Hardy up off her lap so George could see him.

Cricket pointed at the truck. "It's Hardy. He's sick. Please."

George lowered the gun slightly and squinted through the truck's window. "Well, why didn't you say so?" He dropped the gun to his side. "Get him in here."

Hardy was unconscious and unresponsive. Cricket hauled him out of the truck and carried him over one shoulder down to the cottage. Darcy ran and held the door open, and Cricket huffed his way into the living room. The small room was cozy but cluttered. A large sofa, a few chairs. Side tables and bookcases were piled with papers, books, magazines. The small kitchen at the back of the room looked outdated but tidy, except for the sink of dirty dishes. George's bird announced their arrival by crying "Ouch!" and bouncing nervously around its cage by the front window. Darcy wondered if they had done the right thing by bringing Hardy there.

George pointed to the back of the cottage. "Back to the left. Lay him on the bed. I'll get my things."

Darcy followed Cricket through the living room into what looked like George's bedroom. Cricket practically threw Hardy on the unmade bed. Darcy rushed to Hardy's side.

"Be careful," she said.

"He's heavy. You try carrying dead weight."

Darcy rubbed Hardy's forehead and turned and looked at Cricket. "Do you think, just this once, you could try not hating me."

Cricket chewed the inside of his cheek.

"I know it's here somewhere," George yelled from the other room.

The sound of cabinets opening and closing echoed through the small space.

"You're right. I'm sorry." Cricket rubbed the back of his neck and stared down at Hardy. "I'm scared."

"Me, too," Darcy said softly.

"I knew it was in there somewhere." George came in with his old, black doctor's bag in tow. He sat on the edge of the bed and removed a small light from the bag. He lifted Hardy's eyelids one at a time and peered inside. "And you two are…?" He returned the light to the bag.

"I'm Cricket. This is Darcy. We're—"

"Friends of Hardy's," Darcy finished.

George fished inside his bag and pulled out a stethoscope. He lifted Hardy's blue shirt and poked around his chest, listening.

"What happened?" George said, looking at Cricket.

Cricket shrugged.

"He was exposed to dandelion toxin again," Darcy said.

George removed the stethoscope from his ears and stood up. "What do you mean, again?" he said, squinting behind his glasses.

"It was Mama, Nurse Troxler. He was trying to save her." Darcy felt tears flood the back of her real eye. Cricket was staring at her in disbelief.

George pushed his few remaining white strands of hair back into place and looked down at Hardy.

"Is there...something you can do?" Darcy asked.

"I'm afraid not. He either recovers or he doesn't. There's nothing I can do for him."

Cricket turned and slammed a hand against George's closet door. He hurried out of the room. The front door banged shut, shaking the small cottage.

Darcy stifled a sob with her hand. She stepped up to the bed and looked at Hardy's lifeless body. His scrubs were soaked through. Sweat pooled on his forehead. This wasn't happening. She couldn't lose another person who she—

She spun around, anger seeping from her every pore. "You're a doctor! How can you do nothing?!" she screamed.

"I'm sorry," George said, looking at Hardy. "He's been exposed to some mighty powerful toxins. His body will either use it for good, or he'll die."

Darcy closed her eyes and swallowed the sob that wanted to escape from her throat. There was nothing left to do but hope and pray. She opened her eyes and looked at George. "I'll need a washcloth and some cold water."

George nodded and left the room.

**

Hardy felt his body launch into awareness. His body ached, and his head felt like an overinflated basketball. *What day is it*? His eyes fluttered open. He was in a strange bed. Startled, he sat straight up and pushed himself backwards into the headboard. *Where am I?*

His eyes dashed around the small room; dresser, mirror, chair, closet. Window, left wall. Door closed. He didn't remember anything. He was only wearing his blue scrub pants. His shirt and shoes had been removed. Okay—scrubs. He must have been at Hill Home. Did he pass out again? No, that was wrong. There were pictures of people on the wall. Hardy got out of the bed and stood in front of the dresser's attached mirror. He rubbed his fingers across his beard. He needed a trim. His eyes were bloodshot. His normally tan skin was pale. He looked like crap.

Hardy's eyes traveled to one of the pictures hanging next to the mirror. He stood in front of the picture and blinked several times, trying to clear his head from the clouds. The black and white picture was a group shot. Three young men and a woman in black graduation caps and gowns—tassels around their necks. All smiling—their arms around each other. Something about the man on the left end looked familiar. It was the eyes.

He turned and surveyed the rest of the room. A pile of dirty clothes. The nightstand next to the bed was piled with books. Why couldn't he remember anything?

He moved to the door and put his hand on the doorknob. Something flashed in his mind, a déjà vu—the door was locked, he couldn't get it open. What door? The thought made him feel anxious. He twisted the knob and was relieved when it turned freely.

He pulled the door open and peered out. The living space

was small. The kitchen at the back, living room at the front. An old cottage by the look of its beamed ceiling. He heard a clatter in the kitchen. Someone was removing mugs from a cupboard. Three, to be exact. Their face hidden behind the cabinet door. A hand closed the cupboard and turned around. It was George. He noticed Hardy right away.

"So, you survived it. Come on. You'll need this." George turned to grab a coffee pot from its brewer. He started filling two of the mugs.

Hardy didn't move. *Survived what*?

"What are you waiting for, an invitation?"

Hardy dragged himself over to the counter and pulled out a stool. He sat, and George pushed a mug toward him. Hardy absently took the mug into his hands and stared at the black liquid. George raised his mug and slurped.

"What happened? Why am I here?" Hardy asked.

"You don't remember?"

Hardy shook his head.

"You should drink. You're probably dehydrated."

Hardy glared at the steaming cup. The smell was like stale cigarettes. He felt nausea rising from his stomach into his throat.

George gestured toward the mug with his head. "Go ahead. Drink up."

Hardy lifted the mug to his lips and held his breath. He took a swallow and immediately began coughing. "Man...that's...awful." The bitter taste made his stomach churn. He wondered where the bathroom was.

George smiled. "That right there will set you straight."

Hardy set the mug down, shaking his head. "No,

thanks." He pushed the mug out of smelling distance. "Are you going to tell me what happened, or are you just trying to kill me with your lousy coffee?"

"You'll probably get a better idea from her." George pointed to somewhere behind Hardy.

Hardy turned and looked into the living room. A thread-bare, white blanket covered a small lump on the couch. Darcy's blonde braid hung off the side. "Darcy?" he said quietly.

"Brought you here yesterday with another friend of yours."

Hardy watched the blanket rise and fall in rhythm with her gentle breathing. He strained to remember. There was nothing.

"What other friend?"

"Weird name—Crockett, or something like that."

"Cricket."

"That would be it, yes."

Hardy turned back to George. "Where is he?"

"He left. Said he had to go home—cover for you. He's supposed to come back this morning, bring you clothes. If you made it through the night. You're very lucky."

Hardy knew he should be more anxious, concerned. But since he couldn't remember anything, he felt nothing but a weary awkwardness that came from standing bare-chested in George's kitchen.

Hardy's stomach growled. He absently rubbed a hand across his bare stomach, trying to remember the last time he ate. He was famished, but the idea of food made him feel nauseous.

"Listen, George. I haven't had a chance to thank you

for…you know… helping me out of a jam the other night."

"Think nothing of it. Though I think it would be wise for you to stop snooping."

Hardy instinctively searched the room for a police scanner, but didn't see one. "Where's the police scanner?" he asked suspiciously. That's how Hardy was becoming now, suspicious. Just like everyone else on the island.

George pursed his lips. "I might have made that part up."

"Might have, or did?" Hardy felt a twinge of the mistrust he had felt with George after the Hill Home fiasco. With no police scanner, how could George have known that the police had come to Hardy's house? Better yet, how did he know that Charity was his prom date?

George headed back to the coffee pot to top off his mug. "I've been keeping tabs on you." He turned and leaned up against the kitchen sink. "It's not what you think," he said, holding up a hand. "I was worried."

"Worried?" Hardy asked. Finding it hard to believe that George would worry about anybody.

"After what happened to Olen, I thought I should keep an eye on you."

"So you've been spying on me," Hardy said, indignantly.

"Spying is such a strong word."

"Cut the crap, George. I'm not up for one of your games." And he wasn't. A slow throb had started at the base of his neck, and all he really wanted to do was crawl back into bed and pull the covers over his head.

"Calm your shorts. I only asked one of my police buddies to keep an eye out. When he heard your name come up at the station, he gave me a buzz."

"And Charity?"

"Right," George said. "One of the guys in the Romeo Club works a security detail at the Governor's office in Greystone."

Hardy studied George's face. It seemed truthful enough. Still… He wondered if he could trust him.

"I want you to call off your dogs," Hardy said.

"Fine. Message received."

George took a glass out of one of his cabinets, filled it with water from the sink, and handed it to Hardy. "Here. This might sit with you a bit better."

Hardy turned to check on Darcy. She hadn't moved an inch.

An awkward silence settled between them. Hardy sipped his water. He decided to ask George about the picture hanging on his bedroom wall.

"Um…that…um picture in your room…"

"Recognized Olen, did you? The four musketeers. That's what we called ourselves—our little group," George explained.

"The four musketeers?"

"Yes. We were all part of The Program. The lovely lady in the picture is your grandmother, Sarah. She died shortly after she gave birth to Tom. Olen was crushed, of course." George slurped coffee loudly from his mug.

Wow, Hardy's grandmother was a doctor, too. "What about the other man?"

"Ah, Dr. Finch. The dark horse."

Hardy held up a hand. "Wait. Cain Finch?"

"That would be him."

"But he works at Town Square."

George raised an eyebrow. "So you know him?"

"Well, no. Not exactly."

"Finch lost his license to practice. It was an ugly little affair, I'm afraid."

"What did he do?" Hardy asked, trying to imagine the distinguished Dr. Finch doing anything wrong.

"Finch used our dandelion research on a patient—it was your grandmother, Sarah. All the medical board knew was that a patient died in his care under mysterious circumstances. That was enough to charge him with gross negligence."

Hardy rubbed the back of his neck. Maybe that was why Olen had fled to the woods and left his life behind. "I don't understand. Why would Finch do something like that?"

George shrugged. "Finch is the only one that knows for sure."

George was staring off into space now, like he had traveled all the way to the past and was having a hard time finding his way back.

Darcy stirred on the couch. Hardy left George in his daydream and walked quietly to Darcy's side. He stared down at her angelic face.

"She stayed up all night with you." George took a long slurp of his coffee. "She was determined to get your fever down. Didn't leave your bedside until the fever broke around 4 a.m."

Darcy's hands clutched the blanket under her chin. She looked so peaceful. Something stirred inside Hardy. What was it? It was something. If only he could remember…

279

Darcy's eyes opened. When she saw Hardy, she threw the blanket off and jumped up, wrapping her arms around his neck. She was still wearing her work scrubs.

"Thank, God." She pulled back and felt his forehead with her hand. "No fever." She grabbed his face. Hardy knew what she was going to do. She wanted to scan his eyes. He gently grabbed her wrists. "I'm fine, Darcy."

Darcy's grip on his face tightened. "Humor me, please."

Hardy dropped his hands and looked into her eyes. She hesitated. They were looking at each other now. There it was again—something. His stomach lurched like he was plummeting on a roller coaster.

Darcy blinked and refocused on his eyes, scanning with her blue eye. She quickly let go of his face and took a step back. "I'm glad you're okay."

"I hate to disturb you two lovebirds, but you're both likely in one big heap of trouble," George said.

Darcy's face flushed, and Hardy wondered why.

"What is he talking about?" Hardy asked.

"You don't remember anything?"

"No."

"Nothing?" Darcy said, looking disappointed.

Hardy shook his head.

"Mama is dead," Darcy said sadly.

"Your mother?"

"No. Nurse Troxler."

"What? How?" Hardy asked.

"You better sit down and let me explain."

Hardy felt a shiver spread across his body and realized he was standing there shirtless. "George, do you have a shirt

I can borrow?"

"I'll see if I've got something." George left for the bedroom.

"Darcy, I'm sorry."

"For what?" she asked, her eyes questioning.

"I don't know. I feel like I've done something wrong."

She reached out and slipped her hand into his. "You didn't. You tried to save Mama."

"I did?" Hardy searched her face for the truth. Instead he saw...?

"Sorry, my painting shirt is all I have clean." George handed Hardy a denim shirt covered in splotches of multiple paint colors.

Hardy quickly shoved his arms into the shirt and buttoned it up. His arms stuck out below the sleeve.

The sound of an approaching vehicle sent George quickly to the door. He picked up his shotgun that was propped up against the wall and eased the door open.

Hardy felt himself stiffen. *Why should he be afraid?*

A car door slammed. Pebbles crunched beneath feet.

"It's your buddy." George propped the gun back up against the wall.

"Did he...Is he?" Cricket's voice asked from outside the door.

"He's fine," George said.

Cricket stepped through the door. He was holding a plastic grocery bag. Whatever concern Hardy had heard in Cricket's voice quickly evaporated into a scowl when he saw Hardy.

"You sure know how to scare a person, you jerk." Cricket

pushed the bag into Hardy's chest. "I brought you some clothes. The splatter look went out in the 80s," he said, eyeing Hardy's shirt.

"Thanks."

"Look, I covered for you with your parents. I said we were having a sleepover for old times' sake. Senior year and everything."

"Did they buy it?" Hardy asked.

"Duh, yeah."

"Thanks. I owe you one."

"Yeah, whatever," Cricket said, his eyes shooting daggers at Darcy.

"Darcy was about to explain what happened yesterday," Hardy said.

Cricket didn't say a word. He planted himself in a worn chair with a flat cushion next to the couch. Hardy sat on the couch with Darcy, and George sat in an old rocking chair. Darcy explained everything. The overheard conversation of Trevor's. Finding Mama in a locked room. And what she only saw and heard in pieces. A black box. An argument. A struggle. Hardy on the floor. All of it ending with her dragging Hardy to Cricket's car, sweaty and delirious.

When Darcy finished, she was almost in tears. They all sat quietly for a few minutes. Hardy leaned his head back against the couch, struggling to remember, fighting the drumbeat that was sounding off inside his temples. It all seemed vaguely familiar, like he could see the edges of it, but not the whole picture.

"This is all your fault, Darcy," Cricket said sharply, breaking the silence.

Darcy stood and wrapped her arms around her thin body.

"Cricket...don't," Hardy warned. "Everything happened because of me, not her."

Cricket flew out of his seat and moved toward Darcy, spreading out his arms. "What? Am I wrong, Darcy? Didn't all this start when you worked up some idea in his head that his grandfather was murdered? Hardy could have died!"

Darcy's hands flew to her mouth. Her brown eye was filling with tears.

Hardy put himself between Cricket and Darcy and put a hand on Cricket's shoulder. "Stop."

Cricket pushed his hand away. "No. I won't stop. I blame her, and there's nothing you can say to change my mind!"

"Darcy, don't listen to him," Hardy said, reaching out to her.

Darcy ran past him and out the front door.

Hardy chased after her. "Darcy!" She headed straight into the woods like a scared rabbit. "Darcy! Stop!"

Hardy tried to run, follow her into the woods, but quickly realized he could barely hold himself up. He stopped and placed a hand on a tree to steady himself. His breaths were coming short and fast. Darcy disappeared into the trees. He gritted his teeth and slammed his hand into the rough bark. She was gone.

He sank to the ground and leaned against the tree. He looked up through the treetops—the leaves swayed with the wind. *There's wisdom in trees.* Hardy heard Olen's voice as if the wind carried it to him. He stuck his head into his hands. His life was falling apart bit by bit, and he had no idea what to do. Darcy had made him believe they should do something—*could do something*. So what if he tried to save Mama? Mama was dead. Mrs. Gobble was dead. Olen was dead.

"Moping isn't going to get you anywhere."

Hardy looked up. George was standing over him, hands in his pockets.

"Leave me alone, George," he said, resting his head against the tree trunk.

"Listen. I feel partially responsible," George said.

"How's that?"

"I told you about The DIE Program. It probably got you worked up to do something about it." George held out a hand to Hardy. Hardy stared at it before he grasped it. George pulled him from the ground.

"It doesn't matter. We've got nothing," Hardy said.

"What if you did...have something?"

"Do you know something I don't?"

"No. But Olen might."

Hardy sighed and walked back toward the cottage. "In case you forgot, Olen's dead."

"Olen was a smart man. What if he left you a clue?" George asked.

"He didn't." Hardy thought of the ransacked cabin Darcy and Tate had found. "Unless of course you think someone ripping his cabin apart is a clue."

George stopped in his tracks. "By George—no pun intended. It very well could be a clue."

Hardy raised and dropped his arms. "I don't see how."

George moved closer. "I think it's pretty clear. The Program was there looking for something."

Hardy scratched the scar on the back of his head. "Like what?"

George moved a hand across his mouth. "I don't know, but whatever it was, it must be important."

"Well, if they found what they were looking for, that does nothing to help us," Hardy said, defeated.

"What if they didn't find it?"

"What if they did?" Hardy asked, losing patience.

Hardy wasn't in the mood for going down George's rabbit hole. He just wanted to go home and crawl into bed.

"Something to think about," George said, walking away from Hardy.

"Yeah." But the only thing Hardy could think about was the look on Darcy's face right before she ran out of the house. His chest ached. How much longer was he going to be able to keep this house of cards standing? Maybe it was already falling.

Chapter Twenty-six

It took Darcy two hours to find her way home after running into the woods. Partly because she first came out into a field of windmills, one of many spread across the island. When she saw the spinning blades, she knew she wouldn't be able to cross through them. She had tried more than once to conquer her fear. She knew it was irrational. The blades couldn't harm her, they were too high in the air. That's what always made her try. She knew it made no sense to be afraid. She would make it halfway across a field before she would start breathing too fast—right before the panic and fear set in. Then it was too late. Her vision would blur in her real eye, while the other stayed perfectly stable—the world tilting. She would run, falling, tripping over the smallest lump in the ground. Finally, blind in her own eye, she would run like she was looking through a camera lens. Space perception and distance warping and changing with every step. Once, she felt she might not make it out and the windmills would bend down to her and swallow her—take her the way the plane's propellers had taken her father.

No, there would be no trying to make it across this field. Not today, anyway.

Eventually, she found a road she was familiar with. It wasn't long before a widowed, elderly neighbor, Mr. Barrow, returning from the North Island, spied her and picked her up. She fell asleep almost immediately, her head falling against the vibrating window. She felt like someone was driving her through a dream until Mr. Barrow shook her awake.

Darcy rubbed her eyes and blinked. It took her a minute to realize where she was. She looked over at Mr. Barrow. "Thanks for the ride." She grabbed the door handle. A hand touched her arm.

"Are you okay, Darcy?" He asked.

Darcy smiled weakly. "I'm fine."

Mr. Barrow nodded and smiled.

She would go home. Sleep. At least for a little while, she would try to forget. Forget that Mama had died, that Hardy had kissed her and didn't remember, that Cricket blamed her for everything that had happened. When she slept, she was invisible.

She stood outside her door staring at the empty flower box. She promised herself right then that she would plant flowers for her father. The purple, trailing petunias, the ones they had always planned to plant together.

She pushed the door open hoping Nash wouldn't be there. Danny was laid out on the couch watching something involving loud crashes and screams. He sat up when she closed the door.

"Be careful," he said quietly, moving his eyes toward the kitchen.

Darcy listened over the blood-curdling screams on the TV. Pots and pans were rattling. Kitchen cabinet doors slamming. Danny tilted a fake bottle to his mouth.

She nodded and mouthed, "Mom?" It was only noon, and Nash was already drunk.

Danny shook his head.

This was the worst-case scenario. A drunk Nash, with no Mom. When she was around, Nash stayed away from Darcy. When she wasn't… Darcy rubbed her arms and walked quietly back toward the hall to the bedrooms. If she was quiet, she could slip past the kitchen and down the hall without him seeing her.

She could hear him cursing under his breath. A pot slammed on the counter, and she jumped. She tiptoed past the kitchen and tripped on a pair of boots someone had left in the hallway. She fell to the floor on her hands and knees and froze. *Please. Please.* She pushed herself up slowly and sat back on her heels. There was silence in the kitchen.

"Where have you been?" Nash asked from behind her.

Darcy's heart dropped. She stood and turned around. Nash was staring at her, spatula in hand. His eyes were small and red.

"I stayed the night with a friend." She turned to go to the bedroom.

"Hold it right there."

Darcy swallowed.

"Who with? You ain't got no friends."

He was right, she didn't have any friends. She frantically searched her mind for an answer.

"I have a new friend," she said.

"And who might that be?"

"Charity."

Nash tapped the spatula in the air and narrowed his eyes. "Charity who?"

"Hill."

The spatula stopped moving in mid-air. "Ain't that the Governor's daughter?"

"Yes."

Nash pointed the spatula at her. "You must think I'm one dumb idiot if you expect me to believe that you spent the night at the Governor's mansion. Besides, it's not Halloween and you're wearing a nurse's uniform."

Darcy took a deep breath. "Believe what you want." She didn't care anymore. She needed to sleep.

She took two steps when Nash grabbed her and pushed her against the wall with one hand. The smell of burnt bacon drifted from the kitchen.

"You're a liar," he breathed into her face.

Darcy grabbed his arm with both of her hands and tried to push it off. "Your bacon is burning. Let me go before you burn the house down."

Nash grinned. He grabbed her braid and pulled her behind him to the kitchen.

"Let me go, Nash!" Darcy screamed.

Nash dragged her into the kitchen and pushed her out of the way while he grabbed the smoking, cast-iron pan.

"Dad-blast!" Nash yelled out after grabbing the hot pan

without a mitt. Danny appeared in the kitchen doorway. Nash quickly grabbed a dish towel, pulled the smoking pan off the burner, and dropped it into the sink. The sound of breaking glass echoed through the kitchen. Nash turned fire-red and breathed heavily through his nose. He came toward Darcy. She backed into the kitchen table and looked at Danny.

"Nash," Danny said.

Nash spun around and pointed at Danny. "SHUT UP! GET OUT NOW, OR YOU'RE NEXT!"

Danny hesitated. He seemed afraid—he should be. He turned and left. What else could he do? One thing about Nash Atkins: he was good on his word.

For the second time in her life, Darcy prayed she would die.

***

It was late Saturday afternoon before Hardy managed to pull himself out of bed. The sun had finally forced its way through a crack in his curtains and was now shining in his face—a kind of forced resurrection.

He made his way down the ladder and into the kitchen where he was met with the smell of peanut butter and chocolate. His stomach growled in response.

His mother was bent over, pulling a cookie sheet from the oven. She smiled when she noticed him. "Hey, you." She set the silver sheet on top of the stove burners and pulled off her oven mitt.

Hardy moved toward the warm brown circles and

stretched out his hand. Anna slapped his hand and he jerked it back. "They're too hot. Not yet."

"I'm starving."

"I'm sure you are. It's three o'clock."

"It is?"

"I can make you a sandwich."

"Fine." Hardy dropped himself at the kitchen table. "Where's Dad?"

"Out working in the yard."

Good. Avoidance was Hardy's friend.

Anna headed for the refrigerator and piled her arms with Bologna, cheese, pickles, and a jar of mayonnaise.

"Sounds like I've missed a few things," she said, dumping the load on the counter.

"Not really," Hardy said dryly.

Anna removed a loaf of fresh bread from the bread drawer. She turned to face Hardy, putting a hand on her hip. She tapped a finger on her cheek and looked up. "Let's see, a visit from the police, and… I don't know…Charity Hill as a prom date." She raised an eyebrow and stared at Hardy.

"Oh yeah, that." The truth seemed distant somehow, like it was someone else she was talking about.

Anna chuckled. "Yeah, that." She pulled the bread from its paper bag and pulled a knife from the knife block.

"We're just friends. No big deal."

"Uh-huh." She dragged the knife through the crusty exterior. "I would have thought you'd be more excited seeing that you've had a crush on her since second grade."

I would be, but Mama died, and Darcy… "Sure, I'm excited, just not quite awake yet."

291

Hardy watched her layer the Bologna and pickles and finish the sandwich off with a large helping of mayonnaise. "Here you go, your favorite," she said, topping it off with the final piece of bread.

"Thanks, Mom."

She set the sandwich down in front of him and ruffled his hair.

Hardy crammed the sandwich into his mouth. Sour pickle juice ran into his beard. Anna sat down across from him in what was usually his father's chair and rested her chin in her hand. He glanced at her over his sandwich. "Mo…" He swallowed. "Mom. I'm not going to talk about Charity if that's what you're waiting for."

She handed him a napkin. "Can't a mother talk to her son? I haven't seen you in two days."

He took the napkin, rubbed it across his beard, and dropped it onto the table. "Honestly, I thought you'd be more interested in the whole police thing." He dug his teeth into another bite and chewed slowly.

"That was some kind of mix-up. Why would I care about that?"

Hardy swallowed and dug a hunk of bread out of his back teeth with his tongue. "Dad sure did. He didn't believe me. He was ready to pack me up and send me off to juvie without as much as a 'Hold on there, partner'." He embellished the last line with his best cowboy impersonation, watching her face as he bit into his sandwich.

She frowned slightly—probably trying to figure out how to excuse his dad's behavior, just like she always did.

"What do you expect, Hardy? You come home late. You

don't explain your whereabouts. Someone ID's you. I imagine I would have made the same assumptions."

No you wouldn't have, Hardy said with his eyes.

"Your father loves you."

So you keep telling me. Actions speak louder than words, though, Mom. Hardy said what he thought she wanted to hear. "I know."

She smiled and stood up. "How about those cookies? By the way, Cricket called to remind you that you're supposed to meet him in Greystone tonight after he gets off work so you can rent your tuxes."

Hardy stuck the last bite of sandwich into his mouth. *Crap.* He had forgotten all about it. The last thing he wanted to do was ride his bike all the way to Greystone. Yesterday he could barely carry himself a few feet at a time. It was time to put on the charm.

Anna was transferring the cookies to a cooling rack with the spatula. He came up behind her and hugged her. "You know, if you really love me, you would drive me to Greystone."

She continued transporting the cookies two at a time to the gridded rack. "You have a bike. It's my day off. Cricket can give you a ride home."

"Pleaseeee," Hardy said, squeezing her harder. Time to drop the death nail. "Don't you want me to go to the prom? I can't be all sweaty and try on a tux."

"Oh, okay," she relented.

He reached a hand out toward the moving spatula. He managed to snatch both cookies from it and make a mad dash out of the kitchen.

"Hey, you," she said, swatting after him with the empty spatula.

"Thanks, Mom. You're the best. I'm just going to catch a quick shower."

Before he made it halfway to the bathroom he heard, "and a shave!"

***

Cricket worked in Greystone at Briley's pancake house. It was a narrow hole in the wall with nothing but a long counter of stools and a row of small tables against the left wall. It had been branded as "WHERE THE LOCALS EAT" years ago. Open twenty-four hours, Briley's was a big draw in the summer months when people were vacationing and looking for small-town flavor. Hardy was pretty sure that no locals ate there, but even in the slow months the place managed to draw in curious travelers.

Briley's was stuck behind the town hall, so Hardy's mom dropped him off in front of Town Square, right where he had saved Charity.

"Try not to involve yourself in any dangerous rescue attempts while you're down here," Anna said jokingly.

"Very funny." Hardy pushed the door shut and waved as Anna drove away.

He turned around and stared at the square. The outdoor cafés were doing a brisk business which was typical for early Saturday evening. The sky was getting that warm pink glow that came with the sun's descent.

He was prepared to skirt past Viola's statue when he no-

294

ticed Dr. Finch collecting trash in the grassy area around Viola. Hardy stopped in front of the chain link barrier. He hadn't expected to run into Finch, but now that he had, he wondered if this might just be the opportunity he needed to dig a little deeper into Dr. Finch's murderous past with the DIE Program.

"Dr. Finch," Hardy called out.

Finch straightened and turned toward Hardy. He adjusted his glasses and squinted at him. "Yes?"

"It's me, Dr. Finch. Hardy Vance."

Dr. Finch studied Hardy for a few seconds. Recognition spread across his face like one who just realizes a mosquito has landed on his arm.

"Of course. The hero who thinks the Greystone statue is just a fairy tale." Dr. Finch turned and tied a knot into the plastic bag of trash.

"Look, Dr. Finch. I'm sorry. I guess I just never really took the whole legend thing seriously. But I'd be interested to learn more."

Finch climbed over the chain link and headed for the town hall.

Hardy ran to catch up with him. "I'm serious, Dr. Finch. Ever since I worked on cleaning the statue—"

"Viola," Finch said, continuing to pretend that Hardy wasn't there.

"Yes, Viola. Ever since the cleaning, I have become...curious." *Curious about you and the connection to my grandfather, that is.*

"Everyone is curious, Mr. Vance. Come for a tour like everyone else."

"I was hoping to hear more details from you."

Dr. Finch stopped and turned to Hardy with a look of agitated distraction. "What's this really about, Mr. Vance?"

A group of people burst into a fit of laughter several feet away at one of the café tables. A large man at the table of six slapped his hand hard on top of the table. Hardy looked back at Finch who was now frowning.

"I'm going to write a paper." That was a lie, but he needed to appeal to Dr. Finch's fine-tuned intellect. Writing a paper seemed intelligent-sounding enough.

The man was now coughing while the rest of the table continued to wipe the tears of laughter from their eyes. Hardy was getting a weird feeling. Like the square was beginning to tilt.

"A paper?" Finch asked suspiciously.

"Yeah." A sudden wave of heat rushed through Hardy's body. Sweat seeped from his forehead. He couldn't tear his eyes from the man at the table.

The man turned red. His coughing stopped, and he grasped at his chest. Nobody noticed. They were caught up in the moment—they had lost perspective. A small pinprick of light swirled next to the table.

"Mr. Vance? Are you all right?" Finch asked.

Hardy moved toward the light. It was growing, spinning, drawing in the darkness that was settling over the square.

"Mr. Vance!"

Hardy heard Finch call after him, but he couldn't stop. The light turned gray, spinning faster, absorbing darkness, until it became darkness itself. Flashes of memory played in his head. Mama—*should I go, Hardy?*

Hardy ran toward the man who had now tumbled out of his chair onto the cobblestones. "Nooo!" he screamed. The man's friends stopped laughing and looked at each other. Some smiled and stood, staring over the table, wondering if this was part of the act.

The man clutched at his chest and gasped for air. Hardy fell on his knees next to him.

"He needs a doctor!" Hardy screamed.

Hardy felt like he was underwater again. The voices were muffled. He couldn't tell if anyone heard him. They seemed to be in shock as they gathered around the dying man. The swirling light had become swirling darkness and was almost big enough for Hardy to step through.

Arms pushed Hardy aside, and he fell backwards on his hands. Dr. Finch pumped the man's chest up and down like he was pressing a large buzzer. Finch tilted the man's head back, held his nose, and breathed into his mouth.

Hardy could see the bridge building itself one slate at a time into the swirling darkness. Storm clouds churned beyond the bridge building upon themselves, growing. There was no light this time, only darkness.

Finch's hands continued to pump the man's chest. The man's spirit rose from his body and stood staring down at the stranger working on him, his eyes wide with fear. He looked at Hardy, pleading with his eyes. *Don't let me die.*

The bridge was complete now. Something in Hardy's memory clicked into place. He remembered everything that happened in Mama's room. Not as a flashback, but all at once, like a revelation. He looked for the man on the bridge—the overwhelming feeling of love. But there was no man, the bridge was empty.

A black liquid crept across the bridge toward Hardy, pushing between each plank until it enveloped each one and absorbed it into its black abyss. He felt what the man felt…fear. Fear beyond anything he had ever felt before. His heart strained against his chest like gravity had come to claim it. His lifeblood was being pulled from him—from the man. The dying man's face turned to terror as he realized what was happening.

"Save him! Save him!" Hardy pleaded. People in the crowd were staring at Hardy, pointing, whispering. He didn't care.

He stood inches from the white, lifeless version of the dying man. There was nothing he could do.

Finch sat back on his heels. He had given up. Hardy grabbed Finch's shoulder. "One more time…Please." The man's shocked friends looked from Hardy to Finch with a fearful hope. Finch nodded and pressed his hands once again into the man's chest. The sound of sirens filled the air. Hardy staggered backwards through the crowd. A bright light swallowed the darkness. He fell to the ground.

Chapter Twenty-seven

"Here, drink this."

Hardy took the glass from Finch and stared at the clear contents.

"I called your friend like you asked. He said he'll be right over as soon as he finishes his shift," Finch said.

"Thanks." Hardy took a long swallow of water, trying to figure out what had just happened. But the truth was becoming all too clear. He could see people die. A gentle throb began in his temples. What did it mean? Was it permanent? He felt completely drained.

Finch sat down next to Hardy at the large table that sat at the back of Finch's office: the same place where he and Darcy had read about the island's past, about Viola's curse. Now Hardy was sitting face-to-face with a man who was possibly knee-deep in it all.

Finch's face was expressionless, as if he was waiting for Hardy to speak. Hardy continued to lose himself inside his glass of water.

"The man is going to be okay. He's at the hospital now, in case you're interested," Finch said.

Hardy set down the empty glass and nodded. He didn't want to talk about it. He was scared. This time had been different—very different. It had been dark, dangerous. Maybe he had hallucinated. Maybe none of it was real. People go crazy sometimes—it happens.

"You want to talk about what happened out there?" Finch asked.

Hardy turned the glass in circles with his fingers and glared at Finch. "No."

"No, I suppose you wouldn't. After all, you have something to hide, don't you?"

Anxious and afraid, Hardy immediately turned the tables. "No. But you most certainly do. You killed my grandmother," he snapped. He hadn't meant to come right out with it, but his head was still spinning from what had just happened with the man in the square, and he wasn't thinking clearly.

Finch reddened with what was clearly shock. But, being the composed scholar that he was, he quickly recovered and removed himself from the table. He returned to his desk and poured himself a glass of water from a glass carafe.

"I'm curious, Mr. Vance. How did you happen to come across this information?" Finch turned and stared at Hardy over his glass of water.

"An old friend of yours."

Finch set his glass of water down on the desk. "You shouldn't involve yourself in something that could become quite dangerous for you," he said stiffly.

"Is that a threat?" Hardy said fiercely.

Finch returned and rested the fingertips of his right hand on the table next to Hardy. "On the contrary, it's a warning. One that you should pay attention to."

Cricket came bursting through the office door, out of breath. Hardy breathed a sigh of relief. He was sure now that Finch was involved in resurrecting the DIE Program. The only thing that he couldn't reconcile was why a murderer like Finch would work so hard to save the man in Town Square.

"So. Do you want to talk about it?" Cricket asked. "I heard you saved some guy's life at the outdoor café. What's up with you and Town Square? Maybe they'll start calling you the Town Square hero."

They were walking through the square now, heading down the hill to the waterfront where the tux rental place was. The grayness of night had settled in, and the street lamps were lit up.

"This is serious, Cricket. Something happened out there, and frankly, I'm kinda freaking out about it."

"What happened?"

"I was talking to Finch by the statue when my eye kept being drawn to this group of people eating at one of the café tables."

"And?"

"And that whole weird thing that happened in Mama's— Nurse Troxler's—room started happening again. The guy grabbed his chest and fell to the ground. The whole town square started spinning. I could see him dying... *Feel* him dying. It's hard to explain."

"Maybe it's an after-effect from being exposed to the dandelion toxin," Cricket said.

"It doesn't feel like that, though. It feels like I possess it somehow. Like it's a part of me." Hardy didn't know how to explain it.

"Like a sixth sense," Cricket suggested.

"Yeah. Exactly like that."

Cricket laughed. "Welcome to my world."

"What? You think I'm like you now?" Hardy asked.

"Well, not exactly like me. But yeah."

"But I wasn't born with this like you were."

"Remember the story you told me about the cattle?" Cricket asked. "Some of the cattle died, but some got stronger after eating the dandelions. Maybe you always had the gift, but it was buried or it was too small for you to notice. But now that you've been exposed...you got stronger."

Hardy hadn't even considered the possibility that this was something he had always had. It's not like he had ever been around dying people before. But right before he found Olen dead, hadn't he felt his skin crawl? He remembered thinking the feeling was strange. And there was the flickering vision when Cricket's dog had died, and with the squirrel at Olen's cabin.

"It feels like a curse," Hardy said.

"Well then, I'm cursed, too." Cricket stopped and placed a hand on Hardy's shoulder. "It's not so bad. You saved the guy's life, after all. Everyone else wanted to give up." Cricket dropped his hand.

"The thing is… I felt myself dying…when…you know, I was standing next to the guy. There was something dark coming for him, and it wanted me, too."

Cricket rubbed the back of his neck. "Okay, you're right. That's creepy. Just make sure you never follow the dead."

Hardy smiled. "Yeah." But he remembered Mama and how he wanted to go with her.

"Hey, what was up with that Finch dude? Things looked kind of intense when I came in," Cricket asked.

Hardy told him about Finch's connection to Olen and the DIE Program.

"Whoa. You think he's the one behind all this?" Cricket asked.

"It's starting to look that way."

***

An hour later, the black tuxes had been fitted and rented for next Friday's prom. Hardy's tux was black with a lilac vest and tie. Cricket's, black with gray vest and bow tie. Any excitement that Hardy had had over his date with Charity had vanished over the past few days. He felt like he was just going through the motions.

Outside, dark clouds had rolled in. The smell of rain was in the air. The sky had completely darkened, even though sunset was still an hour away. The wind had picked up and thunder rumbled in the distance. It was clear that a big storm was moving in, so they took off in a slow run, trying to make it back to the truck before the sky let loose.

Giant drops blackened the cobblestone sidewalks. One landed in Hardy's hair, wetting the whole top of his head. He could smell the salt-tinged air coming off the ocean. The wind whipped between the buildings. They ran through Town Square: waiters and waitresses were frantically trying to close café umbrellas and clean tables before the storm hit. All the tables that had been full of customers earlier were now empty. Loose trash swirled and slammed against shop windows.

They sprinted around the corner that led to Briley's back alley. They had barely made it inside the truck when the sky released its fury. Buckets of rain pounded against the windows. They sat in the loud cocoon trying to catch their breath.

Hardy rubbed the fat drops of water out of the top of his head.

"Talk about perfect timing. Ten more seconds and we'd have been toast," Cricket said between exhales.

They tried to wait out the storm, but when it showed no signs of stopping, they headed for home.

From inside the car, it looked like it was raining sideways. Cricket's wipers swiped full blast. Water slung from the windshield only long enough to show the road for a few seconds before the water completely enveloped it again. Cricket was leaning over the steering wheel and concentrating on the few feet of visibility that he had. They rode without talking. Storms had a way of doing that to you.

The past few days had been more than what Hardy felt like he could handle. What did a normal day even feel like? He wondered if Darcy was okay. He hadn't even checked to make sure she had made it home after she had run off into the woods at George's house. She had taken care of him all night. He wondered what kind of friend he was to Darcy. He wasn't a friend. That was the truth. He treated her the way he treated everything that wasn't part of his plans—as an inconvenience. Something to be dealt with, but nothing important enough to care about. But he did care. Yet he didn't understand why he did. And he definitely wasn't acting like he did.

Hardy stared at the road in front of them, concentrating on the white lines. The lines seemed to be the only thing that existed outside the truck. Then he saw something. Or thought he saw something in the middle of the road. He only caught a glimpse of it through the slicing of the wipers. It seemed to be moving. As they got closer, the ghostly apparition appeared right in the middle of the road—a small, thin body in a white dress, hair matted with rain—black, wet eyes staring out of skull-like sockets.

"WATCH OUT!" Hardy screamed.

Cricket swerved and ran off the road, barely missing the eerie, pale figure. He slammed on the brakes. The truck fishtailed in the wet, grassy bank and did a one-eighty, jerking to a stop. They were now facing the direction they had just come from.

"Holy crap," Cricket said, throwing the truck into park. He dropped his shaking hands from the steering wheel. "What was that?"

"I don't know," Hardy said, craning his neck to look out the back window. He couldn't see anything through the blinding rain and blackness. "I think someone was in the middle of the road."

"Or something," Cricket said, sounding spooked.

"We should see if they're okay."

Cricket looked at Hardy through the green glow of the truck's console lights like he was crazy. "You expect me to go out there and find out if some creepy whack job is okay?"

Hardy did what he always did when he got nervous—bit his nails. "We can't just drive away."

"I beg to differ."

"I think it was a girl. Maybe she needs help," Hardy said.

"Or maybe Viola is haunting the island looking for two good-looking guys to kill with an ax."

"You watch too many horror movies. Besides, whoever it was wasn't carrying an ax."

"Fine. I'll wait in the car. I'm not going out there," Cricket said.

Hardy sighed. Was he really going to do this? Take another risk that would inevitably lead to more trouble? Still, he couldn't leave knowing someone was out there in the storm, alone, walking in the middle of the road.

"Can you at least turn the truck back around so I can see?" Hardy asked, looking out the back window of the truck.

"You're really going to do this?"

Hardy didn't answer. He didn't *want* to do it. But he was starting to realize that sometimes a person needed to step up regardless of how he felt.

Cricket grunted and shifted the truck into drive. He turned the wheel left and slowly pulled the truck back out onto the dark road. They sat there for a minute with the headlights blaring straight ahead, the wipers thumping. The rain cut through the lights of the truck like butter.

"I don't see anyone, do you?" Cricket said nervously.

"Not yet. Drive slowly."

"Okay, but I swear if a man-eating zombie throws itself on the hood of my truck, I'm throwing you out the door, and I'm out of here."

Hardy placed a hand on the dashboard and leaned forward, straining to see through the curtains of rain. At least now the wind had let up, and the rain was falling in straight lines instead of sideways. "Just drive."

"Just sayin'," Cricket said.

"Yes, okay. Feed me to the zombie."

Cricket inched forward. Secretly Hardy hoped the person had left the road for safer ground. He wasn't in the hero mood.

"I don't see anything," Cricket said.

"Keep driving."

As the truck's lights pushed through the darkness, nothing appeared except white lines and black, wet pavement.

"Coast is clear," Cricket said.

Hardy knew he didn't imagine the wet figure. It had to be there somewhere. There—something, an outline. A person's back. It looked like a young girl by the small build. She was walking slowly, stumbling in the middle of the road. Her long, wet hair was plastered to her back.

"I'm freaking out," Cricket said loudly.

"Get closer." Something about her seemed familiar, but Hardy couldn't quite put his finger on it.

"Okay, but I'm not getting out of the truck under any circumstances."

They got within ten feet of the girl when she stopped, turned into the truck's lights, and collapsed into a heap on the road.

Cricket slammed on the brakes. Hardy threw the door open and ran toward the lifeless body. The rain soaked through his clothes within seconds. He fell on his knees next to the body. The girl's back was to him, the pink soles of the feet bare. He had a sinking feeling, like he was going to be sick. He gently turned the frail frame toward him. The right side of her pale face had a red gash from the edge of her eye, down across her cheek. Her lips were blue. He immediately recognized the white face. *No. Oh, no.*

"Who is it?!" Cricket screamed through the rain, leaning over the door of the truck.

"It's Darcy!" Hardy stared down at the white, wet lashes. His head filled with anguish. A sense of overwhelming hopelessness engulfed him. He couldn't tell if tears or rain were pouring down his face.

Chapter Twenty-eight

Hardy lifted Darcy from the road and ran to the truck. She felt like a small child in his arms. He slid into the passenger seat and pulled the door shut.

"What the heck happened to her?" Cricket asked, noticing the gash across her face.

"Do you have a blanket or something?" Hardy asked, cradling her head in his arms.

Darcy's skin was so white he had to wonder if any blood was running through her veins. The only indication of life was her warm breath on his fingers as he pulled the wet hair from her face.

Cricket jumped out and fumbled through his storage locker in the back of the truck. He returned with a gray hoodie.

"Sorry, this is all I got."

Hardy took the hoodie and covered Darcy.

"What do we do now?" Cricket asked.

Hardy went numb. He knew who had done this. *Nash.*

"Should we take her home?" Cricket asked.

"No," Hardy snapped. *Not to that monster. Not ever again.* "Let's take her to Tate and Vivia's. They don't live far from here."

"Doesn't she need a doctor or something?" Cricket asked.

"Vivia will know what to do. Just go, okay?"

"Okay. Yeah."

The rain had changed to a steady drizzle. They rode in silence listening to the thump of the wipers—a morbid sound that reminded Hardy of the thud of dirt being thrown into a grave. Darcy shook in small quivers. He let his hand rest on her face, hoping to bring some warmth back to her cold skin.

I'm so sorry. The same three words ran over and over again in his head. What kind of person hits someone like Darcy? He couldn't help feeling like this was somehow his fault. She had been walking barefoot in the middle of a storm in just a thin, white dress. His heart filled with anguish.

Cricket pulled in front of Tate and Vivia's cottage. Lights were visible through the front windows.

"Go tell them we're here. I'll bring Darcy," Hardy said.

When Cricket knocked, the outside light came on. Hardy watched Vivia listen to Cricket and stare out at the truck. She disappeared briefly and came out with a large umbrella. She opened Hardy's door and looked down at Darcy's lifeless figure.

"What happened?" Vivia asked, looking horrified.

"I don't know," Hardy said. But he did know.

"Bring her in. Come on," Vivia said.

"Thanks, Vivia."

She nodded and held the umbrella over the truck's passenger door while Hardy pulled Darcy's body back into his arms. Vivia walked beside him, protecting him and Darcy from the rain. Like it mattered now: they were soaked through.

Vivia followed them into the cottage. Cricket took the umbrella from her and set it by the door.

"Take her into our bedroom and lay her on the bed," Vivia instructed.

Hardy could feel the frustration building inside him. *Why is this happening? Why is this happening to her?*

Hardy laid Darcy's limp body on Tate and Vivia's floral bedspread. He didn't want to let her go for fear of losing her forever. He stood like a statue at the edge of the bed, looking down at her battered face. The mark across her face was dark red and puffy. Vivia ran around the room gathering who knew what. She disappeared into the bathroom. The sound of water falling into an empty tub soon followed.

Darcy murmured incoherently and began moving her arms and legs. Hardy sat down next to her on the bed and grabbed her restless hands. "Darcy, it's okay."

She suddenly gripped his hands so tight, he instinctively tried to pull them away. Her eyes flew open and darted back and forth like a trapped animal. She clawed at his hands like she was drowning.

"Darcy. Look at me. It's Hardy." He tried to pry his hands out of her death grip.

Her eyes finally connected with his, and her grip loosened. "Hardy Vance," she whispered.

He tried to smile. "Yeah. Hardy Vance."

She shot straight up and pulled at his wet shirt. Her eyes widened. "Nash," she said, panicked.

He rubbed her arms. "It's okay."

Darcy pushed herself to the edge of the bed. "I have to get out of here. He'll come back."

Hardy tried to keep her in the bed, but she was frantic and pulled from his grasp.

Vivia emerged from the bathroom.

"I have to get out of here," Darcy repeated, burying her hands into her wet hair.

Vivia took over immediately. She pushed Hardy back and grabbed Darcy by the shoulders. "Darcy, I'm Vivia. You're safe now."

"I'm safe?" she asked, confused.

Vivia nodded. "Yes. You're safe."

Darcy threw her arms around Vivia. Vivia held her, stroking the back of her wet head.

"Hardy. Wait out in the kitchen. Boil some water for tea," Vivia said.

Hardy backed out of the room and closed the door.

***

Darcy eased herself down into the warm water and let it cover her like a blanket. She leaned back against the cast-iron tub, careful not to put pressure on the bruise on her back.

She closed her eyes and let the lilac-scented water drift into her senses. *This is what it feels like to be safe.* She let Vivia lift her arms and legs and washed them with a hand so tender, Darcy wondered how such a person existed in the world without being crushed by it.

"Sit up now, Darcy," Vivia said.

Darcy slowly lifted her body up from the water, her eyes still closed. She wanted to remember what it felt like to have someone care for her in this way. She didn't want the computer part of her telling her how deep the water was, or Vivia's life history. She wanted to feel without her eye telling her facts she didn't care about right now.

Darcy felt Vivia hesitate when she came to the tender spot on Darcy's back—the place where she had fallen back against the kitchen counter after Nash had hit her across the face. Vivia slowly but gently covered the bruise with the soapy washcloth.

"Do you want to talk about it?" Vivia asked.

"I don't know. I never have before."

"You're safe now. No one will hurt you here," Vivia said, gently rinsing Darcy's back with warm water.

There was that word again—*safe*. Darcy realized that she did feel safe. Maybe for the first time in a long time. "He didn't used to be like that."

"Your father?"

"No. My older brother, Nash."

Vivia squeezed shampoo into her hand and worked it through Darcy's hair with her fingers.

"What changed?" Vivia asked.

"Nash had a good job with the Greene Island energy company. He mouthed off one too many times and was late more than they cared for. He got fired, then he got angry.

313

Thought the world was out to get him. He started drinking heavily. The only work he was able to get was as a farmhand."

"I see," Vivia said. "Can you go under the water so I can rinse your hair?"

Darcy slid under the water and held her breath. Vivia gently pulled the soap from Darcy's hair, then lifted her by the shoulder and handed her a face towel. Darcy dabbed her face dry and looked at Vivia kneeling next to the tub. She was beautiful.

"I would like to ask you a personal question if that's okay?" Vivia asked.

Darcy nodded.

"Is this the first time this has happened?"

Darcy looked down at her immersed hands and shook her head.

"We need to report this, Darcy."

"I figured they already knew about it. What would be the point?"

Vivia stood and dried her hands on a towel hanging on a rack behind her. "Ah, yes. Your eye."

"I guess Tate told you?"

"I'm sorry, yes, he did. We don't keep things from each other."

"It's okay. I'm glad you know."

Vivia knelt back down next to the tub. "Listen, the fact that someone may have seen past incidences on your video feed is not the same thing as reporting it. That's up to you to do."

"It's okay. I deserve it."

Vivia grabbed Darcy by the shoulders. "It's not okay. It's never okay. Ever."

Darcy looked into Vivia's eyes. She couldn't stop it. Her eye took over. Vivia's stats immediately started popping up. *Vivia Brooke Wilson Vance. Twenty-five. Married. Elementary school teacher. Mother — Mary Wilson. Father — Andrew Wilson.* Then, there it was — the police report.

"Vivia. I'm sorry. Your father..." Darcy stammered.

Vivia retreated to the sink and stared in the mirror. "I was wondering how long it would take you."

"He hit your mother," Darcy said.

"Yes."

"You got in the way," Darcy continued.

"I can't have children."

"I'm..." Darcy was at a loss for words.

"Did I deserve that, Darcy?"

"No, Vivia."

Vivia turned to Darcy. "Exactly."

***

"How is she?" Cricket said from the living room sofa.

"I don't know," Hardy said quietly, heading into the kitchen.

"I'm glad it was us who found her," Cricket said.

Hardy took the tea kettle from the stove and filled it with water. "Yeah."

"You blame me," Cricket mumbled.

Hardy set the kettle on the burner and shut his eyes. "Yes...No...I don't know."

"I was mean to her. I took advantage of her."

Hardy turned the burner to high.

"Listen, I didn't know about...her situation," Cricket said.

"You mean that she has a lousy, no good excuse for a human being brother?" Hardy said, watching the burner turn red. He didn't know if it was the heat from the stove or anger that felt like a fire raging on his face.

"You knew?" Cricket asked.

Hardy turned around. "Yeah. And I did nothing. I'm no better than you."

Cricket stood up and came over to the kitchen island that separated the two rooms. "I'll make it up to her, Hardy. I swear I will. We should go to her house right now and kick some—"

"Nobody's going anywhere," Tate said from the cottage's back door. "Where's Vivia?" Tate glanced at the closed bedroom door and set a lunch box down on the kitchen island.

"Darcy's here," Hardy said.

"Uh-huh. Care to elaborate?" Tate asked.

"Her brother—"

"Her brother hit her, and now we're going to go over there and beat the crap out of him the way he did to her," Cricket blurted out.

Tate held up a hand. "Whoa there. You aren't going anywhere."

"You can't stop us, Tate," Hardy said, backing up Cricket.

"Is that right?" Tate took a deep breath and let it out slowly.

"Yeah, that's right. You may be able to stop one of us, but not both of us," Cricket said.

Tate laced his fingers together and pushed his arms out, cracking all ten knuckles. "Well, we'll just see about that."

Chapter Twenty-nine

Vivia laid dry clothes on the bed for Darcy. "Here are some clothes. I'm going to get you some hot tea."

A loud crash followed by two thumps shook the bedroom floor. Darcy pulled the borrowed robe tighter around her neck and stared at the bedroom door.

Vivia held up a reassuring hand. "It's okay, Darcy. I'm sure it's nothing. Don't be afraid."

"What if it's Nash?"

Vivia put a hand on the doorknob. "He doesn't know where you are, remember? Stay here. I'll be right back."

Vivia stepped into the living room and closed the bedroom door. Hardy and Cricket were both on the floor. A red-faced Tate had his left knee in Cricket's back and Hardy in a choke hold under his right arm.

"What in the world is going on out here? This hardly seems appropriate, Tate Vance."

Tate held his position, trying to keep a hold of the

squirming bodies of Hardy and Cricket. "Before you go jumping to conclusions, you might want to know what these two bozos were planning," Tate said.

Vivia put her hands on her hips. "Well, let one of them go so I can hear it."

Tate released Hardy who fell back on the floor and coughed.

"Out with it, Hardy," Vivia said.

"We were going to go to Darcy's house."

"And do what, exactly?"

Hardy coughed and didn't answer.

"Tate," Vivia said.

Tate kicked Hardy with his free leg.

"Ouch. Okay. We were going to beat up her brother."

Vivia sighed. "Unbelievable."

Tate took one last dig into Cricket's back with his knee and stood up. "I still got it."

"Don't think you're off so easy, Tate Vance. You scared Darcy half to death," Vivia said.

She marched over to Hardy and stood over him. "Get up." Hardy had his arms crossed over his face and seemed not to have heard her.

"Get up!" Vivia snapped.

Hardy rolled to his knees and stood slowly. Vivia pointed her finger in his face. "This is serious. I don't have time to worry about you two infants. Do you understand?"

"Yes," Hardy mumbled.

"Yes, what?"

"Yes, ma'am."

"Fine." Vivia turned to Cricket who was propped up

against the couch holding his back. "Cricket?"

"Yes. Yes. Got it."

The tea kettle started whistling. "Good." Vivia headed into the kitchen to make Darcy's tea.

"I told you I could take the both of you," Tate whispered to Hardy and Cricket.

***

After Cricket took Hardy home, he drove back to Tate and Vivia's cottage. He cut the lights and engine and coasted up to the front of the cottage. The place looked dark except for a small hint of light coming from the right front window. A nightlight, maybe. He guessed that's where Darcy was sleeping.

He rubbed his hands together and started second-guessing his decision to come back. But he just couldn't go home until...until he told Darcy he was sorry. He had treated her like someone lesser than, and she had let him. He had to make things right. It was selfish, but he needed to clear his conscience.

He leaned his head back against the back window and took a deep breath. He left his body and rose up and out of the window of the truck. He traveled like a mist through the front gate, down the stone path. He stopped at the cottage door. Why did this feel like breaking and entering? There was a part of him that was telling him it was wrong to sneak into someone's home without them knowing it. He reminded himself that technically he wasn't really in the house.

He melted through the front door. The light was on over

the stove. He quickly glided into the second bedroom. The light of the moon seeped through the window blinds and cascaded across the bed. Darcy was sleeping on her side.

Cricket had tried to communicate with people before when he was out of body, but he had never been successful. It didn't matter. He would try again.

He slowly drifted up to the ceiling above the bed. Darcy slept with her hands underneath her face like she was praying. Cricket lowered himself down until he was just above her face. He let his being touch her cheek. *I'm sorry, Darcy.* He tried to convey his feelings to her, if only in spirit.

Darcy didn't move, not even a slight twitch. She just continued to breathe lightly in a peaceful, gentle rhythm. Cricket was disappointed. He thought maybe this time it would work. That if he wanted it bad enough he would be able to...do it. He pulled away and flew through the window out to his truck.

Darcy was lost in sleep when she touched her cheek. It was warm. "Cricket?" she murmured from a groggy half-sleep. "I forgive you," she whispered, and drifted back into her dream.

Chapter Thirty

He stood outside his car at the top of the cliff and stared out at the dark water. The storm, along with its heavy rain, had passed through, leaving the blackest of night and a moonless sky. A light drizzle fell now. The white breakers flashed like dim beacons. He waited for Trevor.

Trevor had become careless. He was a liability that The Program could no longer afford.

Headlights split the night air and turned into the secluded cove. The silver Honda pulled up next to him. Trevor rolled down his window.

"You're late."

Trevor took a pack of cigarettes from the front pocket of his blue scrubs and tapped one out into his hand. He pushed in the car's lighter. "Yeah, well. Duty and all that," he said sticking the end of the cigarette into the corner of his mouth. "What's so important that we had to meet on a night like tonight?"

"I haven't been too pleased with your recent activities."

The lighter popped out. Trevor held it up to his cigarette. He took a long drag and blew the smoke out the window. "You're going to have to be more specific."

"Let's start with you calling the cops when you caught Hardy and his friends in the woods."

Trevor stared out the front window of his car into the beams of his headlights. "They were trespassing."

"Did I ask you to stop them?"

Trevor took another long drag on his cigarette and this time exhaled into the windshield. "I did what I thought was best."

"I don't pay you to think. I pay you to follow orders."

"Okay. I'm sorry. Won't happen again."

"Then there's the incident with Mrs. Gobble. Your jealous stunt could have killed Hardy."

Trevor smashed the cigarette out into his ashtray.

"And let's not forget Nurse Troxler."

"It's not my fault your precious Hardy and his girlfriend bashed the door down," Trevor snapped.

"The truth is, Trevor, you're becoming messy, careless."

Trevor smiled. "So, you going to fire me, Pops? I've got enough on you and the Governor to blow this thing wide open."

"You're right. You do. It's unfortunate that I'm going to have to take steps to make sure that doesn't happen."

The cockiness evaporated from Trevor's face. It was replaced with a look of cautious surprise.

"Steps?" Trevor asked nervously. "Now listen. I'll do better. I'll—"

"I'm sorry, Trevor."

Trevor's face turned red with terror. He struggled to put the car into reverse.

"I'm afraid this is goodbye."

He jabbed the needle hidden in the palm of his hand into Trevor's neck and watched him slowly close his eyes and slump forward into the steering wheel. The mild sedative would make the job much easier. He forced Trevor back into an upright position and reached across him, slipping the car into drive. He bent over and picked up a brick-sized rock, and tossed it onto the gas pedal. He stood back and watched the lights of the car disappear off the cliff.

Chapter Thirty-one

On Sunday, Tate and Vivia took Darcy to the police station. Tate had called Hardy that afternoon and told him that social services had taken over and placed Darcy in a foster home. She wouldn't be allowed to return home as long as Nash was living there. Vivia had wanted Darcy to stay with them, but since they weren't family, the request was denied.

Hardy had spent the rest of that day lying in bed staring up at his bedroom ceiling wondering if he would ever see Darcy again.

Now it was Wednesday, and he wondered if he was hallucinating when he saw Darcy's blonde hair cresting the hill. Cricket was carrying her backpack and her lunch tray. Hardy rubbed his palms on his pants, trying to keep himself from jumping up to meet them.

He heard Charity say something, but he was too focused on Darcy and Cricket to catch what she said.

"Huh?" Hardy asked absently.

"I said—"

Charity's voice trailed into blah, blah, blah. Cricket set down their trays and let Darcy's backpack drop from his shoulder and fall to the ground. Darcy's hair was braided and wrapped around her head like a yellow halo. The mark on her face was covered with make-up. She looked—well.

"What's up?" Cricket asked, sitting down.

Hardy and Darcy's eyes locked, and they smiled at each other. Hardy realized he was staring across the table at what were probably his two best friends in the whole world. He was happy they were all together again.

"Are you and Megan coming to my party?" Charity asked Cricket, severing the moment.

"Psst. Yeah. We wouldn't miss the best party of the year," Cricket said.

That seemed to make Charity happy. She started peeling the skin off her grapes with her long, pink fingernails. Charity ignored Darcy, but then again, she always did.

Hardy just wanted to be alone with Darcy so they could talk.

Luis arrived and forced himself in between Darcy and Cricket.

"Bros and ladies," he said, sitting down.

"Hi, Luis," Charity said.

Why was it that everybody liked Luis except for Hardy? He found himself glaring at Luis.

"Are you coming to my party Friday night?" Charity asked.

Luis had already opened a milk carton and was mid-chug. He finished and crushed the carton with his large hand.

What a pig, Hardy thought, taking a bite of his chicken sandwich.

"Definitely. Plus one, right?" Luis asked.

"Of course. Who's your date?"

Yeah. Who is the lucky girl? Hardy wondered.

Luis put his arm around Darcy. "You're looking at her."

A piece of chicken stopped halfway down Hardy's throat, and he started choking. He put a fist to his mouth, his face swelling from a lack of oxygen.

Charity slapped him on the back. "You okay, Hardy?"

The chicken shifted and moved down his throat. "I'm fine," he said in a strained whisper.

Hardy was stunned. *When did Luis even have time to ask her?* Hardy looked at Darcy for some kind of explanation, but she avoided his gaze. Why shouldn't she go to the prom? Hardy was going. He felt like he had lost something. But he had no idea what it was.

***

"Hey." Hardy heard Darcy's voice above him as he worked the combination of his bike lock. He pulled the lock from its spoke and stood up.

"Hey," Hardy said.

"You want to go down to the beach so we can talk?" Darcy asked.

"Yeah. I do."

They rode their bikes to Dunwoody beach and took the steps down to its sandy shore. The sun was high and clear.

The emerald ocean churned with soft, silver peaks of light. A band of blue-gray rested on the horizon, topped with clouds shaped like lumps of whipped cream. Small clusters of people, hiding under their umbrellas and straw hats, dotted the beach. Young mothers stood at the shoreline watching the water nip at the heels of their screaming children. Older couples with stiff, determined arms skirted past the children and continued their brisk walks.

Hardy and Darcy left their shoes by the steps and followed their shadows down the beach.

"So, how are you?" Hardy finally asked, after they had walked in silence for several minutes. He decided he wasn't going to ask her about Luis and the prom.

"I'm fine," Darcy said.

"I'm sorry about…"

"I know."

"How is it…you know…at your foster home?"

Darcy turned toward Hardy but continued to walk. "They seem nice. They have a four-year-old boy. He walks in the room, stares at me, and leaves. I think he's trying to figure out who I am."

"But they're treating you okay?" Hardy asked.

"Yes. And Vivia is keeping in touch."

"That's good."

Hardy felt awkward. Guys weren't good at this emotional stuff, or maybe it was just him. He thought about taking her hand. He could keep her safe if he held her hand. Darcy reached over instead and tucked her hand under his arm, as if she knew he needed it.

"We should talk about Hill Home," Darcy said.

"Darcy, I don't think we should." Darcy stopped walking and put a hand on Hardy's chest. "Don't say we should give up. I won't."

"But with everything that's happened. I just thought…"

"You thought wrong. It's up to us to expose what's happening to our elderly—what happened to Olen." Her eyes searched his, looking for understanding.

Hardy laid his hands on Darcy's shoulders. "Are you sure?" He knelt down slightly so he could look her straight in the eyes.

Darcy nodded. Hardy dropped his hands to his sides. "Okay. I'm still in." *But I won't let you get hurt again. I can't.*

They continued to walk, and Darcy slipped her hand back under Hardy's arm.

"I have no idea what we should do now," Hardy said.

"I've been thinking about that."

"I'm all ears."

Darcy smiled, and Hardy wondered if perhaps she thought he had big ears.

"Remember how I told you I had overheard Trevor on the phone?" Darcy asked.

"Uh…that whole day is a little sketchy."

"Trevor said, *She won't be a problem after today. Tell the Governor not to worry.*"

Hardy squinted at the sun and scratched the back of his neck. "Yeah, but I mean it's the Governor we're talking about here. How could we possibly find anything that would implicate him? Unless we figure out who Trevor was talking to." Hardy's mind spun with possibilities. "I wonder…"

"What?" Darcy asked.

"Nothing. It's just… I think Cain Finch could be involved. Maybe it was him on the phone with Trevor."

"Why would you think that?" Darcy said, sounding confused.

Hardy realized there was quite a bit that he hadn't been able to tell Darcy. So he told her what George had told him about Finch. How Finch was part of The Program and had lost his medical license when he was implicated in Hardy's grandmother's death. He covered everything that happened in Town Square with the man having the heart attack. He described the overwhelming darkness, how Finch saved the man's life and how Hardy had passed out. He ended it with the threats from Finch warning him not to get involved.

Darcy's eyes narrowed with concern. She grabbed his face and pulled him close. He knew what she was doing. She stared into his eyes, her blue eye twitching back and forth. Then she felt his forehead, pulled his head down and checked the area of his head where the stitches had been, like a monkey preening its friend. She pushed his head up and took a step back.

Hardy expected this from Darcy now, so it was starting to feel normal. "Am I going to live, Doc?" He smiled.

"I'm worried about you," Darcy said, wrapping her arms around herself.

"Don't be. Cricket thinks it may be permanent. Ya know…the whole seeing dead people thing," Hardy said, trying to lighten the mood.

He watched the worry on Darcy's face turn into realization. "Viola."

Hardy frowned. "What do you mean...Viola?"

"Her descendants—"

"Oh, gee. Not that again," Hardy said, digging his foot into the sand.

"What else could it be?"

Hardy raised and dropped his hands. "I don't know. Dumb luck."

"And Cricket being able to leave his body? I suppose that's dumb luck, too?" Darcy asked, smugly.

Hardy grazed his hand across the scar on the back of his head. "Okay, so I don't have all the answers, but it's a big jump from dumb luck to inheriting this crazy mess from Viola."

Darcy shrugged. "It's as good an explanation as any. This happened to you after the incidences with the dandelions."

"So I'm cursed now?" Hardy asked.

"I guess some people might consider what is happening to you a curse. But if you use it for good, like you did when you saved the man, then it's not a curse."

"I didn't save him," Hardy said quietly, staring at the sand seeping through his toes.

"You didn't let them give up."

"Maybe. I don't know. I didn't save Mama, though," Hardy said, staring out into the ocean. His face tightened with sadness. He hadn't admitted how much witnessing Mama die had affected him. He didn't want to cry in front of Darcy.

"Maybe she didn't need saving," Darcy said, reaching out to him.

Hardy blinked back tears and nodded. Darcy walked into

his arms and held him. He put his arms around her small waist and buried the tears he was fighting into her neck. The ocean broke around their feet, and he wished the water would take them and carry them out to sea forever. He wondered what he had done to deserve a friend like Darcy. He would try to deserve her. She was his gift, and no curse could take that away from him.

He backed away and cleared his sinuses by sniffing a few times. "Thanks."

Darcy held out her hand to him. "Come on."

"Where are we going?"

"To plan a break-in at the town hall. Finch has a safe behind a picture on his wall."

Darcy took his hand and pulled him back toward the access. Hardy planted his feet. "Wait, I thought you said you didn't have x-ray vision."

Darcy sighed, dropped his hand, and headed back down the beach.

"Yeah, okay, but we're not done talking about this," Hardy called after her.

He shivered imagining Darcy being able to exam every bone in his body.

Chapter Thirty-two

They waited until dark. Now they stood under the arched eaves of the town hall waiting for—Hardy had no idea what.

"Is there any particular reason why we're just standing here in the shadows?" Hardy asked.

Darcy's hair was tucked under a black ski cap to match her all-black attire. She was leaning against the brick arch and staring straight ahead. Hardy knew by the look that she was accessing something on the net.

"Yes. We are waiting for someone," Darcy said.

Who? Hardy wanted to ask. Instead he said, "Didn't your foster parents ask why you were going out dressed all in black?"

Darcy blinked and looked at him. "I'm a teenager. Black is not that unusual." Darcy refocused in a spot in front of her. "He's almost here."

"Who—?"

"Sorry I'm late," Cricket said, materializing out of the

dark.

"Cricket?" Hardy said, confused.

Cricket rubbed his hands together. "Let's do this."

"Whoa, wait. Why didn't you tell me you asked Cricket to come?" Hardy asked Darcy.

Darcy just shrugged. "We need him. It was a last-minute thought."

"Gee, thanks," Cricket said.

"You're welcome," Darcy responded.

"Whatever. Why do we need him?" Hardy asked.

"I'm starting to feel insulted now," Cricket said.

"Relax. I'm just trying to figure out what the plan is."

"He can go inside and let us know when the coast is clear. There's a guard at the reception desk," Darcy explained.

"Couldn't we just look in the window?" Hardy asked.

"I want to know when he is at the back of the building so there's no chance of bumping into him," Darcy said.

Cricket clicked his heels together and gave Darcy a goofy salute.

"Okay, fine. That's not a bad idea," Hardy relented.

The last thing Hardy needed was to get caught, but this whole new friendship thing between Darcy and Cricket was just—weird.

"It's almost nine o'clock. That's when he begins his next round. Are you ready, Cricket?" Darcy asked.

"Yep." Cricket sat down and propped himself up against the back of the brick arch they were hiding behind. "Remember, don't touch me."

Cricket closed his eyes. His head slumped slightly to the

side, his body grew still. Darcy immediately pulled something out of her pocket and knelt down beside Cricket.

"What are you doing?" Hardy asked.

"Shh."

Hardy heard a cap snap off. Darcy reached a hand out toward Cricket's face. Hardy couldn't see what she was doing, but Cricket hadn't moved, so he was still inside the building. Darcy stood up and backed away.

Hardy bent down to get a closer look. Even though it was dark, there was enough light from the square's street lamps to see what Darcy had done. He stifled a laugh with his fist.

"He's going to kill you," Hardy said.

Darcy stood with her hands on her hips admiring her work. "He had it coming, don't you think?"

Hardy was grinning now. "Yeah. I suppose he did."

Cricket's lips were the perfect shade of bright red. Darcy shoved the tube of lipstick back in her front pocket.

"Is this why you asked him to come?" Hardy asked, still smiling.

"No. This was just a bonus."

Cricket's eyes popped open. He gasped for air and hiccupped. "All clear, he's headed to the back on the other side of the building." He jumped to his feet and brushed his hands off on his shorts.

Hardy choked on a laugh and started coughing. The image of Cricket in lipstick was more than he could stand. Darcy's face was like stone.

Cricket patted Hardy on the back. "You okay, man?"

Hardy nodded, unable to speak.

"Come on. We'd better hurry," Cricket said, heading for

the door.

Hardy whispered to Darcy, "How long are you going to let him stay like that?" She smirked and kept walking. He was beginning to like this new Darcy.

They huddled around the main entrance. The rectangular keypad glowed next to the door. Hardy had no idea how Darcy planned to get them inside.

She stepped up to the keypad and pulled two slim pieces of metal out of her pants pocket. She pushed them into the small keyhole of the keypad's lock. Within seconds, the panel to the keypad unlocked.

"Whoa," Cricket whispered.

Darcy reached into her other pocket and pulled out a tiny cord. She pulled down her eyelid and stuck one end into her eye. She connected the other end to something inside the keypad. The cord twitched while her eye moved back and forth. There was a click and the door to the town hall released.

"Cool," Cricket said quietly.

Darcy pulled the cord from her eye, detached the other end from the keypad, and pushed the panel back in place. "Let's go," she said casually, like nothing was out of the ordinary.

Hardy's heart raced with admiration. Darcy was a girl James Bond, except cooler.

They slipped inside. No sign of the guard. So far, so good. They ran quietly through the lobby and down the hall to Finch's office. The hallway was dark except for a few dim lights seeping from the frosted glass windows of some of the office doors.

When they got to Finch's door, Hardy tried the brass doorknob. "Locked," he whispered.

Darcy took her razor-thin tools, leaned into the lock, fiddled, and the lock clicked.

"Remind me to ask you how you know how to do this stuff," Hardy murmured.

Once they got inside, Hardy gently closed the door and flipped the lock. A small desk lamp with a green glass shade burned on Finch's desk. The rest of the room was shadowed in darkness. Hardy turned on his palm-sized flashlight and headed straight for the picture behind Finch's desk where Darcy said the safe was. He put the flashlight in his mouth and gently removed the picture from the wall, setting it on the floor. A small, black safe with a combination dial and a lever handle stood between Hardy and the evidence they hoped to find that would link Finch to The Program and hopefully the Governor himself.

He took the flashlight out of his mouth and turned to Darcy. "Okay, do your thing."

"Can I just say, this is like the coolest thing, ever. I mean, we're like Mission Impossible here, people," Cricket said.

"Shut up, Cricket," Darcy and Hardy said at the same time.

Darcy stepped up to the safe and studied it for what felt like forever. Hardy wondered if they had done all this for nothing. Cricket stepped up next to him to get a better look, but Hardy could barely look at him with his shaggy, blonde hair and red lips. Cricket looked like a creepy clown doll from one of those slasher films where the doll comes to life in the middle of the night holding a butcher's knife.

Darcy finally reached up and slowly rotated the dial. Hardy held his breath. After a few left, right, left combinations, a click echoed through the room. Hardy exhaled slowly.

Darcy grasped the silver lever and pulled down. The safe swung open.

"Ladies and gentlemen, we are a go, I repeat, a go," Cricket said.

Hardy shined his flashlight into the safe. A large stack of neatly organized folders appeared to be the only contents. He reached inside and carefully pulled out the stack. There were at least twenty folders. "Well, I guess we'll have to go through all of them."

"We better hurry. What if the guard comes?" Cricket asked.

"The door is locked, genius," Hardy said.

Hardy headed to the table at the back of the room with the stack of folders.

"He probably has a key, though," Cricket added.

"Would you stop worrying about it and help look through these folders?" Hardy asked.

"Fine. But I swear if we get caught—"

"Isn't it a little late to be worrying about getting caught?" *Clown face.*

"Here." Hardy divided the stack into thirds, and they all dug in.

"What are we looking for exactly?" Cricket asked.

Cricket was really starting to get on Hardy's nerves. He forgot how hyper Cricket could be sometimes.

"You'll know when you see it."

"Copy that."

Darcy pushed through her folders like a bionic droid. Her blue eye blinked at each page.

Hardy buried his head back into his folder. Cricket started whistling like he was taking a walk in the park. *Ignore him, Hardy.* He rubbed his eyes with his thumb and index finger and tried to refocus on the papers in front him. Darcy kept flipping pages and blinking her eye at warp speed. He was having a hard time concentrating.

Most of Hardy's folders were personal. Genealogy research, several unfinished editorial pieces. Maybe he was wrong about Finch. It was possible that Finch just thought Hardy was digging up the past and was warning him against it.

Darcy closed her last folder. Hardy nodded in Cricket's direction. "Please, take some of his."

Darcy reached across the table and grabbed the rest of Cricket's stack.

"Hey!" Cricket said, watching his folders disappear from underneath him.

Darcy devoured another folder. "Hey, I think I've got something," she said, scanning the page in front of her.

Cricket held up a gray notebook. "Hey, I found Finch's journal. He had tea with Mrs. Beechum at Courtney's tearoom today. Apparently, she was delightful."

"Shut up!" Darcy and Hardy echoed each other.

"What is it, Darcy?" Hardy asked.

"Look." Darcy slid a yellowed newspaper clipping across the table. Cricket scooted his chair over to get a better look. It was a picture of three men in cowboy hats. One was holding the reins of a horse. They were standing amongst a field of dead cattle. The caption below it read, "Six hundred cattle were killed by an unknown weed en route to Greystone cattle market."

"Good grief. This is straight from the story George told us about Olen as a kid." Hardy wondered if any of the men in the picture were his great-grandfather.

Darcy nodded.

"What else is there?" Hardy asked anxiously.

Darcy began flipping through the rest of the folder and then stopped cold.

"What? What is it?" Hardy pushed.

"A death certificate."

"For who?"

"Olen's, from the drowning."

A light broke through the glass of the office door. The clack of a knob turning broke through the sound of shuffling papers. Cricket and Hardy turned toward the door. The rattle of keys set Hardy's heart racing. "Crap."

"What now?" Cricket muttered desperately.

"Hide!" Darcy said in a loud whisper. They quickly shut the open folders. Darcy grabbed the stack and ran to the safe.

Hardy's flashlight landed on a door next to the bookcases. He scrambled toward it. The sound of a key sliding into its lock sent him into full panic mode. He whipped the small door open. It was a narrow coat closet—barely enough room for one person. He pushed all the empty hangers to the side and stepped in.

"Make room," Cricket said, grabbing the door Hardy was

trying to shut.

"No room," Hardy whispered harshly.

The gears of the office door lock released.

"Too late." Cricket pushed his way into the tiny closet and pulled the door shut. They were chest-to-chest in a closet big enough for an ironing board. Cricket's red lips were inches from Hardy's.

Hardy clicked off his flashlight. "Great," he whispered.

"Did you want me to get caught?" Cricket asked, blowing his pancake breath in Hardy's face.

Yes. Hardy wanted to say. If only to see the look on the guard's face when he saw Cricket's red lips.

The office door creaked open. The guard's flashlight seeped through the cracks of the cramped closet. Hardy hoped Darcy had found a good place to hide. He couldn't let anything else happen to her.

The close quarters, mixed with Cricket's sweet, syrupy breath made Hardy start to feel light-headed. He wasn't generally claustrophobic, but this was pushing it. Plus, he didn't want those red lips anywhere near him.

"You tell these people to turn their lights off, they never listen," the guard complained.

"Oh, no," Cricket whispered. "I think I'm going to sneeze."

"Shh."

Cricket started sucking in air. "Ah—"

"Don't you dare," Hardy whispered furiously.

The guard's heavy footsteps boomed against the wood floor. Next they heard the grating of the desk lamp's chain being pulled. The room went dark.

Cricket took a huge breath and then, "AH-CHOO!"

"Who's there?!" The guard yelled out. A flashlight clicked on and light poked in and out of the closet's seams.

"You have got to be kidding me," Hardy hissed.

"My bad."

Without any further communication, Hardy and Cricket burst out of the closet and made a run for the door. This wasn't the first time they had ever made a run for it, but that was a long time ago in a barn with an angry farmer who didn't appreciate the trespassing.

"Stop right there!" the guard called after them.

They stumbled into the hall. Cricket tripped over Hardy's feet and fell. "Come on," Hardy said, grabbing Cricket by the back of his T-shirt. Cricket scrambled to his feet, and they sprinted side-by-side down the hall toward the exit.

"You two, stop!"

Hardy could hear the guard breathing heavily behind them, keys jangling at his hip.

Cricket whooped and laughed all the way down the hall and through the lobby like it was all a grand joke. Hardy pushed Cricket into the front door, and they rushed into the safety of the night. The guard would call the police, but Hardy was pretty sure he'd only seen their backs.

They ran until they were completely out of sight and in the back alley of Briley's where Cricket had parked his truck. Hardy leaned up against the passenger door and closed his eyes, trying to catch his breath. He opened one eye and glanced at Cricket who was standing at the back of the truck bent over his phone.

"What are you doing?" Hardy asked.

"Letting Darcy know where we are."

Hardy let his head fall back against the truck. "You better hope she made it out."

"Yeah. Yeah. She'll be fine. You saw her, she's like a stealth ninja."

Hardy was too tired to be concerned, at least not yet, anyway. All he could really think about was why Finch had a death certificate for Olen. What did it mean?

"You almost got us caught back there," he reminded Cricket.

Hardy bent over and put his hands on his knees and looked over at Cricket. The lipstick was smudged now. It was smeared up one side of Cricket's face. Hardy started to spill the beans when Darcy appeared from around the corner. He straightened and sighed in relief.

"Thank goodness. Are you okay?" he asked, meeting Darcy at the back of a truck.

"I'm fine."

"How did you get out?" Hardy asked.

"As soon as the guard left the room to chase two bumbling idiots, I slipped out of the room and out a back exit."

Hardy and Cricket both pointed at each other. "He did it."

"I know it was you who sneezed, Cricket," Darcy said.

Cricket frowned. "Why do you assume it was me?"

"Because you were probably having a reaction."

"Psst. To what? Hairy face over here?" Cricket asked, shoving a thumb in Hardy's direction.

"No, not him."

"Then what, Bond girl?"

"You should look in the mirror." Darcy smiled.

Hardy sighed. "Look, can this wait? I need to know about the death certificate."

"No. I want to know what's so funny," Cricket said, annoyed.

Darcy smirked.

Cricket walked past Darcy's smug face and bent down to look in the side mirror of the truck.

"What the—?" Cricket wiped his mouth as hard as he could. He looked at his hand and smelled it. He turned around and glared at Darcy. "You. You did this?" he said with clenched teeth and narrowed eyes.

Darcy shrugged and smiled.

"I'll kill you."

Cricket ran toward Darcy. She laughed and took off. They were gone.

Hardy got inside the truck and rested his head against the back window. *No problem, guys. We're only talking about life and death here.*

Hardy expected their little game of cat and mouse wouldn't take long. Cricket might be a good sprinter, but he was no long-distance runner. After what Hardy had witnessed with Darcy's bike riding, she would no doubt leave Cricket in the dust.

Sure enough, twenty minutes later, Cricket grabbed the handle to the driver's side and slid in behind the wheel.

"Got away?" Hardy asked.

"Yep," Cricket said, starting the truck. He threw the truck in reverse and begin slowly backing out of the alley. "Thanks for having my back, by the way."

Hardy grinned.

Chapter Thirty-three

The next day, Hardy and Darcy met Cricket after school at Briley's pancake house. There was no chance of discussing anything at lunch with Charity and Luis hanging around.

Hardy and Darcy sat across from each other at a table in the back of the restaurant near the bathrooms. Cricket approached the table with two plastic menus in his hand. He dropped them on the table and took a seat next to Hardy.

"You're lucky I got a leg cramp last night," Cricket said to Darcy.

"You wouldn't have caught me," Darcy said flatly.

"Okay. Let's put the drama aside. It's not like she took a picture or anything," Hardy said.

Darcy smirked.

Cricket stood up. "Okay, that's it."

Hardy grasped Cricket's arm a little too tightly and pulled him back down into his seat. "Chill. We don't have time for this."

Cricket jerked his arm out of Hardy's and reluctantly settled in his seat.

"I'm sorry, Cricket," Darcy said.

"What about the pictures you probably took with that eye of yours?" Cricket said gruffly.

Darcy held a finger in the air. "Hold on." She stared off into space, her blue eye twitching. "Erased."

"Satisfied?" Hardy asked.

"Yeah. I guess."

"Good," Hardy said. "Darcy, tell us what else was in that folder."

"Okay, well, besides the old newspaper clipping on the cattle deaths, there were articles and clippings on Olen's drowning, and the death certificate I mentioned. But there was something weirder—obituaries—people who have passed away at all the different Hill Homes on the island. I never got to the bottom of that stack."

"You still think Finch is involved in all this?" Cricket asked.

"I don't know." Hardy said, drumming his fingers on the table.

"Didn't you say he accused you of having something to hide?" Cricket asked. "He's obviously worried about something."

"Huh. George did mention that maybe whoever killed Olen might have been looking for something, since the cabin was ransacked," Hardy said.

"And Finch wants whatever it is," Cricket said, filling in the blanks.

"Maybe. Darcy, what do you think?" Hardy asked.

"What's the connection, though? Trevor's phone call implicated the Governor," Darcy insisted.

Cricket held out his hand, displaying his large, gold class ring. "Ladies and gentlemen, you may now thank me and kiss the royal ring."

Hardy and Darcy stared at Cricket, wondering what kind of game he was playing.

"You underestimate me, my children," Cricket said.

"Just spill it," Hardy said impatiently.

"While you were rudely telling me to shut up in Finch's office, I was perusing his journal."

"Yeah, yeah. Tea and crumpets. So what?" Hardy asked.

Cricket breathed on his ring and polished it on his shirt. "Not *just* tea and crumpets. Finch had a visit with a VIP after that. And not just that day, several in the last month."

"Well, who?" Hardy said, tired of Cricket's dramatic reveal.

"The Governor himself."

Hardy and Darcy looked at each other in shock. "What if Finch killed my grandfather?" Hardy said, falling back into his chair.

"What now?" Cricket asked.

Hardy felt a fire burning inside him. He didn't care what it took now. They would get whatever evidence they needed, and they would tell the world.

***

The plan seemed perfect. They would be in the Governor's mansion Friday night after the prom. Cricket would run interference while Hardy and Darcy snuck into Governor Hill's office. Darcy would access the Governor's personal computer, download any incriminating evidence, and then they would take it to the police, news media, anybody who would listen.

Hardy's mom was tying his bow tie. "Hold still," she said.

He was already sweating, and he hadn't even left the house yet.

"Are you okay, honey? You seem a little peaked," Anna asked.

He stared at the ceiling while Anna's fingers moved at his neck. "Just nerves, that's all."

And it was nerves. But not because of Charity. Because he knew tonight was his only opportunity to get justice for Olen, Mrs. Gobble, and Mama.

"There," Anna said. "It's been a while since I tied a bow tie, but I think I managed it."

Hardy tilted his chin down to look.

"You look so handsome. Oh, my…" Anna took a step back and covered her mouth with her hand. Her eyes started watering up.

"Mom…"

"I'm sorry. It's just…you're going to college off the island soon...and, well...I'll miss you."

Hardy closed the distance between them and embraced her. "I love you, Mom."

"I love you, too." She took a step back and rubbed non-existent lint off his shoulders. "Now go. Go have fun," she said, managing a smile.

"Okay. I will."

"You're meeting Charity at the school?" she asked.

"Yeah. She had to be there early since she was on the prom committee."

"Oh. Let me get your corsage for Charity out of the fridge."

The front door opened, and Tom came in. He took in Hardy's tux without any reaction. Hardy shared the awkward silence with his father before Tom spoke.

"I expect you to behave responsibly tonight."

"Yes, sir."

"Okay, then. Have a good time." Tom walked past Hardy into the kitchen.

Hardy almost called after him. He was pretty sure now that Tom was not involved with Olen's death. Whatever *truth* Olen had wanted Tom to tell Hardy was likely something else, or nothing at all. Besides, it didn't matter now. No truth could be worse than the one he was facing right now.

He wanted to tell Tom everything. All of it. He wanted to pour his heart out and have Tom put an arm around his shoulder and tell him everything would be okay. He didn't want to need Tom. He kept telling himself he didn't need him. The truth was, a part of Hardy desperately did.

"Here you go." Anna handed him the white wrist corsage. "And, you'll need these," she said, dangling a set of keys in front of him.

"Thanks." Hardy leaned down and kissed his mother on the cheek. "Mom, if I have ever done anything to disappoint you or Tom, I'm sorry."

She lifted a hand to his face. "Sweetie, you've never disappointed me or your father."

Yeah, but I might after tonight. They would know everything. The lies. By exposing the Governor and Finch, he was also exposing himself.

***

The theme for the prom was "Friday Paris lights." The gym had been transformed into the streets of Paris, complete with a very large, lighted Eiffel Tower.

Charity spotted him right away and hurried to greet him. She was dressed in a strapless, short, floral dress. She wore a crystal headband in her short hair. She lit up the room with her million dollar smile.

"You look beautiful," Hardy said.

And she did. This was Hardy's dream. It should have been one of the best days of his life, but knowing that her father was responsible for the murders of innocent people, and that Hardy was getting ready to blow her world apart, changed everything.

He opened the box with the corsage. "Here, this is for you."

Charity smiled and held out her wrist. His hands shook as he slipped it on her wrist, but she didn't seem to notice.

She held her arm out and admired it. "It's perfect. Thank you, Hardy." She took his hand. "Come on, let's dance."

So he held Charity in his arms, her head resting on his chest. They danced under a canopy of thousands of miniature lights in front of the Eiffel Tower. There couldn't have been a more romantic setting.

Throughout the whole dance, Hardy kept his eye on the gym doors. He had seen Cricket with Megan, but there had been no sign of Darcy and he began to worry.

Just as the song ended, Luis came to the door with a beautiful blonde on his arm. Hardy wondered where Darcy was until he realized it *was* Darcy. Her hair had been completely straightened. She wore a short dress with gold sequins on top and pink tulle on the bottom, and gold high heels. He couldn't believe his eyes. The long skirts and Bohemian tops were gone. She was...beautiful.

Hardy swallowed. Luis headed for the punch table, leaving Darcy standing alone.

"I'll be right back, Charity," Hardy said.

"Okay. Don't be long."

He pushed through the stiff suits and perfumed dresses toward Darcy. He stopped in front of her, and they looked at each other for a brief moment before words were spoken.

"You look—" they both said at the same time.

Darcy smiled and lowered her eyes.

"You look...great," Hardy said.

She looked down at her dress and rubbed her hands down the pink tulle. "Vivia did it all. You think it's okay?"

"Definitely okay." *Better than okay.*

He realized he was staring at her. He wanted to take her hand, lead her to the dance floor, and disappear into her arms.

"You ready for tonight?" Hardy asked, forcing himself to blink.

"We have to do this, Hardy."

"I know."

"Are you okay?" she asked.

"I will be."

Luis returned with two clear cups of pink punch. He handed one to Darcy. "Bromeo," he said, "doesn't my date look fantastic?" Luis drank his punch in one gulp.

"Yes, she does," Hardy said, looking into Darcy's eyes. "Anyway, I better get back," he said, shooting a thumb behind him.

"Okay, bro. Catch you later," Luis said, raising his empty cup.

When Hardy looked back, Darcy was laughing at Luis who was exaggerating some stupid dance move.

Hardy found Charity sitting at a table with her friends and their dates. But, instead of engaging with the others, Hardy spent the rest of the night keeping an eye on Darcy. He just wanted to make sure Luis treated her right. It was concern for Darcy. That was it, wasn't it? Concern? Why did it feel like something else? The kind of thing that made him want to punch a wall.

He wished he could say he would remember every moment of his one and only prom. That he enjoyed basking in the limelight of being on Charity Hill's arm. But he was just numb. After tonight, everyone would know the truth about what was happening to the old people on the island, and his parents would know everything he had been keeping from them—the deception.

He had a sick feeling in his stomach that felt like he was about to enter Judgment Day. Would his parents even listen to him, believe it had all been for a good reason?

He thought he didn't care about anyone but himself, but

something had changed. He thought of the worn, tired faces of the people at the home—the ones he felt a kindred spirit with. Now, he would risk everything for those faces, those souls that deserved honor and dignity. They had done the one thing that Hardy had yet learned to do—live.

He was by himself at the table now, and that was perfectly fine with him. He swallowed a mouthful of punch as some sappy love song echoed through the gym. Why did it feel like he was nursing a broken heart? A voice came out of nowhere, "So, who is she?"

Hardy hadn't realized anyone had sat down next to him. She was a redhead with green eyes and a splash of freckles across her nose. She wore a red dress. Bold move.

She held out her hand. "Emma. Emma Snow."

Hardy grasped her hand. "Hardy." He recognized her from her column in the school newspaper. "You're on the school newspaper, aren't you?"

She twisted her punch cup absently on the table. "Yes. I somehow manage to write riveting articles about student life at Southeast High."

"Oh, they're not so bad," Hardy said, wondering if Emma would be talking to him if he wasn't at the prom with Charity.

Emma raised her eyebrows. "Wow, a reader. Those are few and far between."

"You'd be surprised."

"I already am. So, who is she?" Emma asked.

"She?" Hardy looked around them wondering who Emma was talking about.

"The girl you've been staring at all night. And I don't

mean Charity."

"Is it that obvious?" Hardy asked, feeling busted.

"Only to astute individuals, which would eliminate a good two-thirds of the room. So your secret is safe." Emma took a swallow of punch.

"She's…um…I don't really know."

"Yes, you do," Emma said, crunching a piece of ice in her teeth.

"I do?" Hardy asked, perplexed.

She smirked. "Duh. You been watching her all night. You have a thing for her."

"She's just a friend," Hardy said. But he was starting to think she was more than that.

"Maybe. Or she's more than that," Emma suggested.

Hardy felt his face flush. It was like Emma was reading his mind. "And…um…exactly how would I know if it's *more than that*?"

Emma smiled. "Hmm. Well, it's all very subjective. But let's try this. Do you want to kiss her?"

"What?!…I don't know. Maybe." Was he really having this conversation with a complete stranger?

Emma laughed like it was all so clear. "Maybe?"

"I don't want to hurt her," Hardy mumbled, looking away.

"Uh-huh," Emma said, sucking another ice cube out of her cup.

"What does that mean, uh-huh?" he asked.

She swallowed her mouth of crushed ice. "You should tell her."

"Tell her what?" Hardy asked, exasperated. *You know*

what, Hardy.

"Do it before it's too late. Her date's pretty cute." Emma set down her empty cup and stood. "Well, I better go find my loser date my parents set me up with."

"Who is it?" Hardy asked.

"Russell Westwood III," Emma said, straightening her dress.

Hardy grimaced. "Ouch."

"Yeah. My thoughts exactly. Dad's always working the business connection. What's a girl going to do?"

"Good luck," Hardy said.

"You, too. And listen, don't wait. You never know if there will be a tomorrow. No regrets."

Emma held out her fist, and Hardy bumped it with his. "No regrets," he echoed.

He watched Emma walk away and wondered if she was right about his feelings for Darcy.

He stared into his cup and swirled the remaining punch. He was about to finish it off when he heard Olen's voice echoing through his head—*There's wisdom in trees… You best listen when wisdom calls out to you…* Hardy sprang from his seat, his heart racing. How could he have been so stupid? What if Olen had been trying to tell him something? A clue, like George said.

Olen's favorite tree was that old rotted-out oak they buried him next to. If Olen had wanted to hide something that no one could find, that would be the perfect spot. *You best listen when wisdom calls out to you…* That had to be it. Whatever the Governor and Finch had been looking for was in the rotted hole of that tree.

Hardy pushed his way through the crowded gym looking for Darcy. He found Cricket and pulled him aside.

"Have you seen Darcy?" Hardy asked frantically.

"She just left with Luis."

Hardy stuck his hands in his hair. "Why did you let her leave?"

"They left for the party. What's wrong?"

He grabbed Cricket by the shoulders. "I think I know where Olen may have hidden whatever The Program was looking for."

"Seriously? Where?" Cricket said.

"An oak tree—right where we buried Olen in the woods. It has a hole in it. It was his favorite tree."

Cricket removed Hardy's hands from his shoulders. "O-kay," he said slowly. "It seems a little far-fetched, don't you think?"

Hardy sighed. "Look, I don't have time to go into it. Just trust me on this."

"All right, then. What are we waiting for? Let's get out there," Cricket said, jabbing Hardy's shoulder.

"I could be wrong," Hardy said, biting into a hangnail. "We still have to try to get something on the Governor."

"This is fantastic. We're going to nail their—"

"Yeah, okay. One step at a time," Hardy said.

Charity suddenly linked her arm underneath Hardy's. "It's time, boys. The limo is waiting."

"Limo?" Hardy asked. He needed his car for a quick get-away.

Charity smiled. "It's taking us to the party."

Neither he nor Cricket would have a car. "Charity, I really need my car," Hardy said, breaking into a sweat.

"Nonsense. Let's go." Charity dragged him by the arm. "My driver will take you anywhere you need to go."

Hardy looked to Cricket for help. Cricket shrugged and went to find Megan.

Chapter Thirty-four

To say the Governor's mansion was big was an understatement. Hardy stood in the foyer thinking that just this section alone was probably bigger than his whole house. A winding staircase led from the foyer to the next level, taking the eye to the grand, domed ceiling that stood above them. It was like something from a French château. Cherub-like figures draped in billowy sheets floated among the clouds.

Hardy and the rest of the group from the limo followed Charity through the foyer down a long hall. The steps of his black dress shoes echoed off the marble floor. Sweat beaded on his forehead. If only he could take off the monkey suit. It felt like his tie was getting tighter by the minute.

They ended up in the grand kitchen that rivaled some of the best restaurants with its large, stainless appliances and real, wood-burning pizza oven. Charity made introductions to her mother, an older, slightly taller version of Charity. Hardy wiped his sweaty palm on his pant leg and shook her mother's hand. There was no sign of Governor Hill.

The party was outside on a huge, multilevel veranda that overlooked a lighted swimming pool. In a word, it was stunning. White tablecloths covered table after table of food. One table even had an ice sculpture of a lion—the school mascot. A local band had set up to one side and was performing a sound check.

Cricket grasped Hardy's shoulder. "This place is off the hook."

"Just don't forget why you're here."

"Don't be such a buzzkill. At least try to enjoy yourself."

"I don't think that's possible. I'm too nervous. What if this whole thing blows up in our faces?"

"Have you forgotten who's in charge of creating the distraction? It's going to be epic."

"Charity will hate you for it," Hardy said.

"You think I care? I'm going out with a bang. No one's going to forget this party—ever."

"Fine. Just don't blow it."

"That's the whole idea," Cricket said smiling.

"What is that supposed to mean?"

"Don't worry. I've got Luis on it as we speak."

Hardy held up a hand. "You know what—I don't want to know."

"Nope. You probably don't," Cricket said. "You just worry about your little girlfriend."

"Charity?" Hardy asked.

"No, Darcy."

"Darcy is not my girlfriend."

"Uh-huh."

Hardy rolled his eyes. "Whatever. Speaking of Darcy. Why isn't she here yet?"

Hardy spent the next hour following Charity around, clueless about what he was supposed to be doing as her date. Luckily, she wasn't big on dancing, and he only had to endure making a fool out of himself twice.

Cricket had disappeared. He still hadn't seen Luis or Darcy. He had started entertaining the idea of punching Luis's face in when he finally spotted Darcy coming through the kitchen's French doors. He excused himself to Charity and made his way toward Darcy.

"Where have you been?" Hardy whispered fiercely. "I've been worried sick."

"You don't want to know," Darcy said.

He frowned and crossed his arms. "Actually, I'm pretty sure I do." *Especially since you were with Luis.*

Darcy looked puzzled. "You're angry?"

Hardy raised his eyebrows, waiting for an explanation.

Darcy apparently decided to ignore his strange behavior. "I know where the Governor's office is." She motioned with her head toward the far left corner of the house. "See the tall windows at the end?"

Feeling silly, Hardy uncrossed his arms and tried to refocus. "Yeah."

"That's where it is."

"How do you know?" he asked. They needed to be careful now. No mistakes.

Darcy hesitated. "I have x-ray vision when I can get close

enough."

The blood drained from Hardy's face. He stared at her unable to speak.

"That response is exactly why I lied about it. My family thought I could see them naked."

Hardy instinctively shoved his hands under his armpits and narrowed his eyes. "Well, can you?"

Darcy sighed. "Not like you think. Besides, I've already seen you naked."

"Oh, and that makes me feel so much better," he said sarcastically.

She grabbed Hardy by the arm. "It should. Come on. Let's go."

"What about the distraction?" Hardy asked, stumbling after her.

"Don't worry, it's coming."

"So, how does the x-ray thing work exactly?" Hardy asked.

"I'm not talking about this right now, Hardy. Can we please focus on the task at hand?"

"You're right. Sorry."

Right when they got up to the doors of the kitchen, there was a loud explosion, followed by the sky lighting up like New Year's Eve. Then, a long series of firecrackers popped off like a machine-gun by the pool. Everyone was running and tripping over each other to get away from the fiery blasts. If that wasn't enough, Luis got up on the pool diving board in just his underwear and screamed, "CANNON BALL!" He ran and dropped into the pool like a guided missile. Water drenched the shocked students scrambling to get away from the firecrackers.

"Awesome," Hardy said.

Darcy led him through the kitchen down a dark, back hall. Hardy was pretty sure he heard more splashes in the pool. Charity's party was going down in flames. Hardy couldn't help but grin. Maybe Luis wasn't so bad after all. He was helping them, and he had no idea what was going on. That was a true friend.

They stood at the large, white door. Darcy appeared to be scanning the door.

"We're good. No one is in there," she said.

Darcy's hand moved toward the knob. Hardy grabbed her arm and slid his hand into hers. "Wait," he said.

"What is it? What's wrong?" Darcy asked, looking concerned.

"Thank you—for doing this," he said quietly.

She stared down at their clasped hands. He realized he was stroking the top of her hand with his thumb.

"We should...you know...get in there," Darcy murmured.

"Yeah...um...right...we should...you know." Hardy dropped her hand and opened the door. *Brilliant, Hardy. Just brilliant.*

Most of the office was shrouded in darkness. A small lamp burned to the left in a sitting area staged with two leather club chairs and a small antique table. Once Hardy's eyes adjusted, he could see that the room ran the entire length of the house—long and narrow, lined with bookcases and gold-framed paintings. To the right, a large table surrounded by rolling chairs sat in front of the long windows facing the backyard. Heavy drapes blocked what Hardy could only imagine was total chaos outside. Right in the center of the room stood the Governor's desk—ornately carved and ostentatious. Just like something one would expect to see in an office of a head of state. And on top of the desk, the computer screen loomed in front of them like a monolith rising from the depths of the sea.

"There it is," Darcy whispered.

She removed her high heels one at a time and dropped them to the floor. Hardy followed her to the computer. The desk was spotless. Not one paper or pen in sight. Darcy pulled the Governor's rolling chair back from the desk. She reached inside the top of her dress, pulled out a cable, and inserted one end into her eye and the other end into the side of the computer.

She touched the keyboard once to pull it out of sleep mode. This was it. They were either going to blow the lid on the Governor and Finch, or they were going down in flames.

The screen flashed to life, and the images on the screen moved so quickly he couldn't make out anything. Darcy's eye was darting back and forth—the fastest he had ever seen it. It was not only exhilarating, it was one of the coolest things he had ever seen. No, it was more than that. It was her. He did feel something for her, and he had been trying not to because he felt like someone unattainable like Charity was what he should want. He was wrong.

"Darcy?"

"Not now, Hardy."

"Did I mention how beautiful you look tonight?" He drew closer and reached out a hand to her hair. It felt like woven silk.

Darcy didn't budge. The screen continued to flash, move, scroll.

He put his hands on her shoulders and swept aside one side of her hair.

"Hardy."

"Darcy, I need to tell you something," he said next to her ear.

"Don't do this, Hardy. I can't…"

He put his cheek against hers. The screen went black. Darcy pulled the cable from her eye and turned into his arms, rising to her tiptoes. Their lips flew to each other. She grabbed his face, he took her in his arms. Everything he had been denying came in a flood, and he drowned in it. Why had it taken him so long to realize her…this…them?

Darcy's heels dropped to the floor, and their lips parted.

"You have really bad timing," she said breathlessly.

"I'm socially awkward."

Darcy smiled. "I know."

"You're beautiful, you know that," Hardy said, placing a hand on her cheek.

"We should probably save this for another time. I've got what we need," Darcy said.

"You're right. Let's get out of here."

Darcy unhooked the cable to the computer. Hardy took her hand. She stooped to grab her shoes.

Hardy reached out a hand to the doorknob when the door abruptly opened. Two bodies shadowed the entrance. The door slammed.

Chapter Thirty-five

"Why am I not surprised to find you two here?"

Governor Hill, even at this hour, was still wearing a dark suit and tie. He walked behind his desk and begin typing on the keyboard. His goon—bodyguard, also in a dark suit—held a vice grip on Hardy and Darcy's arms.

"Hmm. It looks like someone's been busy snooping."

"We were just, you know, trying to get a little privacy." Hardy thought lying was at least worth a shot.

"And miss the fireworks going on outside?" Hill came back around the front of his desk. "Bring me the girl."

The guard pushed Darcy toward the Governor. She fell in front of him on her knees. Hardy struggled to get out of the guard's excruciating grip on his arm.

"Get up," Hill said to Darcy.

Darcy stood. But not as the shy, awkward girl Hardy had first met. She stood tall, with a fierceness that Hardy was just beginning to realize she possessed.

"Where are they?" Hill asked.

"Where's what?" Darcy said flatly.

He backhanded her across the face.

"NO!" Hardy screamed.

Darcy held her cheek in her hand, then slowly looked back to Hill and stared stoically into his eyes. "My brother hits harder than you, but then you knew that already, didn't you?"

"Don't play with me, young lady. Unless you'd like to see your boyfriend over there get hurt."

"Don't tell them anything, Darcy."

The man holding Hardy quickly turned into him and landed a large fist into his gut. Hardy fell to the floor, gasping for air.

"I know you downloaded files. Where are they?" Hill asked again.

Darcy looked at Hardy with worried eyes. All Hardy could manage to do was shake his head.

Hill nodded toward the guard. The guard picked Hardy up by the collar of his jacket and landed a fist into Hardy's kidneys. Hardy dropped into a heap on the floor. He drew his legs into his chest and struggled to breathe. He had never felt such searing hot pain.

"Stop!" Darcy called out. "I'll tell you what you want to know."

"That's better," Hill said.

"You won't get away with this," Hardy gasped.

Hill picked up a crystal paperweight from his desk and tossed it from hand-to-hand. "You should have kept your nose out of where it didn't belong."

Hardy raised his head from the floor. "How could you do this to people, old people?" he spat.

Hill smiled and set the paperweight back down on his desk. "A leader has to make tough decisions and do what's best for its people. How can I justify spending thousands of dollars on people who aren't going to get better? Unless we find a way to reduce costs, you and your children will be left with—well, nothing."

Hardy held his side and pushed himself up on one knee.

"So, this is about money?" Hardy asked, still breathing heavily. "You're killing old people to save money?"

"Everything is about money. But not just money. The future of this island. It's nothing personal, Mr. Vance, it's business." Hill removed his jacket and laid it on his desk.

Hardy gritted his teeth and glared at Hill. "You killed my grandfather. That makes it personal."

Hill unbuttoned a sleeve and rolled it up. "Your grandfather was—a loose end. I had nothing to do with it."

"You allowed it to happen!" Hardy yelled, rising to his feet.

"I don't expect children to understand the complexities—"

Hardy sprinted toward Hill and grabbed him by the throat. Hill pulled at Hardy's hands, his face red from the crushing force of Hardy's fingers. "You'll pay for this!" Hardy screamed.

Within seconds, the guard had pried Hardy off. He felt a crushing blow to the head. Everything faded to black.

Chapter Thirty-six

Hardy felt himself rising out of a hazy mist of no sound, dim lights, and a solid thumping coming from inside his head. His whole body felt like it had been crushed by a steamroller. He tried to move, but his hands were bound tightly behind his back. He was tied to a chair in a room lined with wine bottles from floor to ceiling. It was cold.

He tried to twist around. "Darcy?"

"I'm right behind you."

"Are you okay?" Hardy asked, struggling with the plastic ties that bound his wrists.

"I'm fine. It's you I'm worried about."

Hardy could feel a large, painful knot at the base of his head. "What happened?"

"His thug knocked you out with a 16mm. I told them where I downloaded the files."

"Darcy, why?"

"I had to. They were…hurting you."

"It's over then," Hardy said.

"Not necessarily. It will take them a while to retrieve all the documents. I embedded each page into thousands of pictures of old people."

Hardy managed a small laugh that made him grimace in pain. "Only you would think of something like that."

"Yeah. I'm genius in that way."

"Then we still have time. Can you contact Cricket?"

"No. They shut me down. I only have a vision app running now. You'll have to think of something else."

Hardy let his head fall to his chest. What were they going to do now? This was the kind of stuff where people's bodies got shoved into trunks and then disappeared. What was worse was that Darcy didn't deserve any of this. It was his grandfather who was killed, not hers. And now all these feelings for her had started surfacing. He closed his eyes and clenched his jaw. For once, he just wanted to do something right.

The door opened. Hardy didn't know who he was expecting, but he certainly wasn't expecting him.

"Well, you two have gone and gotten yourselves into quite a pickle," George said from the doorway.

"George! How did you...never mind. Untie us, quick," Hardy said.

George fished inside his khaki pants pocket and pulled out a small pocket knife. He cut the rip-ties from Darcy's wrists, then Hardy's.

Hardy immediately took Darcy's hands and rubbed her red wrists. "You okay?"

Darcy nodded and tried to smile.

"Your buddy Cricket called me. Said you disappeared. He seemed kind of panicky, so I thought I should come," George said.

"How did you get in? The security around here is like the CIA," Hardy asked.

"Ah, you underestimate the old man. I came to fetch my grandson who stayed out past his curfew. And then, maybe I got lost in this big, old house looking for him."

Hardy smiled. "George, I never thought I'd be glad to see you."

"You really know how to flatter a guy."

"We have to get out of here," Darcy said.

"Come on. I think I know a way to slip out unnoticed. There's a service entrance down the hall from here," George said.

"I should find Cricket first," Hardy said.

"Too risky," George said.

"He's right. They don't know anything about Cricket. He's safer away from us," Darcy said.

"Okay, yeah. Let's go," Hardy said.

They hurried to the end of the hall and slipped out of the basement's service entrance. The door led to a concrete loading dock with two bay doors. Two men in dark suits stood next to a truck that had *Two Sisters Catering* written on the side. One of the men cut out a slice of apple with a small knife and stuck it in his mouth.

Hardy and Darcy hesitated. "Not to worry," George said quietly. "They're only the muscle. Just act normal, like you're supposed to be here."

They followed George down the steps. The men stared in

their direction, but said nothing.

"Well, I'm sorry. I got turned around and brought you out the wrong entrance. It won't kill you to walk, you know," George said loudly.

When Hardy didn't say anything, George jabbed him in his side. Hardy winced. The bodyguard had done a good job on Hardy's mid-section.

"Oh, um…Thanks a lot, Grandpa," Hardy said robotically.

George glared at Hardy over the top of his glasses.

Okay. So he wasn't an actor.

George raised a quick hand of greeting to the men, which they ignored. They seemed only mildly interested in the small dispute. Hardy eyed the radio hanging on the belt of the man without the apple. He half-expected to hear *code red, code red* blare from the man's hip. The men would be obliged to stop them. But then that was Hardy's vivid imagination taking over. They walked around the house and piled into George's car without incident. They were even waved through the gate. The Governor was unaware that they had escaped from the basement.

Once they were out of the gated complex, Hardy breathed a sigh of relief and undid his tie.

"I don't know how to thank you, George," Hardy said.

"Eh, it makes me feel young again, busting you two out. Being old has its advantages. People never suspect you of anything."

Hardy chuckled. "I suppose that's true." He turned to check on Darcy in the back seat. "I'm sorry the night turned out this way, Darcy."

"It's not over yet."

"What do you mean? We came out empty-handed," Hardy said.

"The information is still on the cloud where I put it."

"Yeah, but they'll find it and erase it."

"It will take a lot longer than a couple of hours."

Hardy shook his head. "No, Darcy. We're done. I can't let anything else happen to you. If we try and access the documents, they'll be right on top of us before you know it."

Darcy sighed. "Fine."

"There is something, though. Something I haven't told you yet," Hardy said.

"What is it?" Darcy asked.

"I think I might have figured out where Olen hid what his murderer was looking for."

Darcy leaned forward and grabbed the back of the seat. "Where?"

"He had this thing he always said: There's wisdom—"

"In trees," George finished.

Hardy was surprised. "Yeah. How did you know?"

"I've heard it from him before," George said flatly.

"Anyway, I think that may be where he hid what Finch was looking for."

"Finch?" George asked, glancing at Hardy.

"Yeah. Cain Finch. Your dark horse. He's had a suspicious interest in all of this. We think he may be working with the Governor."

"Is that so?"

Darcy laid a hand on George's shoulder. "Can you take us to Olen's cabin?"

"Of course," George said.

"It's too dark, Darcy. We should wait until morning," Hardy said.

"We may not have that long," Darcy said.

Hardy didn't want to admit it, but she was right. He was naïve to think this would all just go away because they escaped. But if they had other evidence, even if it didn't explicitly implicate the Governor, it could be enough. If they got something on Finch, they could tie him to the Governor with Finch's journal entries. Hardy was beginning to feel hopeful again.

"You're right. But we can't just go out there stumbling in the dark," Hardy pointed out.

"You kids are in luck. I keep emergency supplies in my trunk. I have two big flashlights that will cut a path of at least twenty feet," George said.

Hardy smiled. "All right, then. Let's do this. George, head toward Southeast High. Do you have any qualms about driving your car down an old railroad path?"

George tapped the steering wheel. "You've seen where I live, kid. Old Betsy here has seen a dirt path or two."

"Old Betsy?" Hardy asked.

George raised his bushy, white eyebrows. "Every car's got a good name. I bet you got a name for yours."

"He doesn't have a car," Darcy said.

"Let's just focus on getting Betsy to the woods," Hardy said.

"You got it." George gunned the car, and they sped into the night.

***

Hardy was half-carsick by the time George had maneuvered the huge Cadillac down the dirt trail. Riding a bike on it was much different from riding in a car. The vast amount of holes that George had managed to hit were easily avoided on a bike.

"Told you Betsy could handle it," George said, once they were all out of the car. "Let me grab the flashlights." George hobbled to the back of the car and started rummaging around the trunk.

Hardy reached out for Darcy's hand. "Are you okay? You know...without your eye working like you're used to?"

"I'm with you. How can I not be okay?"

Hardy drew Darcy into his arms, and she slid her arms around his waist. He buried his hands into her soft hair and told himself things in his life were going to be different from now on. He wanted to stop running from his life and start living it. If that meant staying on the island, then he would stay.

She took a step back and looked at him. "Can I ask you a question?"

Hardy smiled. "Yeah, sure. Anything."

"Is this...you and me...because you feel sorry for me, or something?" she asked, rubbing her arms.

"What? No, Darcy."

"Because if it is, you can stop now while you can."

"Why would you think something like that?"

"I know Charity was your dream girl. I can't live up to that."

Hardy bit his lower lip. "Give me your hand." Darcy lowered her eyes and placed her small hand into his. "Look at me," he said. She lifted her eyes to his. "You've got it all wrong. The truth is, she can't live up to you."

Darcy nodded and a tear fell from her eye. "I take it she can't pick a lock?" she asked.

"Not even close," he said, kissing the top of her hand. "Your hand is freezing: are you cold?"

"A little."

He removed his jacket and held it open for her. She slipped her arms into the sleeves and turned around. He drew her into his arms and held her so tight he thought he might crush her.

A bright light burst into the night and lit them up like a circus act.

"Okay, you two. Get your hormones in check. Let's get this thing done," George said.

Hardy released Darcy, and George handed him the other flashlight.

"Are you sure you're up for this, George?" Hardy asked.

"I'm old. Not dead."

"Just watch your step."

They did well enough through the woods down to the boat. Rowing downriver, however, was major spooky. It seemed as though eyes peered at them from behind trees. Everyone was on edge. No one said a word until they were at Olen's cabin.

Hardy hadn't been to the cabin since the day they buried Olen. Coasting up to the bank filled him with a sense of dread. Olen was gone. Murdered. Now they were returning to where it all started and where Hardy hoped it would all end. He prayed there was wisdom in trees.

Anxious and hurried, he missed the jump to dry land and his freshly polished shoes landed in the cold, shallow water. He pulled the front of the canoe onto the rocky shore and helped Darcy and George out.

"Up here," Hardy said, shining the flashlight up the hill into the dark shadow of the trees.

He led the way, with George bringing up the rear. His feet squeaked inside his wet shoes. He tried to ignore the uncomfortable feeling.

When they reached the top of the path, Hardy shined his flashlight on the empty cabin. It was a dark statue—quiet—foreboding. The only life it had known—gone.

"What's the hold-up? Let's get on with it," George said impatiently.

He had forgotten how cranky George could be.

"This way," Hardy said, heading into the woods to the right of the cabin.

Sweat broke out on his forehead despite the chill in the air. Things looked different at night, and he began to wonder if he would be able to find the tree. He stopped and tried to get his bearings. He turned in circles, shining the light into the woods. Everything looked the same at night.

"What's wrong?" George asked.

"I don't know. I'm not sure I can find it in the dark."

"Well, we're not stopping now, kid."

George's attitude was starting to grate on his nerves. "Just give me a minute, okay?" Hardy shined the light on the forest floor and up into the trees. There was no dirt path you could just follow. You just knew the way by direction and trees that during the day had color and dimension. At night, everything was flat.

"I think it's this way," he finally said, shining his flashlight to the left.

"You think?" George snapped.

"Feel free to lead the way at any time, George," Hardy said.

George held up a hand and looked away. Hardy pushed forward into the darkness. Eventually, he began recognizing some of the trees by their massive sizes. He was sure they were close. When they passed a large boulder, he remembered. "It's right up here." His heart raced with anticipation.

He reached the grave first. Olen's grave. Weeds had already taken root and were taking over the dirt-filled mound. Ashes to ashes. Darcy approached from behind and slid her hand under his arm. She understood that this was hard for him.

"Where's the tree, kid?" George barked.

Hardy spun around, tired of George's insensitivity. "What's your problem, George?"

"Not a big fan of the woods at night," George responded.

"Fine. Whatever." Hardy approached the large oak. The rotted hole stood ominously in front of him. The idea of sticking his hand inside it ranked right up there with sticking it in a toilet.

He shined his light in the hole, half-expecting to rouse a bat or owl or something equally undesirable from its sleep. Nothing moved. No glowing eyes stared back. It appeared to be empty. At least he hoped it was.

He slowly stuck his hand inside the hole. He immediately hit some kind of moist bottom that felt crumbly and soft.

"Anything?" Darcy asked.

"Not yet." Hardy moved his fingers around some unidentifiable objects that he sincerely hoped weren't some creature's abandoned remains. He felt along the cavity wall, up and down its rough sides. He was beginning to feel he had been wrong. He was so certain. The message seemed so clear.

He made one last pass over the bottom, but this time he dug into the decaying debris. That's when his fingers caught onto the edge of something—a pointy edge. He cleared the dirt around it and felt a flat, smooth surface. He grabbed the edge of it and pulled it from the tree. He held it in front of the flashlight and shook off the remaining dirt. It was a clear plastic bag with papers in it.

"Oh, my gosh," Darcy said. "You were right."

"Maybe. We don't know what's in here. It could be anything."

Hardy handed Darcy the flashlight. "Here, hold this."

He pulled apart the bag's closure and removed a stack of paper joined by a single staple. He dropped the plastic bag and held the paper close to Darcy's light. He read aloud.

"To whom it may concern: I, Olen Vance—"

Hardy stopped abruptly and looked over at Olen's makeshift grave. Overcome with the emotion of knowing that Olen expected him to find this letter, Hardy wondered if he could continue.

"Go ahead," Darcy said, placing a reassuring hand on his arm.

Hardy coughed into his fist to clear his throat.

"—do hereby leave this letter as a testament of truth. A truth that I am unduly ashamed of but find that I have been a party to, nonetheless.

Secret medical research done under the umbrella of what was called "The Program" was entered into in hopes of finding a cure for the incurable through an unlikely resource—Greene Island's little-known toxic dandelion. I witnessed its power to kill and its power to save. It was the power to save that was meant to be harnessed for future generations. But, as the research unfolded, it became evident that those saving qualities were unable to be isolated. Too much depended on an individual's genetic markers and not the dandelion alone. Unable to identify what those genetic markers were and who in fact might have them, we found ourselves at the proverbial dead end.

It was at this time that a new directive was issued by the powers to be. DIE—Direct Instant Extermination was born, and the research became fully focused on the ability of the toxic dandelion to kill. There were those of us who vehemently protested this new direction, but sadly our numbers were few. Only four of us had the courage to speak out against it. Despite our complete disdain of the new direction, the four of us stayed on willingly, in hopes that we could slow the progression or, better yet, determine how to stop the DIE research. It wouldn't be wrong to say that our very lives were at stake. Forced obligation was more than accurate to describe our reason to cooperate.

By the end of that fateful year, I was able to discover the key to removing any chance of survival after exposure to the dandelion, thus making the toxic dandelion one hundred percent fatal. Ironically, this discovery came a few days before Sarah gave birth to our son, Tom. My great joy quickly gave way to fear when I discovered a betrayer in our midst. We stood outside the door of my wife's hospital room when he informed me that my breakthrough discovery must be shared and that he had only pretended to side with us in order to obtain what they had all hoped I would discover. I stood in the face of the worst kind of man. One who chose to live by selfish ambition instead of truth. So shocked was I by the discovery of this betrayal that I quickly removed myself to the lab to take into custody the research I had hidden in my office. With the research safely tucked away in my briefcase, I hurried to gather my wife and son. When I arrived at the hospital I found Sarah dead in the very bed where she had birthed our son—a dandelion seed grasped in her hand. I was a fool to leave her in order to secure the research. Her death was no doubt meant as a warning. My only concern then and now was ensuring the safety of my son. I knew Tom's life would be in danger as long as I withheld my research. Unwilling to give up my son or my research, we disappeared. I made it look as though I left the island with Tom. I, of course, stayed on the island, thinking it the least likely place they would expect to find us.

It is now under what I assume is my death that this letter has been found and that I can finally rest assured that The Program can no longer use the life of my son as leverage to obtain the key to the destruction of a man's life. I suppose I will be judged for not speaking up sooner. History will be kind or unkind to me, but no one can fault a man for loving another more than his own self. It was for my son that I did what I did. I am neither proud nor ashamed of my actions.

I owe my deepest apology (if he is still yet living) to Dr. Cain Finch. Being the only one left of our four, he was subsequently *implicated in my wife's death and stripped of his medical license. I was unable to reveal my whereabouts in order to clear his name, and for that I am sorry. I will only hope that, being a fellow protector of life, he will understand why I couldn't come forward without risk to my life and my son's.*

You will find attached to this letter my research. I pray now that someone will find the courage to destroy it once and for all. I suppose fear and pride kept me from doing so, and for that I am sorry.

My final wish is that if the betrayer and murder of my wife still lives, he will finally pay for his sins, though no amount of justice can undo that which has already been lost. I now release that name to the bearer of this letter — that of George Bolt."

When Hardy saw the name, it felt like he was being punched in the stomach a thousand times over.

Without saying a word, George calmly raised his arm and pointed a gun at Hardy. "I'll be needing those papers now."

The weight of Hardy's colossal mistake hit him like a hammer. He had been wrong about Finch. He had been wrong about George. His heart burned; heat spread through his body like a furnace. He covered half the distance between him and George and pointed a finger. "You killed Olen."

"Hand over the papers," George said calmly.

"Or what?" Hardy asked. "You're going to kill me, too?"

"If I have to."

"I trusted you," Hardy said fiercely.

George shrugged. "Sorry, kid."

"So, all that at Hill Home was…was…what?"

"I needed to find his research papers. I knew Olen had likely kept them. But when a search of the cabin didn't turn anything up, I figured you were my next-best shot. Olen always did have a flair for the dramatic. Frankly, I'm surprised you figured out where he hid them. You're not the brightest bulb in the bunch."

"Shut up!" Hardy screamed.

Hardy looked at the paper in his hand. How could he have been so stupid? It was right in front of him the whole time, but he didn't see it. How was he ever going to look at Darcy in the eyes again? He had let her down, himself, and everybody else whose lives had been taken from them.

George held out his hand. "The papers."

Hardy stuck his hand in his pocket and felt the cold metal of Olen's lighter. *I'm sorry, Olen. You believed in me and I let you down. I'm going to make it right now. For you, and for me.*

He pulled the lighter from his pocket, flicked the lighter open, and struck its wheel with his thumb. He held the papers out, bringing the flame inches from its edges.

George's eyes grew wide with fear. "Stop right there, or you're dead."

"Hardy, don't!" Darcy pleaded.

Hardy had gained the upper hand. George didn't want the research papers destroyed. "What is it, George? Huh? You underestimated me. Now who's the brightest bulb?"

"Last warning, kid." George's finger moved on the trigger.

Hardy moved the flame closer to the paper. "Kill me."

"Hardy, No!" Darcy called from behind him.

But Hardy couldn't hear her pleas. He was angry. He was tired of losing. He had the chance to win, and he was going to take it. When he was afraid, he was brave. "At least I will die knowing you didn't get what you wanted. Olen will have the last laugh."

George's tense face relaxed into a grin, and the gun shifted to Darcy. "Then, I'll kill her."

"I wouldn't do that if I were you," a familiar voice said from just behind George. Tom stepped out of the shadows with a rifle shoved against his shoulder, his eye aiming down the barrel at George. "You may or may not hit the girl, but my gun most certainly will not miss you."

George's eyes darted to the side trying to see Tom, but he kept Darcy in his sights. There was a crack, a blast, and two flashes exploded into the night. George stiffened and fell to the ground, his flashlight rolling from his side.

Hardy spun around. Darcy stared in horror at George's lifeless body. Thank God she was still standing. George had missed. Hardy closed the lighter and dropped the papers to the ground. Tom approached the body slowly. He bent down and placed two fingers on George's neck.

What Hardy knew would come next, came. George's spirit lifted. Strangely, he smiled at Hardy. Light burst from the darkness. Hardy raised his arm to shield his eyes from the blinding light. A bridge built itself one slat at a time like falling dominoes. A strong wind pushed against Hardy, yet nothing moved around him. The bright light slowly faded to foreboding darkness. George's smile quickly turned to wide-eyed horror as he no doubt felt what Hardy was already feeling. The awful chill and the pure terror of what was coming.

The darkness twisted and formed itself into a thick liquid that raced violently toward the bridge. The churning blackness wove itself up and down through the bridge's planks like a snake until it engulfed George's body and spun around him like a tightly wound cocoon. Hardy watched as George's hands frantically clawed against the black web that ensnared him. His face pressed against the enveloping horror in a silent scream.

Before Hardy knew it, the blackness oozed to the ground and spread like crawling vines around his feet. He felt the indescribable pull of evil. His lifeblood straining against it. His hands clenched into fists as it crept up his legs. A tentacle wound around his thigh and up his chest. It stopped and pulled at his heart, fighting to take it. His head flew back, and he grimaced in pain. He couldn't move. He was paralyzed. The words of the man on the bridge in Mama's room flooded his brain as the tentacles spread and dug into him. *Don't be afraid. Don't be afraid.* Hardy whispered the words. The fingers of the dark shrieked and retreated as if burned and disappeared into a hole of darkness. The woods returned to normal.

Hardy grabbed a handful of shirt next to his heart and looked down. He was alive. His heart racing inside him. He breathed a sigh of relief.

Tom was still bent over George's body. "Is he...?" Hardy tried to ask, even though he knew the answer.

"Dead? Yes," Tom said, standing. "Are you okay?"

Hardy rubbed a hand across his mouth and nodded. He had never been so glad to see Tom. "How did you find...?

How did you know?"

"Cricket called me when he couldn't find you or reach Darcy."

"So you...know...everything?" Hardy asked. *All my lies?*

"Most of it. The short version, anyway."

Hardy paused, waiting for Tom to erupt in anger. Instead, Tom dug a boot into the ground next to George and rubbed the back of his neck.

"How did you get here—without a boat?" Hardy asked.

Tom flung the shotgun across his shoulder. "Son, I lived in these woods for fourteen years. I know them like the back of my hand."

Hardy stooped down and picked up the stack of paper that would change all their lives. He ripped off the top sheet and handed it to Tom. "I think you should read this." Then Hardy did what Olen had entrusted him to do. He cleared a small area with his shoe and lit the edge of the remaining papers—Olen's research. He waited for the fire to take hold and released the burning papers to the ground.

The light from Darcy's flashlight suddenly tumbled to the ground. "Hardy," she said, her voice shaking.

Hardy rushed to her. Her face, illuminated by the fallen flashlight was as white as a ghost. She stood completely still—paralyzed, holding her stomach. He placed a hand on her face. "What is it? What's wrong?" he asked. "It's over."

She looked into his eyes. He had never seen her look so afraid, not even on the night he found her in the road. He put his hands on her arms. "It's okay. It's over now."

"I'm sorry, Hardy." She looked down at her hands.

He followed her frightened gaze to her stomach. He

slowly pulled her hands away. They were covered in blood. A dark stain was seeping through the delicate pink tulle.

"No. God, no," Hardy said.

Darcy's eyes rolled into the back of her head, and her body slumped forward. She fell into his arms. His knees buckled beneath him, and they collapsed to the ground. "Darcy! Please, no!" Hardy's chest tightened, he couldn't breathe. He tried to cover her wound with his hand. Tears were already falling down his face. Darcy's head fell backwards, her bloody hands falling out to her sides. There must be some mistake. George had missed, hadn't he? How could this be real? It was over. They had won.

Tom ran over and knelt down next to Hardy.

"Tom, please help her!" Hardy said through a veil of tears. "I can't...I...Oh my God." Hardy sobbed and rocked Darcy in his arms. *I'm sorry, Darcy. I'm sorry.*

Tom laid down his gun, lifted Darcy out of Hardy's arms, and took off, running into the woods.

Chapter Thirty-seven

"You should go wash up," Tom said from his chair.

Hardy looked down at the dried blood on his hands. "What's taking so long?" he asked, pacing. "They've been in there for hours."

"I'm sure they're doing everything they can."

He stopped pacing and faced Tom. He realized he resented Tom's sudden interest in his well-being. "Why are you here, Tom?"

"What do you mean, why am I here? You're my son."

Hardy looked at the ceiling and rubbed the back of his neck. "When I found those papers in the tree trunk, the first thing I thought of was that Olen had trusted me. That he had believed that I could figure out what happened to him."

Tom was bent over his knees looking at his hands. He looked up and nodded at Hardy.

"The thing is, Tom. That was the first time—" Hardy paused and took a deep breath. "That was the first time I felt like someone believed in me."

"Are you sure you want to do this right now? You're upset."

Hardy laughed and held out his arms. "Yeah, Tom. I'm upset. But right now, I'm scared. And when I'm scared, I'm brave. So, yeah. I want to do this—right now."

Tom continued to look at his hands. "The truth is, I never knew how to be a father."

"I really don't want to hear excuses."

"Just hear me out," Tom said, staring up at Hardy.

Hardy crossed his arms and gave Tom a quick nod.

"Olen was...I don't know. A lost soul. He rambled around that cabin like he was just going through the motions. He was alive, but it was like he had died a long time ago. I think the loss of my mother broke his heart. He treated me more like a student than a son. He educated me, taught me how to survive in the woods. At the time, I thought that was a normal father-son relationship. Then one day, a man showed up at our door. He'd heard there was a doctor living in the woods that might be able to help his sick daughter. He was from a poor village, one where people kept to themselves. Olen took his bag, and we followed the man through the woods to his village. For the first time I thought, why can't we live in this village? Olen treated the girl. Told the mother how to make chest compresses from eucalyptus leaves. He smiled at the young girl. Held her hand, rubbed her forehead. I was jealous of the girl—the attention Olen gave her. It wasn't until later, when we returned to the cabin, that I became angry."

Tom's face reddened with emotion. His eyes filled with

tears.

"How was it that a man who was supposed to be my father had shown more love for a little girl whom he had never met than for his own son? So, I asked him like I had asked so many times before why we had to live in the woods. I thought if he would just trust me enough to explain, then maybe I could at least understand why we were living the way we were living—like two lost souls drifting through life. He gave me the same vague answer he always gave—he was protecting us. I knew then that I would leave." Tom pulled Olen's last words from his jeans pocket. "Only now do I understand."

Hardy knew he should feel sorry for Tom, but he didn't. He turned away from Tom, unable to face him. "Then why did you do the same thing to me?" he choked. "Treat me the way Olen treated you?"

"I don't know."

Hardy spun around. "You really suck at this, you know that!"

Tom stood, red-eyed, and took a step toward Hardy.

Hardy held up a hand. "Don't. I really needed you, you know. I was going through all this stuff, and I had no one." Tears streamed down his face.

"I hate myself, Hardy. I do. I can't give you what you want."

"And what is it that you think I want?"

Tom wiped a hand down his face and stared at the ground. "That's the thing. I don't know."

Hardy bit his lip in frustration and paced in a two-foot circle. "You can't be this clueless."

Tom just looked at him—his eyes filled with anguish.

Hardy stood directly in front of Tom. "I just want you, Tom. Do you understand? A father. You don't have to have all the answers. You just need to be that part of Olen that smiled at that young girl, held her hand, rubbed her forehead. You just have to be there for me."

Tom nodded. "Would you accept a broken man as a father?" Tom asked, lip quivering.

Hardy finally felt the barriers between him and his father breaking down. If only the tears would stop. "Yes...Yes, I would. Because, I'm broken, too and..." Hardy's voice grew rusty. "I could really use a father right now."

Tom quickly embraced Hardy. They held each other and cried for all the years that they had walked through in silent anguish because of their broken relationship.

When they stepped apart, Tom sniffed back the tears and placed his large hand on Hardy's shoulder. "I'm proud of you and I want you to know that I'm going to try and do right by you from now on."

Hardy wiped his eyes with his thumb and forefinger and nodded. It was a start.

Hardy's mother came down the hall dressed in her blue scrubs with worry in her eyes. After seeing their red faces, her eyes registered a slight look of surprise mixed with relief. She seemed to understand that they had made peace with each other.

"Is she...?" Hardy asked, afraid to hear the answer.

"She's out of surgery," Anna said.

Hardy breathed a sigh of relief.

"She's lost a lot of blood, Hardy. You need to know she's

in a critical condition. The next twenty-four hours will tell whether or not she pulls through."

"Can I see her?" he asked, feeling the tears burn at the corner of his eyes.

"Yes. But you should know—she's on a ventilator."

Hardy wiped his face again. "Thanks."

Tom clasped Hardy on the shoulder. "I'll go with you."

"Room 402," Anna said. "Listen, there's another girl in ICU from Southeast High in critical condition. I didn't know whether you knew her. She's a senior."

"Who is it?" Hardy asked, surprised.

"Emma Snow."

"What?"

"You know her?"

"Yeah. I mean, no, not really. I just met her at the prom tonight." Hardy recalled the last words Emma had said to him. *Don't wait. You never know if there will be a tomorrow. No regrets.* Her words seemed prophetic now, both for her and Hardy. "What happened?" he asked, trying to shake the chill running down his spine.

"Car accident. Evidently, her date had been drinking. Look, I just wanted you to know in case you saw her family or friends in the ICU." Anna reached out and rubbed Hardy's arm.

Hardy looked at his shoes and nodded.

Hardy and Tom stood outside the door of room 402.

"I'll wait out here," Tom said.

"Okay, thanks." Hardy meant it. He could see how uncomfortable Tom was, how he looked nervously from room to room as they passed by each one. He knew it was hard for Tom to be there, but he was doing it for Hardy, and that meant something.

He could hear the whirl and clunk of the ventilator before he even laid eyes on Darcy. He stopped at the end of her bed and stared at her lifeless body. Her hair lay in a puddle beneath her. Her skin was pale, translucent. He scarcely recognized her. If not for the plastic tube moving with the air being pumped into her lungs, he would have thought her dead.

He moved to her side and stuck his hand underneath hers. His tears fell on the top of her hand.

"Darcy. I need you to live," he said, catching the sob coming from his mouth with his other hand.

He couldn't speak any other words. His face flushed with heat and it quickly spread down his arms to his feet. His breathing came in short, shallow bursts. His legs weakened, and he thought he might faint. He grabbed a chair from behind him and pulled it up to the bed. He sat and laid his head on Darcy's arm and tried to breathe with the rhythm of the machine that was keeping her alive. Even now, like this, she calmed him.

Hardy must have dozed off, because he jumped when someone put a hand on his shoulder. He popped up, groggy. It took him a minute to remember where he was. He looked at Darcy's arm taped with plastic tubes, and it all came rushing back. He turned in his seat. Tom stood behind him.

"The police want us to go to the station and give our statements," Tom said.

Hardy looked back at Darcy. "I don't want to leave her."

"I know."

Hardy pushed the chair back and stood up. "You'll bring me right back?"

"Of course."

Hardy stuck his hands in his pockets and nodded. He took one final look at Darcy before he left the room. *Don't die on me, Darcy.*

***

The sun was rising by the time they got back to the hospital. Hardy's eyes burned from the lack of sleep. The police station interview had taken much longer than he had expected. A lot had happened, there was a lot that had to be explained—starting with Olen, Hill Home, the Governor, George.

It was during the interview that Hardy learned that Trevor was missing. He was told there may be more questions. He had no doubt there would be.

The only thing he didn't tell them was the part about being able to see people die. He figured that belonged to him now, and it wasn't something he wanted to share.

Tom took the elevator up with Hardy back to ICU. Hardy told him to go home and get some sleep, but Tom insisted on staying.

As soon as they stepped off the elevator, Hardy began having a funny feeling. Something moved through him—a vibration like electricity. He knew what that meant. He sprinted down the hall, navigating around stranded medical equipment, patients dragging their IVs behind them. Tom called after him.

Ten feet from Darcy's room, he stopped cold. The door to another patient's room was open. He heard the sucking and blowing of a ventilator. He couldn't see who was in the room, but he could see the end of the bed, the tented feet of a patient. A pinhole of light was spinning on the back wall. Someone was getting ready to die. He wasn't sure what to do. If the patient was in ICU, that meant critical.

"There's nothing you can do," came Tom's voice from behind him.

He turned to Tom. "What?"

"About the girl. That's the girl from Southeast High in that room."

"Emma? Yeah, well…I don't know why I stopped at her door." Hardy tried to cover his strange behavior.

"It's okay. I used to think I could save them, too. That's the curse of the thing, isn't it?"

Hardy stepped closer to Tom so no one could hear. "You can…see it?" he whispered.

Tom nodded.

"What? How long?" Hardy was stunned. He never had a clue outside of Tom's dislike for hospitals.

"Ever since I can remember, really. I thought it was normal that I could always find the wounded animals in the woods, that I could see the bird with a broken wing fly away from his body up into the clouds. Not until Olen figured it out did he tell me not to ever tell anyone what I could see."

"I thought maybe I was crazy," Hardy said, feeling relieved.

395

"You're not. I'm a little surprised, though. I haven't noticed it with you before now."

"It's kind of recent." Then it dawned on Hardy. Olen's note to Tom. *It's time to tell Hardy the truth.* "The note from Olen. This is what he was talking about?"

Tom nodded. "He must've noticed something about you while you were there."

Hardy remembered the strange vision he had experienced with the squirrel. Now he knew that the squirrel was probably getting close to death. "Do you ever get used to it?" Hardy asked.

"It's more like you come to terms with it. But it's one of the reasons I tried to avoid hospitals. Every time it's like a chorus of people calling out to me at once." Tom glanced toward Emma's door. "It looks like it will be a while."

"It's hard to walk away...knowing," Hardy said.

"I know."

When they reached Darcy's door, Tom left to go get coffee. A nurse with latex gloves on was changing a drip bag hanging next to Darcy. Hardy approached slowly. "Any change?"

"No. I'm afraid not." Sensing the distress in Hardy's face, she added, "Why don't you try talking to her. Some believe they can still hear you." The nurse smiled and left the room.

So he talked to Darcy. Told her how things were going to be different after she got better. How they would do normal things like go to a movie, eat at a real restaurant, spend the day at the beach. They would make the most of the time they had together before he left for college. He held her hand and kissed it.

***

Cricket showed up about mid-morning. Tom was roaming the hospital somewhere, giving Hardy space.

"Hey," Cricket said quietly.

"Hey."

"How is she?" Cricket asked, nodding toward the bed.

Hardy gently laid Darcy's hand back down on the bed and sat back. "I don't really know. I keep expecting her to wake up or squeeze my hand or something."

Cricket pulled up a chair next to Hardy. "I...um...saw your dad out there. He filled me in on what happened."

Hardy rested his elbows on his knees and pinched his eyes shut. "This is all my fault, Cricket. I was trying to be the hero."

"I doubt Darcy would see it that way."

Hardy was too tired to argue the point. "Maybe," he said, massaging the back of his neck. "Where's Luis?"

Cricket raised an eyebrow. "Evidently, he's scared of needles and faints at the sight of blood."

"Listen, tell him I appreciate all his help...with the distraction at the party. I never really gave him a fair chance."

"Yeah. Sure, okay," Cricket said, giving Hardy's shoulder a firm squeeze.

They sat in silence for a few minutes listening to the wheezing of the machine that kept Darcy alive. Hardy leaned forward and held her hand between his.

"So, how long have you been in love with her?" Cricket asked.

Hardy looked over at Cricket and back to Darcy. He realized that he did in fact love her. When it had happened, though, he had no idea. "I um…"

"It's okay. I've seen it coming for a while. I just wondered if you were aware of it."

Hardy nodded. "I kissed her, you know."

"Yeah, you mentioned that when I showed up at Hill Home to pick your crazy butt up."

"What? I was talking about last night."

"Evidently, you kissed her at Hill Home that night you almost died. You were going on about how Darcy was a good kisser. She insisted you were delirious."

Hardy grinned and laid her hand back down on the bed. "I didn't realize anything had happened. She never said anything."

"Well, she was probably embarrassed." Cricket smiled. "You made a complete fool of yourself in the truck, falling all over her, defending her against me, even."

"Really?" Hardy asked.

Cricket rolled his eyes. "It was a real eye-rolling kind of ride."

Hardy guessed that explained why things felt different with Darcy the next day. Why he felt like something had passed between them.

"Thanks," Hardy said.

"For what?"

"I don't know. Making me smile."

"What are friends for? Listen, I'm going to go." Cricket stood up. "I just wanted to see how she…how you were doing."

Hardy stood. "Thanks."

"You should get some rest," Cricket said.

"I know."

"Call me…if?"

"Yep."

Chapter Thirty-eight

Hardy eventually slept. His mother brought him a cot, against hospital rules. He fell asleep early evening, dead to the world. He was physically and mentally exhausted.

It was sometime in the middle of the night when it happened. The room was dark except for a dim wall light at the head of Darcy's bed. The cold air woke him. He realized he was shivering. He wondered why it was so cold in the room.

He opened his eyes. Darcy was standing next to his cot, looking down at him. She was glowing like a beautiful, warm light. Her hair hung in long, soft waves across her shoulders. She wore a white gown that shimmered like luminous liquid. Her eyes were both brown—both real and deep and dark against her long, white eyelashes. She smiled at him. She was beautiful, like an angel. He thought maybe he was dreaming.

"Hardy, I'm leaving. I wanted to say goodbye," Darcy said.

He quickly sat up and looked over at Darcy's bed. She was still in it, the machine still pumping oxygen into her lungs. He rubbed his eyes. "I'm dreaming."

Darcy smiled. "No, you're not dreaming."

She put her porcelain hand on his shoulder. It was cold.

"I can feel that. But you're not real," Hardy said.

"My body is broken, Hardy. It can't repair itself. I'm bleeding internally. It won't be long now."

His heart leap into a throbbing ball of fear and desperation. He pushed her hand away and rushed to the unconscious Darcy's bedside. "It can't be too late."

"I'm sorry. It is."

He turned to the vision. "Why? Why are you leaving me?"

Darcy shook her head, and tiny pieces of light like glitter fell from her hair. "I don't want to, but I must. It's okay. You'll be okay."

"No! I won't be okay, Darcy! Please don't leave me." His face burned with sorrow.

Darcy linked her fingers together and stared down at them. "Thank you for being my friend." She looked up into his eyes. "It meant the world to me. I can leave this world happy because of you."

"Darcy. Oh, my gosh." Tears fell down Hardy's face. "I love you."

"You love me?" she asked. White, iridescent tears fell from her eyes and rolled down her face like melting wax.

"Yes. Yes, I love you. Isn't that enough?" His chest grew tighter and tighter with anguish.

"I wish it was," she whispered.

"But this can't be it. We just found each other. I can't lose you."

Darcy tried to smile. "You'll never lose me. We're a part of each other now."

"Please don't go," Hardy pleaded.

She started to speak but stopped as if someone had just called her name. "It's almost time. Goodbye, Hardy."

He moved toward her and placed his hands on her cool, luminous face. "I will always love you," he said.

She stared into his eyes and placed her hands over his. "And I, you."

Hardy placed his lips on hers and inhaled the sweet vanilla scent of her face. Their tears mixed together and fell salty and bitter upon their lips as sorrow enveloped their last kiss. Then, like a smoky vapor, she disappeared from his arms, and the alarms from Darcy's machines violently sounded off. Multiple beeps echoed off the walls, growing louder and faster. The overhead lights flew on. Two nurses rushed into the room and frantically worked on the machines, on Darcy. A nurse pressed a button on the wall. "Room 402, stat!"

Hardy backed away from the bed until he hit the wall near the foot of the bed. His knees gave way, and he slid to the floor. A circle of light spun on the wall next to him. He dropped his head into his hands and closed his eyes.

**

Darcy watched as the doctors and nurses needlessly tried to save her. She turned and floated toward the light. Hardy was sitting against the wall with his head in his hands. He wouldn't watch her go. She understood.

It was beautiful—the bridge suspended in mid-air amongst the blue sky and billowing white clouds. She felt peace and an all-consuming love. She floated toward it, feeling the air move through her. Her heavy body was gone, and she felt light as air, free.

She reached the edge of the bridge only to discover that she could move no further. Some invisible force kept her from moving forward. Confused, she pushed on the clear barrier that separated her from passing through to the next life. The entire scene shattered like glass and dissolved into a sterile hospital wall. Like a vacuum cleaner, she was violently sucked into a dark tunnel. She twisted, turned, slammed into the narrow passage that seemed to encase her in a dark void. She wondered how her body wasn't torn into shreds, then she remembered that she wasn't a real body, she was more like air. She remembered what Hardy had said about the darkness that had come for the man in Town Square. She thought she should be afraid, but she wasn't. She sensed *nothing* would hurt her. But *nothing* felt like—someone. Who?

She sped toward a light that shined in the darkness. She grew anxious. The light grew brighter until Darcy plunged through it as if being born in a violent burst. Her destination was not what she expected. She was in a hospital room. Someone else's.

A man and a woman with sad faces sat at the bedside of a girl. They held each other's hands. Red hair. Darcy could see her red hair, long, fanned out to the sides of the girl's breathing tube.

"Hello?" Darcy glided toward the man and the woman.

"They can't hear you or see you," a woman's voice said, sounding distant.

Darcy looked for the source of the voice, but no one else was in the room.

"She's gone," the voice said.

"The girl in the bed?" Darcy asked.

"Yes. Her name is Emma."

"But she still breathes," Darcy said.

"No. The machine breathes for her. She has already left. They will unplug the machine soon."

Darcy didn't understand why she was there. Maybe this was a test of some kind.

"It's not a test. It's an opportunity," the voice explained.

"I don't understand."

"Emma is an only child. Her parents love her very much. You could give them their child back."

Darcy looked at the deep lines of anguish on the man and woman's faces and the hopelessness in their eyes. "Tell me how," she said, wanting to take away their pain.

"You can take her place."

Darcy stared at the girl. Emma was half-human, half-machine. She cringed to think that Hardy had seen her just as this girl was now—half-dead, half-alive.

"I don't understand. How can I take her place?" Darcy had just left her broken body: why was she being offered another?

"You're special. You have a gift. And now you're being given the chance to use it."

"But I have no gift. I'm ordinary. Once I had an eye that could see things, but that was all."

"Oh, but you are wrong. You're a Shifter. You can receive a new body, heal it, if you choose to." There was a pause, as if the voice was letting this new information sink in. "You will have parents that love you. A new life," the voice said, enticing her with the one thing that she'd always wanted. A real family. One that loved her.

A Shifter? A new life? Could it be that simple? Maybe...except... "Except they won't have her back. They will have me."

"Do you think they will care? They will have their precious daughter back. They will love you."

Darcy shook her head. "No, I can't. It would be wrong." *Wouldn't it?*

"Wrong? To save someone from life-altering pain? And what of Hardy? Don't you want to return to your one true love?"

Hardy. His name tugged at her heart. He would want her to do this—for him—for both of them. Her mind fought against her. "I'll be someone else. He won't know me. It wouldn't be the same."

"My darling, he could come to know you. Maybe even love you again. But you must decide. The doctor has arrived."

A doctor entered the room and approached the parents. The man and woman stood. The woman buried her face into her husband's shoulder. He comforted her with his arm.

Darcy felt panic rise in her chest. How could she decide? She didn't even understand what was happening. "Why me?" she asked the voice. "Why can't she live?"

"I told you. She's already gone."

Darcy wanted it. She could feel the deep, gut-wrenching desire growing within her. A new family. The chance at a newer, happier life. One with Hardy in it.

"I'll do it."

"You must hurry, before it's too late."

"Tell me how."

"Float above her and lower yourself into her. The body will resist, but it will relent. You must want it. You must fight for it. Do not be deterred."

Darcy floated to the ceiling above the girl's bed — Emma's bed. Tears were falling down the woman's face. The doctor spoke, but Darcy could not hear what she was saying.

"One more thing. You must never tell anyone you were once Darcy, or it will all disappear," the voice said.

Darcy hesitated. "Who are you?"

There was a small laugh. "Oh my dear. I think you must know by now."

Darcy realized that she did know. "Viola," she whispered.

The doctor moved past the parents to the machine that was keeping Emma alive. There was no time to think this through. She stretched herself out on her back and lowered herself until she hit the body. It was solid and unmoving. She pushed — tried to wiggle her way in. Darcy looked over at the mother. Her hand was on her mouth. Tears were streaming down her face.

"You must hurry!" Viola urged.

Darcy rose a few inches and lowered herself down. The

body gave only slightly. She heard the click of the machine being turned off. She rose again and dropped herself like a hammer. She could feel the top of her new hands, her new toes, but she bounced out again. The doctor pulled the breathing tube from Emma's throat. The parents rushed to their daughter's side.

Darcy screamed and plunged once more, this time melting into Emma. The body was hers. Instantly, she felt heavy, tired, old. It was dark. Unable to open her eyes, she squeezed the hand that was holding hers.

"She squeezed my hand," the mother said desperately.

"It's likely just a reflex," the doctor said.

I'm not dead. Darcy blinked her eyes.

"Is that a reflex?" the father said, sarcastically.

"No. No it is not," the doctor said. "Please step back."

"John, she's alive!"

Darcy listened to the cries of joy. Her eyelids were pried open, and a bright light was shined into her eyes.

"I don't believe it," the doctor said. "I've never seen anything like it."

"It's a miracle, John," the mother said over and over again.

There was a small beep. "I need assistance in 410."

Darcy closed her eyes again. Her throat hurt. Her chest felt heavy, as if someone had laid a ten-pound weight on her ribcage.

"Darling, can you hear me?" The mother asked, rubbing Darcy's forehead.

Darcy cracked her eyes open and nodded.

"You're going to be okay. Your father is right here. We're

both right here," the mother reassured her. She looked at the faces of her new mother and father. They were smiling and crying. Tears of joy and love.

A nurse rushed into the room. The bed was raised, monitors checked, a blood pressure cuff was wrapped around one of her arms. The doctor listened intently to her heart. Once the doctor was satisfied, she stood and stared at her in amazement.

"Do you know where you are?" the doctor asked.

Darcy nodded.

"Do you know your name?"

Darcy nodded.

"Can you tell us your name?"

Darcy looked into the expectant faces of Emma's parents. "Emma," she whispered. "Emma Snow."

END OF BOOK ONE

If you enjoyed this book, please consider reviewing it on www.Amazon.com.